A Tryst of Fate

Diana Kathryn Plopa

All rights reserved. All characters appearing in this work are fictitious. Any resemblance to real persons, living or dead is purely coincidental.

No part of this publication may be reproduced, distributed, or transmitted in any form or by any means, including photocopying, recording, or other electronic or mechanical methods, either now known or unknown, without the written permission of the publisher, except in the case of brief quotations embodied in critical reviews and certain other noncommercial uses permitted by copyright law. For permission requests, write to the publisher, "Attention: Permissions Coordinator", at the address below.

Grey Wolfe Publishing, LLC
PO Box 1088
Birmingham, Michigan 48009
www.GreyWolfePublishing.com

© 2016 Diana Kathryn Plopa
Published by Grey Wolfe Publishing, LLC
www.GreyWolfePublishing.com
All Rights Reserved

ISBN: 978-1628281323

Library of Congress Control Number: 2016946275

A Tryst of Fate

*Karen —
Remember True Love!
Thank you,
Diana Plopa*

by Diana Kathryn Plopa

Dedication

For my husband, Dave, who started me on this journey fourteen years ago.

I love you!

Acknowledgements

I am eternally thankful for those who have inspired me over the years, including…

My life's teachers and cheerleaders:
Jim Bunnell; John Staniloui; Leslie Jacobs; Ken Jannot Jr.;
Lisa Wolfe-Gawel; Aaron Konivisser; Celia Ransom;
Evelyn Zimmer; and Renee Barratt.

My parents: Earl Wolfe & Nancy Walls.
My siblings: Karen Talbot, Rick Mitchell, and Curtis Wolfe.
My grandparents: Earl & Emily Wolfe.

My son, Zachary Bennjamin Wolfe.

A special thank you is extended to my editor,
Kalli Connor, whose insights and attention to detail made
this story much stronger than when it all began!

Prologue

Metal exploded all around them. Glass shattered. The shards impaled the unaware, smearing the afternoon sun with the devastating splotches of torrential loss. The screams of an implausible collection of souls erupted from those sitting in front and behind... not one sounded the same. Not one cried out the same words or prayed the same scripture. It was the most fear she had ever experienced. It was the most painful moment she had ever endured... and it became clear to her in that instant... she would not survive.

She held her daughter as closely as possible, cushioning her head from the oncoming blow, trying to remain calm. She added soft tones to her voice so as not to scare the small child. "Please God, just make it end quickly", was all she could manage her voice to whisper.

As she kissed her limp daughter for the last time, she watched the jagged cavern wall outside the window collide with the two cars in front of her, then fly past her tear-filled eyes with storm-fury. Water began to flood the compartment. And then... searing pain and perfect dark.

Chapter One

*"Man does not control his own fate.
The women in his life do that for him."*
~Groucho Marx

It was three o'clock on Wednesday afternoon when Nathan got a text to meet Paige at the marina. He was a little apprehensive. When summoned to the boat, there was never a hint of what would come of it. Sometimes, it was just a sail around the harbor. Sometimes, it was a job—sometimes sinister, sometimes not. But you never knew... and you never refused. The intimidation of not knowing was like walking a tightrope... forever a little off balance with some influence, but no control. That was exactly the point. It was important for Paige to remain in control... always in control... despite everything else.

Nathan accepted the invitation to the meeting with a simple "yes" reply, and inhaled tentatively. He looked at his watch. She wanted to see him at five o'clock; that would give him time to finish up his current project, catch the blue line to Lewis Warf, and still have time to grab a quick bite. *What could she want now?*

During their association, which started long before her parents' death, Paige asked much of Nathan. Much of it could have been morally disputed; though guided by the perfect dash of incentivizing guilt and a lot of pacifying cash. The rest were primarily menial tasks far below his pay grade. He sensed it was an excuse to keep him close. Her paranoia ran deep and spoke softly. He was sensitive to its whispers.

Nathan was one of the few people who recognized Paige from both sides of the mask. He saw the controlled, sophisticated woman the rest of the world encountered; forever maintaining and building her father's legacy in ways that would make him proud. He also saw the inverse echo... the tumultuous teenager who hid from the mistakes of a past she could not control, at times lashing out with emotions she did not understand. Nathan knew the confusion and frustration of her life but had no explanation for it. Her habitually complex behavior didn't track, considering her comfortable childhood. But, he accepted it and became the curator of her safety, as her father requested. Acceptance didn't make meeting with her at the marina—or anywhere, for that matter, stress-free, though.

Nathan's watch read 4:58pm as he reached the finger dock aside *Wing*. Punctuality was definitely a thing with Paige, and he knew better than to be insolent with tardiness. Paige was already there... sipping something defiant from a glass held high to refract the early evening sunlight. She watched him walk down the dock, but of course, said nothing. It was not her habit to bring attention to herself here. She preferred to be disguised... just another average, although financially comfortable, sailor in the fleet. Marinas were a nice blend of the sophisticated and sublime. Being ignored here was simple. No one took offense to those who were indifferent to their dock mates. Seclusion with all the amenities. She thought it merely nice; and she liked nice.

As he came within three feet of the boat, Nathan waved a hand and called out, "Ahoy! Permission to come aboard?" Nathan had never been much into the pretension of the lifestyle she had chosen to inherit, but here, she demanded it; and since she also signed his paycheck, he indulged her.

"Permission Granted!" Paige called back with an air of playfulness and a genuine smile that she only indulged in this place.

As he grabbed the stanchion and swung his leg on the deck, he thought about how many times he'd been here. *Only three that I can remember... and each time, my life changed.* The first time was just after her father and the Board voted to promote her to CEO. Paige invited Nathan out for a day sail, along with a few of the other minions. He discovered on this trip that she had selected him as one of the "chosen few". He was equally pleased and petrified. He recalled that it felt much like becoming a "made man" in the Patriarca crime family. *An honor, and a curse simultaneously.*

The second opportunity came four years ago when she celebrated his promotion to resources manager with dinner and a night sail with a few of the Board members. Now a sergeant in the "family", he was tasked with not only protecting innovative revenue generating projects, but her personal secrets as well. It was a weighty assignment, keeping the Figureheads and the Potentate at equilateral distances, yet proportionately well-informed. It took all the shrewd negotiations he could devise to avoid creating cracks the gentle façade of either the company or the woman. *It cost me more than a little sleep to get it right.*

Nathan's third visit to the harbor brought with it the devastating news of her parents' passing, just fifteen months ago. He'd taken over the funeral arrangements and made certain that her image had not been compromised during the grieving. It was her father's dying wish that she be well protected, and Nathan planned to do his best to fulfill that wish. He'd been Mr. Lambert's valet for several years and was very fond of the man. He was strong, clever, and compassionate. Those traits, plus the astounding skills he possessed in the business world, made him a difficult man to deny.

Even so, it was a tenuous line for Nathan to walk ... devising just the right level of outward professionalism and still retain some level of decorum that did not paint Paige as an unemotional bilge rat. She didn't make it easy, spending about five months impersonating a bipolar diagnosis. In the beginning, she lost herself to misery living with the shades drawn tight, eating nearly nothing, and screaming at every opportunity. Once that stormed had passed, her jubilant responses to miniscule triumphs far exceeded the inappropriate. The household staff was replaced three times as her paranoia of secrets becoming public manifested in anger, while a quarter-point jump in her stock portfolio brought on a champagne and caviar celebration. Paige's phases between mania and depression kept Nathan continuously guessing and re-tooling. There had been no tell-tale signs of shifting winds, and yet, he managed to keep her reputation on an even keel.

These last few months were a bit more tranquil. He was comfortable with her displacement of confidence and defiance, in equal measure. The tide had receded and calm had returned. Now, on this fourth harbor call without a horizon in sight, he wondered, *what sweet chaos will try to capsize me this time?*

"Welcome aboard." she said, offering her hand, which he took in his, uneasily. "Have a seat, help yourself to a drink. We have much to discuss. Isn't the view beautiful here?"

"Indeed." Nathan had learned early on that fewer words kept him without regret.

"Well, let's get right to it." Her eyes held a sparkle that set Nathan into worry mode. Her plans and schemes, which usually profited her happily, rarely worked out well for those on the periphery. He was wary of what was to come.

"As you know, I've been searching for some time for a more effective approach for our marketing program. Three months ago, I sent Aaren on a quest for a new social shaman to shepherd a resurrection the company's public persona. After quite a diligent search, she connected me, through several SKYPE sessions, with a brilliant gentleman named Thomas Laird," she said, picking up a page from an open file on the table next to her. "He comes highly recommended, a veteran writer with the Detroit Free Press. I'm told he was a wizard with reporting disasters, always putting a spin on things that increased readership rather than alienating them. That's exactly what we need here, don't you think? Our marketing program has grown stale... we need someone to jazz things up just a little bit. We had a final Skype call two weeks ago; and everything seems in order. Legal checked his background. He starts on Friday. I want you to keep an eye on him. Make sure he understands the company... but also, make sure he understands the town, too. You know just as well as I do that in order to bring all our plans to fruition over the long haul, he will need to understand not only our business, but our culture as well."

"I'm not quite sure what you're asking of me, ma'am. I mean, I get that he'll need a mentor to get through MouseTrax and its infrastructure... but I'm not sure what else I can do..." Nathan detected an eerily strong undertow in her request. He wanted to be certain of her intentions and her expectations. Getting it wrong could not only put his job - but his reputation - in jeopardy. "What exactly do you want me to do?"

"All right, Nathan, let me put it to you plainly. I need you to watch him. Make sure he is the man we want and need in this capacity. If he produces the kind of effects that have been insinuated to me, our profit margin could triple in the next year. Give him as much rope as he needs to string up others, but not enough to hang himself. Understand? I want to make sure he gets everything he needs to make waves and propel us into the next decade with our competitors cheering. Spare no expense... Spare no networking opportunities. Make what he wants to happen... happen. Oh, and keep this away from the Board. I don't need their infantile meddling complicating things. Am I clear?" Nathan silently nodded his comprehension.

Paige set down her drink, stood and descended the galley ladder. When she returned, Nathan stood and she handed him a noticeably padded, plain, white envelope. "This should make up for any inconvenience you may encounter."

"Of course, I'll take care of it." Nathan said, a bit reluctantly. He liked succinct directions; and this was far too vague for him. This new guy, Thomas, had just become Paige's new pet project, and Nathan had just been made his keeper. This had every mark of not ending well... and yet, it had to; Paige just demanded it, and there was little she was ever denied.

"Are you hungry? We could go to the clubhouse and get a bite, if you're interested." Just that fast, Paige had shifted gears again.

"No, thank you; I grabbed something before I came over, and I'm meeting up with friends in a little while for St. Paddy's day stuff." Although he had no choice in accepting her assignments, that didn't mean he had to spend his personal time with her. He knew there was more to this woman that she often kept under the surface; and more he suspected, to this particular assignment, but it was dangerous water to navigate without invitation, fraught with unknown rapids and invisible reefs. He realized he had to leave it alone for now, but it gnawed at his gut. It was too much uncertainty. He preferred gentle stability over impromptu risk indulgence.

"Suite yourself." she said, sitting back in her deck chair, and taking up her drink once again. "I'll see you at the office on Monday. I'm out tomorrow and Friday. Call Aaren or my cell if there are any developments." It was over. He had been dismissed.

"Very good. Thank you." Nathan said, quickly disembarking, heading back down the dock toward the security of the city streets.

****

From the boat, Paige noticed the crimson and amber hue beginning to streak against the western sky. She recalled the old mariner's adage; "red sky at night, sailor's delight". She took it as a good omen. She let a wry smile sneak past her lips. *My plan is beginning to take shape. Even Blackbeard would be proud.*

Chapter Two

"The words of the prophets are written on the subway walls and tenement halls and whispered in the sounds of silence."
~Paul Simon

After returning from a brief stint in Boston to search for an apartment, Thomas met up with his buddies at the Rathskeller to celebrate St. Patrick's Day and debate the virtues of mass transit over mountains of appetizers, and pitchers of green beer. "I've only been there a month, and already I love the place! I ride the T everywhere; I sold my Taurus to a dealership by the time I'd taken my third subway ride. Think about it; no car payments, no insurance, and no upkeep. It's perfect!" Thomas was almost giddy. His friends looked at him strangely. This was nothing new. Rarely did they "get" him.

"But what about personal freedom? That's lost. I mean, you really can't go out anytime you want and go anywhere, right? Your life is restricted to where and when the train goes." Stan was a die-hard Chrysler man, and through slurred speech was again, towing the company line. Thomas understood. Chrysler put food on the table; but it frustrated him sometimes that Stan was so closed-minded. Stan was not a fan of change, he didn't adapt well.

"Wrong! I can go anywhere I want, nearly any time of day. Okay, I'll grant you, the T closes down between two and five in the morning, but really, who's awake at that hour anyway? And, I can go from one end of town to the other for seventy-five dollars a month, with unlimited access! You can't do that here, the gas alone from the suburbs to downtown everyday costs twice that; and don't even get me started on what it costs to park in Boston! Mass transit is a good idea. I've never understood the Michigan bureaucrats who claim to support a smarter economic plan, yet continually vote down effective mass transit.

"Listen, I know that for decades, Detroit's economy has rested squarely on the shoulders of the auto industry - but I've gotta believe there's a compromise in there somewhere. Couldn't the Big Three create a future for our economy in transit trains *and* cars? For an industry that is so hell-bent on "moving forward", it seems that they aren't really moving at all. If you ask me, I think we're being held hostage by the UAW's pension plan." Thomas continued.

"Oh, come on," said Stan. "It's not that bad and you know it. You just got a new toy to play with and now you've got to convince us to leave our sandbox, throw out our old army men, and play with your new-fangled gadgets. Well, no thank you. I like my sandbox. There's no point in fixing it if it ain't broke."

"But Stan..." Thomas began to take this conversation to the next level, when Tim stepped in.

"Thom, let it go. Stan's smoking the Chrysler corporate dope and he's drunk. Just let it go." Since high school, Tim had always been the designated driver, and the referee. "Tell us more about this new gig. What are you doing out there, anyway? It can't be as sweet a deal as you had going at The Freep."

"Actually, Tim, it's not all bad. I'll still get to write, just without all the drama and exhaustion of chasing down leads and traveling cross-continent, and nobody's dying. This company, MouseTrax, is pretty progressive, and they have some interesting and unconventional ideas for their new marketing plan. The technology sector is growing, and I'm curious about where it may lead. Creating marketing pieces for them will be a lot like writing science fiction. The money's not bad, either. Boston's a pretty cool place. You guys'll have to come out and party this summer. I hear Fourth of July is insane."

"Are you sure you're not just running away, Thom?" challenged Stan. "I mean, really; new job, new place, new identity; are you sure you're just not running away?"

"Oh knock it off, Stan! The man's entitled to a little peace after the torture of the past year, don't you think?" Mark, usually a very calm and reserved person, at that moment, sounded like he might throw something. Stan heard the tone in Mark's voice, saw the glimmer of heat in Mark's eyes, shrugged his shoulders and retreated back into his beer.

"Look guys, I've got to get outta here," chuckled Thomas. "I've got an early flight in the morning, and I've got to show up ready to go on Friday." The last thing Thomas wanted right now was to dredge up the horror of the past year. "Thanks for the party, I'll be seein' ya."

Thomas hailed a cab and headed back to the house in Indian Village. It would be the last night he would ever spend in the house that he and Gillian bought together... the place where they created a home, and raised Eryn. But all of that was gone now. The only thing remaining of that part of his life were a few boxes left for the storage locker, and a couch, which neither would claim, and so they left it behind for the new owners.

As Thomas sank into the soft cushions that once cradled his happy family, wishing he hadn't indulged in that last pitcher of beer with the guys, the image of Paige Lambert on the SKYPE screen leapt into his brain. She'd followed him like a specter... her face, her voice, even some of her mannerisms... he was certain she was Gillian's doppelganger. *Get a grip Thom.* He chastised. *It's just this house. Your new boss is nothing like Gillian. No one could ever be like Gillian. Give it up.*

Chapter Three

"I have had dreams and I have had nightmares, but I have conquered my nightmares because of my dreams."
~Jonas Salk

When the phone rang, stirring Thomas from a fitful sleep, the clock at his bedside read 1:12am. He knew the Metro airport didn't start flying until seven o'clock. He called in a favor from a chopper pilot, a friend at a local TV station, and another from a private jet pilot he knew from his college years. He would land in Kremmling by five-thirty.

Sitting in the Gulfstream's cabin, watching first the Great Lakes and then the Great Plains laid out beneath him, the comfort of the past was gone. Now, in his silent suffering, he heard only the crashing of metal... the breaking of glass... the screaming of the tortured. He had heard it all before; he'd covered many stories like this in the past. Today was different. Today it was personal. All he could do was pray that Gillian and Eryn had somehow, impossibly survived.

The view outside the taxi's window screamed chaos as it prowled through the streets. This usually somber town was engulfed in defeat, as if a nuclear bomb had ravaged the city and decimated every board, brick, and line of mortar. It was a difficult ride from the airport to the Red Cross relief center. Through the early morning haze, Thomas saw every one of the sixteen thousand souls known to Kremmling, and many more from the surrounding area, congealed in the city square in a massive huddle of fear, sorrow and semiconscious sacrifice. People clung together in the middle of Main Street, weeping. Ambulances and fire trucks marked with Denver insignias passed by in a rage of red lights and howling sirens with network and local TV crews following closely behind. Had he been there as a journalist, the scene would be perfect fodder for Thomas' next column, but this time he couldn't detach.

Waving his press pass to gain access past several detours, the insanity all around reminded him of the week he'd spent, just five years earlier, covering the earthquake in Peru that killed nearly sixty-seven thousand people. The only road that got close enough to Gore Canyon, Grand County Road, was cordoned off, there was no access to the train that didn't hold a patrol of guards. The Red Cross relief center, set up at St. Peter's Catholic Parish, was just a half mile or so ahead. But the officer at the last road block refused to let him pass.

"Hey buddy, there's no access through this way. Go back to the town square and wait with all the rest of them. You're not going any farther." The burly officer pounded his fist on the car's hood to punctuate his seriousness. *Rookie move.*

Thomas hung his head outside the window and called to the man. "But officer, I've got a deadline... can't you just make one exception, please? We've got reports of Detroiters in the crash, and if I don't bring home the news, it'll be my job." Thomas tried hard to hide his emotional deluge, working the press angle to the best of his benefit.

A second, more composed officer walked up to the scene. "What's going on here?"

The first officer looked to his sergeant; "This guy is with the press, Sarge. He wants to get closer to the scene, but I told him that he needed to turn around."

The sergeant looked at Thomas and said, "Bob here is right. We can't let you get much closer, press or no. It's just too dangerous."

"But sir; this is important. Family members are waiting for some news of their loved ones. Think about if it was you... missing your wife and daughter down there... you'd want to find out the truth, wouldn't you?" Thomas fought hard to hold back the tears welling up in his eyes. His mind's eye flashed to a scene of Gillian and Eryn lying on the ground, wedged underneath a pile of steel debris. He blinked hard and refocused his attention on the pair of police officers that would determine his future.

The sergeant looked to his rookie and back to Thomas. His eyes softened and his tone grew nearly wistful. "Well, okay, but you'll have to go on foot from here. The roads have been closed all night, and they're tightening up on who comes and goes."

The rookie scowled; "but Sarge... we can't allow this reporter to..."

"Calm yourself, Jonsie. I'm sure that one more set of boots on the ground won't cause any more chaos than they already have down there." The sergeant looked back to Thomas. "Watch yourself, it's craziness down there." There was a gentleness about the sergeant that made Thomas take note. He knew that somewhere, this guy had family... and the rookie, Thomas knew, was just doing his job. This wasn't personal, although to Thomas, everything that happened to him today was personal.

Thomas handed the driver a fifty, slung his duffel to his shoulder, sprang out of the car, and pulled his notebook out of his coat's inside pocket. "Great, thank you! You guys have got a tough job here, and I really appreciate it. Hey, can I get your names? I'd like to look for you when I come back up the road, you know, get your take on the story for my article?" Thomas was grateful, and the only way he could really thank the officers was by giving them their fifteen minutes.

"Sure," said the sergeant. "The name's Jenson, Alex Jenson, and this is Matt Jones. We'll probably be here for the next twenty-four. Our force just isn't that big, you know?" There was a simultaneous elation and apprehension in the sergeant's face, talking with reporters was never predictable. Everyone likes to be seen as a hero in a moment of crisis... he just hoped he wouldn't regret this move.

Thomas began his brisk walk down Main Street, which quickly turned into a rapid trot. He just couldn't get there fast enough. *How much time have I already wasted staring through the sea of lost souls at each checkpoint, hoping to see her? Could I have already lost them?* The thought scraped at his brain and brought a torrent of tears. He stopped for a moment outside the Mercantile to regain his composure. *Breathe, dammit! You've got to get your act together if you're going to find them.* Thomas pulled a photo from his wallet to remind himself of the reality that he was working to regain. It was the visual mantra he had to cling to if he was going to find them.

At last, he found St. Peter's, and made his way inside. The undulation of crying, screaming, and flaring tempers nearly knocked him over. The arched sanctuary walls reverberated with the echo of every sigh, every whimper, and every angry roar. Sure, he'd been to plenty of these scenes in the past; but this time he was enveloped in it, sinking heavy like quartzite in quicksand. Thomas made his way as quickly as he could to the office. It probably took just a few minutes; but wearing his emotionally laced cement boots, the short walk seemed to take Thomas hours.

The woman behind the desk looked to be about sixty and exhausted. She wore the traditional volunteer's red vest, her hair was haphazardly tied at the nape of her neck, and her eyes were heavy with the dark circles of not enough sleep. She had stacks of papers in front of her and a telephone hanging off her shoulder. As she was wrapping up her conversation, Thomas despondently made an effort to get her attention. "Excuse me, ma'am. I'm looking for my wife and daughter; they were on the California Zepher out of Sacramento. The news anchor said I should come here."

The woman, whose name badge said *Nancy*, thrust a form and a pen into his hands. "Fill this out and bring it back to me. We can't identify anyone until the form's been filled out." Her gaze never left the desk, and her monotone voice betrayed the sincerity Thomas was sure she had yesterday afternoon when this whole thing began. *She's detached and overwhelmed, a protection mechanism, I'm sure. Did she even hear my voice?* He needed a new approach. He stepped away from the window for a few minutes and gave the people behind him their chance at the desk. He returned then, with a little more energy and his investigative persona.

"Hi, I'm Thomas Laird, Detroit Free Press;" he said, flashing his press pass in that 'I have clout' way that always seemed to be most effective on overworked volunteers. Nancy looked up from her desk, and over the rim of her glasses, face slightly flushed. Her small-town exuberance for any sort of media attention could not be contained; although much to her credit, she worked hard to keep it hidden.

"What can I do for you, sir;" she asked with a slight titter in her voice. Thomas put his press pass back in his pocket and readied his pen while flipping a page on his note pad, in exactly that romantic way she had seen countless reporters do in the movies and on TV. *This guy looks like the real thing.* Nancy was just a bit star-struck, eager to see how her name might end up in the papers.

"Well, as I said, er, Nancy; I'm from the Detroit Free Press, doing a story on the swift response and difficult work of the Red Cross Volunteers. Every other paper will be doing stories on the victims, and yes, they're the important focus in a story like this;" Thomas leaned into the window, lowering his voice slightly. "But so often, the volunteers, good people like yourself, never get the acknowledgment they so richly deserve. Do you have just a few moments to talk?"

Nancy pulled over another volunteer to take her place at the desk, invited Thomas into the office, and led him to a cubicle in the back of the room. Twenty minutes later he had learned all of the details he needed. He discovered that the most critical cases were being airlifted to Denver, and the severely injured passengers were being taken to Kremmling Memorial Hospital. Those who were more stable were being treated at West Grand High School, because the hospital only had nineteen beds. He learned that they had set up a make-shift morgue at the town's Masonic Lodge. Nancy gave him the names of both the Kremmling Town Supervisor and the Red Cross Supervisor in charge of bereavement and connecting families with their loved ones.

I've been a crisis newspaper reporter for nearly fifteen years. It never ceases to amaze me just how forthcoming people can be if you appear interested in their mission and play to their ego just a little bit. "Nancy," he said, with genuine sincerity; "I really want to thank you for taking the time away from your work here to talk with me. We hear so little about the wonderful work that the Red Cross does in a crisis like this, and I feel that now, after speaking with you, I have a much better understanding and I can pass that along to my readers."

As he got up to leave, Nancy put her hand on his arm; "Wait here one moment, would you please?" When Nancy returned three minutes later, she handed him a laminated index card with a Red Cross insignia on one side, and printed identification credentials on the other. "This is for you. It should get you past all of the security checkpoints and into the more guarded areas of the operation. We really appreciate you taking the time to let the people back in Detroit know just how important our work is. Usually, volunteering where we are needed is its own reward. But a little positive press now and then certainly makes our jobs easier."

"Thank you, Nancy. I'll do my best to get the message out." Thomas hugged Nancy, not really knowing if he would ever make good on his promise... he truly wanted to, he was genuine in his appreciation, he just didn't know if he would... or could.

Pocketing the pass card and his notebook, Thomas shouldered his duffel once again, and headed to West Grand High School, the first stop on his list to survey the triage victims. He really wanted to hit the hospital first, but the school was closer; and he knew that if he was going to have any hope of finding his family, he had to be as swift and as logical about his search as possible. *I've already wasted too much time.*

The scene at the high school was mass hysteria. The news reports put the number of passengers and crew at just over three hundred, and it seemed as if every one of those souls had a band of at least a dozen family and friends searching for word of their survival. Add to that the mix of reporters, EMS workers and regular townsfolk looking on, and it was as though a gang of zombies and a battalion of soldiers were battling for control. Thomas reached the blockade about twenty feet from the door, flashed his Red Cross card, and was magically waved through. Not even one questioning word from the rent-a-cop who was manning the floodgate. It's not that the guard didn't want to do his job effectively, he simply didn't have time; there was a horde of angry mobsters headed in his direction.

Thomas made it into the receiving area, and noticed rows of people, three or four deep, gawking at what appeared to be a blank wall. As he was able to get a little closer, Thomas saw that what they were staring at were several sheets of paper taped to the wall with double-column lists of names, printed in capital letters. These were the survivors, the ones who had made it to the relative safety of triage instead of the uncertainty of critical care and air-evac. The lists were grouped by classroom and arranged alphabetically. *The Red Cross really is the epitome of organization.* Thomas scanned the sheets with the rest of the hopeful, checking each list three times to be sure, but not finding Gillian or Eryn among any of those cited.

There was a simultaneous sigh of relief and jolt of fear that overtook him in that instant. This was the perfect example of a 'defining moment in time'. *Either my family is safe in another treatment facility, or gone.* Gone... he couldn't imagine... He backed away from the wall and meandered toward the door once again. Outside, he slumped his exhausted body into a Greyhound bus stop bench across the street. He pulled the photo out of his wallet again, for strength. It was that ridiculous snapshot he'd taken on Christmas morning. Gillian and Eryn stood in front of the tree, each in their matching red flannel pajamas, holding a brightly wrapped box. Gillian wore that gentle smile that always knocked him off his feet; and Eryn hopped on one foot, giggling almost beyond control, a silly little sprig of hair falling across her face. It was a perfect moment. He couldn't bear the thought of losing them. *They're alive, they just have to be.*

"Okay, what's next?" Thomas pulled out his notebook to review the details that Nancy had given him. The Masonic Lodge had been set up as the morgue space, and the hospital was treating the critically wounded. Each stood at opposite ends of town. The path he took now would reveal his future, and his sanity. "It's pointless to head toward the morgue... if they're... well, there's nothing I can do. So, the hospital it is." Voting for possibility just as Gillian had taught him, he pulled his disheveled soul from the bench and headed south.

Finding a car would be impossible. Although the derailment had happened nearly twenty-four hours ago, the town was still in shut-down mode, and the streets were polluted with too many people and too much anger. Foot traffic was the only option. *Fortunately, Kremmling is a small town, just three miles across. Walking is reasonable.* What frustrated Thomas most was the time lost. It was selfish, but true; driving would have brought his misery to an end - one way or another - much more quickly.

There were five checkpoints Thomas had to get through in order to reach the hospital, and surprisingly, his magical Red Cross pass worked magnificently. When his weary body triggered the automatic sliding door at Kremmling Memorial, the aromas of the place hit like a heavyweight boxer's blow. A pungent blend of antiseptic, pure oxygen, blood, mourning and anger spun his head into an emotional vertigo. With one hand trailing against the wall, it took him a few moments to regain his balance as he walked through the halls, searching.

When he finally reached the nurse's station, one might have thought he was a passenger on that ill-fated train rather than a well-seasoned reporter. Thomas was exhausted. His clothes dripped from him like the rags of a war-torn peasant child; his duffel bag hung from his shoulder weighted with the burden of too many lonely nights on the road; and his face and forehead were mopped in sweat.

"Sir, are you all right?" came the voice of the nurse standing behind the desk.

"My name is Thomas Laird," he heaved. "I'm looking for my wife and daughter. They were on the Zepher out of Sacramento." His voice was barely a whisper, hoarse from all the crying and screaming at God he'd done on the hike across town.

"What are their names, sir?" inquired the nurse with a mater-of-fact tone.

"Gillian and Eryn Laird." The words escaped from him in a doubtful whisper.

"Can you spell the last name for me, please?" asked the nurse.

"L-A-I-R-D. Please, are they on your list?" The nurse flipped several pages on her clip board, and finally poked a finger at the page with a resounding thud.

"Yes. Laird, room sixteen. Go down this hall, turn left, and it's the second door on the right."

"Thank you." Euphoria stung through Thomas like a thousand volts of electricity. *They are alive!* He stumbled down the corridor and finally found it; room sixteen. He paused a minute outside the door, not sure of what he might find inside. Taking a deep breath, he gently pushed open the door and walked in. A nurse appeared to his right, just stepping out of the small bathroom, paper towel drying her hands.

"Can I help you, sir?" The nurse was young, probably in her mid or late twenties, most likely a recent graduate from nursing school. She wore a crisp white uniform and had her hair pulled up on top of her head in a small bun; a stethoscope draped around her neck, and a note pad stuck out of one pocket. Her name tag read *Doris McCann, RN*.

"My name is Thomas Laird. I was told my wife Gillian and daughter Eryn were here."

"Yes, sir; may I see some identification, Please?"

"Of course, thank you for asking." Thomas produced his driver's license. The nurse looked to the card and back to Thomas' war-torn face.

"Thank you, sir." The nurse handed his ID back to him and then led Thomas behind the curtain. He saw Gillian lying in the bed before him, sound asleep. A breathing tube was thrust down her throat and several slender IV tubes ran from poles on either side of the bed, dripping medicines and nutrients into her listless arms. Her face and head were covered in bandages and her left leg, slightly elevated on a pillow, was wrapped in a plaster cast from hip to toe.

"She's had some abdominal bleeding, which the doctors were able to control with surgery; a broken femur; and multiple cuts on her face. She has about forty stitches in her head from where the doctor pulled out several large shards of glass, evidently she was sitting near a window. The doctor has been watching her closely for signs of other internal trauma and concussion. But so far, her heart, lungs and kidneys seem to be functioning properly."

It was difficult for Thomas to see his normally exuberant artist wife so passive and unresponsive. *She's alive! That's enough, for now.* Standing at the foot of Gillian's bed, marveling at the wonderment of modern medicine and his own elation at her survival, his bubble deflated as he noticed the empty bed next to Gillian's. Turning to the nurse he asked, "What about our daughter, Eryn? She was on the train, too. The nurse at the front desk told me she was here."

The nurse looked down at her clipboard with eyes that teared up as she read the note. Averting her gaze, and in a quiet voice, she said simply; "I'm sorry Mr. Laird. Your daughter didn't make it."

****

Thomas' body exploded with convulsions. Sweat dripped from his forehead, his hair soaked the couch pillow. "Damn!" He looked around the house, reorienting himself. "Detroit... not Kremmlin... Get a grip, man." He walked to the kitchen and filled a glass with cold water from the tap. "Shit, Gillian... why won't this insanity stop?" he whispered.

After a shower, and one last walk through the house he shared for six years with a family he knew he would never get back, he slowly closed the door and stepped away from the only sanctuary he'd ever known. After a brief detour at the real estate office to hand off the last of the paperwork and the keys, he made his way to the airport, then to Boston, and a new life. Well, *let's hope this doesn't completely suck.*

Chapter Four

"You're this rat in the American maze, working your way towards the cheese, which is a job."
~Kevin Costner

Friday was Thomas' first day at MouseTrax. He wasn't quite sure why they'd started him at the end of the week, but he was grateful that he could ease into his new surroundings and then have a few days to catch his breath. As he walked the halls to his office, following the receptionist's instructions, Thomas was greeted surreptitiously by Paige Lambert. She said only a few, quiet words in passing as Nathan appeared behind.

"Don't worry about her," he said as they walked down the hall together. "She can be a bit persnickety sometimes. I'm Nathan Hackthorn," he said, offering his hand. "Welcome aboard. Here's your office. It's not much, but at least you've got a door instead of just a cube."

"I'm sure this will be fine, thank you." he said, shaking hands with Nathan. Thomas was a little uneasy in situations that didn't involve burning buildings, screaming women or SWAT teams in full battle gear. He hoped he wouldn't be out of place for too long. It had been quite a while since a desk was his station in life.

"Well, you should find everything you need on the desk; the password to your computer is on that green card. The key to your office door is there, too. Oh, and if you click the "help" icon on your desktop, you'll find the company handbook and the time clock procedure." Nathan held out his business card and offered it to Thomas. "I'm going to be your acclimation buddy for the next couple of days, just to help you get settled. So don't worry about it if things go a little slowly at first. I'll string you along. Just nose around... find out where things are for now. I'll come back in a bit and take you on a tour and introduce you around." Nathan smiled with what seemed to be authenticity... he hoped.

"Thanks, Nathan. I appreciate it." As Nathan left, Thomas sat down and tried to make sense of his workspace. He wasn't very sure what would come of this new adventure... but he knew that he had to make the best of it; at least until he could somehow find a way to get back to Gillian. *Now what?* Thomas looked around the desk and noticed very little paper, which made sense, considering that MouseTrax was a computer firm... but he also didn't find any clues regarding his job assignments. He flipped on the computer, logged in, and poked around. The desktop was filled with the usual stuff... but nothing that might give a hint as to what he was supposed to do next. Just as he was about to click over to the timecard procedure tutorial, a window appeared with an email.

From: Paige Lambert, MouseTrax, CEO
To: Thomas Laird, MouseTrax, Marketing Manager

Dear Mr. Laird,

Forgive me for not spending more time to personally welcome you aboard; but as you might imagine, my schedule is extremely full.

We are pleased to have you join the team, and are confident that your expertise will assist the growth of MouseTrax. I am sure that you are curious as to your specific duties. Nathan Hackthorn will be guiding you through your orientation of the company, and assisting you in becoming familiar with our policies and procedures. However, I have a project that I expect will hold your immediate attention.

    We are currently in a marketing conundrum. We need to enhance our public relations presentation to the industry at the next conference in Worchester, at the end of July. Our biggest competitor is MicroTech out of Maine. Both of our companies have been working on a developing nano technology, which we believe will revolutionize the future of diagnostic medicine. Although still in the developmental stages, perhaps as many as five years down the pike, we are certain that our technology will be released to the market first, and in full operational mode, rather than the beta mode our competitors promise.

    Please begin work on a program that will introduce this technology and its intended use, applications and interface with medical practitioners and the benefits to their patients. The program should be approximately thirty minutes long, and encourage audience engagement. In addition, we will need approximately 250 - 500 words for a brief trade article, as well as two commercial spots; one 30 seconds, and the other 60 seconds in length. Nathan can connect you with the appropriate individuals in R&D, as well as give you access to white papers to give you background information.

    I expect to see preliminary results, which we will tweak as necessary, in my inbox no later than June 1st.

    Your work has come highly recommended, and we are expecting tremendous results.

    Regards,
    Paige Lambert

Thomas clicked *save* on his desktop, and sat back in his chair. *Not even in the building for an hour, and already... this. It's a good thing they don't expect too much.* He sighed heavily. *Well, if this is how it's going to be, I'd better figure out how to get paid.* Thomas spent the next forty-five minutes going over the computerized timecard system and completing his payroll information; then sending it off to the Human Relations director via email, as instructed. Thomas wasn't completely digitally incompetent, but as someone whose career had been established in the world of paper, this digital approach was going to take a little getting used to.

A few minutes later, Nathan returned. "So, are you up for the grand tour?"

"Sure, Nathan. And, I'm going to need your help in getting some information on the nano project. I just got an email from Ms. Lambert, and..."

"So, she's put you to work already, eh? Not a problem. I'll get you squared away. But a word the wise; don't take her attitude too seriously. She's got a gruff exterior - all business - and she's worse on the inside." Nathan laughed as though he'd just told the best inside joke ever heard. Thomas chuckled politely, but still felt lost. "Don't worry about it." Nathan said. "Let's go show you around the maze."

The two men walked out the office and turned right. They traveled down one corridor after another. There were small signs on the walls indicating the direction of each department - which was good - because there was no way Thomas would have been able to navigate without them. *This really does feel like being a mouse in a maze. Wonder if I'll ever find the cheese.* Thomas thought. *What have I gotten myself into?*

Two hours later, after a slight detour to the nano development wing and a brief conversation with the manager, Grant Sanderson, who promised to send production information to Thomas' email; Nathan and Thomas headed across the street to a restaurant for lunch.

"So, what do you think so far?" Nathan asked after they had ordered.

"Well, it's a bit overwhelming right now," Thomas said with a bit of a sigh. "But I'm sure that in time, I'll figure it out." He was dubious, but wanted to at least sound optimistic on his first day.

"Well, don't take too long to dig in. Lambert's not one for waiting. One of the reasons she named the company MouseTrax, aside from the obvious computer connection, is because she enjoys running the place at the speed of mice... scamper, scamper." Nathan again, laughed at his own joke; but the humor of it was lost on Thomas.

"I'm used to fast-paced jobs." Thomas said. "There's nothing more intense or time-driven than the newspaper business... especially when working the disaster desk. But this is completely different."

"What do you mean by disaster desk?" Nathan asked, raising an eyebrow.

"Well, anytime there was a disaster or tragedy, I was one of the guys that wrote the story. Earthquakes, forest fires, hurricanes... you name it—I've covered it. And let me tell you, there was never a lack of story material. My editor was really good at sniffing out the places and times when people suffered the most; and he'd send me in—vulture for carrion—to get the story, humanize it and get it back before the next day's release." Thomas took a sip of his beer, reflecting on the mayhem his old life produced. He took another sip, and let go a reluctant scowl.

"It sounds like things moved pretty quickly. How did you deal with it all?" Nathan seemed sincerely interested, so Thomas explained.

"You learn to weave and bob a lot; you disassociate a lot; and you tend to take on the personal mantra that 'there but for the grace of God, go I'. Most importantly, though, I had to move quickly; get in, get the story, and get out without becoming emotionally involved." Thomas illustrated the explanation by running two fingers to the center of the table and back to his place again. "For that, I was glad that I had immediate deadlines. In the newspaper world, if it bleeds, it leads; but also, if the bodies have grown cold, it's not news anymore." Thomas took another bite of his burger. A stale quiet hung between the two men for a few moments.

"That must be a great way to make a living." Nathan said, sarcastically, sipping his beer in what seemed to be a gesture of remorse.

"Yep. That's why I left. I just got burned out. Living at that pace, and seeing the world through the broken hearts and homes of the people you write about, with absolutely no concern for their personal humanity or privacy—just to get a story—it wears pretty thin after a while. I had to get out before I collapsed completely. Other guys have done it—lost everything and ended up crawling into a bottle; with no connection to their own humanity anymore. I didn't want to be one of those guys." Thomas said, a bit of hollowness in his voice. "I want to write about the things that are moving forward, building up... I'm done writing about the things that are falling apart. It's just too depressing."

"Well, it looks like you've come to the right place." said Nathan. "Our nano project alone has so much potential to build a better life for people who need it most... people with medical issues that, if detected early, might mean improving their quality of life forever; not to mention giving their family a bit of a respite, as well." Nathan took another sip of his beer as though he were toasting Thomas on New Year's Eve. "We've got plenty of other projects, too; lots of connections to improving the educational system, the transportation industry, and entertainment, too. There is a lot of good going on at MouseTrax. It should be a nice change of perspective for you." Nathan said, signaling the waitress to bring their check.

"I sure hope so, Nathan. I've been living in the shadows for so long, there's fungus beginning to grow where my enthusiasm for life once lived. That's got to change." Thomas punctuated his statement by draining his glass and placing it back on the table with a defiant thud.

The two men stood as Nathan dropped money for the bill and tip on the table. "Oh, I don't think you'll have any problems here, my friend. Now, sleeping... that may be a problem." Again, he laughed at his private joke.

Thomas didn't get it, again. *One thing at a time;* Thomas thought as the two men walked out the door and back to the office. *First, the job; then the humor.*

Chapter Five

"The tricks of magic follow the archetypes of narrative fiction – there are tales of creation and loss, death and resurrection, and obstacles that must be overcome."
~Marco Tempest

Morning arrived with tarnished light and a rumbling of thunder in the distance. Rain drummed gently upon the window and skylight, reminding Thomas of the little heartbeat that would echo no more. Just as Thomas began to sit up and make peace with the reality he'd hoped was a dream, nurse McCann emerged again, carrying yet another tray of substandard nourishment.

"The doctor will be here in about an hour to evaluate your wife, Mr. Laird. It's quite possible that you will be able to talk with her today. Breakfast is the fuel you'll need to get you both to the next phase of her recovery. Please eat." The nurse set down the tray, checked Gillian's chart and IV drips, and left as silently as she had arrived. Thomas knew that she really had his wife's best interests at heart; but he was having a problem disassociating his anger - and unfortunately, Doris was his scapegoat.

Despite the fact that breakfast was another marginal meal of powdered eggs, nearly blackened dry toast and some fruit cup thing he couldn't quite identify; the coffee was greatly appreciated. Thomas felt the desire for an entire pot, although he wasn't sure *that* would even be enough to get him through this day. Just as he was finishing the unidentifiable citrus, the doctor arrived with nurse McCann close at his heels.

"Good Morning, Mr. Laird," said the doctor, extending his hand. "I'm Edmond Westchester. I've been the team lead on your wife's case." Doctor Westchester was a very tall man, six and a half feet, if he was an inch; with a moustache that outlined thin lips and a wiggly smile. He wore black rimmed glasses and a haircut that seemed longer than it should have been for someone in his profession. His elongated vowels exposed his Canadian roots, but his hands were large, warm and suggested full competency.

"Doris tells me that you've been updated on your wife's condition. She came through the surgery well and from the stability she's exhibited overnight, I think we can go ahead and remove her breathing tube and wake her up. But before we do that, I need to give you the answers you need regarding the death of your daughter."

Thomas took a deep breath and leaned heavily against the edge of the bed, bracing himself for what he knew would be a mortal blow to his courage on many levels. He wasn't sure he wanted to hear it, but he knew that he had to. Gillian would have questions, and he would need the answers.

"Eryn died of a massive brain hemorrhage. She had several areas of blunt-force trauma, we suspect from hitting her head on the cabin wall. Her occipital lobes seemed to be intact, but we saw several indications on the MRI of spinal cord damage, we don't believe she suffered much, as the damage to her spinal cord was immediate and prevented her from feeling any pain.

"When she was brought here with your wife, she was not breathing. We did everything we could to revive her, but the damage was just too extensive. She was pronounced dead shortly after the MRI. But the point I want you to hear, Mr. Laird, is that we believe that she did not suffer. After the first blow, she was knocked unconscious, and felt absolutely no pain. If there is a positive note to any of this, it is that your daughter did not suffer, did not feel pain, and did not understand fear at the time of her death. It was as peaceful an event as it could have been for her, all things considered."

Silent tears flooded from Thomas' eyes. It was a deluge he could not control. Nurse McCann offered him a box of tissues, which he accepted with a nod of his head, for he could not form words. The image of his daughter being so horribly brutalized caught him in a space between absolute rage and profound sadness. The thought of Gillian holding Eryn, completely powerless to stop any of the violence against them, cast a shadow of sympathy over her that Thomas would never be able to express. *How awful it must have been for her to watch it all - certainly much more painful than even her own injuries.*

After Thomas had regained his composure, doctor Westchester continued. "I'm so sorry for your loss, Mr. Laird. But now we must focus on your wife and getting through her recovery. The most important thing we can do for her now is to get her back to breathing on her own, so that her body can begin the healing process in the most natural way possible. We will keep her on pain medication for as long as is necessary, but I would like to see her taking solid foods within a day or two. I don't foresee any neurological damage, but we won't know that for sure until she can speak and move about on her own. Are you ready?"

Thomas wiped his eyes for one last time, stood upright and squared his shoulders. "Okay, I'm ready whenever you are." He knew that the next few days would be the most difficult, but he believed that they could make it through. He believed in their love. He believed in the strength of it. He was ready for whatever Gillian needed, and he would give it to her, as he always had, unconditionally.

      Thomas watched from a safe, out of the way distance, as doctor and nurse removed the breathing apparatus and all but two of the IV tubes from his wife's body. He watched as they administered a drug that they said would slowly allow her to become conscious. He listened carefully as they warned him that she would be confused and perhaps somewhat afraid for the first few moments after waking up. Thomas moved to Gillian's bedside and took her hand in his, cradling it warmly, gently, just as he had the day Eryn was born.

      It took about five or six full minutes before Gillian's eyelids began to flutter and her fingers began to twitch. Thomas spoke to her in soft tones, reassuring her with every ounce of courage he could find. "It's okay, dear. I'm here. You're safe, it's okay. Open your eyes, Gillian. It's okay."

****

      Thomas closed his journal with a defiant thud, and then tossed it aside with expert abandonment. " 'Write about it,' the shrink sad. 'Writing is your healing elixir. Transferring your memories into words will free you from the pain of the past' ". Thomas took a long draw from his double scotch. "What a quack!"

Chapter Six

*"Our greatest weakness lies in giving up.
The most certain way to succeed is always to try
just one more time."*
~Thomas A. Edison

After a long week of making his way through the MouseTrax maze, Thomas was exhausted. As he took the T from Government Center in blissful robotic monotony back to his apartment in Cambridge, he thought about the changes he was making in his life. *Would Gillian like this life better?* He wondered where she was, what she was doing, and if she'd ever take him back. *I have to find a way to make that happen... but first, a hot shower, a hot meal and a warm bed.*

A block or so from his house was a little deli where he picked up a hot roast beef sandwich and a cup of matzo ball soup... the sandwich was for sustenance, the soup for comfort. Throughout his life, even though he was raised in a Lutheran household, his grandmother had always praised the healing properties of matzo ball soup. "Whether physical or emotional, the magic of matzo ball soup will heal you. There's a good reason it's lasted through the centuries, you know." His grandmother's voice came in crystal clear recollection. Even though she had passed some years ago, there were some things about her that would stay with him forever. It warmed his soul to think that she was still looking out for him.

As he trudged the thirty-two steps up to his apartment, he thought about what his grandmother might think of the direction he was headed in now. He hoped she'd be pleased. He opened the door to his apartment and stared at the stacks of boxes lining the living room. Even though it had been over a month since the move, he was having a difficult time adjusting to making it feel permanent. *Oh look, another maze. I've really got to get things unpacked. Now, where'd I put the couch?*

****

Saturday morning, the sun's warmth magnified through the bay window and Thomas realized that he'd spent the night on the couch, his dinner relics standing sentinel on the boxes around him. He pushed the sleep from his eyes and focused on his wristwatch. *Six-thirty. Ugh!* He was still tired, sore and felt like he'd slept in a fox hole overnight. It was oddly comforting. He pushed his way past the boxes, rifled through one sitting near the fridge, and found the coffee. *Ah, coffee, my old friend. Nice to see you made the trip.* In another box, he discovered the coffee maker, and set it to work. *Nothing is going to get done this morning without caffeine.*

Twenty minutes later, the shower, which he'd neglected the night before, and his coffee, were done. Taking a long sip from the steaming strength, he went to work on eliminating the labyrinth from his apartment. By about one-thirty, he'd filled most of the dressers, closets and cupboards and broke down the boxes to deliver to the dumpster out back. His space was beginning to look livable. *A house, but not a home.* The four rooms he now occupied didn't feel much different than the many hotel rooms he'd stayed in over the past ten years... *So sterile without Gillian. I miss you, babe.*

****

"Thomas, I'm sorry, but I just can't do this anymore. I thought I could... thought I could heal, forget, ignore it and move on... but I just can't. Living here - with you - is just too... too hard. I have to go."

It was then that he noticed for the first time the suitcases lined up near the back door. He didn't know how long she'd been planning this - but he knew that those suitcases weren't there when he left for the pub a few hours ago... He tried desperately to change her mind. "No, Gillian; we can get through this - but we need to stay together. I know it's been hard on you, it's been hard on me too; but I really believe that we can make our lives normal again. We just have to believe in each other. Please don't give up - not yet. We just need more time, that's all. You'll see, it'll get better. It has to."

Thomas watched as Gillian walked quietly and calmly to the sink to rinse out her glass. *She seems so empty. It's as if her spirit has escaped and there is nothing left but this hollow shell.*

"I don't see how things can get any better when every day I have to look at her empty room, her bed that never gets slept in; the toys that never get played with. I know you said we could move her things to storage, but I just don't think that will be enough. I can't do this anymore... I can't wake up and look into her eyes - your eyes - every morning and know that I will never be able to hold her, kiss her, laugh with her ever again. The two of you were always so much alike... same smile, same laugh... it's just too hard!" She crumpled on the floor in a lump, tears streaming silently down her face. The loss of her daughter had left her so vacant; she didn't even have the strength to cry anymore. Her face was hollow, like a lost alien on a planet she could not understand. She quivered slightly, and when Thomas came to her side, trying to comfort her; she erupted in a flurry of emotion. "No!" she screamed, pushing him away. "Don't you get it, Thomas? I just can't do this anymore. I have to go!"

Gillian leapt to her feet, slung her purse to her shoulder, flung open the door to the garage, and grabbed a suitcase in each hand, bolting for the safety of her escape. He was dumfounded. He didn't know what to do, what to say. He just stood there, mouth agape, and watched as she threw her things into the back seat and drove off into the night.

When her tail lights were out of sight, he closed the garage door and returned to the cavernous kitchen, weary with emotional exhaustion. *What just happened?* He was still having problems trying to get his brain to make sense of it. He collapsed onto the kitchen floor, in the exact space his wife had occupied moments before, still, emotionless, lost. Fifteen minutes later, after a raging tirade of tears, he finally came to terms with the fact that she was gone, and she would not be coming back.

I can't stay in this house... I have to get out. It was well past eleven; his flight mode was in full force. He grabbed the keys from the hall table, and like her, escaped into the night. About twenty minutes later, he pulled up in front of The Rathskeller. It had been a favorite haunt of his for years. Since just after high school and all through college. He and his writing buddies used to meet here and compare the day's news, and discuss the best way to write it over a couple of pints and some good German food. It had been a safe place for him. He was well liked there, and he felt at ease. But tonight, he was hoping to be anonymous. *No talking, no writing... just a quiet drink and a dark corner. I need to think.*

****

The next morning hit him square in the head, when the alarm rang. The scotch he'd had the night before while staring into the emptiness of his Cambridge apartment made him realize why it was he didn't drink scotch. Stumbling to the shower, he prayed that the hole-drill hammering in his head would stop soon. *It's funny how every I time forget a life lesson, it magically reappears and reminds me of its importance. All I want right now is hot steam on my body, and hot coffee in my gullet.*

The shower didn't help. Coffee didn't either. It was just another reminder of how his life had changed in the past six months. All that he had ever counted on, all that he had ever invested in, the things that built his belief system on, they were all different now. *It's odd how one day can change everything about who you are and how you live. I wonder if I'll ever adjust. Do I really want to?* It was a question that ran through his head on a regular basis. In order to heal, he was told; he had to move on. *But if healing means forgetting and abandoning; well, don't think I want to heal. I suppose Gillian and I still agree on some things.* The battle raged on, day in and day out.

After fumbling in his closet for nearly ten solid minutes and still discovering nothing that he wanted to wear, he gave up and settled for the black jeans, black T-shirt and gray button up that had gotten far more use than they should have lately. Morbid seemed to be his style these past few months; anything else just seemed - fake.

Checking the mail before leaving for the office yesterday, Thomas found an envelope from Mark back in Detroit. Only now, did he feel brave enough to open it. Inside, he found a copy of his last Freep column with a yellow post-it note that read, "Thought you might want this. They ran it on page one. ~Mark."

A Father's Pain: by Thomas Laird

The funeral was on a beautiful Saturday afternoon. The sun was bright and bold, bouncing off the rooftops and the fountain in the town square. Birds glided around, swooping overhead as if saluting their wings in a sign of respectful mourning. The procession, led by the small urn being carefully carried down main street to the little cemetery on the outskirts of town, was followed by a small, somber cadre of people. Some were the townspeople we'd met - Nancy from the Red Cross, nurse Doris McCann and Doctor Westchester from the hospital, and some others who had attended every funeral since the crash. A few of our friends from Michigan flew in to pay their respects, but Gillian's parents didn't make it. Her mother's neurosis was in overdrive, and she was overly concerned—for no apparent reason, other than she seemed to enjoy worrying—about being slaughtered in an accident, too. Gillian's mother was known to be irrational now and again, but this time it affected Gillian more than usual. Rightfully so.

Looking back, I was frustrated with the pace of the day—I knew that respectfully, I had to allow Gillian this time to grieve and begin to heal, but I felt like I just needed it to be over with, so we could move on. Perhaps that's not the healthiest way to cope with the loss of your child - but it was how I had always dealt with things. In, out, done.

Being a reporter, always on a deadline, you learn how to get in, get the story, and get out - before the emotion of the day hit you. It is the only way to stay objective and it is the only possible way to do the job day in and day out - tragedy after tragedy. There were a couple of reporters straggling behind the procession; one from The Chicago Tribune, and another from the Denver News. Both were quite respectful, but it still irked me that they felt the need to continue following us. It had been four weeks, and they just couldn't let it go. So much for respecting "the brotherhood". The bottom feeders were also there - beyond contemptuous, and there were several I'd like to see stripped of their credentials.

Gillian and I followed close behind, gripping tightly to each other's hands, as if disconnecting from one another would send us careening out into space. The horror of our lives still plagued us and we were both just trying to save what was left of our sanity.

Parents aren't supposed to bury their children.

We chose to lay Eryn to rest in Kremmling because it seemed like the right thing to do. Shipping her remains back to Detroit for the funeral seemed too much like using UPS to deliver fish. The impersonality of it all - the disembodiment of our little angel's happy personality - it was too cruel for us. It was a choice neither of us could make. Dry ice, a wooden box, and a plane ride that would have ripped our guts out with every altitude shift. No... it was far better to bury her there, where it all happened. It took a lot of convincing... and more tears than I care to recall... but at last, Gillian agreed that it would be too difficult to bury her close to home, knowing that we could never hold her again. The constant reminder that Eryn was no longer with us would paralyze us. I told Gillian that I felt that we would be spending so much time at the grave site that the rest of our lives would perish, too. She reluctantly agreed. She was understandably conflicted on this decision. But in the end, we agreed that an annual trip back to Kremmling was all we could handle—for now.

Once we'd reached the cemetery, the pastor stepped forward and began his final remarks. He asked us if we wanted to say anything—but neither of us could think of words that could heal us at that moment. We couldn't think of anything anyone could say that would make this horrible day any easier, and we didn't want to offer more mana to the hedonistic journalists. So we remained silent and let those who were trained do their jobs.

The pastor spoke of the innocence of a life taken far too early. He spoke of how important it was for us to remember that Eryn was at peace and in a place that offered comfort and abundant love. He continued to talk about the importance of never forgetting, and accepting the healing process that was necessary. He spoke of a greater plan, of how we don't always understand the plan, but we must trust that it has purpose. The rhetoric was familiar to me. It was the same speech given at every funeral of a tragic accident. Although his intentions were well-placed, his voice was wasted effort. There would be no comfort found that day. Not for us.

    Despite the pastor's best efforts, I was angry. My anger welled up inside my chest with suicide bomber enthusiasm. I gripped Gillian's hand a little tighter and looked into her pained eyes; but she couldn't see me. She could only see the loss of our daughter. She could only see the emptiness of her own heart and soul. Her eyes were vacant - empty - lost. I wished there was something I could do to support her, something I could say, some magical power I could convey through a touch - but it was useless. I could no better eliminate her sadness than she could soften my anger.

    As they placed Eryn's tiny urn into the hole, I stepped up and dropped a small envelope inside the hole. *Write.* It was the only thing I could think of to do. The only possibility for a minor moment of healing. When the urn had reached its shelf, I walked over and dumped a shovel of dirt on it. There was a light thud as the soil began to reclaim its rightful spot in the hole. It was a sound of expectation, a sound of pain, a sound of finality. Gillian came over to my side, kissed my cheek, and taking the shovel, added her own recognition of the end of our daughter's life to the cavern. Then, each guest in turn, helped us bury our daughter. There would be no more playing in the park. No more gentle mornings reading the comics together. No more snowball fights and snow angles. I'd heard that life finds a way back from such devastation, but at that moment, I didn't believe it.

    As we walked back silently toward town, we noticed the sun beginning to set on the horizon. The mix of red, orange, yellow and blue reminded me of a painting Gillian once created after our first honeymoon night. Our hotel room balcony overlooked the ocean, and the sky was alive and on fire. Although I was frustrated that Gillian had brought her paints on our trip, I never regretted her choice after that night. Gillian had captured the moment so perfectly; each time I looked at that painting, which now hung over the dresser in our bedroom, I was instantly transported back to that night. The sky on the night we buried our daughter and that sky we shared together that first night were so very similar. I wondered if I could ever look on the painting again with the same adoration.

Our hotel room was silent with regret, heavy with sadness, stinging with pain, and seething with anger. Neither of us spoke as we picked at the room service dinner provided to us by the management; his way of sending his condolences. It was a nice gesture, but wasted on the grieving parents. We were hollow inside. The echoing screams of our hearts would not allow us the ability to eat.

We left early the next morning, trying desperately to leave behind the anger and sadness. We convinced ourselves that it would be better when we got back home to Detroit, after giving ourselves a little time to adjust and refocus our energy. Yet when we got back home, the media vultures were still hungry, and the fact that I worked at the paper seemed to make it acceptable - somehow because I was one of them - that gave them permission to sensationalize it all.

They were wrong and I was furious. What they expected was a controlled interview with details rich in adjectives, verbs and vivid imagery. What they got was the most terrifying Yetti they could have encountered. The Yetti's wife wasn't too congenial, either. To say that they were caught off guard would be an understatement. But of course, after their initial recovery, they made that part of the story, too. "Angry parents mourn the loss of their only daughter". It was a headline worthy only of *The National Enquirer*, but they used it just the same. The photographers were heinous, stalking us like wild game, filming our every moment of tiresome sadness. We had hoped to come home to heal. Instead, we were poked, prodded and investigated like someone who had just walked out of Area 51. These were my brothers and sisters of industry, and I was ashamed at how they were acting. I was ashamed of myself for the many years I had spent doing the same thing to complete strangers half a world away. I would never look at the newspaper business in the same way ever again.

So we barricaded ourselves in our house, shades drawn, windows closed, phone off the hook for several weeks. We had groceries and anything else we needed delivered, and we used our credit cards to pay for it all. We were racking up debt we weren't sure how to resolve. I'd taken a bereavement leave of absence from the paper and Gillian had called the museum and told them she wasn't sure when she would be returning. Everyone was very understanding, in the beginning - but their kindness soon wore off. By week three, the paper was demanding a story, any story, to justify my paycheck; and Gillian was being threatened with a loss of not just seniority, but her job, too. Treading water in a sea of numbness was punctuated by nightly crying fits. We had no grip on reality whatsoever.

By week eight, it all finally came to a head. We both needed to return to work. Gillian couldn't do it, and lost her position at the museum. Our relationship had been deteriorating since the day we got back from Colorado, and I wasn't sure we could repair it. The fights over inconsequential things seemed to explode on a regular basis. Nearly every day there was another eruption over money, and our own apathy. Neither of us could have prepared ourselves for the emotional toll Eryn's death would take. We thought we were strong, that we could outlast anything. We were wrong.

Gillian came to me one evening, six months after our daughter's death, and calmly explained why she just couldn't go on living with me. I looked too much like Eryn; laughed like her, snored like her. She didn't know how she could heal with all these constant reminders of her daughter haunting her around every corner. I truly believed that we could make it, if we both just put in a little more effort and energy. I tried to convince Gillian but, she just shook her head and said it was just too hard. She couldn't do it anymore.

Gillian moved to an apartment in the suburbs the following weekend, and I was left with the house in Indian Village and a small tabby cat as my only companion. And so, this final column is my exit from the world of journalism, from the world of heartless reporting, from the world of prosperity through pain and suffering. I will move on, I will find a way to heal. How long that might take, or what that might look like, I have no idea. But I am done with living life at a distance... I must reconnect with my soul if I am to survive. Will I write again? Who can say?

****

Two months later, the divorce was final and each were trying to rebuild their lives. The media stupidity had finally quieted down into an almost imperceptible hum. Gillian took an apartment in a suburb just outside Detroit and went back to college. Art had always been her passion, but since the accident, she just couldn't bring herself to pick up her instruments. The brush and chalk that used to dance with abandon in her hands now stood as silent sentinels to her raw, bleeding and bruised heart. She needed to find something else to get her through, something away from children, away from creativity, away from emotion. She chose finance. It was the one thing that she could think of that would completely ignore every sensitive piece of her being and force her into a logical and stoic world, the world which now undulated within her veins. *I've shut down that part of my life, but I still needed a way to eat.* She had picked up a dual major, art and accounting. At the time, her counselor though it a dichotomy that didn't fit. Her parents were elated. So, she went back to school in search of a certification in financial planning. *The cold numbers were a bridge that I'd always seen as a rainy-day option ... now, I'm becoming the bridge builder. I have to do something... it's the only way I can see to survive.*

Thomas sought out a life that didn't involve invading the sanctity of people's lives. He found a cushy marketing job for an up-and-coming technology firm in Boston. He needed to put some distance between him and Gillian, between his memories of Eryn and the place where she was born. It wasn't his ideal job, but then, nothing would be. *Writing - real writing - was all my soul had ever been meant to do, and now, I feel like I have to abandon every instinct I've ever trusted, just to survive. This isn't ideal- but at least I'll eat.*

Chapter Seven

"Everything has been written. Everybody knows everything about me. There are no secrets except the skeletons in my closet."
~Kirby Puckett

    The alarm jolted Aaren from her bed and nearly out of her jammies. Even though she'd been answering the annoying alarm with dedication since she was hired into MouseTrax just after graduation from Boston College, and even though today was Saturday, and she wasn't going into the office, she still detested the electronic braying that disturbed her cherished sleep. But this morning, she would accept and move on, with a full measure of joy instead of disdain. Today, she was going sailing.

    Paige and Aaren had arranged to meet just before noon at the marina. Since they were children, sailing had always been a part of their lives. In elementary school, they'd made a pact to join the Navy together; but that dream faded when they discovered that the Navy had no actual sailboats in the fleet. The differences between power and sail were monumental to these two as girls... and as women. A collection of tall ships, a flotilla of three-mast ketch, with a giant wheel, white billowed sails and hammock berths was their vision of a proper Navy fleet. Anything else just wouldn't do. So they left their Navy dreams behind and settled for sailing on Paige's family sloop; perfecting their tacking and reefing skills, flying the spinnaker at every opportunity. Sailing was nothing, after all, without a little pageantry. One might imagine the women religious devotees of Poseidon or Neptune, and they'd be right.

After pulling out of the marina and setting the sails for a leisurely run over to Nantucket, they brought out a bottle of wine, a wheel of Gouda, Paige's favorite cheese, and a box of delicate butter crackers. Paige sat comfortably at the wheel; Aaren lounged near the port winch, dipping her fingers in the gentle waters, ready for the next tack.

"So, what's going on with you? You seem a little distant." said Aaren. They had been friends since long before either of them could remember… since four or five years old. Aaren was Paige's only trusted confidant, but lately, casual conversation had been conspicuously absent. Business conversation abounded—there was no stopping that nonsense—but the intimacy of their day-to-day had been lost, or at the very least, side-lined.

"I've just been thinking about Edward." Paige replied with a whisper.

"Edward? Why are you digging up that old ghost? It's been what, almost ten years, right?"

"Six, actually. But who's counting?" Paige looked solemn, almost as if she were at someone's funeral.

"So what's the deal? Why are you suddenly thinking about him?" Aaren's eyes were wide with intrigue. Usually, once Paige was done with something, it was over, never to return. "What is it?"

"It hasn't really been all that sudden. He's been lingering around my brain since spring. I just wonder what he's doing, is all... Do you think we could have made it work?" Paige's face took on a sallow hue. In truth, she asked the question, but dreaded the answer. There had been no love lost between Aaren and Edward.

"Are you nuts? Don't you remember how crazy you were around him? He was tilting windmills and you were building bridges. You two were so divergent. I have no idea how you two ever found each other, let alone how you could have ever made it work over the long haul."

"Yeah, I guess you're right. But still..." Paige's voice took on a wavering quality that told Aaren there was something more going on here than just the lingering memory of a man who epitomized the word incompetent.

"Come on, Paige; what's really going on here?" Aaren pressed Paige to the point where she couldn't hide behind avoidance any longer. Her face resembled that of an elementary school principle; stern but compassionate.

"Look, I'm always impeccably dressed, right; even if it's just jeans and a sweater, it's the best money can buy, and it always complements me - perfectly."

"Naturally." Aaren said with a sarcastic grin.

"Okay, I know it's a bit shallow, but you know, appearances have played a key role in my life. Mother and Father always said it was important. I first heard it in middle school, 'remember Paige, if you look the part, you can close the deal, any deal. It's all about appearances.'"

Aaren quipped, "They were right. And truly, you are a successful business woman." She toasted Paige's acclaim with her glass held high.

"Come on, Aaren. I know I'm a smart woman, and although on many levels, my success has been more inherited than earned, I'm still very good at my job. I just wish I enjoyed it more. And I wish I had someone around who actually believed in me as much as my parents did." Again, Paige's eyes became filled with a thoughtful patina. "They were always so supportive... even if it was just blowing smoke; their vote of confidence meant something to me. But since their deaths, I haven't had anyone in my life who truly 'gets' me... no one who sees my vision the way I do..."

"Hang on a minute. What am I, yesterday's dumpster dive?" Aaren was a little hurt that Paige overlooked their years of friendship. In more situations than she could count, Aaren had stood by her side when so many others had ostracized her for the smallest infraction. Though Presbyterian and not Amish, Paige had been no stranger to being shunned. Outside of her parents, Aaren had been the one true constant in Paige's life.

"That's not what I mean, and you know it. You know how important you are to me—you're my only friend. You don't patronize me, and you don't fear me. But you're also not a man. And that's what I'm missing. I'm missing a relationship, Aaren." Paige shifted in her seat, clearly uncomfortable with the confession. "Sure, Edward was sub-standard on more levels than I care to admit, but at least he was a relationship, I wasn't going it alone. At the end of the day, I felt a little bit like I belonged somewhere when I turned the key in the lock. Now, I'm just drifting. A drifting hermit. I don't belong anywhere or to anyone. I just keep trudging through the same ol' maze, never finding the cheese. And at this point, I'm beginning to think I never will." Paige paused for a moment, staring off into the horizon, finding nothing to soothe her soul. She turned back to Aaren and shrugged her shoulders. "Yeah, Edward was a marginal human being, but at least he put up with my baggage and never left me out in the cold."

"Until you left," said Aaren. "

"Well, yes, until I left. But even then he was still being reasonable. I would have given up on me at that point, too. I doubt I'll ever find that again." Paige closed her eyes and tilted her head to the clouds. She inhaled deeply, as if resigned to her fate.

"Oh come on, Paige. You can't believe that. I'm sure that there are plenty of men who would love to be with you."

"Yeah, but do I want to be with them? That's the real question." Paige took a quick inventory of the wind and set her glass down. "Ready to tack!" bellowed Paige.

"Ready!" shouted Aaren.

"Helm's a-lee!" Paige turned the wheel, Aaren jumped from the port to the starboard side, and began to pull furiously on the port winch; dragging the jib across the bow. There was a slight luff in the sails until the mainsail filled full with wind, and they were once again, on the move. Aaren tied off the sheets, and relaxed comfortably at a twenty-degree heel; splashes of water occasionally lapping over the starboard side rail.

"I mean, come on," continued Paige; "Most guys meet me and only see my bank balance. I would like a little more than that; and I think I deserve it." The fire was in her voice again. "Edward wasn't evil. Sometimes he could be nice. And he had enough of his own money that mine didn't mean anything to him."

"Edward was not that terrific, you know. You'll find someone else; someone better." Aaren reached over and thumped Paige's knee. "You just need to be open to the possibilities." Aaren tried to sound comforting, but even to her own ear, she sounded a little condescending. She didn't mean it that way; it was just the way it came out. Of all the people Aaren knew, there was a part of her that thought Paige had the least amount of reason to complain - about anything.

"Looking back, I guess maybe it wasn't really all that great a relationship. How did we expect it would be? He lived in DC, carrying political torches for causes I couldn't relate to, and I lived here, spending my time climbing the Bostonian corporate ladder, right behind Father. It was a pursuit Edward couldn't make sense of. I remember how maddening it was for us in the beginning, all those long weeks endured alone just to look forward to short weekends spent commuting, so we could spend a brief few hours together." Paige chuckled at the memory. "It was crazy, but it seemed so right at the time. We really wanted to be together that badly. But then, who knows why, it just got... easier. It got easier to avoid the commute than to make the effort to be together." In her head, Paige heard the long whine of the Amtrak train in the distance, remembering that time in her life as if someone had recorded the soundtrack.

"The truth is, I discovered that it was okay to have him for just a few hours at a time. He was a huge distraction. I had so much I wanted to do, and with him somewhere else, more of it got done. I certainly didn't get to where I am today because I was comfortable playing the part of the dutiful wife. And, honestly, I was happier when we were apart. I was oblivious to it back then, but now, it all seems so transparent... Maybe we were just too young and too foolish..."

Although she considered slipping in a snide remark about Edward... she'd never approved of the political rodent... instead, Aaren let Paige talk. It was clear that she needed to vent, and at times like these, Aaren knew it was best to let her pump out her bilge without complication.

"Thanks to Mother and Father, and their connections, I didn't have to sacrifice a great deal to get what I have now. Although, the marina membership and the brownstone didn't come cheap." Paige took another sip from her glass as if the point needed punctuating. "DC life wasn't for me; and it's not like we were really having all that much fun. It was a good way for us to get what we both wanted at the time. We had our careers, the prestige of our places in the community, and plenty of money. It all seemed so simple. Users using." Paige fixed her gaze out to the horizon for a long moment. "And now that I think about it, we didn't really have all that much in common." She let go a long sigh.

"Let's face it, Paige; he had awful taste in clothes, didn't understand the concept of reading books for pleasure, danced like he was having convulsions, and ate weird foods. To tell you the truth, none of our sorority sisters were surprised when you two finally broke up. But I must say this about him... I almost never saw you two argue. That must have been nice."

Paige laughed again, this time, a full bodied chortle. "We never really spent enough time together to argue." She took another moment in memory... or was it remorse... she wasn't sure. "It's pretty sad, really. The only thing left of my relationship with Edward is a quagmire of memories punctuated by a few old photographs and papers tucked away in a box in the back of a closet someplace." Paige drained her wine glass, poured herself another, and helped herself to another hunk of cheese. Aaren did the same.

"Six years later, and the problem is, now I have a house full of stuff, a sizable bank account, a corporate title, but none of the happiness my parents had once promised me would come. Lots of the trappings that go with the title, but no peace, and no personal fulfillment. And no one to share the photographs with along the way. So, Edward is in Washington still carrying torches for causes he believes in, righting great wrongs, making a difference... And I'm still alone, in Boston, surrounded by shadows of apathy, and toys, and people I've grown tired of... still left wanting more."

"And you think a man will help you fill that void?" Aaren said, reaching over to help herself to another handful of cheese.

"No, I don't think anything will fill the void. I think the hole that lives in me was dug a long time ago; I'm guessing probably on the day I was born. But I'm beginning to think that having a man around—or maybe just a few nights of disassociated sex—might make things a little easier to take. It doesn't matter how much money you've got, Aaren, loneliness is still loneliness; and it's not as much fun as you might think." There was an uneasy silence between them for a few moments as they tried to mask it again with more cheese indulgence.

Why me? was the whisper that infiltrated her brain. *It's just not fair.* Since her parent's death, despair was far too common an emotion in Paige's life. And even though she had begun to feel comfortable with it, she still resented it. She resented that it was one of the only things left in her life that she had little control or influence over; no matter how many self-help books she read, or how many therapy sessions she endured. This was her life, and she hated it. She had a deep-seated desire to change it, but she didn't know how.

"I have a secret, though." giggled Paige, the wine doing its job nicely.

"Okay; so, spill it." Aaren said, happy that the conversation was finally shifting.

"I think there might be some potential in our new marketing manager, Thomas Laird."

"Really, why him, Paige? What haven't you told me?"

Oh, so very much. "I'm still not really sure how our friendship started ... I vaguely recall some sly banter we exchanged early on in his collaboration with the company, back in April, which is intriguing to me, mainly because he was able to keep up. So few can. But I can't be exactly sure. It seemed like such a long time ago, and I guess it's not really all that important now."

"Why Thomas... what is it about him that makes you think you might want to invite him into your world?" It was odd for Paige to take a risk with anyone, and never with an employee. Aaren sensed there was something deeper going on... but she couldn't put her finger on it. *Strange that this is the first time she's mentioned him. We don't usually keep secrets.*

"All in all, he's not a bad guy. Since he's been at MouseTrax, he's proven himself to be something of a media wizard. He's extraordinary at turning a phrase to put just the right spin on anything; be it good news or bad. Not your average marketing guy; he's witty, personable and sort of eclectic. Hiring him turned out to be one of my better ideas." Paige prattled on like some teenager making tic marks on a laundry list. "I've been watching him. He's the guy everyone calls when they need to find just the right angle. He has an uncanny knack for getting problems dissolved almost instantly; helping those in need save their jobs, and the company's image. Shape-shifting, it appears, is second nature to him. He's well dressed, but not too pretentious; he's sublimely provocative. At the office, he always seems to have a pad of paper and pen in his hand, feverishly writing; all the while talking down an irate department manager, and making it all seem like a day at Disneyland."

"Wait a second, you said at the office. Have you been seeing him outside of the office?" Aaren was stunned.

"Well, yeah, a couple of times, but it's not that big a deal." Paige tried to shrug it off, hoping Aaren would drop the issue.

"Not that big a deal? Paige, you never date! And more importantly, you never keep secrets from me. That must mean this is a pretty big deal. How long have you two been seeing each other?"

"Come on, Aaren; it's not that monumental. I've dated since Edward - it's true, they were all morons - but I've dated. I didn't say anything because I just didn't want this guy to be added to my resume of deviant diversions. I thought that if it didn't turn out to mean anything, then he could just dissolve, like all the others. Really, it's not that big a deal."

"You didn't answer my question. How long have you been seeing each other?" Aaren chided.

"Not long. Just a couple of weeks." Paige offered sheepishly.

"What have you been doing with him?" Aaren prodded.

"Oh, you know, the usual stuff. The Pops, we went to the science center once; oh, and I took him sailing."

"You had him on the boat!" Aaren nearly exploded with giddy excitement. "You never invite guys on the boat. It sounds like this might be getting serious," she chided with a playful nudge of her foot. Aaren knew Paige well enough to know that the one more tack they had to make before reaching Nantucket Harbor would not yield the entire story, but she thought she'd nag just a little bit more—just short of enticing Paige into performing a man-overboard maneuver. "What is it with this guy, Paige? Tell me what's going on! Just how far has this gone?"

"It's not that big a deal, Aaren. It was just a day sail. And you know, in the final analysis, he's simply cute. And that's not a bad thing. I could use a little cute in my life these days," she said, punctuating the remark with a toast to the clouds. Her voice dropped, almost out of Aaren's hearing; "but I need to be careful, here. This could come back to bite me. I really shouldn't be dating people from the office. I can't afford to get pegged with a harassment suit or a restraining order by some over-emotional twit who thought he could sleep his way up the corporate ladder. Spending a little time with this guy is fun, but anything more than that and the hassles would be too big to deal with..." Paige took another sip of wine and nibbled more cheese. She looked to the blue waters and said, "But he is cute, I'll give him that."

Chapter Eight

"Only in the agony of parting do we look into the depths of love."
~George Eliot

Exhausted after an overwhelming day, Thomas was looking forward to becoming comatose on the train as it ferried him back to Cambridge. He enjoyed the sensation of his brain on autopilot as he stared aimlessly at the landscape. It was a decadent experience that wasn't permitted back in Detroit, home of the engaged engine. Yet tonight, despite his fatigue, something nagged at him. Instead of boarding the T, he left the station and started to walk home. His body was fidgety, his brain wouldn't shut down, and his emotions were all over the map. It was six miles to his apartment, and still, he felt compelled to walk the distance. He had enjoyed the recent recluse of his memories… but now, his limbic system was running at full speed again. The images and voices flooded back with a vengeance.

****

"What… What happened?"

"The notation I have in your wife's chart indicates that your daughter suffered a massive brain trauma, nothing more. I'm sorry, sir." The nurse put her hand on Thomas' shoulder, trying to comfort him as best she could. But it was of no use. He could control himself no longer. His despair had finally broken through the levy, and it rushed out now with hurricane force.

"No!" Thomas screamed at the nurse. "Not Eryn!! She was only four years old. Oh my God, Eryn..." Thomas fell into the chair in the corner of the room, sobbing uncontrollably as his wife continued to sleep, entirely unaware. Thomas continued to weep until he, too, succumbed to his own exhaustion. Nurse McCann covered him with a warm, wool blanket and simply let him be.

Rousing to the aroma of marginal hospital food, Thomas opened his eyes to find Nurse McCann placing a tray of Pot Roast Surprise on the table next to his chair. "You've had a rough day, Mr. Laird. You should eat something." Her voice was kind and soothing, even though Thomas still hated everything she represented. His daughter was dead, and no amount of kindness could fix that.

Rubbing the sleep and frustration out of his eyes and stretching the kinks out of his back, Thomas asked, "What time is it?"

"Nearly seven-thirty. You've been asleep for about three hours."

Thomas stood up, gathering his energy to focus on his wife. "How's Gillian?"

"She's been doing well since the surgery. She's stable and getting stronger. The doctor says that he may take her off of the sedatives and remove the breathing tube tomorrow. You really should eat, Mr. Laird. You wife will need all your support when she wakes up tomorrow." Nurse McCann left then, closing the door behind her with a soft click.

Reluctantly, Thomas ate his food, staring out the window at the picturesque Colorado countryside, sun fading behind the ridge. As he watched Gillian's chest rhythmically rise and fall, a wash of sadness came over him unlike anything he had ever felt before. His wife lay in the bed nearby, clinging to life. *How close had I come to losing her, too? She must have been so frightened. And now, we've lost little Eryn. How am I going to find the words to tell her? I don't have the courage to claim her body on my own. How can I find the strength to tell her mother that she's gone?* The questions seared worry lines around his eyes and in his heart that would never leave. *How will we ever recover from this?*

****

Thomas spent that night in spasmodic sleep, curled up on the empty bed that once held his darling child, pillow clutched to his chest. Doctors and nurses came in every few hours to check Gillian's vital signs, draw blood, and collect urine samples. It was about midnight when an orderly tried to get him to leave, but he quickly learned that the term "visiting hours" was one Thomas vehemently ignored; and no one bothered him again.

Chapter Nine

*"You can always find a distraction
if you're looking for one."
~Tom Kite*

After three months, Thomas still didn't have many friends at MouseTrax. A company, he learned, that was known for its easy release of employees that didn't "fit the mold", Thomas wasn't interested in building the kind of friendships here that he had in Detroit; and truth be told, he still wasn't convinced he was staying. After a very short time, he had learned that the people here were different, stoic, distant. Couple that with the fact that no one was certain just how long they would last; deep friendships weren't on the priority list. There were many in the company who accepted this personal disconnect as just a part of the deal. They foraged superficial friendships with the complete understanding that they probably wouldn't last. It was all very shallow, yet somehow, it worked. It reminded Thomas of the cliques in high school. Lots of flash but no substance or longevity. Thomas was still too raw from the end to his life with Gillian in Detroit, so he kept his distance. He went to work, did his job with the modicum of civility required to move projects forward... but not much else. He and his boss, Paige Lambert, started some weird fling together... all quite superficial and inconsequential, and that's exactly how he wanted it. It was just a distraction; he refused to get emotionally involved.

The risk was too great. She seemed to agree and so they had no reason to make it public.

The one exception to his life of virtual solitude was Nathan Hackthorn. Nathan had been around for a while... more years with the company than he cared to discuss... and longer with life. He was a retired philosophy and journalism professor from Harvard, and only took this job after he discovered that retirement did not meet his daily requirement for brain stimulation. As he had mentioned to Thomas in one of their first meetings, longevity and future planning were not part of the equation when he joined MousTrax. "My future is more than secure, and longevity... well... it's all about the short game now. At this stage my life it's about finding something to get me up every morning and keep me entertained. Most days, this place does it for me. I've got no complaints."

****

One evening, Nathan and Thomas were sitting in the little cafe around the corner from the office, having dinner together. Nathan noticed that Thomas was unusually quiet. "Hey, what's up with you today? Cat got your tongue?"

"Oh, sorry. I'm trying to figure something out, is all." Thomas apologized.

"Well, spit it out. It's not nice to keep an old man in suspense, you know."

"Do you know Paige Lambert?" asked Thomas.

"CEO of the company, yeah, she's kind of tough to miss. What's the story?" Since discovering that Thomas had been a writer in his past life, Nathan often used this phrase to prod him along when conversations were uneasy for him; and it always worked.

"Well, we've started something... not really sure what it is just yet... but it's something." Thomas' eyes were fixed on his fish, as though it hid the secret to some new puzzle.

"I'd say so." The fries Nathan navigated to his mouth made it... but in the abrupt movement, some of the ketchup didn't. "Dating the boss?" Nathan said, wiping his shirt with a napkin. "That's quite the surprise. The thing is, that simply doesn't happen around here. There's a strict policy, you know. Not a rule against fraternization among employees... nothing that archaic; but Lambert herself, she's got a rule."

"What do you mean?" asked Thomas.

"Well, you see, Lambert doesn't date much. It's rare to see her with anyone—ever. She works really hard at not mixing her business life and her personal life. No one really knows all that much about her personal life... truth is," Nathan leaned in to Thomas as if he was divulging a great secret. "No one's brave enough to ask." Nathan reclined back in his chair, as he mustered up the details. "Some of us have seen her walking through the art museum or going to the Theatre, or attending concerts with the Boston Pops. But she's always alone. She does these things not necessarily because she enjoys them... rumor has it that secretly, she does, though I'm doubtful." A stern look crossed his face. "She can be such a hardass... but for Lambert, it's a great way to see and be seen. She's always on. Always selling the image of the company, and herself. It's probably something she learned from her folks. They were that way, too. In the summer, she strolls along the banks of the Charles and she picnics in the Common, like a lost little puppy looking for a home, but once you get up close, you discover she's really an alligator. She's as accessible as possible, but never really engages with anyone unless they recognize her and want to talk shop. And she's always alone. So, to hear that you've been spending personal time with her outside of the office, is well, unusual, to say the least." Nathan raised his eyebrows, then furrowed them again. "What's going on?"

"I'm not quite sure. We don't really go anywhere, dinner mostly, take-out delivered to her brownstone. She doesn't say much, but always wants to hear about my time as a reporter. She asks a lot about the old writing assignments I went on, and the stories I've written. But whenever the conversation turns a little personal, she shifts gears really fast. We've had dinner together half a dozen times already and I still know basically nothing about her. But she seems to have a cistern of anger boiling just beneath the surface, you know? She's a tough one to figure out."

"So, why are you doing it? What's the point? Are you worried about job security, or something?" Nathan's question sounded like it came from the priest who taught at his elementary school. Thomas couldn't help but answer with the absurd.

"Oh, the sex - definitely!" The two men laughed. "No, but really; that's all it is. It's the epitome of casual. There are times that I feel like her pool boy. There's no emotional substance to it. It's just a casual distraction. But that's okay with me. I don't see it going anywhere, and don't really want it to. But I gotta tell you, a little female companionship sure is nice once in a while. It gets pretty lonely sometimes. And the fact that she looks a little bit like Gillian, well man, that doesn't hurt."

"I hear you." said Nathan. "My wife's been gone nearly fifteen years, and the days do get lonely." Nathan paused for a moment as though he might have had something more to say on the matter; but let it go quickly, trying to find a little levity instead. "But, I'm too old a fart to start playing that game again." Nathan offered a sly smirk, and upended his drink; waving to the waitress for a refill.

Chapter Ten

"The keys to patience are acceptance and faith. Accept things as they are, and look realistically at the world around you. Have faith in yourself and in the direction you have chosen."
~Ralph Marston

One Saturday after a game at Fenway Park, Nathan and Thomas moved their party from the ball diamond to Nathan's backyard barbecue. It had been a difficult game for Thomas; the Red Sox were playing the Detroit Tigers, and he was conflicted all day with which team he wanted to win. In the end, the Sox won, seven to three. Nathan was rejoicing with his home team, and throwing playful jabs at Thomas during the T ride home. Thomas took it all in stride; his friends back in Detroit were much more brutal about this stuff than Nathan could ever be.

When the chicken and ribs were happily sizzling on the grill and the beer had been jubilantly dispensed, the two sat down to enjoy the unusually warm fall afternoon, and a few game recaps. After twenty minutes or so of men being boys, Thomas grew withdrawn and quiet, drinking his beer and watching the clouds rolling overhead.

"Hey, Thom;" said Nathan. "What's the story?"

"Is there anything you miss about your life teaching at Harvard?" asked Thomas.

"No, not much. That part of my life had run its course. No regrets, no what-ifs. I'm good with it. Why do you ask?" Nathan flipped the ribs, half of him keeping lunch from going up in flames, the other half analyzing as he listened. The philosopher in him never seemed to rest.

"I've been thinking lately about all the things and people... people mostly, that I left back in Detroit. I'm starting to rethink my choices. At what point are you allowed a "do over"? At what point to you say to yourself, 'I had a different ending in mind, and now I think I want that'; and then go back and get it? At what point does your "do over" expire?" Thomas was rambling. He knew he was being insufferably vague, but he figured that if anyone could get through his blundering rhetoric to the point he could not find, it would be Nathan. After all, he was a trained professional in the art of rhetoric, no matter what form it came in.

"Well, I suppose that would depend on what it was you wanted to "do over". Nathan added more sauce to the ribs and chicken, giving Thomas a moment to digest the question. "Relationships, jobs, hobbies - those are manageable "do overs". Sex change operations, not so much." Nathan shot a wink at Thomas, secretly hoping that wasn't his desired "do over". "Why not drop the curtain and tell me what's going on?"

Over the next hour or so, Thomas told Nathan about Gillian, Eryn, and the train crash. Nathan waited patiently, trying not to interrupt Thomas, giving him the opportunity to cleanse. Nathan had the feeling that Thomas still carried a lot of guilt and he wanted him to have a safe place to land when the detox was over.

"We were there for two months. Gillian's recovery had been slow yet deliberate. She was still an emotional wreck; and who could blame her. The realization of no longer having her young daughter playing at her feet, whispering secrets in her ear, and laughing wildly at everything was a near-impossible thing to adjust to... and under the same set of circumstances, any other mother might have given up and checked out. It was true, Gillian was distant, sad, and almost completely non-verbal; but at least physically, she was making good progress.

"It was two weeks after the doctors released Gillian from the hospital. She and I were living in the small hotel in Kremmling until she was cleared to travel. I tried every day to talk with her and get her to come out of her damaged shell... but it was effort made in vain. Gillian was in so much pain. Although I knew her grief was beyond overwhelming; still, I couldn't help feeling a twinge of anger and sadness myself when she refused my touch. I lost my daughter too. I need comforting too. I didn't know how much more of her rejection I could forgive. It was becoming harder and harder for us to be in the same room together.

"In an attempt to avoid her sadness and the guilt of not being able to help her, I began taking long walks to the crash site. With my reporter's eye I watched as daily, they cleared more and more of the wreckage from the gorge. Then, I would retrace my steps through town that I took on that night I found Gillian lying in the hospital bed... trying desperately to find some reason for this madness. I could find none.

"Then, I was faced with a new problem, and I found myself spending time with Nancy. She was comforting and sincere in her attention. She was the perfect counselor; familiar yet anonymous simultaneously.

"In the first month, Gillian had been unable to face the truth of Eryn's death. She was just so wrapped up in the hope that someday soon, Eryn would come bounding through the door, stuffed duck in hand... she could not allow a funeral.

" 'Yes,' she said. 'It is a difficult thing to stare that reality in the face. It must be very painful for her - and for you.' Nancy was gently consoling yet never condescending. I was grateful for her kindness.

"But soon, the doctor cleared Gillian for travel. It was now at the point where we have to deal with Eryn's funeral and get back home. Gillian had her work at the museum; I had my work at the newspaper. We had responsibilities. People were counting on us to return to our commitments. Yes, our friends and colleagues had all been quite understanding - given the circumstances - but we had to go back. It was time. We couldn't hide in Kremmling forever. I was sad, angry, hopeful and despondent in a single moment.

" 'It's true, she said gently; 'Your lives, no matter how shattered, need to find a way to keep going... heal, and move forward. I'm sure your wife will adjust as best she can. Just make the decisions that need to be made, and be there to comfort Gillian when she needs it. You may not recognize her needs every time. Just be there and do what you can. I'm sure it'll be enough.' I tried, really, I did."

"After a last long walk to the crash site, now completely cleared of train crash debris, I went back to the hotel to explain to Gillian that I had Eryn's remains cremated and made funeral arrangements. It is time for us to move on; go home; get back to living.' I told her.

" 'You did what?' Gillian's voice was shrill and her face went white.

" 'Gillian,' I said, 'we need to do this. It's not fair to make Eryn wait any longer. We have to let her go." I worked hard to be comforting and understanding... but there was a twinge of frustration in my voice that Gillian did not miss.

" 'How could you do this without me?' she raged. 'How could you make such assumptions about something this important without talking with me first? How could you?!' She was just about as furious as I'd ever seen her."

"I tried to understand her pain... but mine came through instead. 'You weren't doing it,' I screamed; 'and someone had to! Since the day this terrible thing happened, I've been trying hard to understand you... to comfort you... to help you heal. But damn it, this has been hard on me, too! Did you ever think of that? Did you even once consider the fact that I'm hurting? Eryn was my daughter, too, Gillian. And it's cruel of you to be so selfish!" Thomas was lost in the memory, recounting all the sorted details. Nathan was patient and let him purge the pain in his own time.

"The moment I said the words, I regretted them, but I couldn't hide how I felt. I'd never lied to Gillian in all the years we'd been together, and I couldn't start—no matter how much the truth might have hurt her.

"Gillian backed herself into a corner and she sunk to the ground, pulling her knees to her chest. Slowly, I walked over to her and sat on the floor in front of her. I took her hands in mine and rested my forehead on her knees. We sat there for a long moment in silence. The sadness between us was heavy. Finally, I spoke, my voice a gentle whisper. Gillian's eyes did not meet mine, and her hands still trembled. 'The funeral is tomorrow at two,' I told her. 'The small cemetery in town is very pretty... lots of trees. I found a nice little wooden urn, very simple, but I had them line it with flannel. I know how much Eryn loved soft things. I went to the morgue to make sure she was dressed in something cute. I found a little pair of jean overalls and a pink fleece shirt, with pink socks to match. I know she would have loved it.' I paused for a moment, hoping a small smile might be found on Gillian's face. There was none. Only silent tears in unrelenting waves.

" 'Did you... see her... before?' Gillian could barely get the words out.

" 'Yes, I told her."

" 'Was she...' Gillian couldn't finish the thought. Her fear and sadness prevented the words from being spoken.
"'No.' I told her, as gently as I could. ' Our daughter is gone, honey.' "

" 'I need to see her.' Gillian said with an uncertain desperateness in her voice.

" 'That's not possible, sweetheart,' I said. 'Cremation was the kindest option... for both of you.' I knew that what Gillian would have found in Eryn's broken little face might haunt her for decades to come, and I was trying hard to save her form that pain. 'Just try to remember her the way she was... happy, full of life, smiling... that's how you need to hold her in your heart, not... not like this.'" Thomas broke into tears from the harsh memory of that afternoon. He didn't think he'd ever go there again, but here he was, recanting it all in perfect reporter's longhand to a man he'd only just recently met. It boggled his brain. *The stuff you'll do to heal – it's nuts.*

"At the funeral, Eryn's tiny urn was gently laid to rest in the dirt tomb. I placed a small pink envelope next to the roses Gillian's mother had sent. Inside the envelope was a short note. I'll remember what I wrote that day until the moment I take my last breath.

My Dearest Eryn,

I am so sorry you and Mommy fell off the bridge. I wish that you could have come right home after your visit with Grandma and Grandpa in Seattle. I know how much it must have hurt, but the ouches are all gone now. I know you are in heaven, safe and smiling now. I miss you very much. Remember that I will always love you.

XOXO, Daddy.

"When we returned from Colorado after Eryn's funeral, we came home to a barrage of reporters and news trucks camped out in front of our house. The reporters were like vultures, swooping and circling over the ripest carrion. 'How are you feeling? Can you tell us what happened? Do you plan to take any legal action against Amtrak? What will you do now? Do you think you'll have any more children?' Their questions were heartless and cruel; delving into our inner sanctum like it was a day at Disneyland. Even in all my time as a reporter spanning the corners of the country, writing about the horrors of life, never once did I degrade myself or those I wrote about by being so insensitive. It was difficult to ignore.

"We spent the six months after the accident trying to grieve, but the newspapers just kept drudging up the pain, time and again. Because I worked for the local paper, I was their poster child news story. It was always about how awful it must have been to be a young married man, a father for just a short time, to have all that ripped away in an instant. They wanted every detail, every painful tidbit of sound-bite fury, scintillating media drama sure to bring someone an award, if not several. They came after Gillian too. I tried, but he couldn't stop them.

" 'Come on, Mrs. Laird...' they'd prod; 'give us just a little sound bite... we've got stories to file. You know the routine. Your lives are fair game now, your husband is one of us – that makes his life an open book.' The reporters were relentless. Gillian became more incensed with each passing moment. If she'd had a weapon, I wouldn't have trusted her not to use it. Her rationality had left when she gave up her daughter.

" 'Bullshit!' Gillian screamed. 'Just leave us alone!' But it didn't stop them from knocking on the door every day and calling at all hours of the night. She'd had enough. Try as I might, I couldn't stop the frenzy; although in time, it did subside, if only a little.

"The time went by grudgingly. Too many reporters, too many stuffed animals around Eryn's favorite tree in the front yard left by well-wishers from her school, the museum, and the paper. Each time I tried to go out and clean things up, trying to make room for a future that wasn't a constant reminder of our daughter's death, the tributes would reappear. It was as if the community had decided the Laird's mourning period; and they had determined that our family shouldn't be done yet. I was thankful, at least, that the stories about us in the papers had decreased. Finally, they had been reduced to a tagline at the bottom of a column whenever another local family lost a child in some sort of tragedy. But there was still the occasional insensitive reporter, trying to print a new angle.

"Gillian exploded in a rage one afternoon when, after returning from the grocery store. A reporter had the audacity to ask, 'Mrs. Laird, have you noticed a change in the family grocery bill now that Eryn is no longer eating at your table?'"

"Wow!" said Nathan. "That takes balls."

"Yeah. She picked up the hedging sheers from the sidewalk and threw them at him, bellowing obscenities and barking, 'Get out of my life!' I came home to get her into the house just in time. Who could have blamed her? Anyone in their right mind would have taken his head off, too. But the incident landed us in court with a tedious visit with the magistrate. Fortunately, all we endured was an invoice for the reporter's sixteen stitches and paparazzi's version of the story in the next day's paper. When we got home that night, all I could think was, This *whole thing has changed Gillian forever; and I'm not sure she will ever recover... ever really get back to being the woman I fell in love with. I hope she will - but I just don't know, it's frightening to think how this is changing her.* I miss her so much."

"That's rough, kid. I'm so sorry you had to go through all of that." Nathan's tried not to sound condescending, but he wasn't sure his intent at true sincerity was coming through. *Surely, Thomas has heard it all before.*

"Neither of us really knew how hard it would be to heal from something like that. I just expected that we'd stay together and figure it out. It never occurred to me how impossible that would be for Gillian." Thomas paused for a moment, finding his words in the beer he'd just cracked.

"Once I checked into what she was thinking and feeling, it became impossible for me to pretend anymore, either. My whole world changed. I couldn't think, barely ate, didn't sleep, and my writing went the way of the dinosaurs. It was a colossal crash and burn. Gillian moved out, quit her restoration job at the museum and took a job at some finance firm in Rochester; that was her wacky mother's influence, I'm sure." Thomas' snide remark made it clear there was a rift there.

"I was left to sort through the debris alone—again. I was miserable." Thomas was rambling again, but he couldn't slow down the runaway horse now. "Finally, I decided that I needed a new start. I sold everything, and came out here. But what I didn't count on was how hard it would be to let go of my life with Gillian... my life the way I had envisioned it... forever. I need to get her back, Nathan. I need to get her to understand that we were meant to be... really understand it the way that I do. She believed it once... I need to get her back to believing it again. I just don't know how." Thomas drained his beer, and pulled a couple more from the cooler, handing one to Nathan.

"Well, it seems to me that the way to get Gillian back is to remind her of what she loves most about you and your life together. She's never going to forget Eryn... chances are neither of you ever will... but I think there are two things that will bring her back to you. The first is, don't ignore the topic of your loss, should it ever come up again. It may or may not—some people manage their grief with bouts of selective amnesia." Thomas nodded. "But I think the thing that's going to be more powerful for the two of you than anything is to remind her—and you—of your lives together before Eryn was born. Think about the things that you used to do together... the things you used to talk about... those special moments that brought your hearts together in the first place. Those are the things that will bring the two of you back to the road you were once on, my friend. That foundation is what will be your strength. After that, everything else is manageable."

Thomas leaned back in his deck chair, stared at the now darkening sky, and thought about this for a long time. Nathan gave him time to process, as any good friend would.

"Alright," Thomas finally said. "I can see how reminding Gillian of our past life together is important—for us both—but how do I do that? It's not like I can just call her up and say, 'Hey, Gillian, remember that great night when we did that great thing? Remember how in love we were? Let's do that again.' She won't even take my calls." Thomas sank into his chair as if he was four years old again. He was having a hard time with the idea that there was a secret decoder ring out there someplace... and Nathan seemed to know what it was... but he didn't. It made Thomas fearful that he didn't have the answer this time.

Nathan allowed Thomas to wallow in his despair for all of about thirty seconds. "Look, you write, right?"

"Well, sure," replied Thomas. "I worked for a newspaper for years, and I've got a couple novels that I was working on tucked in a drawer. But I don't see..."

"Write to her." Nathan's words came out almost in a whisper.

"What, you mean letters?" Thomas was confused.

"Why not? You said that the two of you used to sit up late at night, like teenagers; you telling stories, her sketching... why not try that again? I know it won't really be the same thing as sitting on the bear-skin rug in front of the fireplace—there's a distance between you now. But if she was as enamored with your storytelling as you remember, it might be the perfect way to reach out to her now." Nathan paused for a moment to allow the concept to sink in. "Think about it; it's the safest thing for Gillian. There's no confrontation. No risk of the pain of her past cornering her in a room she cannot escape from because you're standing in front of the door. Instead, you just give her a sweet, gentle story that she can open and read whenever she feels brave enough. And you'll be right there in the thick of it. You and the love you have for her will breathe deeply with every word she reads."

"Do you think she will write back?" Thomas was beginning to see that this idea might have merit. He missed telling Gillian his stories.

"Maybe, maybe not. Does it really matter? Isn't the real goal here to become a part of her life again? You'll need to start over—from the very beginning. You need to be okay with being a small, gentle part of her life at the start... you can't hit her full-force and expect her to come running into your arms. That only happens in the movies when the world needs to be tightly tucked into bed after two short hours." Nathan drained his beer and set down the empty. "Think about it. It took you years to build the marriage you had. It's going to take some time for her to remember why she did that in the first place. She's still trying to find a way to heal from losing her daughter, her marriage, and the memory of the love that you once shared together. She's got to walk this path slowly. Go back and visit her through your pages... court her... re-grow your love over time. If you take the time... love her from a distance with all the tenderness of your first days together... if you go slowly, you've got a better chance that she *will* remember and love you back."

"That sort of makes sense, Nathan. But what about Paige?" Thomas looked like he had been given the chance to play with an old beloved toy, but didn't want to put down the new one in order to do it.

"What about her? She's just a distraction, right? There's no real love there. I say keep her—for now. There's no sense in you becoming a hermit again. Gillian doesn't want that guy, right? Just go along as you have been; work, have sex with Lambert occasionally, and write to Gillian. Putting all your emotional energy into Gillian, without Lambert as a sexual release valve, I think is a mistake. You'll know when it's the right time to stop one to pursue the other. Trust me on this one, my friend."

****

On the T ride back home from Nathan's place that night, Thomas thought hard about what Nathan was suggesting. *This would mean re-opening the wonderment of our past in such a way that doesn't also pour salt on the wounds that are still so fresh. It also means that I will need to find a way to get back to writing with the same passion I had before my days at the paper... before words were symbols of all that had been lost in life.* He would need to dig deep, write with integrity, creativity; and hardest of all, open himself up to the risk of her rejection... again. *Writing is the easy part. What if she doesn't respond the way I hope she will? What if it just makes her hate me all over again? I'm not sure I can take that.*

Thomas had all his Detroit connections neatly wrapped up. He'd left everyone and everything behind, and he felt good about it. He was in Boston - and the T was his chariot. It's not far from his office across from Government Center to the small two-bedroom Cambridge apartment he calls home; he enjoys the ride. It gives him time to think, time to take in the dichotomy of the Massachusetts skyline, and to revel in the beauty of the Charles at dusk. *Cambridge is a wonderful place, filled with the wisdom of Harvard, the spontaneity of a myriad of students constantly challenging the status quo, and the quiet Sunday afternoons where the boulevard along the Charles is exclusive to bikes and joggers.* Peace was long in coming to him; but finally, he was beginning to experience it here, among the quaint shops and historical buildings that screamed inspiration to him near daily.

Forever. It was a promise they had once made. He could not let it go; but he didn't know how he would keep it, either. It was a frustration that followed him. He tried to find ways to escape. He tried haphazardly dating Paige with no real emotional investment - but still - Gillian was in every moment, in every memory, in every look into the future. *I know she's supposed to be here with me. I have to find a way to get her back.*

Thomas' life wasn't complete unless he was writing. Of course, he'd always known that - long before Gillian had pointed it out to him; and certainly long before Nathan had reminded him of its importance. It was how he took his soul's temperature. It was how he stayed sane, and since losing Gillian and Eryn; he'd lost his writing, too. *No matter what I've tried, it won't come back to me. The work I do at MouseTrax isn't really writing... it's more like phrasing. Marketing's about bullet points, not about stories.*

****

It took ten days for him to find the answer to the challenge Nathan had put before him. It came when he was walking along the Charles one Sunday afternoon, watching the lovers sitting on blankets, sharing picnics, oblivious to his presence. *Nathan's right. I need to write to her.* He would take the risk to open his heart once again. *She's worth it... she's always been worth it.*

He sat down that night and picked up his pen again. The words flooded across the page surprisingly easily... memories of his time with Gillian. He wrote about the evils that he knew had always existed, and probably always would. He added the people, both good and bad, that he had encountered along the way, changing the names to protect the guilty. It was a collection of self-discoveries, and self-indulgences. And it worked. Over the autumn months, he found it easier to leave his torment behind, and he began showing up for life again.

****

Autumn had come to Cambridge. The leaves were turning from green to burnt umber and burgundy. Storefronts were displaying the latest in Halloween paraphernalia and historic buildings were decorating for the approaching Thanksgiving holiday. The tourists flooded through the streets. Places like Old North Church and Franklin's print shop were favorite spots. *It's always a surprise to me the draw the old churchyards have on the tourists. They seem to be enamored with the reality of the gravestones. It's as if for these visitors, the heroes of our past are still alive. Our country's history becomes real here - and somehow - they felt the connection.* Thomas had often considered writing a novel about the phenomenon of Boston's link from history to today. But at this point, it was still an idea that only lived as notes on a few index cards, tucked in the third left-hand drawer of his desk.

Today, as he walked the banks of the Charles, he knew it was time... he had to reconnect with Gillian, and somehow, get her back. He knew that their love was strong enough to survive anything the universe had to throw at them. Despite what Gillian felt emotionally, Thomas knew that together, they could also endure and make it through the horror of their past, too... *but we have to do it together.*

Thomas had become a writer because the spoken word often failed him. He needed to write. He needed to write to *her*. It was how they had stayed connected through all those long weeks of separation when he was away on assignment covering one human tragedy or another. It was how they remained in love through all the Hallmark holidays where a simple card with a trite expression of his love never quite hit the mark. And now, he knew it was how they were going to find their way back to each other.

When he got back to his apartment, he pulled out a sheet of parchment and a feather pen. He contemplated them for a long time. *If we are going to heal together... it needs to start with my words. Today.* He took a sip of wine, for courage, and began to write. He edited it several times, as was his habit. After three hours, and more drafts than he cared to admit, he folded the letter and sealed it in an envelope. He set it on the desk, ready to deliver the next day.

Dear Gillian,

I have missed you so much. Your touch, your smile, your gentle understanding of all the things I don't do so well; and your exuberant encouragement of the things that I do well. I need to write to you. I miss writing to you. I miss sharing my day with you. I know that you are still angry and sad about losing Eryn and the way the press handled everything... and most of all, I know that you are angry with me for not protecting you from the evils of my profession. I should have done more to keep them away. I should have done more to fend off the Peregrines of the Detroit paparattzi. I'm sorry that I didn't do enough... couldn't be enough... for you... for us.

I want to try again. We once made a vow to spend the rest of our lives together. I am determined to keep that vow, and I think you want that, too. We were amazing together. We were incredible parents and wonderful people - together. Apart, we're nothing. At least I know I am. Just nothing. I'm lost and alone without you. Alone, I am fragmented. With you, I am whole. I love you. I love us. And I think we should try again.

Eternally yours,
Thomas

When he re-read the letter the next morning, it sat in his hand, awkward and uneasy. "No... this isn't right. I have to do better..."

Chapter Eleven

"Naturally, love's the most distant possibility."
~Georges Bataille

Gillian spent the morning at her desk bewildered and more than a little irked, computer screen flickering before her, a stack of quarterly tax returns piled around, each with a folder of receipts to review. The sun beamed warmly through the large plate-glass window in blatant deception of the brutal autumn winds howling just outside. She was so tired of Michigan and its complete disregard for the calendar. Winter was still three full months away, but here it was, snowing!

Her day had not started out well. The madness began with a call from Geof at nine o'clock, which was difficult, at best. They'd been seeing each other only a couple of weeks, and he was getting annoying. They spent occasional weekend evenings together, going to movies and dinner – nothing especially spectacular. He'd been calling nearly every day since they'd met, though he never seemed to have much to say. It was beginning to irritate her. She wished he'd just spit out whatever it was he wanted and be done with it. She was tired of his "pay attention to me" games. There was enough to handle dealing with the upcoming anniversary ... she didn't need this nonsense, too. She would need to break it off with him. No great loss there, but still, it was just one more frustrating detail. So to get it over with, she invited him to lunch.

He stood when she reached the table, kissing her cheek and gently hanging her coat on a nearby hook. "Gillian, how have you been? You look fantastic!" Geoff was being annoyingly nice. It was going to make disappearing him much more difficult.

"Thanks, Geoff; you too. Have you ordered yet?" she asked, picking up the menu the waitress had left.

"Nope, I was waiting for you." It was as if he'd become six again. It was nauseating.

"Well, I don't have a lot of time, I've got a mountain of work, and a meeting at two..." Gillian nodded to the nearby waitress to get her attention. The waitress noticed the distress in her eyes and scooted over to the table.

"Hi there, what can I get for you?" asked the waitress.

"Hi, um, I'll have the Greek salad, Italian dressing; thank you," said Gillian.

"And for you, sir?" she asked with practiced panache.

"I'll have the same. Thank you." The waitress took their menus and scuttled off to drop the order slip in the kitchen before waiting on her next table.

"It was great to talk with you this morning, and quite the nice surprise to have lunch. We don't usually see each other during the week; this is nice." Geoff reached across the table and took Gillian's hand, squeezing it gently.

"Um, yeah. It's good to get out of the office for a change," she said, pulling her hand from his and reaching for the water glass. She was growing more uncomfortable as time went on. She prayed the chef would double-time her salad.

"Yeah," he replied. "My day's been nuts too. Lots in the hopper... a really big contract I've got to process or it'll be my commission in the toilet... and I'm getting ready for that trip this weekend. Yep, lots to do." Geoff took a sip of his water, and leaned back, trying to emulate calm chaos, and failing miserably.

"That's great." Gillian feigned support. In actuality, she doubted he had anything in "the hopper". *He's never been hungry enough to go in search of prey; he's more like a mantis, wait until it lands. Anything else is too much work.* But she was happy to be reminded that he was going out of town this weekend. The extra distance between them after she dumped on their relationship would help him forget – at least she was hoping it would.

"Will you excuse me for a moment, please?" Gillian left the table with a smile, heading for the restroom. On her way, she relayed her secret to the waitress, and asked for her salad in a box, softening the request with a generous tip. The waitress was happy to help, especially after seeing the $20 bill now resting in the palm of her hand.

"Um, Geoff, we have to talk..."said Gillian as she returned to the table; "I'm really sorry, but I just don't think things are working out between us." Geoff's smile faded quickly. "Don't get me wrong, you're a nice guy and all... it's just... this isn't working for me. I've still got too much baggage, I guess."

Geoff looked down at the table, sighing heavily. "I was afraid of something like this... we never get together for lunch."

Gillian signaled the waitress. "Look, it was nice... but it's just not right... not right now, anyway. Have a good trip. Have a nice life." The waitress handed Gillian her box as she stood, reached for her coat and turned one last time to Geoff. "Good Luck, Geoff."

As Gillian left the diner, she glanced back at Geoff where he sat dejected, untouched salad on the table in front of him. She wondered how long he would sit there before realizing that she'd actually left. He looked lost and alone. Gillian felt sorry for him a little bit. But this was not a man she could ever spend any real time with. There was only one man for her – and he was gone. She hated herself for leading Geoff on... hated Thomas for leaving... and hated herself even more for not hanging on tighter.

****

It was Friday afternoon, two o'clock, and the war was on. It had all started innocently enough as a small skirmish; a call to review the troops. The task ahead: promote those who were valued contributors to the campaign, and relieve those who did not measure up to expectations. It was a biannual event, "a necessary evil", as the partners explained it. She hated every moment of it. Since leaving the art world, she had fought the fights that would bring her benefit, without regret or compulsion to weakness, rejecting any impulse to creativity. However, standing by, silently taking notes while the boardroom blowhards decided the fate of loyal workers based on some digit-deviant armed with a collection of charts, graphs and projections—all without a thought for the names and lives behind the numbers—repulsed her. Out of nothing more than a sense of self-preservation, she played her role in this disgusting diatribe; invariably becoming the instigator of the elevation from battle to war. She fought hard this day, for her conscience would allow her to do nothing less.

The final head on the chopping block was Clara Stewart. Gillian was in the thick of this battle because she believed in underdogs. She believed that rough-cut diamonds were the most beautiful. She believed that energy and drive meant more than debutantes with degrees. Clara represented all that Gillian believed America stood for. A single mother, without college to back her up, was making her way as best she could in the secretarial pool of a disenfranchising corporation. She made a minuscule wage, and yet was able to attend every Saturday afternoon little league game. Clara embodied every character trait Gillian had ever believed in. Gillian was determined; Clara Stewart would not lose her job today.

Through the next hour or so, Gillian butted heads with some of the most influential and powerful people in the realm - and won. Clara would keep her job; and so would Gillian. Vindicated and exhausted, she made her way home thinking that the effort was worth it. Today, she stretched out, took a risk, and became a little bit more of the Gillian she envisioned would one day smile back at her from the mirror which hung in her again happy home.

****

What a day! Gillian dragged herself up the front steps of her condo, fumbling in her purse for her keys. It was one of those days where she was pulled in several directions, and got little accomplished. Too many meetings, too many deadlines, her car was in the shop - again. How she hated the lack of intelligent mass transportation in Michigan. She'd forgotten her mother's birthday; and to top it all off, the agency sent her a dimwitted secretary who couldn't make a decent cup of tea to save her life! All she wanted now was a little dinner and a hot bath - if only she could find those blasted keys! At last she discovered them in a side pocket. "Ugh! Not even custodians have so many keys!" A coarse reverberation rolled up from her throat, and she tried each one in turn, until finally, she found the right one, and clicked it into the lock.

Tripping over the mail in the foyer, the stupidity of the day magnified tenfold. She was weary with the frustration of it all. "I miss the mailbox at the old house ..."

She dropped her coat on the banister and tossed her keys on the hall table. She scowled at herself as she passed the hall mirror and wandered out to the kitchen; kicking her shoes off as she went, completely ignoring the mail. Anyone watching would have thought she was six. And right now, that's about how she felt. Disheveled, angry and well beyond calm, she'd simply had enough!

Pouring herself a small sifter of brandy, she noticed the DSO tickets peeking out from behind a magnet on her refrigerator. "Rats!" she huffed in disgust. "I forgot about that! Damned benefits! I'm really not in the mood for all that nonsense tonight." She thought for a moment, "I'll give Alex a call, maybe he'll take them off my hands."

Alex, a good friend since high school, was a development engineer for Fanuc Robotics, and had seen her through a lot in her life. *The insensitive socialist in college, through Thomas and the wedding, Eryn's death - he's always been there,* and she was grateful. He was one of the few people in life who knew about her past and didn't hold her hostage for it.

After several minutes of struggling to remember his number, the phone chirped in her ear as she waited for it to connect, sipping impatiently at her drink. One, two, three... and then, finally. "Alex, yeah, it's Gillian... listen, how'd you like tickets to the DSO tonight? I don't know... a benefit of some sort, my boss gave me the tickets... but after the day I've had, I just don't think I could stomach it all... Really, you'll take them? Great! You're a lifesaver! Curtain's at eight; pick 'em up anytime. Yup, you're welcome. See ya later."

She hung up the phone with a small sigh of relief. It was important for those tickets to be used; if her boss discovered the seats were empty, she might never see them again. The symphony was one of the few pleasures from her past with Thomas that she allowed herself; one of the few nice memories she didn't sequester. *Sometimes, I still miss him.*

Gillian opened up the freezer, pulled out one of those near-disgusting "fat-free" frozen dinners, and popped it into the microwave. She wasn't officially on a diet; but this was so much easier than cooking, and it gave her the illusion that she was staying healthy. "Seven minutes ... perfect. Achilles! Dinner!"

She reached for the small can on the top of the fridge, and at the sound of the electric opener, a sleek black cat came running. Winding between her legs and meowing loudly, his gratitude quickly became annoyance. "Oh, knock it off, cat! Here's your dinner, now go eat." Exhausted and irritable, she plopped down the cat's dish and walked out to the foyer. Just as she reached the pile of mail on the floor, the chime from the microwave called her back. "It figures."

Stretching awkwardly to reach it all, she scooped up the pile of catalogues and letters, and dropped them on the foyer table before she headed back to the kitchen. She pulled her dinner out of the microwave, grabbed a fork and her brandy and settled down to eat. She'd gotten nearly four bites down when the doorbell rang.

"Who is it?" she bellowed in a huff, making her way to the front door for the second time.

"It's Alex." She opened the door and invited him in.

"That was fast," Gillian snipped. "Did you find a date, too?"

"Of course! Was there ever any doubt?" he said, bowing before her.

"Here are your tickets, Sir;" she said in her very best usher's voice; "We hope you enjoy tonight's performance of 'Rich and Flaunting It On Parade'!" She handed him the tickets with mannerisms that would have been the envy of the countless wait staff she'd encountered throughout her childhood while being forced to accompany her parents at the club.

"Why thank you, Miss," Alex responded in his very best snob's voice. "I'm sure we will be delighted by such a splendid presentation."

Their laughter echoed through the sterile condo, adding a glimmer of life to a typically overly stoic household. She caught herself, in a fleeting moment, thinking how nice it was to hear herself laugh again… it had been a while. *Not since Thomas and Eryn…*

Alex left then, again, bowing deeply to her. She gave a quick curtsey and an even quicker "Bye!" and let the door close abruptly behind him. She watched his car pull away from the house, picked up the mail, and walked back toward the kitchen. A moment later and she was again sitting before her dinner, now grown cold, sorting through the bills. "Phone, dry cleaning, car insurance, mortgage, electric, car payment, Visa, American Express… how I hate the end of the month!" Bills meant writing checks, and she hated writing checks more than anything. It was a confining practice that reminded her of the cold tangibility in which she lived, and the art she had abandoned. *I'm not going to deal with this tonight. The paperwork can wait.*

She dumped her dishes in the sink, gave Achilles a little nudge, flipped on the CD player in the living room and trudged upstairs to soak in a long, hot tub. She just wanted to soothe the day's stupidity away… forget the whole thing. *It's Friday night, after all, I'm entitled.* Two steps up and she was immediately calmed by the singing strings of Mozart, his music was a fascination that stayed with her well past the days of her early teens when her uncle had first introduced her to it. She didn't know why, but Mozart's music always brought her great peace.

A smile came to Gillian as she slowly seeped into the warm, fluid comfort of her bathtub. Floating gently amidst the bubbles and steam, she closed her eyes, thinking about men, relationships and why she didn't currently have one. Achilles sat perched on the edge of the tub, curious about the crackling bubbles drifting around Gillian's shoulders. Occasionally, he would pass his paw through one and recoil from the surprise of its destruction. As was part of her nightly ritual, she settled in to have a sincere conversation with her only confidant, Achilles. He would never betray her, never repeat what she had said to someone who didn't matter, and certainly never throw her words back at her in a moment of heated debate. Achilles was safe, and he made feel Gillian that way too.

"Well, Mr. Whiskers, I'm not sure what I'm supposed to do now. Soon, it will be time to go back to Kremmling, back to that place... that horrible place. But I have to go - for Eryn. It's important. After everything we've been through together, I can't just abandon her now. I know I've moved away... but I can't leave her... not yet." Achilles nudged his nose against her forehead, setting her into a near-Vulcan mind-meld state of mind. It was as if the cat were giving her permission to empty whatever was in there, and let it go down the drain with the stagnant water and dissipating bubbles.

"It's been a long time... nearly six months..." Her eyes welled up with tears, and the cat sat back and let them flow, statuesque in his support. "I miss her so much... I miss them both... so... much." She could barely get the words out. Losing Eryn from her life was devastating - a piece of her inner soul was ripped from her that day. Missing Thomas was... was like a piece of her heart languished in turmoil, never fully broken, and never fully healed. Thomas was too much a part of her to forget... to let go... thinking of him - no matter the context, good, bad or indifferent - was too painful to endure. He had become a ghost to her, and yet, his spirit lingered forever on the periphery of her life. "It's why I can't move on and find someone else. No one else could ever fit the hole he left." And no one else would ever understand the mordacious memory a simple photo of her daughter could produce.

"I think I'm done, Achilles. It's just too hard... I'm... just... done." She sobbed for a long time, unable to stifle the sadness that had now overtaken her. As she began to calm, the cat leapt from the ledge of the tub, clear that she had no further expectation of his attention tonight. Gillian caught the sliver of his tail slip around the door frame as she released the water from its comforting duties. It had failed to bring her the solace she was counting on, and she was disappointed. She brought her knees up to her chest, sulking through the final trickles of what could have been relief - but wasn't. Her back tensed and her arms ached. Her head pounded and her eyes stung with the tears of a memory she could not purge. When the moisture was finally evaporated from her skin and her body trembled from the chill, she reached for her bathrobe and stepped out, turning to offer one last scowl of discontent toward her failed emotional asylum.

She avoided the mirror; sure the specter of past lives un-lived would chase her demons closer to the surface, and plodded head down, to her bedroom across the hall. She pulled on a pair of flannel pajamas, hoping to find some snippet of comfort - but was instead plagued again by the memories of flannel, Eryn, and that one, happy Christmas morning when Thomas was euphoric over absolutely nothing. She could easily recall their happiness, but hers was elusive since the accident. Like watching the movie of the life she had once led and having no memory of it. The fog never dissipated; and she feared that it someday would.

As she pulled back the blankets on the bed, Gillian gazed across the room at the small table in the bay window. Upon it lay the sketch pad, pencils and pastels that she'd placed there when she had moved away from the house. She convinced herself that it was okay to pull them out of the box, after all, art was a part of her soul, she couldn't give it up completely. And yet, there they sat. She couldn't bring herself to dust away the cobwebs, let alone open the pad and put a pencil in her hand. She longed to feel the freedom of the colors and the adventures of the lines that once lived well in her soul... but they were lost to her now. Limitless primaries and secondaries merging in shadow and contrast with innovative perspective had given way to stagnant formulas and strict controls. "This is my life now. Survival has replaced happiness. Surrender has replaced hope." Gillian drew the covers to her neck and flipped the switch on the bedside lamp. Darkness had now enveloped her; and although she hated it... at least it had finally become familiar.

****

It was two in the morning when Gillian awoke, pulled on her slippers, and headed back down to the kitchen, the previous day's unfinished business still nagging at her. That was the excuse... but the truth was that she hadn't been sleeping well since leaving Thomas. She was lucky if she got a full six hours in one stretch without it being interrupted by some horrific dream or overwhelming loneliness. *I thought that moving away from the house would help. But it didn't.* The condo where she now stored her life felt distant and cold.

"Well, since I'm awake, I might as well be productive." She knew she wouldn't be able to get her Saturday morning started until she'd cleared the rubble from the kitchen sink and erased last night's postal stupidity. It made her crazy to see that stuff piled up on the table. She stopped to glance out the living room window. "Great. Rain. Well, at least it's not snow." Disconnected from what she once thought was beautiful, Gillian watched the reflection of the street lamps in puddles. She noticed each and every droplet as they seemed to fall in slow motion and collect on the pavement.

It was a melancholic rain. And for a moment, she was lost again in a sympathetic fog... someplace between here and there.

It was Achilles who brought her back to reality as he rubbed up against her legs. She bent down, picked him up and held him close to her chest as she padded near silently across polished faux-mahogany floors into the kitchen. "Well cat," she said stroking his long black fur. "What do you think? Think I'll ever find someone to be with forever? Could that ever really happen to me? Nope." she said to his green-eyed stare; "I don't think so either." Gillian nuzzled her nose with his, seeking out his soulful comfort.

As if on cue, Achilles jumped silently from her arms and curled up under the table in front of the heat vent. Glancing up at the clock, she made herself a cup of cocoa and walked over to the kitchen table. She still had several untouched envelopes awaiting her attention. Amongst the stack, she found a belated birthday card from a long distant college alum; a letter from her mother chastising with heaps of guilt her decision to remain in Detroit for the holidays rather than traveling to Seattle to visit the rest of the family; and a strange, unfamiliar envelope with a Boston return address.

As she picked up the letter and inspected it carefully, the music from the stereo she'd left on for company brought her piano solos by a not so famous player she'd met at a shopping mall concert. He had a serene yet optimistic style about his music. She liked that. It was just the mood she was hoping to find tonight. Sliding her finger deftly across the envelope's seam, she released the parchment from its hiding place.

"Parchment? No one uses parchment anymore. Well, Achilles, it's two-thirty; let's see what this is all about ..." Gillian sat, sipping at her cocoa, dumfounded by the letter before her. She hadn't even begun to read its contents, and still, she was mystified. "Calligraphy... parchment... no familiar return address... a

Massachusetts postmark on the envelope." Her analytic brain was going full force... And then she began to read...

"Fair Lady, wouldst thou stop and chat a while? I am Sebastian, Blacksmith of the Realm."

Her immediate response was one of anger. "What the Hell?!"she screamed. The cat ran from the kitchen to places unknown, saving himself from the perceived peril. "He doesn't get to do this anymore. He lost the privilege to write me letters and tell me stories when he left. How dare he?!" She threw the letter on the table, furious with his inconsiderateness. "Didn't he think about how this would affect me? Didn't he know how hard this would be for me? He sure should have!" She stormed to the living room and threw herself on the couch, clutching a pillow, beside herself with anger and remorse.

Achilles tentatively sidled up next to her, nudging her with his signature peacefulness. Her heart softened a bit, and she apologized. "I'm sorry, I know it's completely irrational, but it still hurts. And after the disappointment of Geoff, I guess I'm a little on edge. I'm sorry I scared you." She nudged the cat's nose and he purred his forgiveness.

"I need to get out for a while." She grabbed her coat and keys from the front hallway. "I'll be back soon. Watch the house."

Gillian walked about three blocks in the rain before her blood pressure began to feel normal again. The walk helped. It gave her perspective and allowed her to put a little distance on her memories. She knew Thomas meant no malice. He never did. She made her way back to the house. "Maybe he deserves a second read." It was a phrase they had shared, particularly in election years – a reminder not to make judgements about people until their message was read completely. She grabbed a towel from the powder room and vigorously rubbed the rain and anger from her head.

Sitting at her kitchen table and holding the letter once again, a broad smile crossed her lips and she stifled a joyful tear. There once was a time when Thomas told her stories... wrote her letters... and always, he had signed it "Sebastian". She quickly turned to the last page to see that indeed, it was Thomas who had written the letter. He gently scribed his initials in the bottom right corner, just as he always had, to let her know it was him. It was their secret code. Their private portal to a place only the two of them shared. It had been so long since she had been there with him, she'd forgotten the path. And now, he seemed to be leading her back. She missed his stories - and although she considered throwing the entire envelope away out of self-preservation - she just couldn't. The pain he brought back to her was palpable but so was the memory of his love and the wonderment of his creativity. This most certainly had the potential to be a lot of fun, if she would just allow it. Carefully, keeping her heart at a distance, she read on.

"I was born a simple peasant boy, son of Tobias, Blacksmith of our village. After his passing, I inherited the foundry, and it is my great pleasure to serve you. It is rare that a fine gentlewoman, as most certainly you are, should pay attentions to a common man in the likes of me. And for your many accommodations, I thank you. Your kindness has brought sweetness to my day and a smile to my face."

Such exhilaration ran through her as the words played out before her eyes. She hadn't felt joy in a long time, and she was pleased with how easily it had returned to her. She was fearful that it never would. Still, she was cautious. Dismantling the walls of protection now was not in her best interests. The path before her was dark. She needed to travel slowly, carefully... she had no idea how close she was to the edge. She lifted her gaze to the cat in whispered pondering. "Is it even possible... could he still care about me after everything I put him through?"

As she sat waiting for some wise answer from her emotional compass, her eyes began to wander. They drifted up to discover a similar pair starring back at her. There was a distant flicker of light from the neighbor's house, created an odd reflection and in it she saw three identical pairs of eyes gazing back at her. It was an eerie feeling... like the reflection of her sub-conscious, recording and judging her every move. It was an unsettling feeling, yet strangely comforting. It almost made her feel as if she weren't really alone. Somehow, this small moment brought her back to every lovely memory of Eryn and Thomas. And tonight, together, their eyes shared the same vision of possibility, reflecting in the night sky. Off in the distance, she heard the screeching of tires and she waited for the crash of crumpled metal... but none came. The only sound that followed was the incessant yapping of an over-zealous St. Bernard puppy confined to her neighbor's backyard.

Her eyes and her thoughts drifted back to the letter. "Why would he send this?" Her question was to everyone and to no one; to herself and the cat. The letter continued.

"Lady Gillian, your thoughts are plain to me. Please do not concern yourself with your worth unto me, for each is worthy in their way. If not for your family's efforts and protection, my mount would not make the steep trek up the narrow pathways of Espial Ridge nor carry me through the dense forest of Pique Ardor. It is I, who am honored to make thy acquaintance, my Lady."

A faint smile crossed Gillian's lips, and she whispered to herself, "Oh, Achilles, he's still got it."

"You are most likely wondering what brings me so far from my homeland. You are perhaps thinking it may be a Quest or other such mission that beckons me hither; or perhaps a holiday? Sweet Lady, my purpose is quite simple. I came in search of you."

Gillian gasped in astonishment. She thought her desire for his return was a secret. *How could he know?* Adrenaline rushed through her. Was it excitement or fear? *Is there a difference?*

"Many a minstrel have returned to the Realm with a host of poems and songs praising favor to a fair maiden who lives upon the peninsulas of the five blue lake's crashing wake. They tell of her beauty and insight, of her sweetness and light. Night after night have I listened to such tales of serene perfection to be found in the chestnut eyes of a Lady ... the Lady Gillian. They say she walks with moonlit shadows and summer winds; that her heart sings with the voice of a nightingale. She has a touch so gentle; she can hold a young butterfly in the palm of her hand. And so, Dear One, it is, indeed, for you that I have come. For as I have seen, all their words were spoken true.

"Dearest Gillian, never shall we part; not when summer winds blow others across the torrent waters in search of thee; not when autumn leaves cover the mountain passages in a blanket of red and gold; not when the winter winds howl cold and icy upon your window pane. Never shall I abandon thee."

It took Gillian a moment or two to fully recuperate and regain her composure. A letter from Thomas was the last thing she had expected. *A letter from Thomas, written like... this... unimaginable.* Her cheeks flushed and her hands trembled. Her heart was pounding so strongly, she thought it might send her into cardiac arrest. *It's been a long time since Thomas talked to me this way. At least, not since those first letters so long ago in college.* This was the romance she had missed. She'd assumed that they'd both forgotten it. Staring blankly at the page before her, she was jolted back to life when the last line of prose materialized through her tear-blurred vision.

"You shall always be my Lady. My Love. As Ever, And Always. ~Sebastian."

If indeed Gillian's heart sang, it was certainly crooning tonight! *I can't believe that after everything, the Thomas I love is still out there.* She wondered if it was real... and if it was... would it last? Since leaving the art world, the men she came in contact with by her mother's introduction were arrogant, stuffy highbrows with absolutely no interest in relationships or romance, or literature, for that matter. Just money, and cold, sterile accounting formulas. Her world is now populated by emotional morons and prolific degenerates. *Thomas will never be one of them.* It was then that she allowed herself to acknowledge how much she missed him. She wondered, *Will he write again?*

She turned to Achilles, now perched on the windowsill. "I can hear mother now... *'Now dear, we, I mean your father and me, we both understand that at one time, you truly loved Thomas. But that time has gone. Starting up with him again will only cause you more grief. Do you really want to put your overly fragile heart through that again? I mean, after all, how much of your heart could possibly be left to break... I mean, first Eryn and then the divorce. How much more do you need to go through to learn to stay away from hurting yourself that way?!'*

"Yeah, mom would have a field day with this one. And although I hate to admit it, mother's deprecating voice might be right. Rats! I hate it when she does that. This is a lovely letter. But I'm just not sure I can do this again. It's too hard. But ... I can't just let it go, either. I have to do something."

Achilles blinked at her with an absent attitude.

"I should at least write back... let him down gently. It's the polite thing to do. We do have all that shared history; that can't be ignored. I'll tell him that too much has changed between us, and we have to let go.

"What could have made Thomas think that I am remarkable enough to write to again? Ours was not a nice ending... could this be guilt or is he playing some kind of cruel joke? No - Mom would be right on this one. I should stay away and say nothing. The whole thing will just go away... eventually... I hope."

Achilles stared at Gillian with his perfect cat green eyes, and his perfect cat statuesque posture, saying absolutely nothing. "Some help you are!" She was pacing now... creating circles through the kitchen, into the living room and back again. Defeated, she sat down, staring blankly at the letter. Achilles was not impressed and went back to his cat nap near the heat vent.

"Achilles, wait!" A shot of lightening erupted within her and the cat startled. She leapt from her seat and ran to the living room, nearly losing her footing on the slick floors like a cartoon character, as she rounded the corner. There it was, on the coffee table... *The Wizard of Alcazar*. She'd been entranced by this book for about three decades, reading and re-reading it over and over again, and now was frantically flipping through its pages as she made her way back to the kitchen. "I know it's in here. Here it is, *Espial Ridge*. I knew that sounded familiar, it's a place in the book!" The intensity of the moment again pushed her eyes across the page. "He remembered, Achilles. He actually remembered!"

A warm fondness flooded through her veins. She hadn't felt this loved in a long time. And yet, somehow she still thought it could be a trap. When it was all over he would be laughing, she would be crying, and then he would be gone again. "It's a cruel joke, Achilles... I just can't do this."

Finally, she looked at the clock, noticing that it was nearing four-thirty. The sun would be up soon. She made her decision. "Write him back. Write. Him. Back. There's no other way to do it. But it must end here."

Gillian searched the kitchen drawer for something to write on. She only found lined loose leaf paper and a blue fine-point Sharpie. It wasn't how she wanted her last correspondence to appear, but on such short notice, it would have to do. *The haste of it will underscore my message to make it stop.* Gillian was surprised that her hand was trembling as she held the pen to write. She took another sip of her third cup of cocoa; for courage.

"*Gentle Sir, because you have stepped out on my way, a new joy rushes through me unlike any other I have ever felt. Truly, you have awakened love within me once again. How I wish we could spend an eternity together. Though I know we must tread softly upon these new paths we have foraged, so as not to disturb the gentle balance. I wish to be here for you, forever awaiting your return. However, there is no moon this eve, and the night grows dark. I fear the monsters of the night will consume me. We cannot meet again, for the danger is great. Yet, I shall smile and think of you. Fare-thee-well.*"

Gillian tentatively folded the paper into thirds and placed it within the envelope as a deep sigh escaped from her chest. "Well, let's hope that did the trick, eh Achilles?"

On the outside, she printed "Thomas Laird" and his postal address in simple print. One last look, and she sealed it shut. As she fixed the stamp, she noticed that the music in the house had long since evaporated into the mist of moonlight, and she was again alone with her thoughts and the echoes of her bland surroundings.

Hesitating with the front door's lock, she mused to herself, "I must be out of my mind." Looking out the front door, she saw no one watching. She opened the door, dropped the letter in the mailbox and shut the door, afraid she might be caught in a moment of weakness.

"Oh fudge!" said Gillian, with a shallow groan, her back against the door. She sank to the floor and muttered to herself memories of a life of happiness with Thomas. Then, as she felt the stomach punch of losing Eryn once again, she disappeared into a chaotic weeping she could not control. Try as he might, even Achilles could not distract her pain. Her mother's voice was right. Getting involved with Thomas again would only bring more agony to her life. She'd had enough. *I was just starting to heal. I can't step backward now. I just can't.*

After fifteen full minutes of frustration and sadness, Achilles finally broke in. Exhausted, her eyes closed and she inhaled, letting out a long sigh. Trance-like, she opened the door and retrieved the letter, dropping it on the hall table with a mixture of sadness and hope. She scooped up Achilles and headed up the stairs. All she wanted now was to forget everything she'd ever known and fall asleep. She allowed the cat to jump from her arms onto the bed, as she pulled a Melatonin tablet from the bottle in her nightstand drawer. She'd come to rely on the sleep aid a great deal since the divorce. It had always been difficult for her to sleep in an empty bed; and even more so when the nightmares plagued her. She was useless and depressed without sleep. This little white tablet was her solution to capturing sleep while avoiding the demons of addiction. *It's just a stop-gap measure, until a more permanent solution can be found.* This time, she took two.

Restlessly, she slid her eyes closed and sank into the warmth of her flannel comforter's pocket of softness. As she drifted off to sleep, her heart sketched out a picture of Thomas as a rugged knight dressed in a long tunic of evergreen and gold, with a broadsword at his side. She imagined him with his amber eyes; brown hair draping the nape of his neck, a warm goatee cradling his strong chin, and a sincere gentleness that added wonder to his conversation. In the innocence of her mind's playground, she envisioned the quests he'd been on; the distant lands he'd traveled through; and the people he encountered along the way... gypsies, giants, trolls, minstrels, pirates, sorcerers and noblemen of every variety. A marvelous ballet of fantasy flew through her imagination, danced well to the music of a flute and lyre played somewhere in the distance... the bright, festive banners of the towns and villages; the pomp and circumstance of life at court; the endless summer skies dotted with majestic cotton clouds, the beautiful emerald canopy of an enchanted forest. For several hours, she slept more soundly than she had in months, pleasantly lost in a dreamscape of perfect distraction.

****

As the bright, afternoon sun streamed through Gillian's bedroom window, basking her pillows in a surreal Hollywood haze, she glanced at the numbers on her bedside clock to realize she'd slept well past two... a feat not accomplished since her days at CCS. She rarely slept well these days, forever plagued with the frustrations of business and "keeping up appearances". *But last night was different. I'm still quite sure what to think of it all. What new adventure is coming... I'm not sure I want to know - but I'm not sure I want to miss it, either.* She hadn't had "girlish" expectations for a long time, and she was enjoying it. It was a nice escape. Last night she found a long-lost solace as she dreamt of knights, dragons, unicorns and castle towers meeting with the afternoon sky. Yet, she was still wary. *I'm sure this can't last... why should it? What we had is gone, isn't it?*

As she brought her brain into the new day, Gillian moved in a hangover haze. Though she didn't yet know the consequences, she was determined to hold on to this fleeting peace for as long as fate would allow. She thought about Thomas as she dressed, still caught up in the intrigue of his letter and why he had chosen now to write after all that she'd put him through.

Gillian pulled on a favorite pair of old jeans and an over-sized teal cable sweater from the cedar chest at the end of the bed, truly understanding how nice it felt to be free from the polyester and silk of her everyday nine-to five. As she descended the stairs, she encountered Achilles half-way down and paused to sit with him for a moment. "So cat, what do you think about all of this? It's pretty scary, I'll admit. But there's something that feels right about it, too. I just don't know." She stroked his fur gently. He left her lap, heading toward the kitchen, breakfast was long overdue.

As she rounded the corner from the staircase into the vestibule, she caught a smile pass her by in the mirror. "Well, that's new." It was genuine, and that was what made her notice it. She dared not linger on that thought for too long, for fear that it might disappear again.

Over a brief brunch of an English muffin smeared in butter - a luxury she would not have normally allowed herself - sausage, juice and the morning paper, Gillian thought about how badly she wanted to be someplace else. She was at her wits end. The stress of office politics and that "daily grind" had mowed her down this week. Too many meetings, too many complaints, too much stupidity! This was one of those weeks when she'd questioned why she spent all that money on her "fall back" degree in accounting when a certificate in baby-sitting would have done just as well. "It's time to get away, unwind, just turn it all off for a while. It's two-thirty, and I need to disappear. It's time to cut the strings and become invisible for a while - if only for a day. Yes Achilles, it's time for a Hermitage!"

She fished through her purse, found her cell phone and deposited it defiantly in a hallway bureau drawer. *I won't be needing this.* She deserved a first-class hermitage and she was determined to take it. But first, she had to pick up her car from the shop. She made a quick phone call for the dealership's courtesy car, pulled out some extra food and water for Achilles, and threw a few things into a duffel. She quickly went through the checklist - *heat turned down to seventy, cat safely in his carrier, all the windows closed, phone forwarded to voicemail.* "I do believe we're ready!"

Moments later a car could be heard honking impatiently outside. Gillian shouldered her duffel bag, and locked the door behind her. As she turned her glance back to the door, she saw an envelope flapping in the cool afternoon breeze. As she pulled it from the door jam, she noticed a little note that read, "*wrong address*", scribbled across the envelope. She checked the return ... *Yes! It's from Thomas. He must have sent these the same day as the one I read last night... I wonder why?*

Giggling under her breath, she pulled the letter gently from the door and ran her fingers across her name, again in calligraphy, on the front of a parchment envelope. The driver honked impatiently, and she skipped down the front steps. She tucked the envelope into her duffel... forcing herself to wait. The anticipation of it was intoxicating to her, and she was bound and determined to have as enjoyable a day as possible. Through the typically slow ride through town, she allowed herself a few moments of indulgent imagination.

"I can imagine being drawn along cobblestone roadways in a handsome coach, Thomas by my side. Ah... I'm completely transported through time. It's nice. And there is a lot to be said for nice, wouldn't you say, Achilles?" she whispered to the cat. For a few brief moments, it didn't matter that the car was filled with a disgusting blend of aromas; cigar smoke, the driver's open Tupperware container of tuna salad and the completely useless pine air freshener that swayed from a little string on the rear-view mirror. She continued her quiet conversation with the cat.

"I can smell the fresh open autumn air of mountains, lush wild flowers and a hint of wood burning from a campfire in the distance. The rows of burned-out drug houses are now castle towers and small cabins dotting the open farmlands." Achilles purred in gentle agreement.

Her sweet daydream was foiled, however, with the bray of the driver's voice sodden with slurred rudeness. But she couldn't let go of it completely... how could she? The world was being overrun with trolls, and her taxi driver was just one really good example.

"Hey, Lady, I said we're here; ain't you been listen'?" All at once, she was again barraged with the foulness of the car and the noxious driver. With pleasure, collected Achilles, her belongings and got out, happy to be rid of the disgusting troll.

The dimwit at the "*We're The Best With Broken Cars Repair Shop*" insisted he knew nothing about her car, let alone which one was hers, or even where she might find it.

"I'm sorry, ma'am. I just don't know nothin' 'bout your car. What color you say it was?"

Clearly, he was not a good hire. Frustrated and becoming more than a little enraged, she demanded to see the manager. "Look, I paid you people good money to fix my car, and I want it now! Maybe your manager knows something about it?" Gillian's patience was waning quickly.

"My manager?" droned the attendant with what would have appeared to her as his best Igor imitation.

"Yes, can you go get him, PLEASE?"

"Uh, I guess so." She watched as yet another troll lumbered off to find his boss.

"Stupid people shouldn't breed," she hissed, trying in earnest not to scream those words after him. Keeping her composure today was indeed, a great challenge. *This is not what I wanted to be doing today.* She was more than a little annoyed that these stupid complications were keeping her from where she really wanted to be. Her patience was wearing thin, and her antagonism was beginning to drizzle out of her composed demeanor. As the man in charge approached her, she noticed that he was also a troll. Trolls were easy to spot. They all had the same wore-torn brainless attitude, with the physicality of orangutans. It surprised her that she hadn't seen calluses on his knuckles from all that dragging on pavement. *God, the world is being over-run with trolls. Is there no end?*

She didn't work at hiding the heavy sigh which escaped from her throat as they talked about her missing vehicle. After exchanging the customary unpleasantries about sub-standard employees and poor management, the senior troll admitted that he did have her car, and more importantly, it was fixed. Having established the crux - solved - they moved on to quibbles about price. It was a brief discussion; one that would have lasted much longer, had she been in the mood.

Once the nonsense was over, she handed him her AMEX card and once having pocketed the receipt, was again on the road. The Michigan scenery seemed to stretch out before her in slow motion. At long last, she was beginning to feel relaxed and comfortable.

West Port Marina was about an hour away, nestled in Ontario, on the banks of Lake St. Clair. Once over the bridge, the large glass and concrete office buildings gave way to quaint cottages with white fences and swaying tree-lined roads. Children rode bikes and played roller hockey in the streets, seemingly oblivious to the world around them. Dogs barked at passersby and Grandparents sat talking with neighbors on their front porches. It was a Canadian Norman Rockwell moment, if ever she'd seen one. It was nice. Gillian loved it here. There was something about the feel of soft, wet sand squishing between her bare toes and the smell of crisp air that somehow said home to her. A flood of childhood memories lived here and she loved to visit them often.

****

When Gillian arrived at the marina, she became aware that her stomach was playing some version of a minuet in growls, and so she stopped in at the little restaurant to grab a quick bite. She cracked the windows and let Achilles out of his crate. She put a small dish of water on the floor, closed the car door, and went inside. The urge to open the envelope tugged at her brain, but again, she delayed her gratification... enjoying the foreplay of waiting.

Although the restaurant at the Marina was a familiar place to her, the faces around her seemed strange and distant. She saw no one that she knew, not even wait staff, though it seemed there were some who knew her - or at least knew of her. *It's an eerie feeling, being watched... but then, I have to admit, I'm watching them, too.* The Grille was filled with people of every age and station in life. Families with small children attempting to have a dignified meal, with little success. Lovers wrapped around each other in window seats as they gazed out upon the water, talking in hushed voices of what wonders their life together will hold. Businessmen entertained clients, trying to make the sale, all the while silently calculating their commission, and the tip. There were also those odd collections of visitors who were completely ambivalent to the others who shared their table - and everyone else in the place, too. It was a fantastic menagerie of souls, and yet... she still felt strangely alone.

After quickly, yet discretely, devouring a cup of chowder and a ham sandwich, Gillian picked up Achilles and headed for the boat. The sun lilted low on the horizon, casting a steel-turquoise glow to chrome masts reaching toward a cloudless sky. Ducks paddled busily around hulls in search of small fish or bits of food visitors were kind enough to leave for them. Walking along docks long grown gray and weather beaten, she noticed small red squirrels hopping through freshly mowed grass and seagulls soaring high overhead. *This is such a beautiful place. Peace and tranquility live well here.*

At last, she arrived - slip twenty-two; the name, proudly displayed on the stern in gentle sunlight hues read *The Artist's Way*. The name was stolen from a book she'd read long ago, when she'd first begun painting at the museum. She thought, given how much time she spent sketching on this boat over the years, the name was a good fit. She hoped the author, Julia Cameron, would understand.

She stopped to sit for a moment on the bench in front of her slip, Achilles in his crate, at her side. It was a solemn ritual, taking a few moments of unfettered time to simply enjoy the beauty of nature untarnished by the evils of the financial world. It was important for her to mark this time, the division between here and there, to keep it sacred. Achilles meowed, and she talked with him, to quiet him. Quiet was necessary before they boarded.

"Sure, *Way* is a small boat, just thirty-five feet from stem to stern, and the only thing Uncle Earl left me, but I love it just the same. I remember Earl being so fond of sailing. I'm happy he shared that joy with me. I am so thankful. I relished our time spent on the lake under sail like fine chocolates that would never melt. Pure childhood wonderment. I love this place. My brain just seems to work better out here. It's a place where I can leave the money world behind me and just sink into the simplicity of life. *Way* is rigged for single-handed sailing, you know. It's perfect. I don't have to rely on crew... it's just you and me, cat. No demands, no deadlines, no bellowing executives; just the optimism of a never-ending horizon reaching out to lands not yet explored. I think a lot about sailing away forever... but, well, you know."

Although Gillian had a radio and GPS on board, which really don't count because of the safety requirement, *Way* was deemed a technology-free environment. She had only the essentials; an alcohol stove, a small dorm-sized refrigerator, and a propane shower that shared space with the head. Whenever possible, she enjoyed living such a scaled-down version of life. It reminded her of those things that needed to remain sacred. Things like peace, solitude, self-reliance and a strong connection with nature. These things had been missing in her life since Eryn's death, and her divorce from Thomas. She hoped that by coming here, she could somehow reclaim them... *if only in this moment.*

Things on *Way* were just as she had left them last time out. Her cave had not been disturbed. That fact alone brought her great comfort. *It's a nice feeling to know that there is still one perfect sanctuary left in my life, untouched by tragedy.* Climbing aboard, she tossed her duffel in the forward cabin, released Achilles, and pulled out the parchment envelope, laying it gently on the galley table. She reached for the radio and flipped on her favorite evening show. It was a menagerie of soft love songs hosted by Alan Almond, and his low, gentle, hypnotic voice. Pillow Talk, his signature show had been a part of her life for as long as she could remember. She was grateful to herself for having recorded all those shows in her teen years. Even though he was gone now, he was still with her every time she clicked "play". The combination of his velvet intonation, the tranquil melodies and the easy rocking of the boat made her feel perfectly entranced in a wonderland of bliss.

****

It was about ten o'clock when Gillian poured herself a cup of cocoa, changed into a pair of comfy red sweats, an old *DIA* t-shirt, and battened down the hatches for the night. By the warm glow of amber cabin lights, she regarded the envelope for a long while, considering whether or not she was ready. She reached once again for Achilles and his non-prejudicial comfort. She pulled him onto her lap, gently stroking his fur.

"Could it have just been a fluke? Maybe, by now, he's rethinking the whole thing... maybe he's sitting at home right now, thinking himself a fool for writing to me. I hope he keeps writing. But I'm scared. How crazy is that?!" The cat stared at her with placid eyes; kneading her lap to make himself more comfortable.

It had been so long since anything had excited her, she longed for daily happiness again. She missed it so much. Her mother's voice came to her again. "This is a dangerous game, Gillian. Sure, you two were in love once, and it might have lasted. But after losing Eryn - do you ever really think the two of you can be together again after all that pain? You'd better be careful young lady."

Achilles slinked off to the aft quarter berth for the night. It was his favorite cave. Finally, she slid her fingers under the flap and released the page. She took a sip of her steaming security, unfolded three pages, and began to read.

Dearest Gillian; please forgive this intrusion. For I am in an impassioned state of pure exhilaration. I believe I have come to know more of your beauty than the minstrels could ever invoke in their ballads. I feel a certain kindred with you, Sweet Lady; and I hope you share my vision. I wish to know so much more of you. Please, if you will, speak to me of the wonders that dwell within your soul. Tell me about you... what you value, desire, love. I wish to know all of you... the very heart of you. Share with me your secrets, Dear One, and I shall keep them safe for all time. Or if you will allow, I shall tell you another tale.

A small giggle slipped past her lips. Expectations are not always enjoyable, unless, of course, they become reality. Gillian vaulted to the V-berth, pulled the sketch pad from the forward locker, and began to draw like a woman possessed. It had been a long time since she'd felt sheltered enough to sketch. But there was no denying it. When the Muse called, she had to answer. *I haven't heard the call in so long...*

It is a tale of greed and generosity. Perhaps when you hear my saga, you shall feel more secure in our friendship. Wilst thou tarry a moment and hear this vexed dissertation? If yea; you are kind, gentle Lady, to offer such patience. It is the story of a young bride, her despicable parents, and the vile man they demanded she wed.

Gillian's hands were quivering with excitement as she began to sketch the story Thomas revealed. Her stomach had that new-love nausea that usually follows a first kiss. It was a game they had played often, early on in their relationship. He would tell her stories and she would sketch the scene. Still, she felt a little uneasy. "Remember what Uncle Earl said - *'Creativity comes from within, not from all the books you've read or classes you've aced. True creativity, the kind that people will respond to, comes from the heart.'* I remember the basement, filled with boxes holding those treasures. We talked about publishing a book... but then... the train..."

Gillian braced herself against the memory, refilled her cocoa, and sat back to read... and sketch.

Chapter Twelve

"It is by doing down into the abyss that we recover the treasures of life. Where you stumble, there lies your treasure."
~Joseph Campbell

"Snow... again! If I see one more blasted snowflake... this is insufferable! The end of April and twenty-nine degrees. Shouldn't it be spring by now?"

It's just past midnight, Darrian snores recklessly in a nearby berth. By the glow of a small kerosene lantern, Sabina writes in her journal, pouring out her anger, frustration and desperation upon the pages of a blank book she picked up at the stationary store in Vancouver before they left. She thought it would be the beginning of a novel. She was wrong. She didn't have the energy for that kind of creativity. Journaling was what kept her sane these days.

Sabina sails with her husband, Darrian, a man she hates, upon the frigid, glacier-laced turquoise waters. "Tuesday, Day Twenty: It's been nearly a full month of long and exhausting days at sea and I don't think I can endure much more before I lose my mind completely! The choppy blue waters and screaming winds... though difficult to endure are not the source of my discontent. It's true, the waters here are aggressive. Each crash of wake against bow, in concert with the howling wind, sounds like the rehearsal for my funeral dirge. Yet, these waters and foul weather are not the reason I hate life so much. In fact, there are days when seeing the peaceful shoreline filled with glaciers and an occasional grizzly scavenging for supper are the only things that bring me a bit of solace, despite the wave nauseous rocking. These sights remind me that life finds a way - life will go on. That's the best comfort I can find these days. No, it is with *him* that I take issue! Okay, I hate the cold weather, too. But he... is... ugh!

"Salmon are the most popular fish in the waters around Juneau. That's why we came. Darrian seems to think that he can make a living at this fishing thing. Personally, I don't think he thought it through completely. Obviously, he didn't have the Discovery Channel back home. Didn't he realize that fishing in the Gulf of Alaska was torturous, not to mention cold?! King salmon run in May and June, pinks from mid-July through August, silvers from August through mid-September. Sure, he'd done that much research. But he should have bought a better boat. Between the creaky floorboards and forestays coming loose all the time, it's a wonder this thing sails at all. A sailboat? Really? For fishing? That was pretty stupid. This thing is for weekend jaunts, not capturing buckets of sea creatures waiting to be eaten. But, when you consider the source, this is about the best expectation imagination can create.

"Mother and father tried to convince me that a marriage with Darrian would bring great wealth to our family. Yup, that's my parents, always trying to live vicariously through me - or anyone else who will let them latch on to their lives and bank account. They explained in painful detail how fishing is such a lucrative business, and that Darrian was man enough to handle the lifestyle. But what about me? This is not what I had in mind for the rest of my life... or even the next month... but of course, no one listened to me. I must admit, it was a great escape hatch, marrying Darrian... and I'll find a way out... somehow. He won't keep me here forever! It's survival of the fittest, and I refuse to allow Darwin to prove me the weaker combatant in this fight!"

Life on the water was pure torture for Sabina, a far cry from the romantic notion of sailing around the world with the man you love. Yet the difficulties of her days with Darrian came nowhere near the agony she had endured at the hands of her parents over the previous seventeen years. An only child, she was continually blamed for the troubles of their marriage, the changes in the weather, and for not being born a boy. Often, she felt the stinging pelt of a switch or strap across her thighs and backside as payment for mistakes made... mistakes all children make. She found no comfort in her mother's arms. Her mother made it clear that Sabina was a most untimely inconvenience in her life. Sabina spent her days in school and her nights tending to chores and whatever pitiful desires her parents conjured. There was little time for play or such simple pleasures as strolling through the fields in search of wild flowers. She was nothing more than a slave to them; and a bothersome one at that. It irritated her father to no end, that Sabina was focused on her studies, forever seeking out new things to learn and master. Soon, she had surpassed his intellect, and this infuriated him.

One afternoon, at a meeting with her teacher, her parents were given the rare news that Sabina had won an award for her writing and recitation. "You should be very proud of your daughter, sir." said her teacher. "She's made great strides to succeed with her education. Her creative writing, especially, is exemplary. She truly deserves this award." Sabina's parents feigned happiness as they accepted the envelope with the fifty dollar prize tucked inside, but even though her name was on the certificate she held in her shaking hands, Sabina knew there would be hell to pay when the family got home.

"What did you think you were doing, young lady!? I strictly forbade you to enter that ridiculous writing contest, and you went behind my back and did it anyway. Have you no respect for your parents? You have made us look like fools, with no control over our own child. You're repugnant and disobedient, and I'll not stand for that kind of behavior in my house!"

"It was just a small writing contest, father; nothing of consequence," Sabina pleaded. "I thought you would be proud to receive the award... I thought the extra money might be a welcome gift."

"Nonsense! What you've done is proved yourself the upstart who needs to supplement her father's income with nonsensical pursuits. Now the entire town will think that I can't provide well enough for my family, and I need to rely on my daughter's support to keep us flush."

"But I thought I was being helpful!" cried Sabina.

Sabina's father struck her across the face, leaving a bright red splotch from chin to ear, effectively reducing her to tears and thrusting her deep into humiliation. "You weren't being helpful, you little wretch! You've now tarnished my reputation... I will never recover from this stain upon our family. All who hear of this will now believe that you – an insolent child – can achieve greater things than her father. Who knows now, if anyone will ever trust me or my work again." He sent her to bed hungry and wondering if she could ever do anything that would please him.

Sabina's mother sunk into the shadows, ignoring that primal instinct to defend her daughter, for she was afraid of what he might to do her if she crossed him. *Better to stay quiet and safe. Sabina is young... she will recover much more quickly than I.*

As a way to counteract the defeat her parents felt, they reminded Sabina on a continual basis how unworthy she was of even the most basic of pleasures... and at seventeen years old, she had heard these messages so frequently that her own voice was beginning to repeat them. She had to get away... out of desperation... out of self-preservation. So she married Darrian; with the hope that things would be better. *Surely, anything will be better.*

"If only I had the strength to really say what I felt. But children in backwards towns are not granted such liberties - even grown children. I should have discovered Vancouver long before now - perhaps it would have saved me. It was the morning of the wedding when I finally figured it all out. But by that time, it was too late to do anything about it. All my life, Father has beaten me down, in every way imaginable. He has always been the one in control - although much of the time he demonstrated a lack of control. He used my fear of him to manipulate me and keep me doing just what he wanted, ignoring my dreams and desires completely. After all, what I wanted was counter-productive to what he wanted... total control. He was frustrated with my desire to change things for myself and be brave about beginning new adventures.

"As I think about it now, truly I believe that his anger was misplaced. I think he suffered from self-loathing. He had said as much when he was drunk and didn't know I was listening. In talking with Mother one night, he said he would like to be the kind of person who could trust himself to take the kinds of risks that could propel his life forward, but he was afraid. He was jealous of my bravery and self-assurance. The only way he could counteract his own inadequacies was to try to beat my confidence out of me. If I appeared to be less of a person, he could still win. He could save face and remain greater and more respected than his child. How warped is that?

"He was one of the few people in our town who did not believe that the lives of their children should shine brighter than their own. His own insufficiencies, his own insecurities kept him from admitting that his daughter was worthy of the praise and attention her friends and teachers gave to her. Beating me into submission and controlling me with fear was his only recourse. I remember on a few occasions, while receiving a generous whipping with a switch he had handy, he actually told me this piece of wisdom. 'The first one is to teach you a lesson; all the others are simply to make me feel better.' Intimidation was his favorite pastime. If he convinced me that I would never overcome my fear, he could remain victorious and no one would ever know that he lived a lie.

"Mother just went along with the whole plan out of a sense of self-preservation. If Father didn't take his anger and emotional-flatulence out on me, it would have been to her that he would turn his fist next. In her mind, I am sure, she rationalized that I was younger and more resilient than she. I could withstand it all, and recover with minimal long-term damage. She was wrong. She has always been wrong. The accomplice in the deed is just as guilty as the barbarian who committed the heinous violence. There are no statutes of forgiveness for those who deny what is right and acquiesce to save their own hides. It is simply cowardice."

"Oh, Darrian may have a fat trust fund, and I'm sure that at some point he may have been an attractive, even semi-intelligent person. But he's far from being an impressive man today; very far, indeed! Somehow, his DNA took a dive into the gene pool, and hit the cement deck instead. He's a depraved man ... a repulsive, horrific little fisherman. Even the fish turn their heads away in disgust when they find themselves captured by his nets. Indeed, dying, as his dinner is sweet reward compared with the humiliation of living as his pet.

"Each night he comes to our bed smelling of rancid fish and pungent salt water. He's a crude man with a baneful temper. I don't believe he's ever shaved with any accuracy, he rarely bathes, many of his teeth are missing and his breath bears a foulness which defies description! Against all temptation, I withhold, as best I can, the urge to retch all I've ever eaten since the day of my birth whenever he draws near. A feat, I must admit, not always accomplished well. I need to find a new escape hatch; and soon!"

Sabina wrapped a shawl around her back and shoulders to keep out the chill of night. She reached for the small pot and poured herself another cup of tea. These moments of quiet were precious to her, and she was soaking in as much of it tonight as she could. Juneau gets more than eighteen hours of sunlight at the summer solstice in June but less than six and a half hours of sunlight at the winter solstice. Staring out at the stars, she wondered if her brain could protect her long enough to make it to June... to see the sun again. It was hard to be courageous in the dark. Memories of her past pain haunted her in places she could not light. Focusing her energy on anger seemed to be the best way to stay alive these days... otherwise the sadness might consume her into a tar pit so thick with remorse that she might not find a way to swim free.

****

Gillian was hit with a wave of overwhelm. Thomas seemed to be picking into the memories of her first husband... it was so long ago, and yet, he seemed to be recounting it for her all over again. The relationship—hardly a marriage really—only lasted six months and was quietly annulled. But it had been a gruesome six months. She had talked about it only once with Thomas. It was the beginning of their sophomore year at U of M; when she was trying to recover, still very wary of men. Gillian was surprised that Thomas had remembered their late-night conversation from so long ago. She knew he was telling a story. The fact that it was loosely based in her past was forgivable... so far.

Gillian flipped to a new page in her sketch book and kept reading. She wasn't happy that he brought up the old wounds, but in truth, she really couldn't be angry. It was a long time ago and the scars were barely visible today. It wasn't as bad as his imagination made it out to be.

****

"I am only seventeen years old, far too young to be subjected to spend the rest of my life with such a despicable troll. I hate him, yet if it is at all possible, I hate my parents more. How could they demand such a life of their daughter? Weren't all the years of relentless beatings and degradation enough? Did they truly believe I would have so much difficulty finding a husband on my own? Sure, my parents were well paid for their "gift" of me to Darrian. But that doesn't change the fact that I shall be doomed to a life of sequestered misery on the high seas. I'm sure my parents are delighted. It's true; I was forced into this marriage against every ounce of my being. Yet, this may be my only salvation from a life of eternal anguish. In this case, the devil I don't know may end up being better than the devil I know. Each night as the moon rises high and pure in the midnight sky, I pray that somehow I shall be liberated from this wretched fate. Rescue me, someone! Please!!"

Although life with Sabina's parents was abhorrent and more emotional torture than any youngster should have to endure, at least with Darrian, life was a little more predictable. She always knew by his fill of rum or ale and the size of the day's catch, what his disposition would hold. Thankfully, he didn't speak to her much. He went about his business and often left her to tasks below, ignoring her completely. She was quite lonely, but loneliness was a better alternative, considering the only type of attention she might get from him, whatever his mood, was guaranteed to be vile.

****

A week later, they landed in Yakutat. Occasionally, when the trades were favorable and he was in an unusually good mood, Darrian would allow Sabina precious time to go ashore and walk the wharf marketplaces, chatting with the people who lived there. Although he denied her even the most insignificant of purchases, she relished these times. They were her only connection to civilization and kind, free-thinking people. Sadly, these moments of permissiveness in Darrian were extremely rare, and she saw little of the more than two-dozen harbor towns where they had docked.

Yakutat stands alone along the Gulf of Alaska coast, facing the continent's largest glacier across Yakutat Bay. It backs up to hundreds of miles of some of the most rugged and, Sabina thought, most beautiful mountains in the world. The town's six hundred-eighty people also have the pleasure of living right on top of some of the best fishing in the world. The night before they docked, Darrian sat mesmerized at the chart table, a tankard of ale in his hand. "These are the best waters to fish in the entire world! We'll easily seal our catch and meet our quota... maybe even steal a bit extra... in no time at all. I've got a guy in town who was happy to take my offload, pay me a decent price, too. Mark my words, lassie, our future will be rosy soon... don't you worry, we'll be rolling in it soon enough, you'll see, it'll be everything we ever wanted..."

As Darrian continued to babble, Sabina tuned him out. She wasn't interested in fishing or their future. She just wanted out. He continued to read from the piles of brochures he'd collected. It still fascinated her that he could actually read.

"The nineteen miles of the Situk River, east of town, are famed for steelhead and four kinds of salmon: silvers, reds, kings and pinks. Yakutat Bay has big kings and silvers. Several lodges in the area cater in season to anglers and hunters. Commercial fishing occurs in the risky Fair weather Grounds south of Yakutat for salmon, halibut, crab and black cod. Competitions are held each year, with prize money ranging in the hundreds of thousands. I will make a boat-load of money here."

Yet in the next week, cast after cast, his lines and nets came up empty. Darrian did not handle his failure well, and Sabina suffered for his frustration.

****

"Sex is something Darrian professes a gift for... he is wrong. He needed to feel that he can succeed at something... and fishing didn't seem to be working for him. He had to delude himself into excellence somehow." He raped Sabina that night; which was no different, really, than any other night. He flung her on the berth like a rag doll, his strength easily overpowered her. The foulness of his breath and the harshness of his body attacked her at every angle. Her clothing ripped away, she felt the sting of his hand across her face, and she screamed. She fought his stupidity until the horror of his voice commanding her compliance and the sting of four or five more slaps on her backside stunned her into silence. She gave in, went limp, and went numb. *It is often said that playing possum is the best way to save your life in times of great terror.* When he finally released her, she grabbed at her clothes and scurried like a bilge rat to the deck. Weeping silently, she watched the stunning array of the aurora borealis as steel blue, red and orange flashed across the midnight sky. She prayed for death's salvation as shivers and sleep finally consumed her.

****

Yakutat's summer climate is relatively mild and often rainy. The annual rainfall is a staggering one hundred forty-five inches, including the melted water from an average one hundred ninety-three inches of snow cascading in a veritable waterfall down from the mountains. One afternoon, the boat was engulfed in an unusual and torrential storm. The winds thrashed the craft about like a cork in foamy surf. The galley took a hard hit, with jars of preserves crashing to the floor shattering glass and jams about the cabin in a whirlwind of purple and red. The ale keg smashed against the galley ladder, spilling into the bilge with defiant foam that enraged Darrian beyond description. Sails were torn and one of the aft forestays came loose from the hull. The storm had been brief, yet barbaric. They would need to pull into port and make repairs. The storm caused tremendous damage to the ship. It was a foregone conclusion that Sabina would catch a brutal beating for this—as certainly, Darrian had to vent his anger on someone. Never would he admit to any responsibility. *This all could have been avoided had he agreed to my suggestion of docking rather than his insistence to moor out in the bay, away from the safety of port.*

It was just past noon about a week and a half later when they weighed anchor less than a quarter mile from the picturesque seaside town of Cordova. Darrian had to take out time to make additional repairs to the ship and find a replacement for the keg that was lost.

From the small portholes, Sabina could see a group of kayakers gathering at the water's edge with their boats. *How I envy their freedom.* She saw fabulous cliffs that stood as sentinels around the town. Raven smoke billowed up from portly chimneys on the tiny cabins that hemmed the coastline and a multitude of birds soared effortlessly through a crystalline sky. Sea lions and otters played in the shallows, dancing together in a beautiful minuet of peaceful coexistence. *How I long to walk in the valley, losing myself in the new life of wild flowers and... finally... sunshine.* Given the circumstances, she was certain that she would be allowed to walk the docks and replenish their supplies. Even this chore was enticement for her heart to lighten just a little.

However, Darrian was in a particularly foul mood after the poor catch in Yakutat and an ever-dwindling supply of rum; and refused to allow her even a short stroll along the docks. Sabina would have to admire the view from her portal below as she cleaned the galley of the still sticky residue all around her. He was emphatic about her impound on the boat.

Teak usually cleaned up well, but this wood had not been well cared for, and so it took a tremendous amount of work to get it clean again. A light breeze gently splashed salted droplets of sea foam on her face and hands, stinging her brain with the bitter reality of her unmerciful jailer's suffocating grip on her precious freedom. *Will he ever allow me simple human pleasures? Doubtful. He is a man of tremendous control - if not of himself, then certainly of me.*

****

By the cover of darkness, two nights later, their ship was attacked and boarded by a band of howling Pirates. Colorfully clad in dark leather, brilliant scarves and gold chains around copper-tanned bodies, Sabina found them to be enticing and sensual. Slightly frightened and more than a little excited, she watched them through hands hiding her face with astonishment and gratitude. The fact that they walked onto her boat from another era didn't seem to matter at that moment... she would sort that all out later... after...

They beat her miserable husband into unconscious submission with no remorse, and set to work ransacking the boat of all they deemed valuable. As Darrian lay there, bleeding and broken, his body twisted in ways she knew would not be easily healed. *Thank you!* It was Godsend that this rabble had laid siege upon them. *Finally, I'm free of him. Free from his tortuous ways; free from his foul stench; free from a horrible life of submission and captivity.* She let go a long sigh and crept back further under the galley table to wait for the rowdy rovers to be on their way. The pirates moved about the boat hollering and complaining that their paltry reward was not worth so much trouble. And that's when it hit her - *those are women's voices!*

"What scum this man is, such filth, and not enough in his locker to feed us for even one meal! Why did we waste our time?" They kicked him again, just to punctuate the point.

She was stunned and shocked. It was strange to her that women could live in such a way... women - aggressive women - it was unheard of! *I wish Father could've been here for this. They would have easily taken care of him.* The band of Sea Amazons were much too concerned with this business of beat and pillage to notice her hiding just below their feet. *Pillaging is serious stuff, and must be the center of all focus if it is to be done right,* she imagined. *Surely, they are always caught in a time crunch of one sort or another; sinking ships, constables giving chase, screaming passengers... there was always something getting in the way. It must be a harried life, but everyone has to live somehow,* she conceded. Sabina sensed that they enjoyed it. And she enjoyed them - perhaps more than she should have.

On a final check through the vessel for any tidbit of overlooked treasure or small morsel of food, the one who must have been the Pirate Queen saw Sabina sitting motionless under the galley table, clutching her knees to her chest, with eyes marble big. She was frail from malnutrition and emotional neglect, her lip was split and she had a black circle around her left eye, bruised from Darrian's last bout with frustration; and still, she had an intrinsic beauty about her that the Queen could not ignore.

Shaking and whimpering uncontrollably now, after having been discovered, Sabina's mood turned from winsome glee to unbridled fear the instant the leather-clad warrior stepped toward her. She was certain that hers was the next body to be slaughtered - or worse.

"Hey Sam," called one of the others, "Let's get out of here... Coast Guard'll be coming soon."

Sam... Samantha... The name raced through Sabina's head and lodged in her ears - like rubbing your wet finger on the rim of a crystal wine glass - it hung in the air like smoke from the Sistine Chapel.

"Hang on ..." Sam called back, cocking her head in the direction of her comrades but never taking her eyes off of Sabina. She had a slight Russian accent, or something that sounded like Russian; her long jet-black hair flowed freely around her face and her coal eyes betrayed none of her secrets. She wore so much gold that surely, Sabina believed she would sink straight away if she fell overboard. Underneath, she wore a high-neck silk blouse with a rounded collar, blood red. *Is she for real? She looks like a comic book pirate come to life ... except that she's a woman.* Sabina was paralyzed but whether from fear, excitement or disbelief, she couldn't say.

"Come see what I found... a pet for the journey home."

There was a cackle in Samantha's voice that set Sabina ill at ease. *I've already been one man's pet—could being the pet of a woman... a pirate... be any different?* Three other women huddled into the galley, gaping at her like tourists at the butterfly exhibit at the zoo.

"Ickh... what a pathetic... what's that smell?"

"I don't know, I think she's kinda cute," said Sam.

"Are you nuts? She'll be more trouble than your damn cat - leave her be." More comments flew from the women in unison, exploding the silence with shrill discontent. "Come on, Sam, you can't be serious... "

"No, I think I'll keep this one, Regan. She might be just what I'm looking for. Call it an act of mercy... I'm saving her from a life of stupidity."

"Right, like you're known for your heart burgeoning with kindness..." Regan shot Sam a look that Sam reloaded and shot right back.

"Load her up, girls; we're outta here."

****

It had been weeks, maybe even months, since Sabina had enjoyed a hot shower. The pirates, especially Regan, insisted on it - and she was grateful. The fresh smell of soap alone was enough to send her into waves of ecstasy. Even more invigorating was the sensation of scrubbing shampoo deep into her scalp. She must have spent a full five minutes digging her fingernails into her hair, exfoliating dead skin cells and months of wretched Darrian stench. When the last droplet of water had finally escaped down the shower drain, she wrapped herself in a towel and stepped around the corner and into the small cabin they had prepared for her.

Immediately, she was enveloped in the warm amber of teak, surrounding her in a cave of comfort. Green flannel sheets and red wool blankets covered the berth and crisp white towels hung from a nearby rack. There was ample storage, shelves lined with books - a luxury she'd not enjoyed in far too long - and even a hot sink... right in the cabin! She felt as if she'd become prisoner by the manager of a five-star hotel, rather than a band of Amazon pirates! Sabina changed into the clothes the pirates had left on her berth and stared about the room in disbelief. *I guess this is what you get when women are in charge - clean, warm, nice.* Sabina left her cabin and followed her nose tentatively toward the mesmerizing aromas lofting from the galley.

As they sailed north, toward the Kenai Peninsula at an easy eight knot clip, the crew met up for supper. This boat was a huge two-mast schooner with ninety feet of deck and a twenty-three foot beam. It was a huge vessel. At least a dozen sailed her, with plenty of space to spare. The galley was impressive, holding a full refrigerator and freezer, hot sink and a propane stove. Three comfortable tables adorned with a bishop's feast awaited.

How amazing... eating food that has actually been cooked, not just straight out of the can! There's a lot of space here. It seems more like a house - a mansion, really - than a boat. She'd never seen anything like it.

****

A flash of memory came to Gillian. It was early in their college years - their first memorial day together. Thomas had taken her on a celestial weekend aboard a Windjammer Cruise off Nantucket Island. He had recalled for her all of those perfectly romantic details in his pirate tale. It was as if he had written it from the video he'd secretly taken. But there was no such film. It was baffling to her how after all these years... he wrote about it all as if it was yesterday. Not one detail had been left out. Not one moment of softness had been forgotten. She didn't know how he was able to do it. But she was glad that he did. And the drawing she was working on became the window into their past memory. A twinge of sadness ran through her as she realized he might never see it. She pushed the thought aside and continued to read... and sketch.

****

Sabina was famished. The food was enticing - but she refrained from making a pig of herself. She was still unsure of her new captors, and didn't want to offend them. *I don't want to end up like Darrian.* They appeared in waves around the galley, each piling a plate high with food. Sam and Regan had called each other sister - although to Sabina, they looked nothing alike. Fae,

Michalea and Hali she remembered from the siege on Darrian's boat. They dominated the conversation with nautical concerns; charts, courses and sea conditions. The others ate almost in complete silence. *They must be new to this life, or at least less experienced, or maybe they just know their place.* She took her cue from them and said nothing, keeping her eyes lowered. She was afraid, but relieved that she was rid of Darrian at last. *Would he survive his wounds? Would he recover enough to notice her missing? Would he come after her?* She really didn't care. This was the first good meal she'd had in months, and she was enjoying it for all it was worth.

****

They had been at sea for four days. Sabina became much more comfortable with her new band. She learned to pull her own weight. The Pirates were kind to her and allowed her the dignity of her humanity. As they rounded Seldovia toward their reclusive home in the Cook Inlet, Sabina walked the decks for the first time without fear of reprisal. "Each to her own on this ship," Michalea once told her. *It's perfect.*

A few hours later, they were docked in a secluded cove just opposite Nikiski at the mouth of the Inlet. Each woman disembarked, duffel strewn across her back, and headed up a small stone walkway toward the darkness of a forest of wonder. Sabina hung back on the boat, unsure about her next steps. She nervously held a small black cat in her arms, stroking it's soft fur for luck. It was then that her arm was taken up by Samantha, and she was led ashore.

As they walked through the lush forest, Samantha reached for Sabina's hand, and held it tight, as though she was a small child. Perched at the top of the hill, Sabina saw it - the cabin in the woods. *More than a cabin - a log palace -* it was nestled in the low hills and covered by a cloak of evergreen trees. There were beautiful flowers, small animals scurrying about and birds chirping from their nests in treetops so tall, Sabina could only see small patches of blue sky poking through. There was not a man in sight. *This must be paradise.*

The building was magnificent. From the moment she walked in the door, it looked and felt like a museum. There was rich, brown leather furniture with brass studs; brass wall sconces with aromatic candles reflecting their light off crystal vases filled with dried flowers. The scents of lavender and vanilla permeated every pore of Sabina's skin. She felt royal and undeserving. To her left stood a staircase which led to a balcony overlooking the great room. From her vantage point, she could see several doors lining the balcony's edge—*those must be the bedrooms.* To her right, she saw an enormous kitchen wrapped in granite, stainless steel, and dark wood cabinetry. At the far end of the great room stood massive French doors, a portal to the mythic outdoors. She walked closer in reverent silence, and slowly opened them to allow the fresh pine fragrance to wash over her with the shifting winds. Just below the hill, she could see the boat, standing as a sentinel until their next voyage. A gentle smile crossed her lips, as though she'd fallen in love for the first time.

"So you like it?" Samantha's voice floated in like a Russian narrator from a ballet documentary.

"Of course! It's perfect. I never dreamed that places like this really existed!" Sabina exclaimed.

"I'm glad, because I want you to stay," she whispered.

"Stay? You mean with you? Become a pirate?" The notion filled Sabina with a cocktail of emotions. Giving Sabina some time to think, Samantha moved to the stone fireplace near the kitchen, and stoked up a roaring blaze. The flames billowed out, warming

Sabina in a way only the intoxication of brandy had done before. She felt soothed, at peace... at home. *What would my parents say? What happens if Darrian ever finds me here? How can I possibly live in Alaska, a fugitive the rest of my life? Can I handle this lifestyle? Do I really want to abandon men?* In her confusion, she took a step back, looking around with a mixture of awe and fear. "I... I don't know..."

"It's okay; you don't have to make a decision right away. Take a few days... or weeks... to think on it. We've got plenty of time. It's only just now Spring, and the Winter onslaught won't be here for months yet. Take your time. But for now, let me show you to your room." Samantha's voice was calm and soothing. The invitation was becoming harder to dismiss.

They climbed the grand staircase, and as Samantha opened the door to Sabina's room, a wave of shock and near nausea swept over her. She had only dreamt of such a room in the fantasies she had while distracting herself from Darrian's disgusting sexual escapades. She had no idea that it actually existed!

Glorious sunshine danced into the room from a large skylight perched above the central focal point of the room; a fantastic cherry wood king-sized sleigh bed piled high with pillows and a dark blue ultra-soft flannel comforter. It was easy to believe that she would never sleep cold again. As she looked around the room, her heart leapt from her chest as she noticed each piece of perfectly crafted furniture.

Beautiful blue and white ceramic oil lamps were perched on each table-top adding a perfect haze of warmth to the room. In the far corner, a blue-glass hurricane lamp hung in absolute defiance of gravity from a brass lamp stand next to a deep chocolate leather armchair and ottoman which certainly, two could curl up in quite comfortably. In the corner, near the lingerie dresser, stood a large cherry wood framed mirror - floor to ceiling, it seemed to reflect another world... *A portal to Alice's Wonderland... except that Wonderland is on this side!*

This was by far the most extravagant place Sabina had ever seen... and the thought that she was going to sleep here - it boggled her brain. From the fog of amazement and wonder which enticed her senses, she heard the door softly close. Samantha had left her alone to take it all in... to make her decision.   It was an easy one to make. She flung herself on the bed, giggling beyond control.

Of course I'll stay. I'd be foolish not to!

****

When she'd reached the end of Thomas' story, Gillian gently laid out the collection of sketches she'd created from his words on *Way's* galley table. It was as if the sailing weekend of their past had been recreated in her art. The scenery, although not Alaska, was mesmerizing; and the scenes from the boat and cottage, hauntingly familiar. Gillian sat back a moment and starred at the collection of pages - words and drawings – side-by-side. The two seemed right together - *just like Thomas and me.*

Achilles let out a pitiful moan from the aft berth, bringing her back. It was well past three in the morning, and she was forced to admit, the cat was right. It was time to put out the lights and get some sleep. She'd figure out what to do about all this in the morning. But as things sat right now... she was just about as happy as she'd ever been. She hoped it would last.

****

Thomas and Paige had been seeing each other for about six months. It was a strange relationship. She was clearly the dominant one, and that was just fine with him. The last thing he wanted after his tragedy of a marriage with Gillian was to do it the old way again. The emotional turmoil was just too much for him.

Unless it was with Gillian. And that was his focus - getting her back. Paige was just a diversion, perfect for a moment of release when he needed to take a step back from his heart.

Nathan explained to Thomas that Paige was in favor of very short-term, not very meaningful stints with men. A man's purpose in her life was to allow her to fit in at corporate social events; not because she thought having a man in her life impacted her positively. The sex was nice, although completely meaningless to her; which again, was fine with Thomas. He was enduring enough of his own emotional baggage to take on carrying hers, too.

One night, over far too many drinks, Thomas asked Nathan what Paige's deal was. "No one disputes that she's worked hard to achieve everything that she has; but what's with the "moody and distant" game?"

"If you tell her I spilled any of this," Nathan slurred, "It'll be both our heads. Capeche?"

"Oh sure, I'd never leak a source." Thomas replied, eager to hear the backstory to this puzzle of a woman.

"Paige has no memory of her early years. Her life began as an orphan at nine years old, when her mother had succumbed to cocaine consumption. Don't know about her father. After that, she was subjected to living in a home for discarded children. The comfort that she might have found living in a Bolshevik convent didn't exist for her in that wretched place. Instead, she encountered State employed social workers who were more concerned with their own pensions, health insurance and vacation days than with the happiness of children. The staff performed the basic tasks necessary to keep the children alive and healthy - but beyond that, there was nothing. In fact, for Paige, it wasn't that much different than living with her mother in those early years, with the exception of being healthy and eating more regularly.

Within that first year at the home, Paige learned that if she wanted anything - material or otherwise - she would have to wrestle the powers that be to the ground and then run away with her boon before it could be snatched from her tiny fingers. As the years passed, she developed a hardened heart and a mind that disengaged from anything that didn't directly serve her goals."

"Wow," said Thomas. I never would have guessed."

"And her goals were formidable..." continued Nathan; "nearly unattainable by anyone else's' standards... but somehow, she had grappled her way to the top and grabbed the brass ring. When she was finally adopted by the Lamberts at eight years old, her brain was already in 'high achievement mode'. The fact that they had more money than she could imagine, didn't hurt. An Ivy League education was the finishing touch. And now, she is the wonderful woman we all know and love." Nathan toasted to her and swigged down the last of his scotch. Standing, and enveloping Thomas into a neat choke-hold, he said, "And if you tell her any of this, I'll break your knee caps... after she's finished with you, of course."

Nathan let Thomas loose and staggered out the door leaving him in a fog of journalistic recollection. *I think I just got the scoop of the century.*

Chapter Thirteen

*"When people are very damaged, they can often meet
the world with a kind of defiance."*
~J.K. Rowling

Winter had descended upon the world once again. Snow blanketed the New England rooftops in a surreal white acrylic. Thomas was not looking forward to the Holidays. So often those around him seemed to have lost the point and instead, drowned themselves in an inebriated selfishness disguised as sincerity. The superficial attitudes of some of his colleagues were the most difficult to endure. It was as if they had lost the lease on their souls from Thanksgiving to the week after New Year's.

Each year, at Thanksgiving time, MouseTrax hosted what Nathan had called "a reprehensible affair" designed to further divide the "little people" from the executives. The point of this tawdry display was to completely solidify the segregation between the two camps; with no hope of redemption extended to those whose salaries fell below the six-figure mark. More a show of superlatives that could never be obtained than an extension of kindness and good-will, the Holiday Party was traditionally nothing more than an exercise in ego inflation for those who were unworthy throughout the rest of the year. They needed this boost to fabricate the energy necessary to survive the onslaught of stupidity that was surely to accompany spring quotas. It had been the same in the newspaper business. Thomas hated this time of year more than any other. Now that Gillian and Eryn were absent from his life, he hated it even more. *Idiot, you knew this was coming. You should have remembered and found a way to get out of this nonsense!*

The room was filled with the finery of utter arrogance. Men in tuxedos, women in velvet or satin, and diamonds or pearls - each cradling a glass of liquid security and laughing long before the punch line was delivered. *I would have much rather stayed home and worked on my next story for Gillian. At least there, my demons lilt quietly in the background rather than gregariously slurring their hellos and gripping my hand with tragic desperation.*

As Thomas made his way around the room, dutifully displaying his feigned corporate loyalty, he filled a small plate at the hors d'oeuvre table, working hard at being inconspicuous. He would not be confined to the dictates of a society where he eluded no true allegiance. No tails hung off his back and no bow tie strangled his integrity. Instead, a conservative mourning coat and silk long tie accompanied his quietly unpretentious conversation. Thomas knew that this small spec of defiance set him apart from those who handed out bonuses; and he didn't care.

Few things seemed to faze him—and the reporter in him noticed everything. Impatiently waiting for the moment of toasts and announcements before he could make his escape, he maintained his conversation with a geek from the IT department. The moniker they'd saddled Thomas with, "idea man", he knew, was meant to be one of endearment. But somehow it didn't seem to fit him. With all of his knowledge—on top of the mystery he projected—"master scribe" seemed a more fitting title. It was the one Gillian had given him, and after "husband" and "father", the only one that really meant anything to him.

Thomas was only half-listening now, as Ian, an underling in the personnel department, started complimenting his "achievements in attaining a firm foothold on such a tenuous precipice of the corporate mountain." It was all frivolous - empty words from a young resume architect. Thomas nodded, shook his hand and smiled. Sadly, not much more was required of him to complete the ritual; and Ian moved on to his next victim.

From somewhere in the distance he heard a faint clink of metal to glass - and the sound grew louder, as the clamor of conversation ceased. His attention shifted then, to Bob Harrison, MouseTrax's CFO, as he began his yearly wade into the murky waters of political correctness and complimentary speeches. The two things, Thomas realized not long after he was hired, were mutually exclusive in this arena. Fairly well soused, his method at avoiding detection of his inebriated state was to say a few insincere words and then quickly pass the baton to someone else. This time, his torture fell upon Paige. Thomas felt sorry for her. Over a light dinner one night, they discussed how she detested public speaking or public anything, for that matter. She mentioned to him that night that if they were to embarrass her by drawing her to the podium, it wouldn't be pretty. Caught just a little off guard, Paige paused for a moment, and then began. Thomas could feel the energy in the room shift, and he waited attentively for the explosion he realized was coming.

"Thank you, Bob." She glanced quickly around the room at the dozens of eyes now trained on her. Thomas was right. *She's going to blow! A flak jacket might have been a better choice of attire tonight.* He looked for a safe place to take cover, but found none; so he slinked closer to the door for a quick exit.

"I'm happy to be sharing this night with all of you. Throughout the year you have all showed your loyalty and perseverance, making MouseTrax number two in the country for a second year!" As CEO, this was her privilege, but also her disdain. She hated premature celebrations that derailed future stubbornness. Stubbornness was what they needed to stay on top. The obligatory round of applause rose from the room. Paige waited patiently for it to subside.

"I am proud of your accomplishments. Our research and development team has created four new products and obtained patents for two new programming processes. We've accomplished record highs in sales, and productivity has never been better."

Again, there was thunderous applause and a few drunken whistles from the throng before her. She looked over to Bob, who was smiling wide and shaking hands with well-wishers. *Wait for it... she's not done yet.* Thomas glanced around the room, as if on a plane, making sure he knew where the nearest exit was, in the event of a crash.

****

In an act of what would later be called brazen defiance, she made her scandalous announcement. *I need to set them back on task - the lazy executives. They've become too complacent, too comfortable. They've lost their edge. Tonight, I'll get them back on track.* "Now, because you have worked so hard all year; because you have sustained positive growth for MouseTrax despite a very fickle economy; Mr. Harrison, in his infinite generosity, has verified a $3,000 bonus, in addition to your year-end checks, for each and every one of you, with our most humble thanks!"

The roar of cheers that erupted from the crowd nearly deafened Paige. She knew this would not go over well with the Board - already evident by the disparaging looks they failed to hide with false smiles. They knew this meant no salary increases for them in the spring quarter. She hadn't discussed this with them, and they were not pleased. But Paige knew that this kind of recognition was long overdue. The company had not issued bonuses, except to the executive staff, in over five years. She'd studied the spreadsheets. She knew how much money the company was bringing in; and she knew they could more than afford it. Her father had taught her well. Company morale on the lower levels was failing and she needed to resurrect it if they were going to face the challenges of the innovative work of the new kid on the he block, MicroTech. She knew no motivation spoke louder to the grunts than a few extra dollars in their pockets. She also knew this would be a motivating force for her executive team, too. *A little show of disappointment now and again can be a powerful tool in getting those on the entitlement program to work a little harder. Fear of losing their country club memberships and tuition for their kids' private school education will go a long way toward insighting some forward momentum.*

Paige also knew that this single act of generosity would improve morale and triple productivity. It was a point she had often made in the din of board room negotiations, but had always lost. The fat cats were too preoccupied with their investment's return to consider the greater good of a single, simple act of manipulating kindness. But tonight, since Bob had saddled her with the torture of addressing the troops unprepared, she took her retribution. The look on her face told Thomas that she felt good about it.

Paige finished her champagne and made her way toward the door. She was simultaneously faced with the angry and the elated. Workers from every station, some she didn't even know she'd hired, grasped her hand, patted her shoulder, and showered her with gratitude. *I feel ill.* Now, she was faced with somehow navigating through the torrential seas of genuine adoration and the undulating silence of fierce Boardroom retaliation to somehow find the door.

Finally, she located her coat and vanished amidst the overwhelming thankfulness to the security of her Jaguar's resplendent solitude.   Paige drove home that night confident that she had done the right thing - yet confident also, there would be hell to pay Monday morning. Still, she didn't care.

You won't be asking me to give any impromptu speeches again anytime soon, will you, now?

Chapter Fourteen

*"Jump and you will find out how to unfold
your wings as you fall."
~Ray Bradbury*

Sitting in his apartment that night, staring out the window, Paige's act of courage and defiance at the party echoed in Thomas' head. He knew that she would be pulled out on the carpet for her little stunt tonight. When money was concerned, it didn't matter if you held the CEO title or not; the Board would have a few choice words for her. As with anyone in her position, she had three options. She would deflect it, ignore it, or retreat because of it. Thomas would be tasked with the assignment of writing the press release and hiding the Board's displeasure. He'd rather write the truth, but since he still had not yet found a way to return to his old life - his life with Gillian - he would do his duty and keep his mouth shut, for now.

Paige was not one to expect or want comforting, and so Thomas found himself alone, staring at the bottle of champagne he bought with the optimism of sharing it with her. *After all, it is the holiday season, and we've been dating - sort of.* Once again, he was reminded that Paige was anything but a *normal* woman. The boxes, bows and sentimentality most women demand and coo over, Paige denied with indignant repugnance. She was an enigma to Thomas in many ways; a puzzle he had no confidence in solving. This secretly suited him. *My heart still belongs to Gillian. Paige is simply a distraction away from loneliness until I can find my way back to her.*

As he watched Paige's spotlight moment, Thomas was reminded of his own path toward courage, and how there was once a time when he had none. It was their third year, he and Gillian both working on their degrees at the University of Michigan; they had been dating for about a year. He opened the bottle of champagne and drank to the past. As he sipped, effervescence dancing at the back of his throat, he thought back on that time with a small measure of shame. *That was the year I discovered my cowardice.* It had never been so real as when he attempted to propose to Gillian six months into their courtship; an effort which produced a colossal fail. That Thanksgiving taught him a lot about himself, and a lot about Gillian too, or so he thought. He was convinced that if he was ever going to be able to get her to say 'yes', he would need to find his own courage first.

It was the following spring when he took an internship with the Freep and became a beat reporter on the Tragic Desk. His uncultivated and under-educated male ego told him that he needed to prove himself in the big, bad world before he could prove himself to her. Reporting on the most dangerous and devastating stories in the region seemed the best way to transform himself from the mild-mannered, would-be novelist into a highly respected, edgy, adventuresome journalist. He would be a literary hero, bigger than life. *What woman, especially an artist, wouldn't fall in love with that?!*

Thomas poured himself another glass of champagne and made a silent toast: *To Gillian; wishing her all the beauty and peace the season has to offer.* After filling his glass for a third time, he retrieved a stack of parchment from his desk and began to write. Tonight, he would write her the story of those beginning days when his heart first fell. At long last, he would share with her the story she never knew; the one he'd kept hidden all these years.

****

Gillian pulled the letter from its envelope with a mix of exhilaration and regret. Halloween had been the last time she'd received a letter, nearly two months; and she hadn't written back. He hadn't written in so long, she was afraid that her silence was pushing him away. It seemed cruel to continue indulging in the fantasy of his storytelling without responding - but she just didn't feel strong enough to do anything else. She feared that a word from her would make it all disappear. The holidays were quickly approaching and soon, she would have to deal with the anniversary of Eryn's death. In a season when strength and compassion were personified everywhere around her - in the music, the storefront displays, the made-for-TV movies - she felt lost in a sea of bewilderment, unable to fight the tide. She walked through her days zombie-like, trudging through quarterly tax returns and check registers. The only happiness she found was the anticipation of checking the mailbox each day to perhaps discover another letter from Thomas. She knew it was insensitive and wrong to take so much from him and offer nothing in return. But she just felt too frail to respond. Gillian poured herself a cup of cocoa, made sure her sketchbook and pencils were within reach, unfolded the letter and began to read; hoping that she would find some bit of warmth to ease the chill of Michigan's early December winds and the aching in her heart.

****

Devin sat in the airport just outside Chicago, waiting for his plane's departure. He left the hotel early, *to be sure to get there on time*; he convinced himself... but the truth was more than that.

It was a snowy February afternoon and the sun beat down steadily through the large picture windows, dancing off the windshield of a 747 docked just outside. The terminal wasn't very busy, a few passengers here and there, some milling around the duty free shop; but mostly, things were quiet. It was Friday, eleven forty-five in the morning.

It was hard for him not to think of her; the way she smelled, the way his hand fit into hers, the look in her eyes when they said goodbye. He had come to be with Alec for just a short while; it had been prearranged, but that didn't make the difficulty of their separation any easier. Devin had come with a mission. He planned what he would say, how he would look, the candles, the timing, his gracious escape should failure arise; everything… every last detail… for weeks. It was so important that it was done right. If not, catastrophe would certainly rear its ugly head and he'd be worse off than when he started.

Sitting here now, staring at the planes coming and going… well after the fact, he couldn't get the vision of her magnificent amber eyes out of his head. He had seen them reflecting back at him so many times before; but lately, something was different. *Perhaps it was all in my head*… though he was having a hard time believing that was true. *It had to be there. It was much too strong for it to be some figment of my over active, hopelessly romantic imagination.* He had first noticed it… really noticed it… last fall.

Alec had been traveling all across the country with a special impressionist collection as ambassador for the museum. She came to town between her trips to Chicago and Philadelphia to celebrate the holidays with her family who lived nearby. Devin and Alec set up a time to meet and spend a few precious hours together. Devin missed her, their friendship and their commonality. They hadn't seen each other much since undergrad, and now they had found each other again. It was a surprise he hadn't been prepared for, but he was thrilled just the same. *She is so easy to be with. So freeing. She understands me.* It was a true pleasure for him to be with her, for he could relax and enjoy their friendship without the pressures and frustrations of another's expectations. *We could just be. It was nice.* That night, when they were together, tickling and laughing in his apartment in the dim light of late night, he was struck by something that he hadn't recognized before... at least, not admittedly. *I really care for her.*

It had been a long road he traveled, with more heartache than a person should ever endure. During his second year of undergrad, Devin gave his heart and soul to a woman who, after nearly three years and a proposal of marriage, left him alone and empty, not sure of where or how to go on. He vowed never to allow another to hurt him like that again; never allow another to get that close to his heart. It was just more than he could bear. The anguish was painful beyond description and understanding. *The bachelor life is predictable, hassle-free... safer.*

Yet through it all, forever on the edge, comforting him in ways he never thought would matter... was this lady with the beautiful amber eyes... amazing... Alec. The part she played in his life during that difficult period was crucial... though they were both quite oblivious to it at the time. She was always there... to talk... to comfort his tears with soft words and gentle caresses... to help him heal. *It was a remarkable thing she gave me, but at the time I didn't understand the true nature of her gift, nor its beauty and wonderment.*

After their time together on that late fall evening almost a year ago, Devin awoke with a new sensitivity about her. He was determined to discover what, if anything, of these new found feelings were strong enough to develop into something more meaningful, more lasting. So, with a quick trip to the computer store and the installation of some new software, he connected his computer to the Internet. He rationalized that more frequent communication was the best place to begin. It was the next step he had wanted to take with his computer toys anyway, and now, he had the perfect motivation to follow through.

Over the next few weeks, they began writing e-mails back and forth, even though they only lived two hours from each other; with both of their schedules, it was a far more reliable way to stay connected. They wrote little blurbs about life in his city and hers and what they did with their days and nights; she with her work with the museum, he on a quest of creative self-discovery and half-heartedly writing freelance features for his local newspaper while working on a novel he hoped would bring critical acclaim.

Over the weeks that followed, Devin began to look forward to her little messages... though never of any great length - she was a very busy lady. Constantly traveling for her work with new exhibits - he was pleased to receive each one. *It means we're keeping in touch. Staying close... remaining friends.*

He didn't want to let her slip away... not until he knew, and even then... he wasn't willing. Alec had become far too important to him, although he'd be hard pressed to explain that importance with any clarity to her or anyone else. He called her on occasion... just to hear her voice and share some laughter. And he began to miss her more.

In January, Alec wrote that she had just completed escorting a special exhibit from the DIA to the Museum of Modern Art in New York, and her supervisor gave her some extra time off. Through e-mail messages, they agreed to meet at an old theatre they both knew well, the place they'd met as freshman at the University of Michigan, and make more plans from there. This one little thing... the anticipation of seeing her again... created such joy for him. Rummaging through a shoe box of old memories, Devin found an old picture of Alec and set it in a simple silver frame on his desk... he liked looking at her. Her amber eyes glowed with such comfort and confidence... it was a nice reminder of what fun was; what comfort was; what safety was. *I feel so very safe with Alec... Alec would never hurt me, betray my sensitivities or crush my heart with the tragic infidelities of the past. She has a heart of gold, the eye of an artist, the soul of a poet; and I trust her explicitly with my life.* The revelation was remarkable to him. He never thought he could ever feel that way about another woman again, and he reveled in the joy of finally rediscovering these moments. Surprisingly, and without much warning, happiness had come to Devin's world once again.

The night they shared in January was like a dream to him. Snow fluttered down around them creating a picture post card scene. He complained about the cold, but secretly thanked the heavens for creating such beauty for them to enjoy and remember. Their time together was short... too short by his way of thinking... yet absolutely perfect. *Alec was perfect.* The warmth and comfort inherent within her seemed to have grown one hundred fold from their last encounter... or was it that for the first time, he allowed himself to truly see her as she had always been?

When Alec left that night, Devin fought back an ocean of tears and tried not to let her see that for him, things had changed. He wasn't sure how best to explain it to her yet, and they didn't have the time to talk the way he wanted to that night. *No... better to wait... take time to discern what is really in her head and heart, and then talk with her.* He had to be sure that when he asked his questions; he was prepared for the answers - good or bad. He had to be ready for the evil sting of rejection's blade. Until that time came, talking to her unprepared would cause more grief than either of them cared to navigate. Yes, he would wait. Quietly nursing his courage.

Devin thought about it all for quite some time, mulling over every last detail. He wrote about it. He made lists. He ran the conversations over and over again in his head. He dreamt about it. And at last, he finally knew his own heart and mind on the matter. He would wait until the time was right... when he could see her again... when he could see her eyes... when he could have more than a few fleeting moments to find the right words. That's when he would ask Alec if she would spend forever with him.

Devin felt so very at ease with Alec. She continually allowed him to give her all the love and adoration he wanted to offer. She never belittled him for wanting to do it, as so many others in his past had. She never rejected it; she accepted it freely and without invoking guilt or other humiliating methodology to use his emotions to control him or their friendship. Devin was never at fault or wrong because he simply wanted to give to her. Never once, in all the years that they'd known each other, had Alec ever told him that he was wrong for wanting to be friends with her; or as their relationship became more intimate, share love with her. She accepted it freely and without conflict. That was very comforting to him. It was one of the biggest reasons why he had grown to care for her as much as he had.

After about four or five weeks, and a bit of playful nudging from him, the message came by e-mail. They would be together again at the end of March, in Chicago while Alec was there with an exhibit from the museum. It would be a brief overnight trip, just twenty-four short hours, but Devin was certain it would be time enough. Excitedly, he bought his tickets, requested the time off from work and arranged for the safe keeping of his dog. He bought a new suit for Alec's gentle amber eyes and soft, supple hands to enjoy; and a birthday gift, as he wouldn't be with her on her special day in April. When all was in place from his end, he phoned her late one night to learn where he would meet her and the details about their time together.

It was a wonderful conversation filled with sly innuendo and playful puns. They laughed and talked for a little while, happily, without care... both looking forward to their upcoming rendezvous. Near the end of their conversation, the tone in Alec's voice changed to something ominously familiar. She began to change the tenor of their conversation; but she stopped short when Devin asked her not to venture down that road. He'd heard that tone before... and he just didn't know if he had the energy to be that strong again... not on the phone... not without seeing her one last time. She agreed, swiftly changing the subject without asking him why. *This trust we share...* he thought, *it is beyond mere mortal comprehension and I valued it as I valued my soul.*

A few moments later, when he felt he could bear whatever bad news it was - *the truth, experience has taught me, is never as horrid as what I can imagine.* He let go of his insecurities, trusting in her heart and his strength. Devin asked Alec what it was that she'd begun to say. There was a pause that, to him, seemed to last an eternity; and then she told him, as gently as she could, seemingly sensing how what she would say would affect him; "I just can't see the two of us ever getting as serious as marriage... and that is precisely what I am searching for now."

Marriage. After all this time in school and business; it was a real goal for her now. She was working toward it, saving her energy for it. Hoping it would one day come to be for her. But, she just didn't see the two of them in that vision together. Devin took in a long, silent breath... attempting to recover as quickly as he could so that Alec wouldn't notice his disappointment. He didn't want her to know; afraid that it would change their time together in Chicago, or worse, their friendship forever. With brevity, and a lighthearted air, he accepted her statement as common knowledge and almost fleetingly brushed it aside, moving their conversation forward with a gentle laugh.

A few moments later, they said their goodbyes; each reminding the other that e-mail would arrive soon. Devin hung up the phone that night statuesque, as tears streamed silently from his eyes. Emptiness crashed over him with the impact of hurricane fury. Utter bewilderment was now all that kept him from the numbness that he knew would soon follow. In near-manic state, he grappled with the puzzle of what to do next. The coward in him wanted to run and hide, not go to Chicago, not deal with the disappointment Alec was sure to see in his eyes. But something much stronger kept him steady. *More important to me than anything is that I don't lose her friendship and the closeness we share. She is an important person in my life, one whom I respect, admire and believe in with all my heart. No, I'll go to Chicago as planned... spend time with her... and remember every second. I'll cherish our time together... take everything slowly, recording it all in my heart's memory banks, etching every emotion in my soul, captivating it for all of eternity.* Things had gotten away from him before... things he wished he'd never let slip away. *That will not happen this time. I will never let this get away from me. I will never forget. It is too important.* So he got on the plane, Alec's birthday gift tucked safely in his carry-on bag, and went to Chicago.

The two had a fantastic time together. They loved and they laughed... more, Devin recalled, than he could remember in a long time. They ate delicious deserts and sipped brandy and cappuccino. Alec was so very gentle, caressing his soul with each word, touching his heart with each glance, making him feel extraordinary and worthy again. Her eyes were brighter and warmer than he had remembered, perhaps because he couldn't draw his eyes away from hers. He watched her every move, remembering her every little nuance... the way she smiled, the way she typed up reports on her laptop, the way she walked... everything. *I just have to remember. This might be the last time we'll be together; at least, I have to prepare myself for that possibility. Once Alec discovers the true nature of my heart's early morning ramblings, she might put an end to these blissful meetings.* Several times during their evening together, Devin wanted desperately to tell her what was truly in his heart... but he didn't want to spoil the evening for either of them, so he kept silent.

When the dawn finally came, Devin awoke before Alec, just to watch her sleep. It was something special, like time standing still. No one entered their world; no one drew him from his warm, soothing fantasy forcing him back to the cold, harsh reality of life. *I wish this time would last forever.* He snuggled in closer to her, hoping to make it so. He wanted so much to reach out to her, touch her and never stop, but he dared not... for he didn't want to disturb her much-needed rest. In time, he too, drifted back to sleep, dreaming of her.

When the alarm rang and he opened his eyes, he was struck by the perfection of her, even in the morning, which had never been a good time of day for either of them. They greeted the day with coffee and juice and quiet conversation, although just talking was not first on his wish list of how to spend his last few moments with her. Very soon, the time had come for her to go. She had meetings that she couldn't avoid, no matter how much she may have wanted to.

A few last kisses and Alec was gone. Devin sat alone in the hotel room for a while, contemplating the state of his heart. He wrote Alec a note to tuck away in her luggage, in a secret place, so only she would find it, perhaps weeks later. It wasn't an extravagant note... just a little something to tell her *Thank You* and how much he enjoyed spending time with her. Not once during their time together, nor in his brief letter, did he mention his desire to ask his question. *It's just not the right time. Perhaps some other, but not now.* As the door clicked behind him, he tucked the *Do Not Disturb* sign into his luggage... a small memento of the evening he would never forget.

As he sat now, staring out the window of a 747, soaring high over the Great Lakes of Michigan, the engine's dull roar resonated through Devin's entire being, echoing deep inside his soul. The bright sunshine of the day reflected off the shiny steel wing of the aircraft, mocking his pain in its quiet reverie. Spring was trying to get an early foothold, and he was alone and empty once again. *How I'm supposed to make it from here to where I'm supposed to go next, I haven't got a clue.*

    As Alec's birthday drew ever nearer Devin's thoughts dwelled more and more on her and how he missed having her as a part of his life. There was a time, not so long ago, when they shared much of their lives with each other. Both Devin and Alec were moving through phases of their lives which at times allowed them great insight and transformation. They had spent the better part of five years in extraordinary conversations, learning from and guiding one another. She had been a great teacher in his life, assisting him to move forward... to where he was today, and beyond. Devin hoped he had been able to offer at least some token of the same to her.

    The trees upon the horizon, now painted in the gold and magenta of spring, emerged ever taller as the early morning mist lifted above the canopy. The branches of a thousand trees seemed to reach out to the clouds, beckoning their winter blanket to return. Rain fell outside his office window like the unrelenting tears of angels, weeping for what might have been. Rain collected in small pools on the roofs of nearby buildings and parking structures, dancing in the spring air, reflecting his ambivalence back to him.

    It had been several months since Devin and Alec had last spoken, and the part of him that had belonged to her was becoming numb. *Beyond numb.* It wasn't that he didn't love her anymore, quite the contrary. In fact, his love for her was one of the strongest things he'd ever felt. His despondency came from the notion that he could not control the myriad of emotions that poured from his soul like sweet molasses... slow and steady. There was a time when he had reveled in each new taste, indulging completely in the succulent sting of it upon his lips, but no more. Ever so slowly, it passed through him and every inch of him felt it. And then, just as slowly, every inch of him felt it slip silently away, just as the mist crept from the earth. Again and again, it left him empty and alone.

He was growing weary from the undulating silence crying out to him. *I don't know how much more of this I can take.* In an attempt to seek protection from its wrath, he ignored it as best he could. Banishing it to the very depths of his being; extinguishing the fire, dulling the blade. Praying his efforts would stifle the next attack. Yet in watching the world this morning, hope seemed to rise within him once again, like the billowing steam from a large air conditioning unit seated upon a rooftop not far away. It swelled majestically, ballooning ever closer to the heavens, reminiscent of the steam that rose from a warm Jacuzzi he'd dreamed they would share together. Ever closer to peace and serenity - that which he longed for... coveted... dreamed of... for as long as he could remember. *Can I find it? Can tranquility be mine once again?* He was sure someday it could be.

Focus. One thing at a time. He chanted it under his breath. It was a sacred mantra, guiding him ever closer to his greatest desires. *Life happens in cycles; your time will come again. Trust that it will. Find your courage in that.* He sighed heavily as he watched the minions eight stories below struggle through the details of their lives.

Chapter Fifteen

"We need to realize that our path to transformation is through our mistakes. We're meant to make mistakes, recognize them, and move on to become unlimited."
~Yehuda Berg

Aaren and Nathan got the text message at the same time.

Marina. Now. 911

Fifteen minutes later, they walked down the dock together, and as they approached the boat, saw Paige pacing the deck.

"Permission..." Nathan started.

"Oh shut up and just get on board." Paige snipped. They both climbed on board, wary of the hurricane that was to follow.

"Paige, what's wrong?" Aaren asked. It was highly unusual for Paige to be so frazzled. *This must be big. Paige never panics.*

"I've been here all night. Trying to figure this out. Trying to make sense of this. How could this have happened?" Paige was talking out loud to herself.

"Paige, slow down. What's going on?" Aaren tried again to get her to become coherent, offering her a glass of wine, hoping that would soothe her a little.

Paige turned up her nose in disgust. "I can't have that!" Aaren looked puzzled. Nathan stood by silently, as a path of least resistance. He knew the winds would blow over eventually. His plan was to wait out the storm.

"There I was, sitting at the galley table last night, hands trembling, waiting for the timer to ding. It was the most stressful day I think I've ever endured! This is not part of the plan." She looked at Nathan pleadingly. He continued to stand in stoic silence.

"I'm just not ready for this. There is still so much of the world that I don't know and don't understand. I was barely successful at protecting myself from the pitfalls and trials of life. Am I capable of nurturing another soul through all that eighteen years - or more - will bring?" Her voice dropped down to a mere whisper now. "Will I make choices that will work for us both, or will I simply add to the growing collection of negative statistics? In my head, I thought I knew a better way... thought I had a better plan. That's all screwed up now." Paige was rambling and pacing. It was difficult for Aaren to keep up; Nathan didn't even try.

"This had not been a plan, this notion of having a child before having a husband. I was careful. Not promiscuous. Not ignoring my responsibility for birth control. But sometimes in life, things don't always work out as directed on the label. I failed in many ways in my younger years, and the pharmaceutical company with whom I had entrusted my future has now failed me!"

"Paige, slow down! Are you saying you're pregnant?" Aaren was stunned. She knew Paige and Thomas had a little fling going - but this - it was so out of character for her to be this careless.

"Well, yes, I think I just might be; if you're to believe the quick-as-a-bunny-rug-rat detector I picked up at the pharmacy last night. One line, no; two lines, yes. This looks like two lines to me. Have a look for yourself." Paige handed the small plastic future detector to Aaren, who stared at it in disbelief.

"Paige! You're pregnant!" Aaren squealed.

"Yes," said Paige with an air of disgust. "Thank you very much for air-horning it throughout the entire marina. I appreciate that." Nathan smirked. He knew her disgust for public displays she could not control.

"Well, I'm assuming it's Thomas'. Have you told him yet?" Aaren asked. Nathan cringed, working hard to feign surprise at the news of Thomas being the father.

"Of course not! I just told you two. You're supposed to help me figure this out before I tell him." Paige was becoming more frantic by the minute.

"Ladies," Nathan interjected. "Let's just sit down calmly and think this thing through, shall we?" Always fitted with a level head, Nathan could be counted on to harness Paige's energy toward a manageable direction. He exuded calm. He reduced mania to normalcy. It's what she paid him to do; and he did it very well. "In a situation like this, there are usually three standard responses to the question, 'Now what?' I understand, the fourth possibility, marriage, is not an option for you at this time."

"Or at any time!" Paige nearly exploded.

"Right." Nathan replied.

"But, why not? Thomas seems like a reasonable kind of guy." Aaren asked.

"It's just not, okay?" Paige screamed. Aaren was shocked. It was rare for Paige to talk to Aaren that way. "I'm sorry, Aaren; I didn't mean to yell. This is just a really hard thing for me to deal with right now."

"Okay then," said Nathan. "There are three options still available. Let's go through them calmly." He emphasized the word 'calmly' in the same way that a psychiatrist might remind a patient that restraints were a possible next step if she didn't take his advice. They sat gently on the deck chairs, each afraid they might explode on impact. "Answer "A". Adoption. This is the right solution for some people, but it might not be right for you."

"I wouldn't rule it out." Paige said, flatly.

"Okay. Answer "B". Abortion." Nathan offered.

"All right, look," she said, glancing back and forth between Aaren and Nathan. "I am as strong a "pro-choice" supporter as they come. I think that it is ultimately a matter of choice to terminate a pregnancy or not. It is a decision made (hopefully) by both expectant parents in a long moment of clarity unaided by alcohol or extra-curricular pharmaceuticals or the pressure of others opinions. However," Paige took a deep breath. "The idea of eliminating a child simply because it might cause me some level of inconvenience just doesn't work for me. It's not like I've been raped, or struggle with a cancer diagnosis, or have Münchhausen by Proxy Syndrome. There really is no good reason to terminate this pregnancy beyond my own selfishness and perhaps the disapproving eyes of others who didn't agree with my choice to be a single parent."

Aaren noted that this moment of rational clarity at such an emotionally charged time, for Paige, was about as rare as finding an albino Peregrine Falcon living in a daycare center as the three-year-old's classroom pet. She patiently waited to see what was coming next.

"As you are both well aware, I try to live my life in such a way that I am not faced with the dreaded 'if only' creeping out of my mouth as I languish on my deathbed. This is an 'if only' moment if I've ever seen one. I wonder, if I make this choice now, will I even be allowed to have the opportunity to try again before I die? No, I think Answer B is just too final - too evil - too irresponsible."

"All right, then that just leaves one possibility left; Answer "C". Keep the child and do the best with what you have to make a life for yourself and this tiny little creature that will absolutely change every aspect of your life from this moment until the day you take your last breath." Nathan couldn't help it. Philosophy crept into his words with a fervor he'd not heard since his days in the classroom.

"Way to make it super not-scary, Nathan." Paige said sarcastically.

"I aim to please," said Nathan with a gentle smile.

"So, what are you going to do, Paige? What are you going to tell Thomas?" Aaren was somewhere between being elated and being scared for her friend. They had never shared something this monumental in their lives before. In fact, this topic of conversation had never even come up before. It had always been, date that guy or not; sail to Nantucket or Manassas; chocolate or vanilla. These major life decisions had never pestered them... and business decisions didn't count. Now, they had a life-changing event to manage. A new milestone for their friendship. Aaren knew what she wanted Paige to do.

"I think you should keep the child, Paige." Aaren encouraged. "You'd be a great mother."

"Says you. It's no secret you're just a 'babyaholic'. For as long as I've know you, you've always been enthralled with babies and children. Perfect little beings from the moment they are born and they only get better with age. You once told me that 'kittens are good, but not nearly as great as a baby'. Emotional attachments to small humans have always been your Achilles heel." Paige teased.

"It's true. I know very well that after carrying and bonding emotionally with a little person for nine months, there is no possible way that I could play the part of the NFL quarterback, and just hand it off," said Aaren. "I would be in a little white coat, hugging myself, devising ways to dissolve my existence in no time."

"Thankfully, I'm not so afflicted." chided Paige.

"So, what are you going to do?" asked Nathan.

"I'm not sure yet. But, when I figure it out, I'll let you know." said Paige. "Let's go sailing. Get ready to cast off."

****

That night, Paige called Thomas in a panic and demanded that he come see her, she was dangling from that brass ring, swaying uncontrollably in a torrential squall, toes pointed toward hell.

When he arrived at her brownstone, Thomas had barely gotten in the door when she attacked him in a fury of exacting histrionics. "What the hell were you thinking?! Have you lost your mind? This is all your fault! This is a huge problem for me, and I can assure you - I WILL fix it, even if I have to rip you into pieces in the process!"

"Whoa, Paige, hold on a minute. Calm down and tell me what's going on." Thomas moved quickly into the living room, deflecting what could have been a blow to his solar plexus, if he'd lingered too long.

"I'll tell you what's going on... I'm pregnant and YOU are to blame!" Her eyes shot laser beams of destruction toward him, piercing his soul and cutting a swath through that part of him that he thought he had protected. Zigzagging its way through his chest and into his heart, her deadly stare ripped open the scar in his heart that had been cauterized shut. He was at a loss for words. He stared back at her dumfounded, uttering nothing, not even a whisper of disbelief.

"We had a deal, Thomas." Paige screamed with screech owl decibels. "No children! Remember?! You broke that deal, and now we have to FIX this. This is YOUR fault, and I'm not going to let your stupid lack of abstinence ruin everything I've worked for my entire life. If only you could have controlled yourself, kept your zipper in the upright and locked position, we could have avoided all this. But NO! You're just not that smart, are you?! I'm in the middle of the biggest acquisition deal of my life, and I'm not going to let some little whinny brat get in the way. Do you hear me, Thomas? YOU WILL FIX THIS!"

Paige walked over to the bar and poured herself a snifter of brandy and recklessly tossed it back. Thomas wanted to warn her of the evils of alcohol and pregnancy - but thought better of it in this single moment. The lecture would have to wait. First he needed to process... figure out a solution.

Paige ignored the crux that would have ruined her. The truth of the matter was that she assured Thomas that she was on birth control, and simply forgot to take the little white pill one night when her day had been a little more overwhelming than usual and she'd gotten off her daily routine. She'd switched purses the night before, and forgot her pills on the bedroom dresser. But she'd never accept the fault for the mistake, or see the wonderment in how her life could be blessed by the life of a child, if she'd just rearrange her thinking for thirty seconds. Burying the truth was the only acceptable option at this point. She had too much to lose to allow herself a moment of emotional frailty. So she drowned out the voices in her own head by screaming louder at Thomas.

"Thomas, I just can't imagine being a parent. I'm not equipped to be a mother ... I don't have time to spend with a child, nor do I want to... I've got a business to run, for cripes sake! I'm the executive director of one of the world's most influential computer companies. The market is growing so quickly and everyone is struggling to keep up. But not me. I'm the only one not struggling. For once in my life, Thomas, I'm not struggling. I can't possibly split my time between building this company and raising a child. I have no idea what I would do with a baby. It's not like I can bring the kid to work. The Board members would certainly have a problem with a screaming child in the middle of contract negotiations; and I've no intentions on wasting money on a nanny. Thomas, I simply WILL NOT do this. You need to find a solution, and FAST!"

By now, Thomas had had a few minutes to think. What he realized was that this could either be his moment of complete ridicule or blissful redemption. The tight rope he was about to walk could very well land him against the jagged rocks of Gillian's wrath, destroying everything he'd been trying to recreate for them. If she rejected him over this, there would be no second chances. The do-over would go up in smoke. Or, this could be the one thing that could re-build their love, restore their bond, and remind them of what they could be together. *What will Gillian do?* He wasn't sure, but his gut was telling him to trust Gillian and their love. *If I do this right, we could all win... Paige, me, Gillian, and the child.* He needed a plan – and fast.

He indulged in a few more moments of silence, crafting his next move, as he watch Paige pace tracks in the carpet. *I think I've got a quick-fix solution that Paige will buy... and that will give me several months to get the rest to fall into place. I only hope it works.* Paige was difficult and unpredictable... but he knew he had to try. To give up on this was tantamount to emotional suicide.

"I'd be happy to help you save your plan for world domination, Paige;" he said with a condescending tone and more than a gentle smirk. "But you must agree to have this child. Take a leave of absence if you must... run the company remotely from the house in the Hamptons if you don't want to be seen pregnant in public. Do whatever it takes. But if you want my help, YOU MUST HAVE THIS CHILD." Thomas gave her a few minutes to let the idea of actually giving birth sink in while his plan germinated in his head.

Paige sat, disheveled, in the chair in the corner, cradling her brandy snifter as if her life depended on it. When he saw her like that, Thomas felt sorry for her. She'd led a hard life... fate had handed her a thorny bouquet. But, his sympathy soon eroded as he remembered her bulldozer approach to nearly everyone she met. Nearly sociopathic, she lacked empathy for anyone else; and so, he lacked sympathy for her.

"Once the child is born," continued Thomas, "I'll be happy to take responsibility. But I will not idly sit by and allow you to terminate this pregnancy or give this child to a complete stranger. And if you do, I promise you, I will make your life unbearable. You will endure a smear campaign to rival anything you've ever seen. This acquisition deal you love so well - gone! The status you have in Boston society - dissolved! That vision you have of one day receiving the key to the city for all the supposed humanitarian aid your company provides - poof! I promise you Paige, if you don't do exactly what I tell you, and have this child, the marketing campaign I write will have you falling into a chasm of excrement so deep, you'll never be able to claw your way out. It will all be gone, and people will see you clearly for the wretch that you are; do I make myself clear?"

Blackmail was not at all characteristic for him, nor his first choice in a situation like this, but he knew it was his only option. To keep her from spiraling into a whirlpool of self-destruction, and infanticide by proxy, he needed her to fight for what was most important to her - her precious, public identity. It was the only way he knew to save the life of a child - his child. *I refuse to lose another child. I won't survive that agony twice in one lifetime.*

"Fine." Paige poured herself another snifter of brandy from the sideboard and started pacing the room, wearing a deep rut in the floor with her four-inch heels. "Fine," she said again with the sting of every practiced board room negotiation. "Then this is how it will work. You and I will live at my place in the Hamptons until this wretched ordeal is over. I'll take on a new staff and have everything we need delivered. You'll find a doctor or a midwife or whatever it takes to arrange for me to have this thing happen at the house, in complete secrecy. I'll have the IT department set up a remote server at the house, and you'll make sure that my image remains intact."

Paige switched her pacing directions now, treading north and south rather than east and west. When she had finally decided to stop, Thomas was sure there would be a neat cross excavated in the carpeting. *An interesting commentary on the life of the world's most vehement atheist.*

"And in the end, I'll give you the child and a nice chunk of cash to disappear." Thomas felt rank at the idea of being bought, but it was worth it if it saved the life of his child. "Remember Thomas, I'm on the verge of the greatest acquisition of my life, there will never be another opportunity to grow my company to this magnitude. I don't have time for eighteen plus years of distractions; not to mention the financial drain. Success will only come if I focus; and I won't be able to focus with a kid in tow."

"Perfect," said Thomas. "Our deal starts now." He grabbed the snifter from her hands and dumped it into the fichus tree standing nearby. "You'll do everything that is necessary to keep this child alive and healthy; and I'll do the same for your exquisite reputation and image. And in the end, we'll part ways, cutting off all ties and never speaking to each other ever again."

"Right." Paige had a tone of finality in her voice, but clearly wasn't pleased with the deal she'd just struck. She hated making deals when her emotions were compromised - but this time, it couldn't be helped. Simply destroying it now, making it all vanish from her life now, would be so much easier. But she couldn't take the chance that Thomas would make good on his threat. He was one of the best writers in the business, it was why she'd hired him, and after all the time she'd spent with him intimately, he certainly had enough to become her ruination. She couldn't risk it. *He could do some serious damage in just lifting his little finger in the right direction... what might he do with both hands on a keyboard?* She reluctantly accepted the fact that her life would be in someone else's control for the next ten months - *and after that- surgery will prevent this stupidity from rearing i's ugly head ever again!*

"And, I want it all in writing - before we move out to the Hamptons," Thomas said as he made his way to the front door. "There's no way I'm getting screwed in this deal Paige, so I suggest you get your best lawyer on the case. Draw up the papers. Make it a LARGE amount of cash, and make it happen soon, Paige; or you will rue the day we ever met." Thomas walked out and closed the door behind him, letting out a long, soul emptying sigh. His world had just moved in a way he never would have imagined. *Was it the stars aligning or the tectonic plates shifting?* He couldn't really be sure. But what he did know was that starting tomorrow morning, he was never going to see the sun in quite the same way.

****

Paige and Thomas left in the middle of the night on a Thursday. They did their best impression of a secret government agency - wearing all black, moving quickly, leaving no trail. "The house at the Hamptons," Paige said, "is fully stocked... everything you might need. Just bring your clothes, and the rest - we'll either order and have delivered after we get there - or it'll be there already waiting for us. I have a full staff, and we shouldn't run into any problems... unless those pesky tourists get nosy." The area was known for its discretion when it came to the residents, they maintained a healthy distance from one another. The paparazzi didn't dwell there - they didn't dare - but the tourists were nearly as bad; a camera dangled defiantly from every neck, just waiting to pounce and abscond with some privileged soul's privacy.

To avoid this unpleasantness, and to be sure that her secret wasn't revealed prematurely, Paige hired a new staff and let the others go with generous severance checks - once they'd signed confidentiality agreements, of course. As it turned out, this was not a new habit for Paige. The staff accepted it to be an inevitability that lived within every turn of the grandfather clock's key. Thomas felt a little odd about the disposability of these people - until he saw the guilt money she'd provided to each of them, nearly half his year's salary for each.

Paige and Thomas spent almost the entire pregnancy sequestered on the compound grounds, leaving only periodically to indulge in a day sail around the harbor.

Thomas had plenty of space to himself... *this place could house all of New Zealand... sure it's an exaggeration, but still - this place is huge! A helicopter could easily land in the living room...* he didn't personally know enough people to fill the dining room table... and the pool room was more like an indoor spa than simple swim space. The perfectly manicured grounds in the front exuded an air of controlled opulence, while the understated back lawn and delicate patio led to the pristine shoreline. His quarters, a suite of rooms that included a bedroom, office, on-suite, generous walk-in and a balcony with a spiral staircase the led to the beach, held a view that entranced his imagination.

Over the ensuing months Thomas had little to do but check in occasionally on the marketing mayhem back in Boston, and watch over Paige. She was still working the acquisition deal and was wary of complications. She created no drama for him to embellish. She behaved herself, and that left him plenty of time to devote to his writing. Sometimes he wrote to Gillian, sometimes he worked on the novel he'd been neglecting over the past fourteen years. "It's been a long time, old friend"; he mumbled, fingering the pages of the binder before him... strange, after all this time, and under the strangest of circumstances, I have finally found the creative energy to get back to you." He escaped to the west wing of the compound every evening to tend to his passion; and ignore his folly. He wanted to ignore Paige as much as possible - which was easier now that she felt impossibly repugnant - but it was still challenging because she carried his child, and that was a difficult thing to ignore.

His days were spent working on the various marketing programs for MouseTrax projects, while keeping Paige's public image intact. Although he didn't mind going to the office every day, he was certainly enjoying having the luxury of telecommuting. Working with such a spectacular view of the ocean lapping up over the sandy beach, without the throngs of disinterested souls busying about, made the work less toxic, and even, at times, a little fun.

In one particularly creative campaign that seethed out over the span of about four months, he spun a wondrous yarn about how Paige was working on the biggest merger of her life. It was a spectacularly "hush deal" with a team of "very notable" investors which, he told the troops and the media, could result in an acquisition of one of their biggest competitors. He enjoyed writing the play... he only wished he could be roaming the halls of

MouseTrax and walking the sidewalks of Faneuil Hall to hear the gentle hum of the rumor mill build into the cacophony of stories that would have many checking their stock portfolios and updating resume statistics. People always thrived on morsels of embellished truth, he knew that from his years at the Freep. *Give them a tantalizing headline, and they didn't even have to read the column to know the entire story.* "People don't read anymore," his editor once told him. "They skim. You give them the lead, and they'll write the story themselves." Sadly, Thomas found this to be even more true in the corporate world than it was in the private sector. He hardly ever wrote more than four hundred words in a single communique. The bread crumbs didn't need to be very big for the minions to fashion a full slice of toast - with peanut butter.

Aaren stayed behind, spending a great deal of time at Paige's brownstone, making it look lived in - so no one would suspect social infidelity. What people could create on their own, without even the smallest lead, was remarkable. Aaren also stayed at her post at the MouseTrax offices as was expected, sending daily messages and reports up to the Hamptons, to make sure Thomas didn't miss even the smallest ember of coal from the hot bed of the rumor fire. Fortunately, the staff was relieved to have Paige away on sabbatical. Few missed her presence. Even the Board members relished her absence. With her disconnected -or so they thought- they had the freedom to dictate a little more conservatively; and she let them. Paige was a smart woman, and knew the importance of playing the game if you wanted to win big. Thomas had convinced to her that it was best to keep a fair distance to more eloquently perpetrate the rouse of the merger and acquisition. After all, if she was microscopically focused on Boston, the sailors swabbing the decks would become suspicious that she had such bountiful time on her hands. He had persuaded her that distance was essential to make their story believable. It was a difficult thing for her, to be so "hands off" from the daily management of her company... but she could not dispute that fact that right now, it was the best course to sail. It was imperative that her truth wasn't leaked. She endured the frustration of inaction, but not without foisting most of that negative energy back on Thomas or the house staff. It rarely trickled down to Aaren. She was too far away to feel the effects of Paige's occasional nuclear winter; and besides, as her only real friend in life, Paige wouldn't punish Aaren that way.

Once or twice a month, Nathan would arrive at the compound to give Paige an update on projects and report on the general malaise or contentment of the crew. His meetings with Paige were always held in great secrecy, in her private study in the east wing of the compound. Thomas relished these visits from Nathan. It gave him precious time to escape the house for a few hours to swim in the surf and lose his thoughts amongst the salty sea air. He rarely asked what the meetings were about. He simply didn't care. And, he knew that if it required his attention, Paige would make his option to decline an invitation impossible.

When Nathan was finished with Paige, he would spend a little time checking in with Thomas. They had become friends, after all, and he was genuinely concerned.

"So, how's tricks?" Nathan asked one afternoon as he interrupted Thomas with a pair of beers on the deck.

"Same 'ol, same 'ol." Thomas replied. He accepted the beer from Nathan and offered him a deck chair. "Things seem to be going okay here. Paige is following her doctor's orders, eating intelligently, not drinking, and surprisingly enough, keeping her stress levels in moderation. I think this might actually be okay."

"That's great. How are things between you two?" Nathan offered a gently supportive raised eyebrow.

"Oh, that's gone." Thomas said, swallowing a long draw from the bottle.

"Too bad, sorry ol' man." Nathan said.

"No, it's okay, really." said Thomas. "I think it's better this way. She and I didn't belong together anyway. Neither of us wanted it. She wants more professional success and I want Gillian. It wasn't working; it would never work."

"How are things with you and Gillian? Are you still writing to her? Has she written back yet?" Nathan was curious to learn if his advice was working.

"I'm still writing to her, the stories are a great way to connect us again... but no, she hasn't written back. I think she's still trying to process through everything - either that, or she's still so pissed off that she's not reading my letters. But either way," Thomas said, pausing again to take another draw from his beer, "I'm glad you suggested doing it. It's been kind of like therapy, you know? And, it's helping me move forward with the novel, so I guess that's a good thing."

****

Aside from Aaren and Nathan, no one else from Paige's world knew about her true reason for the sabbatical and she was comfortable with that fact. Paige doesn't have many real friends. She had acquaintances at the marina; she was friendly on occasion with shopkeepers in the village near the cottage, and other business contacts that she ran into occasionally at fundraisers or at the opera. They knew of her, but none really knew her. Since her parents' death, Paige's circle of friends dwindled down to almost nothing. "It's not really a big deal, you know. I get so much more done when left to my own devices. People can be such an inconvenience;" was her stance on the matter. Yet Thomas held and inkling that this lie was one she would have preferred to recant.

The bigger story was that Paige actually did have her eyes on a rival company and was planning a hostile takeover. She'd been watching it for some time, the stock was right where she wanted it; the CEO was near retirement age; and she had secured the inside track on their technology team with all the appropriate bribes. "With a deal like this, the potential for catastrophe is large and looming." She explained every detail to him one night during dinner. "I plan to nurse this deal as one might a glass of brandy at a shareholder's holiday party. Slow and steady. I have no intentions of walking across that bridge of stress until all this 'pregnancy business' is over."

Thomas felt a little better that the web of malarkey he was spinning at least had a small shred of truth to it... if only a little. He sat down one night, after Paige had gone to bed, to write a letter to Gillian. He needed to find some way to tell her about the new baby he would be bringing home with him. He had to do it gently... and a story of "happily ever after" seemed just the thing. The fact that Paige's most recent pre-natal tests revealed that the child was a girl, made it seem even more urgent that Thomas give Gillian a friendly "head's up".

The Griffin of Greed

Once upon a time there was a King and Queen who had a lovely life together. They were adored by the townsfolk for being kind, fair and extremely generous. They thought very little of their own desires in life, instead focusing the bulk of their estate's wealth and the intelligence of their best advisors on how they could help to improve the lives of the people around them.

One day, the kingdom's soldiers... they had soldiers because, you see, not all the kingdoms of the world were as magnanimous as they, and safeguarding their people was of paramount importance... brought word of a Griffin of Greed attacking a neighboring village.

"Oh my goodness." said the Queen. "We should do something to help them."

"Yes," said the King. He called their son, Prince Elliott into his study to ask for his help. "Please son, our neighbors are struggling with a horrible plague. A dastardly Griffin of Greed has flown into their lands and it is tormenting them with ferocity. Will you help them?"

"Of course," said Prince Elliott. "They have been good neighbors; and you and mother have always taught me to consider the welfare of others before myself. I will bravely embark on this quest if it means assisting our friends." Prince Elliott's parents were very proud of their son.

And so, the King and Queen sent their son, Prince Elliott, on a quest to slay the Griffin of Greed, which plagued the land.

Prince Elliott, though brave and strong, and good of heart, could not defeat the Griffin of Greed because it was so large and spewed poisonous venom from its serpent tail that perverted the peasants' judgment. The Griffin of Greed's poison made them lust for things that they didn't need or, in most cases, even want.

"You should stop this despicable behavior, apologize and leave this land," Prince Elliott said. "Isn't it obvious to you that the reason you are the last Griffin of Greed in the world is because the others are all long dead? They destroyed themselves by disrespecting the laws of nature, and I fear you will suffer the same fate. You are on a grievous spiral of destruction. This life you've chosen will not end well for you, just as it did not end well for your kin. Acquiesce now and relinquish your hold on these fine people! It's the only way to save yourself. Listen to me, please! I am your friend... I'm trying to help you!"

But the Griffin of Greed manipulated Prince Elliott's words before the townsfolk, and convinced them that it was instead, Prince Elliott who spewed the venom that was causing the plague. "Can you not detect the rouse he is perpetrating? Your hero is none of the sort. He is attempting to foist his will upon you, and drive me away so he alone will command all power. He is not concerned with my welfare. He is not my friend... or yours! He is only interested in your coffers. His dominion over you will obliterate your way of life and contaminate your children against the customs of nature. He is a wretched element of the self-absorbed monarchy, and he only wants to profit from your hard work and devotion to the land. He is not concentrated on sharing the wealth of your toil - only stealing it from you. He will beguile you with false magnanimity... and force you to surrender everything you cherish simply for his own personal gain!"

Out of a froth of fear and blinding anger, an ugly side-effect of the poison the Griffin of Greed sprayed upon them, the brainwashed mob seized Prince Elliott and threw him off the highest cliff in the land, to breach the jagged rocks below, broken and mangled. His death came soon after... which was the only kindness shown him.

When the King and Queen heard the news, they were devastated. They fell into a deep depression from which even their most trusted advisors feared they would never recover. Drowning in their own despair over the loss of their only child, the King and Queen distanced themselves from one another; they slept apart, took their meals separately and even discontinued their royal duties of kindness and charity - from which they had gained such pleasure in the past.

Eventually, the King moved to a different castle on the eastern shores of their land to live out his days doing only what was imperative to keep the country going. Their despair became so great, that the King and Queen could no longer look upon each other, the memory of Prince Elliott's passing a stain upon their souls too great to overcome. Neither the King nor Queen felt happiness in their hearts. Neither one wanted to practice kindness or charity. "Generosity," they reasoned, "is what took our son. We will not make that mistake again."

As the Griffin of Greed flew farther into the kingdom, smearing its ugly sputum of greed over their land, the townsfolk began coveting each other's resources, wealth, and possessions. . With each new day, a wretched conversation replayed throughout the village: "I want your fastest horse, your grandest clothes, your best laying hen." Their attitude was full with entitlement. "I want to have an excess of exceptional things, not because my family needs them, but because I believe I am deserving of them. I will charge you more for my goods and services simply because I can, and there is no other option to satiate your needs. You are stuck. I will take advantage of your disadvantage. You will fail, and I will triumph."

The corruption that ran unshackled through the countryside was overwhelming. The people were creating a corrosive effect with their greed mongering, debilitating their efforts to live comfortably. Neighbors were resentful of one another. Joy had been abandoned. A dark cloud hung over the kingdom and the Griffin of Greed grew in strength and power; tormenting the townsfolk with even larger plagues of deception, as he encouraged their greed.

The King, still bewildered by his own grief, could not be convinced that he had any power to stop the onslaught of greed and pain. When his advisors suggested that he go to the people and reassure them, he was not swayed. "And who will reassure me?" he would ask despondently. It was a dark time for everyone, indeed.

Years passed, and a poisonous cloud of hopelessness hung low over the roofs and barns of the village. The Griffin of Greed breathed in the wretched fog of emotional neglect as its life's sustenance. It slumbered easily, knowing that the people were now so beleaguered with greed that they would never defeat it. It was sure its life would be one of ease and comfort now that the threat of death had been eliminated. "You shouldn't waste your time trying to kill me," it said. "Not when your energy, time and skills to hunt and kill me will never result in profit." The townsfolk believed its rhetoric; and so, never attempted a coup.

The King slogged through every day, wishing with greater regret that he had not turned away from his dearest love. She danced in his dreams, and with each sunrise, he was reminded of her true heart and pure beauty. He still missed Prince Elliott tremendously, but recognizing that he would never be able to bring his boy back, he focused his energy on the last strand of love that still wrapped around his heart. He worked hard at discovering a way to neutralize the Griffin of Greed's assails against the people's will, and one day, return to his Queen.

While walking through the apple orchard with a new friend one day, the King learned that the Griffin of Greed held a terrific secret. His new friend told him that the Griffin of Greed could be defeated by random acts of kindness and planned acts of charity; for the sunlight of good deeds always penetrates the fog of evil.

Resilient in his dedication to reunite with his love, he began a new campaign throughout the land. He traveled the kingdom, imploring people to perform very small acts of kindness for one another. He told them that they had to keep the kindnesses small in the beginning, so that they did not awaken the Griffin of Greed's ire. The townsfolk thought this reasonable advice, and did as they were asked. Once they became more practiced in kindness, he suggested that they increase the magnitude of their charity. They did, and began to build their confidences once again. Soon, they remembered that community generosity, not greed, is what had made their kingdom strong and free.

The King, being robustly virtuous, felt it necessary to take on two very large acts of charity himself, as a way to show leadership to the people... and as a way to demonstrate to his Queen that he had not been lost in the struggle... he had survived, and he wanted to let her know that she could, too.

On a bright, sunny summer afternoon, The King welcomed into his house a small child, an infant girl. She had lost her mother in the war of despair, and was left on her birth day without a caring arm around her. He took her into his house and made her a Princess. He named her Emily. He gave her every necessity and showered her with kindness and gratitude, for her tiny spirit had reinfused him with a sense of purpose, understanding, and love.

The Griffin of Greed felt this large ripple in the pond of its emotional scum, and was injured from it. The smaller flows of kindness offered by the townsfolk added insult to its injury, keeping it awash in the frustration of nagging niceness. Its piteous poison was beginning to have less effect on the people. This enraged the Griffin of Greed, and it took to the skies to spread its venomous spittle upon their houses. Some perished from the sting of its acidic burns; but most took shelter in their homes. They shared happy stories and sacred meals while enjoying the warmth of love's fire, friendship and freedom.

After all its efforts, it had accomplished nothing. The Griffin of Greed became exhausted from its efforts and retreated to its cave in the mountain side, insistent on discovering a stronger magic that would help it regain control.

The King heard of this recent development and he was proud of his community. He learned how the townsfolk had managed to hold the monster at bay and use the medicine of kindness to fight the symptoms of blight. The King was pleased and said, "even more must be done - and now. If we are going to defeat the Griffin of Greed forever," he said, "we must act now, while its defenses are low and our confidences are high."

The King went on a journey to all the borders of his land. He continued to remind the people of the debilitating effects of greed and the healing power of generosity. He was gratified to see how over and over again, people were remembering to help one another, serve one another, and heal themselves through random acts of kindness and planned acts of charity. Because of their efforts, their harvests were more abundant, their infant mortality rates nearly vanished, and their elders were becoming stronger in body, mind, and spirit.

While on his journey, the King noticed that many of the townsfolk did not have adequate education or cultural understanding. He found few schoolhouses, no theatres, no art houses or parklands. He felt sad because he knew that education and culture were what made a people distinctive and adaptive. For a community, having a fundamental understanding of the laws of nature, and then adding to that the ability to interpret situations from differing points of view, offered the advantage of creative problem solving. It was the combination of these skills and kind-hearted living that sustained a village through whatever ordeals may hex them.

Over the next two years, the King began a campaign of education and artistic stimulation throughout the land. He gave vast sums of money to small villages to improve their schools and he invited teachers from all disciplines to share their knowledge. He empowered young adults to continue their education into University. He encouraged the arts by offering contests of fantasy, storytelling, song, dance, painting and sculpture; all with handsome prizes. Realizing that a kingdom must not abandon the skilled tradesman and farmers if they are to remain stalwart, he offered rewards of deeper compensation, holiday time, and free tickets to artistic shows for those who chose to support their kingdom by fulfilling these vital roles. In a time more swift than anyone could have imagined, the people were rediscovering and relishing in daily joy once again.

    When the King arrived back at the castle, his entourage was greeted by Princess Emily and the children of the castle's attendants. They were delighted hear that they would dance in the kingdom's first pageant parade. The King and Princess Emily spent their days in happy reverie, surrounded by a special love that brought them even closer together. It was not the feeling of being a family that did this; but the special love that can only be found in the act of *choosing* to be a family, though not bound by blood.

    A few weeks of exciting preparation passed by, and then the townsfolk lined the streets for the pageant parade. Dancers lead the way, Princess Emily among them, with a marching band close behind. There were wagons filled with art and sculpture, singers performed magnificent arias, and a play was planned for later than evening. After the parade, the townsfolk shared a cookout to celebrate the power of education; creative enlightenment and charity have in bringing people of good hearts together.

    The Griffin of Greed smelled the smoke of their happiness barbecue and wretched from the aroma filling its lungs. "I must stop this!" it roared. It drank the last of its poisonous potion in a single gulp, adding some sulfur for good measure. Then it flew out over the mountain range toward the people. Its intention was to spit its venom upon them and blacken their hearts with the acid of its rage.

    Now the Queen, who had been living far away in the old castle, heard of all these things. She felt the fear and anger in her heart melt away when she discovered that the King was still, in his soul, the man that she had always loved. She called to her attendants, and they began the trek to visit the King, relying on their fastest horses to traverse the distance in little time.

The Queen arrived at the mountain pass just as the Griffin of Greed was beginning its decent into the valley. She blew a trumpet to alert the people, and called out a warning to get them indoors so they could not be destroyed by the Griffin of Greed's hateful spittle.

The Griffin of Greed heard the Queen's warning cries and became enraged. It turned its position away from the village and focused its flight path directly on her. It began bearing down on her, certain that it could wipe her out in one toxic breath. The Queen's attendants fled in fear. They did not want to be burned by the acid of greed. They did not believe that the Queen's good heart could save them.

In that moment, when the Griffin of Greed was nearly upon her, the Queen brought her cloak about her, raised her staff, and intoned the Prayer of Forgiveness. "I forgive the King for pushing me away and escaping to the faraway lands when I needed his love and support the most. I forgive the strangers who didn't know me as they mocked my pain. I forgive myself for ignoring the knowledge that strength comes from love, and not from pain." And finally, in a voice so loud the entire village could hear she said, "I forgive the Griffin of Greed for taking Prince Elliott from us!"

The Griffin of Greed, so stunned and overwhelmed by this bravest act of charity, faltered in its momentum and began to lose flight control. Its wings folded against its body and it spun into a nose-dive toward the Great Ocean. As it plunged past the water's surface, only a puff of smoke and black stain of acid marked the spot where it plummeted into the depths. As everyone knows, Griffins of Greed cannot swim; and so, it was lost forever.

The King came to the Queen and embraced her warmly. He then introduced her to his new family, Princess Emily and all the townsfolk. Instantly, the Queen's heart filled with love for them; and she welcomed them into her arms, and into her heart for all time.

The townsfolk surrounded the royal family as together, with the King and Queen leading them, they said two prayers; the first was a Remembrance Prayer, for the loss of Prince Elliott. For as everyone knows, in order to move forward in life, one must always remember the circumstances - both good and bad - that lead us along our path to love and freedom.

The second was a Prayer of Forgiveness for the Griffin of Greed. For without its teachings about the evil of blackened hearts defiled by greed, and how resentment distorts a life, they would not have recognized the light of benevolence and love. Now, they can bask in its warmth and enjoy their freedom.

The Royal Family and all the townsfolk from the kingdom danced under the stars that night and greeted the dawn of the new day together. They now understood that real magic is in cultural education and thoughtful charity. And *that* magic is what makes a life worth living.

****

Gillian was lost. Lost in his words. Lost in the magic of the story she'd just been told. Lost in her requited love. She began to fervently sketch, but not his story. In reading his, she'd found one of her own. She only hoped that perhaps someday, she would have the opportunity to share it with him.

Chapter Sixteen

"True love cannot be found where it does not exist, nor can it be denied where it does."
~Torquato Tasso

It had been an absolute crisis management Wednesday, with several teleconferences re-scheduled and far too many piles of paper appearing in three-inch stacks on his desk; a "gift" from Aaren's most recent visit from Boston. Exasperated, Thomas wondered, *how can MouseTrax boast their reputation as a "virtually paper-less office", when most days that isn't the case at all.* While it was true most of his daily correspondence and workload was handled electronically, *it still isn't enough. MouseTrax is one of the leading computer companies in the world. One would think that a purely electronic management of tasks and correspondence should be the standard.* The fact that a more comprehensive electronic delivery system wasn't the norm made his job of telling the world that it was, that much harder. *If MouseTrax was consciously working toward that utopian vision, it would be something I could manage. But they're not.* Lying did not come easily to Thomas, and it infuriated him that he could not promote the truth.

He had spent the better part of eight months convincing the clerical and IT departments to work together toward a more effective end, and thereby easing the stress of his job... especially from this distance; but, the transition wasn't as efficient as he had hoped. Even with the new tablet on the market, the Board was still wary of introducing new policies and procedures. Bureaucracies, he knew, were not limited to the government, and this one was just about driving him mad. *Why was it so difficult for the Board of Directors to see the solutions I find to be so simple? The Freep had the same problem... one software package for editing, one for layout... it was ridiculous. And, management's inability to see how the company's revenue could increase if they just took a risk... well, it's a mystery I will most likely never solve.*

It was four o'clock on a blustery autumn afternoon, and he'd simply had enough. In an attempt to lose himself for a few precious moments, he walked out on the deck. The glorious view of the water prompted him to silence his phone and open his notebook. He missed Gillian more and more lately. Spending this time with Paige and her pregnancy, reminded him of Gillian and their time in anticipation of Eryn's arrival. *I miss them both so much. I just wish she knew.* Writing to her was the only thing that kept him sane these days. Each new story was like valium for him. Feeling like he might be touching her, if only from a distance, brought him a calm he'd not felt since before the accident.

His stress level was at volcanic pressures, and he needed to blow off a little steam. He was frustrated and needed to get that out of his system before it did any damage. *To protect us both, I should probably do a little free-writing first - purge the ugliness before it overruns my story for Gillian.* He was careful to monitor his emotions when he wrote to her. Their years together had taught him that she often visualized things about his stories that he didn't always see himself. If this plan to get her back was going to work, he had to be careful with his words. Fumigating through free writing was the best way to do that - get it out - get it done, and move on.

He pulled a page from his notebook and created a passage where a wretched woman (he imagined her to be one of the disdainful Board members) was rejected by a wizard because of her inappropriate advances toward a visiting king. She was doing it to build jealousy within the wizard, but he was unimpressed by her misplaced loyalty and lack of propriety. She needed to be punished; and in this short bit of writing, Thomas punished her well.

Einar was outraged with Asrah's insolence. He had her banished from the kingdom; escorted through the streets to the outskirts in stinging humiliation by the high guard. Devastated by Einar's rejection, Asrah took to filchery and prostitution in order to sustain herself. Many marriages collapsed at her hand, and too many family savings were squandered on one or another of her wretched schemes. For she was, infamously, an unbiased thief with duplicity and treachery as the tools of her newly adopted trade. There soon came such a time as those around her could no longer tolerate her repugnant behavior. They drove her into the dismal swamp of Volant to live out the remainder of her existence in desperate solitude. Over time, the abhorrent way in which she accosted travelers caused the townsfolk to push her deeper into the foulness of the heathen waters which melted the skin from her bones. In quick order, the vultures began to dine on what little flesh was remaining, picking her skin apart inch by inch. Her misery quickly grew with such intensity that presently, her bones evaporated, joining the sludge of the swamp. She was never heard from again.

After closing out the passage and tearing the page from his notebook, calm returned to Thomas' face and he began to write his story for Gillian. This one, unlike some of the others, was not planned. He simply allowed his Muse to continue the free-write energy... permitting his soul to tell a story Gillian would find patience to hear.

****

It had been another long day for Gillian. Tax season was upon her with a vengeance. She'd spent more time pouring over financial statements and expense reports than she was comfortable with - all while feigning sanity. Her mother and father saw that the season was weighing heavily on her, and invited her out to APAC—the Accounting Professionals Athletic Club—for a night of relaxation. The name was nearly a complete misnomer. True, the place held a longstanding tradition of both accounting and athletics... but nowadays, the membership was more interested in the networking aspects of belonging. Money spoke loudly here... almost as loudly as who sponsored you in the door. True athletics had about as much impact here as animal husbandry did... but it was wrapped up in a vibrant package that screamed *Olympic Hopeful... someday.* "Just another stodgy social club," she complained just under her breath; "I'll never fit in here." As she walked the corridor behind her parents, she nodded hellos to people who resembled well-dressed marionettes as some political viewpoint or another yanked their strings. Gillian noticed the photos on the walls. *Crew, croquet, tennis, and water polo... maybe some of these people really were athletes at one point... it might have been nice to know those people... but not anymore. Now, they win gold medals in flagrant misuse of corporate perks, blue ribbons in complete misrepresentation of charitable goals, and silver-etched trophies in creative enhancement of public slander suits.*

"And this is our daughter, Gillian." said her mother from some far-off place.

"Uh... nice to meet you." she said, with a weak handshake and her well-practiced smile of false interest. *Yeah, this is going to be a fun night!*

Gillian suffered through dinner with her parent's friends - acquaintances, really - and was relieved when they decided a night cap at the bar was in order. "I'm just going to walk around a bit, explore and relax a little..." she said, with a carefully placed emphasis on 'relax'.

Her mother smiled. "Why of course, dear. We'll be in the bar, when you're ready." Her father nodded his approval and turned to shake hands with some new mover and shaker of some political bent that he hoped might benefit him at some point in his waning career.

"Oh Thomas..." she sighed. "You wouldn't believe this if you saw it. Me. Here. Ugh!" Gillian made her way past a gaggle of women discussing the latest news scandal of a mayor who deserved to be tarred and feathered for his misappropriation of funds - let alone people, and found a quiet balcony with wrought-iron chairs that held comfy, over-stuffed cushions. She reached into her purse and pulled out Thomas' most recent letter. It had just arrived that morning, but with all the oppressive number wrangling she was forced to battle, she hadn't had a chance to read it.

Thomas' letters were a saving grace for her these days. She was reluctant to admit it, but hearing his stories brought her comfort and consolation in a world filled with too much overbearing stupidity and not enough grace in art. She slid her finger inside the envelope flaps, releasing them from their glue, and unfolded his parchment. "I love that he still writes with parchment," she whispered to herself; "rather than some sterile computer. It's nice to know that there are some things in life that don't change just because a world collapses." She lay the sheets gently on the end table next to her and liberated her small Moleskin sketchbook from her purse. The habit of drawing had returned to her since Thomas' letters began, and she found that she needed to have a sketchbook handy at all times... for she never knew when the Muse would tickle her brain. It was a habit she'd missed since Eryn's death. A habit Thomas had reignited within her. She was grateful. *I hope someday I get the chance to thank him for that.*

Gillian began to read, moving her pencil across the pages of her sketchbook as she did... revealing the images that Thomas was inviting into her head.

****

It was late on a Friday night in September. Peter trudged, half regrettably, into Jake's to get away from the noise... to get away from the silence... just... to get away. With a contemptuous huff, he dragged out a stool from the end of the bar, disappearing into the crowd; finding solace in his anonymity. Leaning in heavily, his navy trench coat and brown tie hung around him like yesterday's discarded rags. He'd gone to war with the day's best bureaucrats... and lost. The battle wasn't one to which he was really all that committed, but still, the defeat had hit him hard. It was just a bit more rubble, topping off the mountain of complete failures he'd accumulated throughout the week. Now, he just needed an evening to re-group and try to salvage what was left of his energy.

"Give me a shot - of whatever's around," he mumbled to no one in particular, though he was certain someone would hear.

Less than a minute later, a stubby glass appeared before him, floating murky amber in the dim light. Without hesitation, he raised it to his lips and gulped down what he was sure would be the first of many in a night of what he cynically called Social Sedative Therapy.

"Give me another," he croaked flatly.

The words echoed from deep inside the bottom of an aching soul. His eyes never lifted from the place they studied... a figure of a woman he once knew, etched in foggy images of mahogany grain. It had been so very long since he last saw her... so very long since he felt her warmth and devotion smiling back at him. Another glass appeared before his quivering hands. Choking back what could have revealed tears, he dealt with it as he had the first; and not a sound was uttered.

The drink must have hit him harder than he had expected, though... for in the distance, he was certain he heard her voice drifting softly above the barroom clamor. He turned to see if indeed it was she... only to catch a glimpse of a faceless woman's sweeping red hair gliding toward the corner table. The crowd had camouflaged her destination. Digging deeper into his well of frustration, he lost sight of where she had gone. *Imagination's playing tricks on me again... it couldn't be her... could it?*

Makenna stood in the corner, near the pool table, surveying the night's fare. She needed one more tonight and then she could call it done. She never worked weekends... ever. That was her time. *I may give them everything else throughout the week, but nobody is going to take my weekends away from me!* She spotted a few possibles around the place; but most were loud and obnoxious, and already more than a little drunk... not the crowd she wanted to close out the week. *They're pushy, unappreciative, always take far too long, and it's never even slightly satisfying. I may have gotten into this for the money, but just as with any sport, if I don't enjoy myself, what's the point in playing the game?*

Then she spotted Peter, hunched over his fourth shot glass at the end of the bar as though someone had thrown him there. He was quiet and unassuming, and didn't seem to want company. *The perfect way to end a perfect day.* She would do her job, collect her pay, and still be home in time for a hot bath, Johnny Carson re-runs, and a hot fudge sundae amidst the soothing bubbles. The smooth leather of her mini skirt folded silently around her thighs as she made her way toward him.

Peter caught her baroque aroma long before she was ever close enough for him to hear her speak. The unpretentious fragrance hung in the air like a child's kite on a crisp autumn afternoon. Lilting ever nearer, it tickled his brain with memories of happiness long since banished. As Makenna slid onto the stool next to him, Peter shifted his gaze to meet hers, for the curiosity of the face that accompanied the bewitching scent was more than he could ignore.

They looked at each other for a long time, as if both had recognized an old friend whose name neither could recall. Makenna had deep-set, perfectly green eyes and the most delicate cheekbones he'd ever seen. She wore little make-up, and what was there seemed almost translucent upon her perfect skin. A silk blouse of the richest violet hung about her shoulders as though it were made especially for her body, clinging in all the right places, relaxed about the waist. Her auburn hair was gathered casually at the nape of her neck, rolling freely down to the middle of her back. She was, in every aspect, perfect. Mystically evoked from every magazine cover he had ever seen. It was hard for him to recognize that such beauty actually existed. His head grew foggy at this inconceivable moment.

A warm sigh rushed through him as Peter gazed at her. She was a breath of sunlit spring youth breaking through the grey gloom of winter's age. "Would you, um, like something to drink?" His voice cracked and stumbled as he spoke, fumbling like a teenager making his first pass at the prettiest girl in school. His heart pounded with such fury, that surely, he felt she could see it straining to leap from his chest.

"Sure," she answered easily. "I'll have one of those," she said pointing to the empty shot glass perched before him. "Do you come here often?"

"Isn't that supposed to be my line?" he said while wagging two fingers at the barman.

"Yeah, well, I thought I'd forgo the conventional stereotypes and take the risk." A smile cracked across his lips for a brief moment, signaling her victory.

"What a day! Wouldn't want to repeat this one." Small talk was not his strong suit, but he thought he'd make an effort; after all, she was exceptional.

"Tough day at the office, dear?" she quipped. His smile broadened now. *Zing! Score two.*

"Battled pirates, lost the gold, didn't even get the girl," he responded with the voice of a sixteen-year-old.

"Don't be too sure... the day's not over yet," Makenna whispered.

Peter was enjoying this game. The mysteriously beautiful woman at his side was a formidable player. "Oh? Are you free?" he tittered.

"Well, no... but I have an attractive lease package." *Zing!* Makenna was in rare form tonight. It's not often that so many opportunities were laid out so neatly right in front of her. *This one's fun. It'll be a pleasant way to end the week.*

"I'm not sure I'm in any shape to drive." Peter said with a bit of a chuckle. "Want to get a bite and talk a while before we hit the road?"

"Why not." Makenna replied. "I didn't have anything else to do tonight."

They moved easily to a nearby booth and the waitress came over to take their order. The waitress gave them a strange look, but it didn't seem to matter. "What would you like?"

"You choose. It's your test drive." Makenna said.

"Well then... we'll take the sampler and... ah, I'll take a Coke." Peter replied. *That part was easy... now what?*

"I'll have the same." said Makenna.

The waitress scribbled down their order. "Thank you," she responded, fiddling with her pen as if she had forgotten how to write. "Um... yeah... that'll be right out." *She must be new,* Peter thought; completely missing the fact that Makenna's was a customary face to the waitress.

Peter and Makenna sat focused on the candle sconce on the wall, silently waiting to see who would take the next step in this gentle frolic they had begun. Finally, Makenna began the narrative where they had left off. Peter's eyes were locked into Makenna's, working hard at ignoring the outside world.

"So, tell me," Makenna began; "Are you married?" She always started her encounters with this question. It may have been a blunt approach, but it always seemed to work for her. She found that most men, when asked, wouldn't lie. *Why would they need to?* She was a transient encounter, never important enough to lie to; and she knew it. Also, it gave her some idea of what was on his mind for the evening, and at least then she would know where things were headed; and more importantly, where they would end up.

"No," Peter sighed. "I've never been married. In fact, I've just recently broken up with my girlfriend."

"Oh, I'm sorry. Were the two of you together long?" Makenna didn't usually care enough to pry into a client's life like this, but there was something about this man that genuinely interested her. She had a strange desire to know more about him.

"Yeah. We were together almost two years. Really, it was on-again, off-again for two years. But we never seemed to drift too far apart from each other. This last time though... I don't know if she's coming back. Something happened; I'm not sure what... a big fight... it was ugly... I'm sorry. I shouldn't be unloading all this on you."

"It's okay. That's kind of what I'm here for." Makenna tilted her water glass at Peter and took a sip.

"Thanks," mumbled Peter.

It was then that the food and drinks arrived. A steaming plate of the most popular appetizers; shrimp, potato skins, cheese sticks, and stuffed mushrooms. They were all Peter's favorites; he could eat only these four things for the rest of his life and be completely happy. Handing a plate to Makenna he said; "Have you ever had the potato skins here? They're probably the best thing on the menu."

"No, I've never had them, but they look great," she said. This sort of transitional conversation Makenna understood was necessary. At this point, she wasn't sure just what Peter was looking for, but she would have bet her satin sheets he hadn't found it yet. She figured she'd let him keep going until he chose to stop. There was a moment of silence between them, and then, in a voice not much louder than a whisper, he asked his question.

"Do you believe in True Love?" he asked, pausing for what he hoped would be a small affect. "Not the kind of love they show you in the movies where everything is perfect and sunshine. I mean *True Love*. You know, the kind of love that's hard won, the kind you can only find with one other person on the whole planet?" His gaze drifted away aimlessly. "The kind of love that lasts through all the nonsense the world can dish out and it never goes away? The kind of love that you can't ever really explain, but you know it's there because it envelops every ounce of your soul? Do you believe in that kind of True Love?" The look on Peter's face was a mixture of anticipation and terror. It was as if he was watching a brand new ship docking in the harbor, but afraid of who might disembark. Afraid of what that new ship might challenge about his comfortably stayed lifestyle.

To Makenna, Peter looked like he was a small boy who had just asked his mother if he could keep the puppy that followed him home from the park. She took a sip of her Coke, sat back in the booth, and began to speak in a tone that, had Makenna not known any better, could have actually been the voice of another person altogether.

"True Love? Let me tell you a little story about True Love...

"You spend your whole life waiting for it. Really preparing yourself for the one day when True Love will finally find you. You heed the advice of your parents, though they don't realize you're listening; and your friends, who aren't really much help because they're just as confused as you are; and you try to be the person that men want you to be.

"You think that tenderness and emotion is what they want to see. That romantic tendencies and thoughtful demeanor is what men really want; though they all brag that they want and get much more. You do anything and everything they ever ask of you, within reason. You are loyal beyond expectation - so loyal in fact that most men don't believe you when you say you are, just because they're not accustomed to such devotion. You even go so far as to change your appearance to match some magazine cover you saw him stare at once. But it's never enough. It's never right. So you change."

Peter's face was crestfallen. He was surprised by her words, caught completely unprepared. His silence gave her the permission she needed to continue.

"You get tough," Makenna continued. "You get aggressive and as independent as you possibly can. You learn to use sex to manipulate emotions and you learn to ignore emotions. You learn to hide what it is you truly need and simply learn to live with what you get. You push away the ones who might enjoy a romantic interlude, only to endure weeks of one-night stands in misery. Finally, you give up completely and relinquish yourself back to the person you have always been, despite what the men might think, say, do, or want. You go back to listening to your emotions and acting on whimsical impulse. And, it's still not right."

Peter nervously gulped his Coke, and signaled the waitress to bring more. Makenna kept talking, barely taking a breath. She was in her own world of frustration, and she wasn't giving up the podium.

"At last," Makenna sighed, "you find a heart that seems to be in sync with yours. You think that perhaps you have finally found True Love, despite all the self-help books on healing doomed relationships that adorn your bookshelves and coffee table. Then, that fateful day comes."

"What day?" Peter asked in nearly a whisper.

"He breaks your heart," said Makenna flatly. "You spend a lot of time asking yourself 'why' and 'how come'. You spend more days and nights alone than you can ever remember and you take to sleeping on the couch because the bed is just too big and too empty. You cry an ocean of tears and decide that taking out stock in the Kleenex Corporation might be a wise move. You decide that if any man is ever going to share True Love with you, it'll have to be someone who isn't too fussy, and is desperate enough to love you as you are; romantic quirks, emotions and all."

"I don't know who wouldn't want to love you. You're pretty spectacular." Peter smiled, but Makenna didn't see it. She was lost now, this ship had sailed and there was a wake at her stern.

"Then, out of nowhere, you finally find someone that you discovered you loved all along, yet you were too busy being stupid to notice. You make a vow to yourself to love him and be loyal to him forever. A flash of the past hits you and you recall that's how you got into this trouble in the first place. So, you change your tack a little bit. You keep your distance, trying not to force your way into his life, yet remaining as close as you possibly can. You remember that the friendship is the most important thing, forever, and you never forget your vow. Then you lose him anyway. Not only does his closeness slip away, but you feel his friendship slipping away, too. You begin to second-guess your relationship with him. You begin to slowly drive yourself mad. You wonder what it is about you that he doesn't like. You wonder if there was anything you could have done differently to make him want to stay. You wonder if you'll ever get the chance to make it right again. Most of all, you wonder if you'll ever see him again; and that is you're worst fear. Never seeing him again.

"So you spend your evenings trying not to bother him and not make a nuisance of yourself. You try to get yourself to accept your fate. But of course, it isn't a fate easily swallowed. So at last, you have a really good cry over the whole mess, and awake the next morning ruing the day you came into the world. Cynicism and bitterness creep into your day one happy little ray of sunshine at a time, and you feel a tremendous sorrow for what you know could have been wonderful, if only it were given a chance to flourish. You would have given your life to please him, and you have... by letting him go. Squaring your shoulders and disallowing any trace of a tear, you tread through your life savoring the beauty you can find in little things, knowing that's all the world has left you. You accept it, realizing that some things were just simply meant to be. But, all that doesn't change how desperately you love and miss him. And that, my friend, is what True Love is really all about."

****

Gillian stopped reading when she realized that the story had changed. It had begun the same way their playful first night had so long ago—except the prostitute part, that was his creative license exerting itself, she knew, but this last part—his monologue about True Love, she realized, was more of the present and less of the past. What she wasn't sure about, though, was the message he was trying to send. *Are these his thoughts and feelings; or is he fishing for mine?* Out of all the stories he'd told so far, this one was the most puzzling to her. *I just can't figure this one out.* She kept reading.

****

"All I really want is someone who'll stay," said Peter. "So often I meet a woman... and she's great and everything... but then she never stays. I can't figure out why. I mean, if it's something I've done, I wish she would say so... then maybe I could stop it from happening the next time." Peter sounded like a confused child, unsure as to how he became covered in mud after he'd been out playing in the rain-soaked yard. In that instant, Makenna almost felt sorry for him... this poor, lost soul, with no one to love him. Almost.

"Haven't you been listening?!" Makenna was stunned at how much Peter had missed. So, she attempted to put it into simpler terms for his pathetic, inebriated little brain to follow. As Makenna continued, she had more than a bit of contempt in her voice. "It's men like you that I don't get. I'll bet that more times than you can count you've found someone who was really dedicated, someone who was willing to stay forever, and you pushed her away."

"Why... why would I do that?" Peter said, nearly whining.

"That's the part I don't get," snipped Makenna. "I've heard so many men talk about how they just want someone who'll stay. Although it's never just that. It's been said that women have an unattainable laundry list of qualifications for inviting a man into her life. Well, let me tell you, men have got their own little laundry list going." As Makenna talked, she ticked off the items on her fingers. "They want someone who'll be completely devoted. They want someone who's subservient to them in bed, yet independent in all other aspects of life. They want someone who'll love them unconditionally. And, most of all, someone who'll want them as much as they want to be wanted - never more, never less. But, when that person comes along, they invariably push her away. Maybe they push her away because when actually faced with that kind of devotion, it frightened them and they weren't sure how to handle it.

"So my guess is, the guy discovers some minor flaw about her... something that just didn't quite fit into his agenda... and he lets her go, or he helps her feel the need to go, based on that one little aspect of her or of their being together that just wasn't right in that moment. Men never think beyond the moment."

Peter looked at her with blank confusion; so Makenna continued. "Perhaps it was that her name or her face reminded him of someone he loved and lost. Maybe she didn't look exactly like the picture of a woman he'd seen in a magazine someplace. It could have been that her bank account balance was more important than who she was as a person. Or perhaps she had a child, or a pet, or a career responsibility that he didn't think he wanted to deal with; although he told her several times that that thing wasn't an issue.

"You see, this guy makes up all this odd logic in his head so it somehow makes sense to him, although to no one else, and he pushes her further and further away. Sometimes it happens quite subtly with forgotten phone calls and missed dates; and other times it's very obvious with mean-spirited words and hurtful anger. But in the end, she's still gone. She's left trying to figure out why he pushed her away; and he's left trying to figure out why she left."

Makenna took a sip of her Coke and paused for a moment. When she continued, her voice was almost a whisper. "And you know, the funny thing is, if he asked her back into his life again, she'd most likely come running, forgiving him completely and being just as devoted as she always was. Until he pushes her away again. They'll come to play this kind of 'yo-yo' game until she just can't do it anymore. Then he'll ask her back once more... only this time, she won't be there.

"That's just about the time he ends up coming to a place like this, staring into the crowd, trying to find her in a sea of people, only to wake up the next morning disappointed, confused and horribly hung over. He, of course, never does find her again. So, he tosses the memory of her away with all the others, in order to be refreshed to work his 'magic' on someone else who believes he's important enough to be devoted to him forever."

When Makenna had emptied herself of the rant, Peter took a sip of his drink, and leaned back in his seat. *It's interesting the things you can learn if you really listen*, he thought.

****

Gillian had her answer. *This is a message for me. In this one small paragraph, Thomas' intent seems to be clearly defined. Together, we have been through something neither of us understood. It looks like he's been working hard to see the problem and the solution from my point of view. Maybe he's convinced that it's his fault... he was the reason we failed and he made the situation worse.* Gillian thought for a long moment, looking over the sketches she'd created out of Thomas' words. *And, it looks like... he's asking me to take the same tack. It's like he's asking me to step into his soul for a moment and look at the world through his eyes.*

Gillian picked up the letter, and took a moment, staring into the nothing around her, trying to see with his vision. Then, she flipped the page in her book, and began to sketch what she saw. When her drawing was complete, she was surprised at what Thomas had shown her. It was a view she had never expected.

Gillian let go a long sigh. She felt like she needed to take a moment and come back to herself before continuing to read the rest of his story. She knew that her parents were probably missing her... wondering where she'd gotten off to. And, she knew that she needed to be present, focus herself, to hear the rest of Thomas' message. *I can't worry about Mom and Dad right now. This is important.* Avoiding the bar, she went to the matr'd to ask for a small plate of cheese and crackers. She felt that she needed to cleanse the palate of her imagination - before indulging in the new emotional cabernet Thomas would offer. With a curious indulgence, the matr'd complied, and she returned to her secret space to continue reading... and sketching.

****

"Is that why you ended up doing... um... what you do... been pushed away too many times?" asked Peter.

"I'm done playing the game their way. I've been down that path more times than I care to recall. My system just couldn't handle the shock of it anymore. It's a lot of work being that devoted. And, it's even more work to be rejected that regularly. It takes a lot out of you. Why should I continue to play the game when I am continuously forced to lose? Aren't I entitled to win occasionally?" She sat back in her seat, two hands grasping her glass. "Playing the game my way, I avoid the risk of all that pain, and at least I get a little taste of winning. Granted, it's not the best possible solution, but for now, it'll do."

In the silence that now hung between them, Peter and Makenna sipped at the last of their drinks. There was such bitterness in Makenna's voice that it cut him to the quick. Oh, he'd heard many women speak these things through the din of midnight sorority sleep-overs, as he had eavesdropped outside open windows; but never once considered that it could be truth. He had never before imagined that a woman could feel just as lost, dejected and frustrated as he did about the entire dating and relationship process. There was such an intense emptiness to Makenna's words and a tremendous pain in her face that Peter found it difficult to look her in the eyes.

Makenna's confession and confirmation of the emotional puzzle they shared meant that Peter would never triumph over her destiny... or any woman's... any more than he could conquer his own. It did make Peter think, though. Although he wanted it, he wasn't sure he could deal with whatever might come next. *Will I ever be strong enough to be what she needs?* "Let's get out of here." Standing, Peter threw a pile of twenties on the table, helped Makenna on with her coat, and together, they walked out the door.

*****

All this time, I didn't think he was paying attention. It turned out that not only was he paying attention... he also got it. He actually understood why I pushed him away. I don't know how to draw that. How do you sketch remorse and forgiveness?

Chapter Seventeen

"All we will ever know and share about love, humility, compassion, and sacrifice – the secrets that will reveal and then resolve old sorrows – awaits us within ourselves."
~Guy Finley

"Paige, what's wrong?" The look on her face was a contortion Thomas had never seen before. It scared him just a little.

"My stomach's just a little off. Just a little cramping." It was four in the afternoon, and Thomas was trying to plan dinner with the chef. He waited for Paige to return from the bathroom. A moment later, he heard her scream. Breaking through the door, he yelled, "Paige, what's wrong?"

She just stood there, hand over her mouth, pointing at the toilet. Blood swam in the bowl; Thomas flushed and led her back to the bed. "I'm calling the midwife." Paige opened her mouth to protest, but screamed out in pain, instead.

When the midwife arrived thirty minutes later, Paige was lying in a left-sided fetal position on the bed, moaning in frustration, pain and fear. A quick exam and the midwife's years of experience told them that the fun and games of sequestered living were over. "The bleeding is a little heavy, but only spotty at this point. Still, I don't think it's something that should be ignored."

"That's it. We're getting her to the hospital - now," he said.

Twenty minutes later, the private ambulance delivered them quietly to the back door of the emergency department and whisked the trio into a private exam room of South Hampton Hospital. Thomas was in awe of the preferential treatment money could afford. He flashed back on Gillian's time at the little hospital in Kremmling, and how difficult it was to get help and answers as quickly as they wanted them. The dichotomy between this time and that was stunning.

The night was spent sleeplessly, with many tests and the faces of forlorn doctors and nurses passing through every hour or so. It was seven o'clock when the resident came in and gave them the difficult news. Within an hour, the decision was made to leave the Hamptons and head back to Boston. "The brownstone is closer to Bringham and Women's Hospital. I know that the doctors in the Hamptons are quite capable, skilled and well trained; but if we're going to do this," said Paige. "I insist on having the best; and the best are at Bringham and Women's."

Helicopter rides weren't new to Thomas… but having one at your beck and call was. It was a swift ride in the elevator to the roof where the rotors of a sleek, black, luxury Augusta Westland AW109 Grand purred in stalwart devotion. It took just a few minutes to get loaded – Paige, Thomas, and the midwife; and then they were airborne.

During the hour flight, Thomas had an opportunity to let his mind race, but he focused instead on the midwife's dramatically changing facial expressions. "What's wrong?" he asked, gripping Paige's hand a little bit tighter.

"Things are looking worse. I'm not sure we can take the chance landing at the airport and then going to the brownstone. I think we should fly directly to the hospital."

"Bringham's... it's got to be Bringhams!" Paige screamed.

The midwife shouted the new flight plan to the pilot as Thomas tried to find comforting words for Paige. "It'll be okay, Paige. Everything's going to be all right." The helicopter banked a little and Thomas' stomach lurched; but whether from fear or altitude adjustment, he wasn't sure.

The staff at the hospital worked with military precision. Thomas now understood why Paige was so insistent on coming here. Clearly they were the best. As they raced out of the elevator and into a private exam room, Thomas noticed a dedicate plaque hanging on the wall across from the nurse's station: *The Lambert Neonatal Wing.* Thomas barked his revelation just under his breath... *Of course she'll get the best care AND anonymity... her family built the place. That's why she wanted to come here!*

They had Paige stabilized three hours later, and although her doctors protested loudly, she was released to her house under the midwife's care. Thomas didn't agree, but since they weren't married, he didn't have much of a say in the matter.

When they arrived at the brownstone, Aaren and Nathan met them at the door. Aaren led Paige and the midwife up to Paige's bedroom, Thomas and Nathan hung back, giving respectful distance to the women. "What the hell happened, Thom?"

"I have no idea. One minute, we're trying to decide on dinner plans, the next... there's blood in the toilet and she's shrieking in pain. The doctors in the ER told us that the baby needed to be delivered soon - some sort of trauma - I still don't fully understand it all. But Paige insisted on coming home, so here we are." Thomas was glad to have a friend nearby. Even after all his years of covering the Trauma Desk, moments like this - the ones that he couldn't detach from - were still difficult for him to process.

"Don't worry, buddy. Things will work out okay, you'll see." Nathan was trying to be supportive, but there was a hint of nervousness in his voice that could not be denied.

Aaren appeared at the top of the stairs. "She's asking for you."

"Which one?" Nathan asked.

"Both." Aaren said.

The men climbed the stairs, wary of what was to come. Paige's habit for summoning people to her presence at the office did not define her reputation as a gentle soul. Even after all the time spent in the Hamptons together, in a more relaxed space, Thomas still felt it - the dread of her demands. As they walked into the room, they saw Paige tucked neatly into the bed, the pout of an impertinent child on her face. The midwife packed up her little black bag, as she gave last minute instructions to Aaren.

"She needs to stay in bed. No getting up except for the bathroom, and she's never to be left alone. I will call in a couple of hours to see how she's doing, and I'll check in with the hospital and schedule a comprehensive exam for tomorrow. Keep her diet gentle, and absolutely no alcohol. And..." she said staring straight at Paige; "Absolutely no stairs! Do you understand?" Paige nodded, but said nothing; a scowl of disdain on her face. Aaren took the prescription paper the midwife handed her with the instructions to give to the hospital when they arrived. The two continued to talk quietly in a corner of the room.

Paige left the child behind and once again became the CEO in charge. "Nathan," said Paige. "I need you to handle damage control at the office. Do whatever it takes - I don't care what you tell them - just don't tell them the truth. I don't think any of us are ready to fight off the bilge rats. I know that I'm certainly not in any shape to deal with their questions and insinuations. Just let me get through this, and then we'll deal with the fall-out. Aaren has what you need to get it done." Right on cue, Aaren took three steps to meet Nathan, and handed him the customary white envelope. No words were exchanged between them.

"Don't worry about it, Paige. I'll handle it. You just focus on having a healthy baby." Nathan was trying to be sincere, but Paige dismissed his words with a huff. It was the first time Thomas could remember seeing Nathan look hurt.

Paige looked sternly then, at Thomas. "Thomas, you are staying here. There's a perfectly nice guest room down the hall; I insist." There was something in her eyes that Thomas had never seen before. Could it have been fear, anger, or something more? Thomas couldn't be sure; but still, he was hesitant about staying at the brownstone. It was uncomfortably close to the office. He knew the ways of roving tabloid reporters. They could be evil and unrepentant. Thomas wasn't interested in dealing with that again. He felt the need to object. "I don't know, Paige. What if someone finds out I'm here... all our plans could be ruined. I'd only be just a phone call away..." Paige waved the other three out of the room, and hesitantly pulled him into her confidence.

"Look, Thomas," Paige said with an unusual quiver of desperation. "I can only remember one other time in my life that I have been this afraid... and I was just a child then; without my mother to protect me. Let's face it, I don't process fear well; I avoid it. At thirty-four, you certainly don't expect me to change now, do you? Avoidance is where I'm most comfortable, if you hadn't noticed." Paige's voice grew more unsteady, and a bit louder. "You got me into this mess. You caused this problem; and you made me promise to see it to the bitter end - so you have to do the same thing. You simply can't leave now!" Her voice had become frenetic. She was completely out of control - and Thomas believed that's what frightened her most. He had no choice but to give in to her demands. The fact was, his first responsibility was to this child. No matter what the effect on Paige's corporate image, her inability to cope, or his connection to the scandal that he knew would eventually come.

The next morning, they went to Bringham and Women's Hospital for an exam and to discover exactly what was going on. The doctors could not determine the exact nature of the problem. Paige's blood pressure was a little low, but they attributed that to stress of childbearing and trying to run a company remotely miles away from her office. She was given strict instructions to abandon her work, for a time, until after the baby was born; and to remain quiet and comfortable at home. Neither of these things were going to happen, Thomas knew. It was difficult for Paige to ignore the company; and the mileage didn't matter. She could be in deepest, darkest Africa, and she'd still want daily sales reports and updates from the R&D people. He knew it would be difficult to keep her quiet, but he also knew that the health of their child depended on it. When they got back to the brownstone, he led her to the couch in the living room and laid down the new law.

"Look, I know how important your company is to you... Lord knows I get it, after nearly nine full months surrounded by your manic attention to it, even while at the cottage, but that's got to stop. The doctors told you to calm down, and that's exactly what you're going to do." Paige tried to interrupt but Thomas cut her off. "Look, I'll make sure that you continue to get your updates, and that you don't lose touch with the company; but you have to promise me that you'll take it easy. No stair climbing. You go up at night and down in the morning, and the rest of the time, you stay on this floor. You've got plenty of space down here. Lots of books to read, movies and music. I promise you won't get bored. And if you do... so much the better. Take a nap." Again, Paige tried to interject, but he didn't permit it. "There will be no arguing. You will do as you are told, or you will end up in a nice, dull room at Bringham and Women's Hospital - with no contact to the outside world, period. Have I made myself clear?"

Paige was a little taken aback by his "take no prisoners, give no quarters" attitude. She'd never seen him so aggressive before. Oh, she'd seen it before on a professional level, but never on a personal one, at least not since this whole thing began nearly nine months ago.. He had always seemed so timid. She liked the change and feared it simultaneously. Paige nodded her head in compliance; not sure of what to say.

"Good. Now, I'll set you up in the living room with the laptop for a little while, just so you can catch up, and I'll get you some lunch... but then you need to rest." Thomas helped Paige off with her coat, and got her settled in on the couch, the laptop and a few files laid out on the coffee table. She immediately went to work checking e-mail and downloading the day's reports. It was as if someone had set a plate of lobster and crab in front of her with a bowl of drawn butter... she could not contain her zeal for the delicacies she'd been denied for the past forty-eight hours, and the anticipation dripped down her chin.

Thomas shook his head and went to the kitchen to pull together something for lunch. He was struggling to keep his emotions in check; and he didn't dare dwell on his inner thoughts for too long. He was afraid of losing himself to fear - the thought of losing another child terrified him - the chance that losing a child to the fault of his own misstep, completely unacceptable. *I have to keep it together... at least until this is all over; and then it will be... well, I'm not sure what it will be... but it won't be this hard anymore - I hope.*

After lunch, Thomas removed the laptop and files from the living room, and offered Paige either the TV remote or a book. At first, she looked at both with revulsion - but then, accepted the book as the lesser of two evils. He covered her with an afghan, and settled himself at the desk to attempt a little writing. Staying close enough to keep a watchful eye on Paige... yet keeping a little distance to maintain his own sanity. They both needed it. Even as big as the Hampton Cottage was, he still felt like they had been living on top of each other for the last several months. Part of that was by his design - staying close just in case there was a problem; and part of that was because she had been extremely needy. Paige hadn't anticipated the hormonal, emotional drain this pregnancy would bring, and she hadn't handled it well.

****

It was three days later when Paige woke Thomas up with screaming that sounded like she was being struck with a cat o' nine tails. He ran to her room to find her doubled over against the mattress, knees on the floor, holding her belly. Blood had pooled on the carpet and her hair dripped with sweat. Thomas reached for the phone and began to dial 911.

"No! No one can know..." Paige wailed.

"Look!" Thomas screamed. "No more of this nonsense! I don't care who knows what, if it will save our child!" Thomas was furious; so much so that he was not willing to placate her any longer. When the operator finally answered, he gave her the address and situation in abbreviated staccato, and quickly hung up the phone, not waiting for further instructions. Thomas worked to get Paige to her feet and dressed. It wasn't Prada; just a housecoat and slippers; but he knew she would be mortified if the EMT personnel found her as he had. Although he wasn't willing to jeopardize the safety of their child, he would do what he could to maintain her dignity along the way. When he heard the knock at the door, he gently set Paige in a nearby wing-back chair and ran down the stairs to let the paramedics inside. He pointed with labored breathing to the top of the stairs, and the team of three hauled equipment and a stretcher up the perfectly polished stairs. He knew Paige wouldn't be happy with the scratch marks, but Thomas couldn't be bothered with that right now.

After they had taken her vital signs, a brief history of the event, and stabilized her; they lugged her back down the stairs attached to the stretcher. The mortified look that crossed her face and a vision of a cartoon character careening down the stairs at a full clip brought a smile to Thomas' face. He chastised himself for the brief indulgence and followed them out to the waiting ambulance. Once they reached the hospital, Paige was wheeled with NASCAR speed to the emergency room, and there, a quick assessment was made. As they whisked her off to the delivery room, a doctor came out to explain the situation to Thomas.

"Ms. Lambert is experiencing obstetrical hemorrhaging. This means that the heavy bleeding she is having is directly related to the baby and the way it is interfering with her internal organs. We're not sure, just yet, but the bleeding may be vaginal and external, or, less commonly, but more dangerously, internal and expanding into the abdominal cavity. Typical bleeding is related to the pregnancy itself, and usually resolves completely; but some forms of bleeding during pregnancy are caused by other events and are difficult to identify. While I know that this is hard for you to hear, you must know, obstetrical hemorrhage is a major cause of maternal mortality."

"Meaning what, exactly?" asked Thomas.

"Meaning that it is possible that if we don't deliver the baby now by C-Section, and stop the bleeding, either one or both of them may die. Now I'm sorry, but I must go attend to her. I'll have a nurse bring you an update as soon as we know something more definitive."

Thomas was left alone in the corridor, wondering what to do next. A horrible flash of that night in Kremmling came back to him in vivid vitality. He reached for his phone and called Aaren. "Aaren, it's Thomas. Paige is at Bringham and Women's... it doesn't look good... obstetrical hemorrhaging. They've got her in the delivery room now... the doctors don't know if they're both going to make it... thank you. See you soon."

Fifteen minutes later, Thomas still hadn't heard anything from the nurse, but Aaren and Nathan were now sitting by his side, waiting with him. A full forty minutes of shared silence had passed when the nurse finally came out, looking for Thomas.

"Mr. Laird?"

"Yes," said Thomas, as the trio stood up.

"Ms. Lambert is out of the delivery room and in the ICU. She is resting, but is still in critical condition. We have been able to isolate the bleeding, and we know that it is lurching from her abdomen. We're doing our best to control it. We've got her on antibiotics to stave off any infection, and she's on fluids and nutrition drips." The nurse was clinical but not unkind.

"And what about the baby?" Thomas' voice was filled with fear and anxiety.

"Your daughter has been taken to the NICU. She was born several weeks early, as you know, and although she is struggling to breathe on her own, which is not uncommon for a preemie at her stage, everything else looks good. She is tiny, but we expect that she will do well."

Thomas, Nathan, and Aaren were relieved and guarded by this news. "When can we see them?" Aaren asked.

"Mr. Laird, you may see your daughter right away; but unfortunately, unrelated visitors are not allowed in the NICU." She placed a pink bracelet around Thomas' wrist with the name, "Baby Lambert", printed in bold letters. "I'm sorry, these children are just too fragile to allow extra people in the room; I'm sure you understand," she said, looking at Aaren and Nathan.

"Of course. Can I see Paige?" Aaren was very worried about Paige. She'd rarely been sick, and to her recollection, never spent time in a hospital.

"Yes, you may. Just give us a few minutes to make her comfortable. I'll be out in to guide you back shortly. Mr. Laird, would you like to meet your daughter?" The nurse gave Thomas a gentle smile, knowing how exciting and scary a moment this was for him.

"Yes, please." Thomas said gently. Thomas looked at Aaren and Nathan with wide, unbelieving eyes, and followed the nurse down the hall.

Chapter Eighteen

"I made decisions that I regret, and I took them as learning experiences... I'm human, not perfect, like anybody else."
~Queen Latifa

It felt so strange to her... no movement, no voice, no emotion... the room was heavy with the pressure of these things lost. Energy had always surrounded her, even in those early days of unhappiness when she was trying to find out who she was, and even in the most intense of negotiation struggles - there was always energy. Sometimes positive, sometimes negative... but there was never just - nothing. Now, the silence and solitude seemed a black hole in her life, consuming everything she was and had ever been. She couldn't feel... couldn't think... didn't know. *Is this my punishment? My tariff for taking too much for granted for far too long? Am I finally reaping the reward of the distance I fabricated between me and the rest of the world?* She had learned now... she didn't vanquish its effects, simply delayed them; and now, they were prolonged. Subjecting her to these final few hours of a slow-motion revisiting of her past, ignoring completely her present. She thought she knew overwhelm... but she had never experienced it like this before. In a flat dimension without the benefit of her five senses - only the sixth, upon which she knew she should not rely. Then... a sound coming to her from the darkness - a familiar melody, but still so far away.

"Mom? Can you hear me?" *Logan. Sweet Logan.* Far away, but coming closer. She reached out, trying to feel his hand, but grasping only empty air. "It's okay, Mom; I'm here." A warm hand slid inside hers, grasping her tightly. She feels the pinch of the tape around the tube in her wrist; sensation coming back to her... finally. Darkness still surrounded her, and she wished for its banishment, if only to see her son's smile one last time. *I'm so very tired, so very confused. Will peace ever come back? Will I ever find redemption - after all these years, am I even worthy it?*

The nurse held her hand and soothed her as best as she could. When Paige's eyes finally opened they flooded with silent tears. That's when she knew, never again, would she see her precious Logan. Her question had been answered - no, she was not worthy. The light came back to her in blurred edges and brilliant prism color. She tried to shield her eyes from the sudden assault. "It's okay, Paige. Just take your time, do it slowly. You've been asleep for a long time... just take it slow."

Finally, the world came into focus. The room was comfortable, beautiful teak walls, a large bay window inviting in the sunlight and blue skies, and there before her, Thomas. How she wished it could have been Logan, but she understood now, that time would never come for her again. She smiled knowing now that even though the end was close, she could leave in comfort. But, there was one last piece of business - one last secret that must be told... this was the most important thing she could do now, and she knew there wasn't much time.

"Thomas, I need you to get something for me."

"Of course, Paige, what is it?" Thomas had spoken with the doctors; he knew that she didn't have much time left. Although she had been beyond difficult these past several months; she did give him Emily, and for that, he needed to thank her the only way he knew how - by giving her a last request and a gentle exit. "Do you want some water, some food - tell me what you need."

"No, none of that—at the house..." Her breathing was labored, it was difficult to get the words out, and only a whisper came from her lips. "In my Grandfather's desk... back at the brownstone... in the top left drawer... find the key... get the blue box."

"Paige? A blue box? Don't worry about that right now, you can deal with whatever that is when you get better... it's not important now..."

"Yes!" In her head, Paige was screaming; but her voice was barely audible. It was frustrating to be so close to invisible. "Get the box, Thomas. It's important - Please!" The nurse came in just then, with a worried look on her face and an urgent attention to computer screens and tubes. It changed the look in Paige's eyes from insistence to pleading.

"All right, Paige. I'll go get it. I'll be back soon. Just rest now." Thomas left, not knowing what this was all about, but knowing that he owed her this one last request.

As Thomas left the room, Paige allowed her eyes to close. The darkness flooded over her; a warm, welcoming force... but she couldn't leave just yet. Not yet. She willed her ears to stay awake, even though her eyes no longer held the energy to see.

****

Thomas ran out of the hospital, waited impatiently for the T to arrive, and surged as fast as mass transit would carry him through the underground to Paige's home in Copley Square. The two miles felt like two thousand. Climbing the flight of stairs before her brownstone was like summiting the Tibetan mountains, as he struggled to leap three steps at a time.

"Keys; these damn keys!" He had never understood Paige's need to keep so many keys, especially since the advent of electronic entry systems. Her archaic attachment to some things, he would never understand. Finally, he found the right one and quickly turned the lock. A mad dash to the study upstairs revealed her grandfather's roll-top desk. Under its protective ribs lived three rows of small apothecary drawers.

"Top left..." As Thomas pulled open the small wooden drawer, he spied it's only contents. A single metal key, a number etched on one side, and on the other, *Boston Public Bank*. He turned the key over in his hands, inspecting it closely. *A safe deposit box key? All of her important documents are kept with the company lawyers. Why would she have this? What could she possibly be hiding?*

As he made his way back to the T station, he called Aaren. "Do you know anything about Paige having a safe deposit box at Boston Public?"

"Yes. She added me as a co-signer just shortly after her parents died, and swore me to secrecy. Why?" Aaren sounded just as perplexed as Thomas.

"You need to meet me at the bank. I'm not sure what this is all about; Paige said something about a blue box. Does that ring a bell with you?" he asked.

"No. She never told me what she put in the safe deposit box. Why is this so important? Shouldn't we be here, at the hospital, with Paige?"

"She asked me to get it, Aaren. It sounded like a dying wish. We have to do this." Thomas was pleading with Aaren now. "Please, help me do this."

"Okay, I'll have Nathan stay with her, and I'll meet you there." Aaren said.

"Great, thank you." Thomas hung up the phone, his mind racing as he tried to imagine what the secret might be.

Another frustratingly slow T ride to Government Center deposited Thomas on the steps of a large stone and glass building. *Boston Public Bank est. 1842* was etched in the cornice above the threshold. This building had once been an old church; or at least the facade had. Newer additions jutted out above and from either side, a striking blend of old and new in what some brain-dead architect thought was an appealing style. To Thomas, it looked like the designers had bastardized all of early American architecture and history, simply to get paid.

He fingered the key in his pocket as he searched out someone in authority. Finally, he found a manager. "My name is Thomas Laird. My boss and friend, Paige Lambert is very ill, and she has sent me to retrieve the contents of her safe-deposit box."

"Do you have the key?" The manager asked in a suspicious tone.

"Yes, of course." Thomas pulled the key from his pocket and cradled it in the palm of his hand as if it were a new-born kitten. The bank manager inspected the key and handed it back to Thomas.

"Are you a signer on the account, sir?"

"No... but..."

"Well then, I can't permit you to open the box, key or no key." The manager began to walk away, when Thomas saw Aaren walk through the doors.

"Aaren!" he called. "This is Aaren Graner..."

"Mr. Thompson; how nice to see you again," said Aaren. "Ms. Lambert has asked us to retrieve the contents of her safe deposit box. I am a signer on the account, and Mr. Laird has the key. I would be happy to have you verify my signature, to speed things along."

The manager led them to the counter. "Please sign here, Ms. Graner." She signed the card he produced, and he disappeared for a moment, returning almost before Thomas remembered to let out the breath he'd been holding.

"Your signature has been verified, Ms. Graner; thank you. Right this way, Mr. Laird." Together, the men walked past the row of tellers and lines of people waiting for their turn; around a cluster of cubicles and down a narrow hallway. A left turn and the pair stood before the massive open door of the bank's vault. To the right, a cage stood guardian over shelves of cash and bags of coins. To the left, another cage protected a wall of safe deposit boxes just beyond its bars.

"Your key again, please, sir." Thomas handed him the key, and the manager opened the cage door, stepped in, and returned with the box cradled in his arms. He closed and locked the cage door behind him and led Thomas away. "This way, if you please." Halfway back down the narrow hallway, the manager opened a small door and invited Thomas in. There was a shelf about waist high, and a single chair. The room was no bigger than a phone booth built for two. The manager placed the box on the shelf and left Thomas alone. "Take as much time as you need."

After a moment of apprehension, Thomas opened the box. Inside he discovered an opal blue stationary box measuring about eleven inches by fourteen inches, and about four inches deep, decorated with white satin ribbon around the edges. There was a gold clasp on the long edge and little hinges on the opposite side, firmly attaching the lid. The clasp held a lock with a hole that he was sure was a keyhole, but it was unlike any key Thomas could imagine. It didn't look quite deep enough for a skeleton key, but it wasn't the right shape for a modern key, either. Thomas was stumped. Glancing at his watch, he realized that he'd been away from Paige for far too long. Collecting the blue box in his arms, he hurried from the bank, Aaren in tow, and they made their way back to the hospital. Sitting on the T during the return trip, the mystery began to nag at him.

Thomas turned to Aaren, "What's in this box... what's with the strange key... and why didn't Paige ever mention this before? Clearly, this is pretty important to her - after all, she's close to dying. If anything, she should have mentioned it to you... but she didn't. I wonder why?"

"I have no idea," Aaren said, shaking her head in dumbfounded disbelief. They rode the remainder of the trip back to the hospital in stunned silence.

****

When Thomas and Aaren returned with the blue box from the bank, Paige was awake, wheezing and coughing as the nurse caught her bloody sputum in a plastic dish. Paige had never been a good patient, and as she grew weaker, that stubbornness became more intense. It was something she didn't see a need to change, for as she had often reminded Thomas, "tenacity is an excellent quality - it gives you the energy to reach goals most people only fantasize about".

Paige saw Thomas come into the room, cradling the blue box in his hands. She waved the nurse away with a grunt and motioned for Thomas to come nearer. The nurse tried to make some sort of protest, but Paige was no longer paying attention, and the nurse, recognizing defeat, took her small victory of no new blood stains on the pillow with her as she retreated back to her other patients.

"You found it!" Paige was excited; but any stranger walking by would have heard her voice and might have thought she was in pain.

"Yes, Paige; but it's locked. We couldn't find a key to match the lock. Shall I break it open for you?"

"No..." Feebly, Paige removed her ring; and that's when Thomas noticed it. The shape of the blue opal stone in her ring was exactly the same size and shape of the indentation for the keyhole on the blue box. She had carried the key to her secrets in plain view every day of her life, and he'd never suspected, nor had anyone else. Aaren stood by, mouth agape. Paige handed him the ring and fell back against the pillows, defeated. "You must find her... her brother... Logan." Paige wheezed out the command as her head hit the pillow and her eyes fell shut.

"Paige, whose brother? Who's Logan?" Thomas looked to Aaren for help, but her eyes held no answers.

"Emily", Paige said with the sternest whisper she could evoke. "Five years before we met, I had Logan. It was a bad time for us... I let him go... gave him away. It was a mistake. But you must find him. Repair the damage I've done."

"Logan?" asked Aaren in a whisper barely heard. "You mean... Edward?"

"How do I find him? Where do I look?" Thomas and Aaren were stunned by Paige's deathbed confession.

"Sanctuary... in Washington DC... The blue box - find him, Thomas. Make peace. Make it right. Please!" The energy drained from her then, almost as if in an old silent film. Paige always had a flair for the dramatic, but this time, Thomas knew she wasn't acting. Alarms sounded from the many computer components surrounding her bed. Doctors and nurses swooped in on her like vultures over carrion. After a few minutes of fury, a doctor joined Thomas, Aaren and Nathan in the hallway and spoke in a hushed voice.

"Ms. Lambert's blood pressure has spiked again. The blood filling her abdomen is not subsiding, and we can't find the source. She is far too weak for surgery. We've given her another round of antibiotics, diuretics and blood pressure medications; but I'm not sure what more we can do for her until her system strengthens; and quite frankly, I'm not sure if that will happen." He looked between the three friends, gravely. "You should say your goodbyes now."

Of course, the doctor was right. The complications from the pregnancy and delivery had raped her, and Thomas knew there may not be much time left. Sleep overtook her then. Thomas gently squeezed her hand and kissed her on the forehead. "Just rest now, Paige. I'll be back in a little while. I love you." Normally, he wouldn't have said those words to Paige... he didn't really feel it... but the thought of her dying without hearing those words from—somebody—made him cringe. He backed out of the room, hoping against all hope that this wouldn't be the last time he saw her. She'd become a friend, and she was Emily's mother, after all. He didn't want to see her leave before...

Protecting the blue box as if it held the secrets to the greatest mystery of all time, Thomas made his way silently through the hospital hallways, replaying her words in his head.

Paige had a son. It was almost more than he could comprehend. It was late, nearly eleven. He was exhausted, and needed a quiet place and a little bit of sleep to process through everything; but he couldn't leave her, not like this.

"You look horrible," said Aaren. "Why don't you go home and get some rest. Nathan and I will stay here with her." Nathan nodded his agreement.

"Home... sleep... I can't... what about Logan..." Thomas was nearly babbling.

"Look, buddy, you've been through a lot," said Nathan. "You're no good to anyone here - especially Paige. Why don't you go home and get some rest. We can deal with the Blue Box Mystery in the morning."

Aaren gave Thomas a warm hug, and Nathan clapped him on the back. "Go home, Thom, we've got this," Nathan said.

Thomas stumbled back to Paige's brownstone, closing the door behind him. He scanned the foyer, the stairway to his right, the living room to his left, and the kitchen directly ahead. The house he had spent the past few days in seemed suddenly distant and strange. He wondered what other secrets had been hiding in the woodwork all these years. He walked into the living room and set the box on the coffee table. He settled himself on the couch, exhausted, and was soon fast asleep. Four hours later, his cell phone vibrated at his hip, jarring him from his deep sleep, it was Aaren.

"Hi, it's me. Paige isn't doing well, you should come down and see her soon. The doctors don't know how much longer..." Aaren's words trailed off into silent tears as he hung up the phone and made his way to the door. He put his back against the wall and braced... *Just like Gillian, all over again...* He could not escape the thought that his history was replaying itself, but with an opposite outcome. *"I lost my daughter and sacrificed my love for the woman who filled my world... I can't sacrifice my daughter again. I must be strong for her..."*

On the way into the hospital, he stopped by the NICU to check in on Emily. She was tiny, and frail, pink and perfect. She would need a couple of weeks to gain her strength, but the doctors had reassured him that she would live and thrive, just as he had hoped. "I'll be back to see her again later today," he told the nurse; and backed his way out of the unit, praying she would still be there when he returned.

****

Thomas spent the majority of the day at Paige's bedside, hoping that she would return to consciousness and tell him more about Logan, and what she wanted him to do next. But her condition was weakening, and although she stirred slightly, she did not wake up. He checked in with the doctors again, before leaving at about eight o'clock, but they had no new updates for him. "Only time will tell," was all they could say. Thomas hoped there would be enough time for Emily to meet her mother before...

He left the hospital to get some sleep, stopping in at the NICU on his way out. Emily was still doing well, the nurses said, and they encouraged him to go home, eat something, and get some rest. He listened to their advice. As he arrived back at the brownstone, and dropped the mail in the basket by the stairs, his phone rang.

"Hi, Aaren," answered Thomas.

"I'm almost at the hospital to visit Paige. I wanted to call and make sure you and Emily were all right before it got too late."

"That was kind of you, thanks. Emily is fine, resting comfortably and breathing without problem; they were able to take her off the ventilator this morning. The nurse told me that she had a good appetite tonight, too. They told me there wasn't really anything else I could do there, and basically, they sent me home. So, I'm at the brownstone now. I'll go back again first thing in the morning."

"What's wrong?" Aaren asked. "There's something strange in your voice."

"Nothing... I just started going through the Blue Box a little this morning, and discovered some interesting information... but there are a few things I need to figure out. Would you be willing to lend a hand? I could really use another set of eyes on this one."

"Of course. I'd be happy to help. When?" Aaren's voice was supportive and strong. He had never seen her falter. He wondered if she ever did.

"I'm exhausted; can we make it mid-morning tomorrow? I'll go to the hospital early to check on Paige and Emily, and then meet you back here. I'll order in brunch. I really need some sleep tonight." Thomas let go a yawn that sounded like it came from a small dinosaur rather than a human being.

"All right, what time?"

"Ten-thirty would be great. That should give me enough time to get the update from the doctors. I just don't think I can handle going into the office just yet. Do you think you can take the day off?" Thomas wasn't sure what he had in the box, but he was certain it would take more than an hour or two to figure out. That's usually the way secrets worked - especially deathbed secrets.

"Not a problem. Paige has got me on a tether, at least as far as MouseTrax is concerned. I won't be missed. I'm at the hospital now. I'll spend a little time with Paige tonight and I'll see you in the morning."

"That sounds good. Thanks, Aaren." They hung up and the silence of Paige's empty brownstone once again enveloped him.

Thomas was grateful for Aaren. Through all of Paige's manic episodes, she had been a source of stability; she was completely trusting of them both, and more than loyal to Paige. He knew that no matter what they discovered, he could count on Aaren to maintain her loyalty to Paige, without blurting rumors to nosy co-workers, no matter how tantalizing the story might be. *She would have made a lousy reporter.* He mused to himself. She always gave him whatever time and help he needed. Since the day they had met, she had been genuinely kind to him. *Kindness. As a stranger in a strange land, it's a rare luxury in my world.*

Thomas left the mystery box in the living room and went to the kitchen to find the take out menu from the corner deli. Pulling it from behind the refrigerator magnet, he dialed his cell phone and placed their order for morning brunch. "Hi; Yes, I'd like two orders of your Challah French Toast and two orders of the Sunrise Special, over easy, with bacon and sausage; can you also add a pot of coffee and a carafe of orange juice, please? Um, delivery, please. The address is 346 Beacon Street. Ten-thirty tomorrow morning? Thank you."

After giving the man at the deli his credit card number and making sure they had the right cross streets, Thomas stood staring out the kitchen window, his mind drifting to islands that had never existed before. He tried to imagine what could have possibly gone wrong in her life that would have prompted Paige to give up her son. And, what's more, give him up to strangers. What kind of a man wouldn't want to be a part of his child's life? It was a senseless crime to him - abandoning a child. And now, Paige had done it twice. *How does she live with herself?* His brain was fuzzy; he couldn't think clearly anymore tonight. He needed sleep. *Perhaps it'll make more sense in the morning.* But deep inside, he knew it wouldn't.

****

Thomas spent the night tossing and turning in the same bed he'd slept well in many nights before, his head was still reeling with the infinite questions he now had the opportunity to explore. As he sat up in bed, trying to get his bearings, the doorbell rang. He quickly glanced at the clock - it was ten-thirty on the dot. *How does she do that?* He pulled on his slippers and made his way down the stairs. When he opened the door, he found Aaren thanking the deli delivery boy, and taking the food from his arms into hers.

"Aaren, let me help you with that." They made their way toward the kitchen, brown paper bags of Mother's Best aromas nested in their arms.

"Thanks. How'd you sleep?"

"Not great. But clearly, I overslept... didn't make it to the hospital this morning. How was Paige last night?" asked Thomas.

"No real change. She was asleep the entire hour and a half I was there. The doctors told me that they hadn't seen any improvement since you'd left. I tried to sneak a peek at Emily, but they wouldn't let me. Nathan took the night shift."

"I feel bad about not making it in this morning. I was so tired last night. I'll call in a little while and check in. They tell me there's not much I can do there right now, anyway." said Thomas. "I knew they wouldn't let you in to see Emily. You've got to know the secret password to see the princess." said Thomas, flaunting the pink plastic band dangling from his wrist with a grin.

Aaren emptied the contents of the bags on the kitchen table; Thomas retrieved plates, coffee mugs, glasses, silverware and napkins. When their plates had been filled and emptied, the Styrofoam and paper discarded to the trash, Aaren asked; "So what's the deal with the blue box Paige gave you? You said you needed my help with something?"

"I looked through the box a little bit last night, and I've discovered that this is a mystery of far greater proportions... the mystery... of Paige's past." Paige's dramatic flair had not been lost on her progeny.

"Paige's past; Thomas, what are you talking about? I've known Paige since pretty much forever. I've been working with her for twenty-five years, and Emily is the only child I've ever known about. Now, in just a few short hours, we've found out that she had a son, and gave it away... what could be more mysterious than that?"

"Well, Paige told us that his name is Logan, right; and that she gave him away five years ago. She told us to contact *Small Hearts Sanctuary* in DC. Then she told me to get the rest from the box. Then she passed out. It's weird. I feel like I'm caught in an episode of *The Twilight Zone* or something."

"Um... Okay... so, where's the box and what's in it?" Aaren's curiosity had begun to swell.

"Oh, it's in the living room. I don't know exactly what's in it, lots of envelopes, stacks of paper, stuff like that. I was so exhausted last night; I didn't really go through it piece by piece. But there's a manila file folder with a wax seal that I didn't have the nerve to open. It looks like secret spy information or something. I thought I'd wait for you to get here, I need a second set of eyes and a level head to help me through this; my brain hasn't been functioning rationally lately; and with my creative mind... I thought it would be a good idea to have someone a little more logical on hand when I really went through it all."

"What are we waiting for, then?" Aaren looked as if she were twelve years old on the morning of her birthday. Since the days of Girl Scout treasure hunts, mysterious boxes had always held a fascination for her.

Thomas cleared the dishes to the sink and picked up the tray with the coffee cups and pot, Aaren grabbed the juice carafe and glasses, and they walked together down the long hallway back to the living room. They paused at the threshold, both gazing tentatively at the mysterious blue box with the white satin bow, sitting in the very center of the table; exactly where Thomas had left it. Thomas was the first to step forward, and Aaren followed silently behind. He moved to the leather chair and sat down. Aaren took her place on the sofa across from him. They both put what they were carrying gingerly on the side tables next to them. The blue box sat between them, as if it were some great ancient archeological find, hiding the secrets of Paige's past and Emily's future.

Pulling the box closer to him, Thomas retrieved the ring from his pocket and held it up to Aaren. "She told me to keep the key."

"Oh my gosh. I still can't get over this. It's the ring I've seen her wear my whole life. I don't think I've ever seen her without it. She got it sometime in ninth grade, she told me. It never occurred to me that it held secrets." Aaren's eyes were so dilated, any passing police officer might have insisted on a urine test to prove her sobriety.

Holding his breath, he inserted the ring into the lock and with a gentle push, the clasp clicked open. He lifted the lid as though he were a technician with the bomb squad... slow and deliberate... carefully, almost painfully slowly. He truly felt like this just might blow up in his face. *Paige, what have you done?*

From inside the box, Thomas lifted out the contents cautiously and deliberately, as if avoiding a trip-wire. He placed each item on the table in front of him: a large manila file folder, stuffed with papers and sealed with wax; a collection of micro-cassettes tied with a blue satin ribbon; half a dozen photos of a sailboat; and a wallet-sized photo of a blonde-haired infant. On the back of the photo, written in near-fading blue ink were the words *Logan Alexander; July 2, 2007.*

Thomas stared at the contents of the blue box arranged on the table in front of him. Paige clearly wanted him to use these things to find Logan, so he needed to really look at everything clearly, detach his emotions for a minute, use his reporter training and instincts, and figure out where to begin. *Impossible.* He scanned through the stack of cassettes. Each was labeled with a date range beginning in 1990 to just a couple of weeks ago. They were preserved in tiny little plastic cases, bound up in stacks of four. The large manila folder held a report of some sort, with the insignia of "Action Private Investigators" stamped on the cover.

Aaren lifted the stack of cassettes from the table. She pulled out a micro-recorder from her purse and began to insert the first cassette. Thomas gave her a strange look. "Paige and I both have one of these, we carry it everywhere, and we have since high school. We use it to take notes in meetings, record stupid people making stupid comments at inopportune times... but most often, we use it to send messages to each other. Paige hated to write letters. She always complained that her handwriting was illegible... but she wanted to keep in touch. So, when Paige went off to Georgetown, she sent me one." Aaren held the recorder in her hands as if it were a secret decoder ring with a history of solving mysteries. "For years, this is how we've kept in touch. She always said that she felt comforted by hearing my voice. She said it made her feel safer to know that our papers couldn't get into the wrong hands. When I asked her about Watergate, she just laughed and said we'd never be that important. We've been doing it ever since."

She leaves a tape on my desk, and a day later, she gets one back from me. But I've never seen these." Aaren clicked the recorder shut, and pressed play. The message that came out was Paige's younger voice, but it was definitely her.

July 5th; It's done. I'm sure it's for the best. Still, I'm very sad. Thank God for Logan.

Aaren clicked off the recorder and looked at Thomas. They were both stunned by what they heard. Thomas got up to warm his coffee as Aaren flipped through the pages of the PI's dossier. A shabby envelope fell loose and fluttered to the table. She opened it and discovered a yellowed newspaper clipping about a train crash in Montana from 2005 and a small, hand-written note.

"Thomas, listen to this...
'April 22, 2005: Metal exploded all around them. Glass shattered and the shards impaled the unaware, smearing the afternoon sun with the devastating splotches of torrential loss. The screams of an implausible collection of souls erupted from those sitting in front and behind... not one sounded the same. Not one cried out the same words or prayed the same scripture. It was the most fear she had ever experienced. It was the most painful moment she had ever endured ... and it became clear to her in that instant... she would not survive. She held her daughter as closely as possible, cushioning her head from the oncoming blow, trying to remain calm, adding soft tones to her voice so as not to scare the small child even more. "Please God, just make it end quickly", was all she could manage her voice to whisper. As she kissed her limp daughter for the last time, she watched the jagged cliff outside the window collide with the two cars in front of her, then fly past her tear-filled eyes with storm-fury. Water began to flood the compartment.

" *'And then... the searing pain and perfect dark.'*" Thomas recited with her in unison.

Thomas dropped into the chair in the corner of the room, feeling six years old. *Sad, Confused, Angry, Betrayed, Played... and a host of other emotions that simply defied description.* He stared at the box and its contents on the coffee table for a long moment. Then he got up to pour himself a stiff drink. *If there was ever a moment that called for scotch, this would be it.*

"Ah... Isn't it a bit early for that, Thomas?" Aaren said with a bit of a tremble in her voice.

He didn't reply, but only poured a second glass, adding; "Here, I think you're going to need this;" and sat back down, taking a long sip.

Aaren gave him a confused look and set her glass on the table. "What's this all about?"

"She knew. All along she knew, and she never said a word. I wondered why out of all the resumes she got, she picked the washed-up reporter from Detroit. That's why I got the interview, the job, her bed... but why? Why me?" Thomas' questions emptied into his next drink.

"Uh, a little help here, please?" said Aaren, more confused than she could ever remember being in her whole life.

"That train wreck - it's me. I mean, I wrote that. It's a piece I wrote just after burying my five-year-old daughter... Eryn... the daughter I lost in that train wreck."

"What?!" Aaren picked up her glass and swallowed hard.

Thomas began to pace the room with Paige's signature cross. Aaren just stared into the carpet, her reality black and blue from the beating it had just received. On his fifth north-south trek, his phone rang. The caller ID told him it was the hospital.

"Ahm... Yes, this is Thomas Laird... Yes, I see. Of course, I'll be right there."

Aaren worked hard to bring herself back to consciousness, but failed miserably at the attempt. "What is it?"

"Paige. I have to go," he said, gulping down coffee.

"I'll go with you."

The pair collected their coats and headed out into the tepid spring morning. Dew played on the lawn and etched outlines on the rooftops of the neighborhood. Summer was arriving early this year. A foreboding feeling hung inside Thomas, and not just because he knew Paige was dying; but also because of all he still had to face. His history would sleep no longer.

Chapter Nineteen

"For me, I always wonder what's worse: an emotional betrayal or a physical betrayal?
That's a really tough call."
~Halarie Burton

"Paige... Why didn't you tell me?" Thomas was lost in a sea of confusion, waves of regret, love and a distant understanding crashed into him in alternating currents. He asked the question, but wasn't sure he'd ever get an answer that made any sense. Too many of the dots didn't connect. Too many of the pieces didn't fit together. There was still so much to know, and the blue box, he was sure, held the answers she would never have the time to offer.

"Thomas... this is my last chance." Paige's breathing was labored. She had more difficulty birthing her words now than she did bringing Emily into the world just two short days ago. She inhaled deeply, struggling to stay present. "Please fix our family...your family... promise me..." She reached for Thomas' hand in one last, desperate plea to help her to see the world as she knew it was meant to be.

"Of course, Paige. I promise." Thomas was revisiting every emotional drain that had come the day they buried Eryn in Kremmling. Living it twice... it was almost more than he could bear.

Paige reached out a limp and shaking hand to Aaren. "Help him, Aaren." Aaren took Paige's other hand, standing as a silent sentinel to all they had shared since childhood. She had vowed to protect what she knew and now she was faced with the task of fracturing her long-held loyalty. "You have all the secrets, all the access... help him make it right, please." Paige squeezed Aaren's hand, her eyes closed against the disappointment that she feared lived in her friend's eyes.

"Paige, I love you as my sister... of course... I will do all I can to help Thomas and Emily... and Logan. Don't be afraid... don't worry. I'll take care of everything."

Paige opened her eyes to allow the tears of years of regret and remorse to flood over her cheeks. Aaren wiped them away with a delicate, loving hand. "Thank you..." Paige could only whisper. She was so near the edge, and she felt she could leave now. She looked back at her friends, one last time; and closed her eyes, remembering Logan's tiny smile. "Emily... is she... beautiful?"

"Just like her mother." Thomas placed a kiss on her quivering lips; and in a last, contented sigh, Paige was gone.

There was an easy calm on Paige's face now. As a final breath left her soul, a small smile parted her lips. After decades of chasing shadows, dealing with devils, and gambling on fate, she had finally found peace. Thomas and Aaren looked at each other, sharing a moment neither would ever verbalize. They felt as children, newly connected in a bond of friendship and a revised history that would stay with them forever. Aaren would become the aunt Emily and Logan would have known in Paige. It would be his last gift to Paige's memory, and the best way he knew to honor Aaren's devotion.

As the machines surrounding them whistled and beeped in a cacophony of insanity, Thomas noted the time, 1:04pm, and gently slid the white sheet over Paige's face. He would let her go now, cocooning a new warmth in his heart as the pool of his family enlarged. It flowed from Paige to the new daughter they'd created together and toward the son he would soon discover.

Thomas was met in the doorway by a nurse holding a clipboard with Paige's DNR. He initialed it, noted the time, and walked toward the door, a silent sentinel to the pain of her heart.

Chapter Twenty

"The story of life is quicker than the blink of an eye, the story of love is hello, goodbye."
~Jimi Hendrix

It was the second day of visitation, and Thomas was thankful that he had been able to keep the casket closed. *At least Paige is able to maintain some dignity through this circus.* The private funeral was set for tomorrow afternoon, and the mourners were still streaming in as if Paige had been some dignitary of legendary prestige. Sure, MouseTrax had a wide global reach, but Thomas hadn't expected all this. Complete strangers with various accents kept offering limp handshakes, expressing their deep sympathies and their hopes for continued success for MouseTrax. Face after face, they all quoted the same, well-rehearsed, empty lines. Not one asked about her family or friends. Their only interest was in the success or failure of the company. Thomas was so exhausted that he simply didn't believe their profusion of concern anymore.

Seeing his frustration, Aaren appeared at his elbow and led him out to the funeral home's patio, past Nathan's ever watchful eye, for a bit of fresh air. The early summer winds blew fresh and crisp. It was a nice change from the stuffiness inside. Through all the madness of the past year, Aaren and Nathan had been the only constants that Paige had allowed, the only people she'd kept on when all her other servants and underlings were either relocated or dismissed and replaced. Paige and Aaren had a long history - back to their childhood - and even though Paige rarely showed it, she was fiercely loyal. Thomas wasn't sure what Nathan's connection was to Paige, but he knew that it had to have run much deeper than an employment agreement. It was only with the birth of Emily and the surprise of Logan that Thomas finally understood what it was that they had shared to make Paige keep them so close. It was a secret greater than any held by James Bond or J. Edgar Hoover; and now it was his.

"How are you holding up?" Aaren's words were gentle and kind. Besides Nathan, she was the only one knew the truth of what the past year had brought into his life. But unlike Nathan, she understood the emotionality of it in a way that he found difficult to describe. She understood that his life would now change irrevocably. She was happy for him and she worried for him. She truly believed him to be a good man, and deserving of such a precious gift; and the chance to begin again. She only hoped that she could help in some small way. *It's what Paige wanted*, and Aaren was determined not to let her down.

"Paige would have hated this... all this fuss over her. I know she would have preferred a quiet, understated ceremony, but when MouseTrax gets involved... nothing is understated. And there's only so much a marketing mouthpiece can do once the Board of Directors gets stirred into the mix. I've got so much to do still... so much to do... I'm worried." Thomas knew how important it was, now that he knew, to find Logan... protect Emily. His confidence was failing, daily.

"It's okay, you'll get through this. You'll figure it out, and when you do, things will be better, you'll see." Aaren's voice was calming and warm.

"Always the eternal optimist. I wish I had your faith. Thanks." Thomas kissed Aaren tenderly on the cheek. His emotionality had been drained to its core these past few weeks, and thankfully, Aaren understood. She and Nathan were the only ones who even made the effort. She had kept their secret, and he was grateful that she would continue to keep his confidence, long after he and Emily were gone.

With absolutely no remorse, one of the stuffed suits from the Board interrupted them, insisting that Thomas return. "You really should come back inside, Mr. Laird. There are many of Ms. Lambert's colleagues in there who want to pay their respects, and it doesn't look good for you to be out here, with her... assistant..." He spit the words with a contemptable sneer that Thomas didn't appreciate. "...and ignoring them. Our first priority is damage control, it is your primary function, after all; and how can we do that when you're out here?"

If there had been something heavy or sharp nearby to throw at the village idiot in that moment, Thomas would have done it without a second thought or a moment of regret. Instead, he took Aaren's hand, kissed it, shot a death-ray look at the suit. He walked back inside to deal as best he could with the throng of repulsive megalomaniacs. A scant few were genuine in their sympathies, but most simply wanted to know what was going to happen to the company now that its CEO was gone. Thomas repeatedly tried to assure them that after things had settled down a bit, a decision would be made. Unfortunately, that explanation wasn't good enough for some. Nathan was standing on the edge of the throng, calm and nearly invisible, as always. Aaren joined him, avoiding the zip line of inconsiderateness. "Watch it," he said to Aaren in a hushed voice, taking her elbow to move her away from the doorway. "He's going to blow."

"But what about our research... What about the nano project we've just started... We really need to get that new marketing plan in place... In this economy we can't afford to drag our feet on this..." The khaki clad engineer was nearly whining and waving his arms in a rabid display, embarrassing both himself and the company to the crowd of onlookers.

Thomas was infuriated. He exploded. "Listen people, my friend, a brilliant business woman, and the woman who for years, signed your paychecks, has just died. I know it's a stretch for you, but can we please show a little compassion?"

Those standing around him skulked back into the shadows, dispersing like deviant prison inmates in the presence of a sadistic warden. On his way out of the room, Thomas passed the funeral director and addressed him in a voice strong enough to resonate through the entire building.

"Will you please deal with my friend's mourners and their stupid insensitivity? I'm sure you have much more experience with brain-dead individuals than I do."

****

It was exactly two weeks after the funeral. Mother's Day would be in just a few days, and Thomas couldn't help but think what a cruel trick it was that Paige had died before truly enjoying the holiday. Doubly cruel, in fact, knowing that twice now, she had missed that special brand of joy. Thomas wished there had been a way to make it right. And now, the only way left to him was to find Logan and reunite with Gillian. Although he still wasn't quite sure how that was going to happen.

The T ride to the lawyer's office was hellatious. The trains were extremely full, and the crowds seemed less friendly than they had been the past year. Thomas felt disconnected and foreign; it was the first time in a long time that he felt, once again, like a displaced Detroiter amongst a throng of wicked-strange Bostonians. This is how he'd felt that first month in town, until his encounter with Nathan. He was glad that Emily was in the safe care of Aaren for this most difficult meeting. He'd never enjoyed lawyers, and the reading of a will is especially abusive. *There always seems to be at least one person in the room that argues over everything. I hope this will be a quick meeting.* He took the elevator to the third floor, and entered the suite.

"Thank you all for coming." This particular stuffed legal suit was one that Thomas didn't recognize. That fact alone wasn't surprising. After all the people Paige had fired and new staff she'd brought on to replace them over the past year, a new lawyer would just be one more security change. Thomas suspected that nothing emotional was tied to the decision to retain him. More likely, he had a good reputation for handling classified materials and secretive activities.

Some of the people in the room, Thomas knew, some he didn't. Of those names he could recall there was the vice president of Research, John Slotnick; and Stephen Nordgren, the vice president of Development. Nathan Hackthorn was there, Thomas knew, for stupidity control. The Board brass feared Nathan, and none would cross him. Tina Franek, Aaren's Secretary was standing in for Aaren.

"My name is Mr. McClish and I represent Ms. Lambert in her final affairs. She left behind some brief instructions, with the majority of her assets held in several trusts. My intent today is to explain those trusts and validate that those of you named can gain access to them."

There was a heavy fog of distrust and intrigue as the men in the room looked around at each other, wondering what would come next. Paige had always been unpredictable, but more so in her business dealings than anywhere else. In the time that he'd known her, Thomas learned that Paige believed the surprise attack, the air of mystery, and the unreliable touchstone, would forever give her the upper hand. Thomas knew that she would not abandon these elements, even in death.

"Let's start with you, Mr. Slotnick and Mr. Nordgren. As representatives of MouseTrax, members of the Board of Directors, and responsible as you are for the company's future, Ms. Lambert wanted to be certain that you had plenty of funding to keep the company successful and financially solvent. Ms. Lambert has established a trust which is fed by a high-yield, low-risk investment account, to be certain that you will continue to have the funding you need to maintain the success of the company. This trust and its investment account are managed by an outside investment firm. You will have access to the funds when they are needed to propel the company forward; but you will not have control over the investment account and how the funds are acquired through those accounts. There must be a three-quarter majority vote on any future decisions regarding any facet of the operations of MouseTrax by the Board of Directors. Suffice to say that the experts in finance will do their jobs, and you will do yours. In this way, Ms. Lambert projects that profitability will follow MouseTrax during your tenure, and well beyond." McClish handed each of them a manila envelope. "The details regarding the trust and the investment firm are conveyed to you in these packets. Please take the time necessary to consider them carefully. Confer with the company's general counsel if you have questions."

The executives weren't sure if they wanted to be pleased or frustrated as they accepted the envelopes from Mr. McClish. They seemed happy to have the funding security... but Thomas knew that they were not so pleased about the fact that they had little control. *Nicely done, Paige.* He knew that she would be giggling from her place in heaven; she loved to watch them squirm.

"Ms. Franek, I understand that you are here on behalf of Ms. Graner, is that correct?"

"Yes, Mr. McClish. She was not able to be here today, and has asked me to act in her stead." Tina's voice quivered a little. She was nervous. She was fairly young, just twenty-two, and still an intern at MouseTrax while she finished her degree at Boston College.

Mr. McClich handed her an envelope. "Ms. Graner has been left a sizable trust as affirmation to her years of loyalty and devotion. Please take this packet to her and instruct her to contact me, my card is inside, should she have any questions." Tina accepted the envelope gingerly, as if it held special secrets Tina would never be privileged enough to understand. "Furthermore, Ms. Lambert has provided a scholarship entrusted to you, for the purpose of completing your educational program to the level of Master's Degree. Ms. Graner is named as executor of that trust; and you should discuss your future educational plans with her." Tina was dumfounded.

"Thank you, Mr. McClish." Tears welled in her eyes. Tina was not expecting to be named in today's proceedings, and Thomas knew that her gratitude would not be expressed today. She had just been given a gift, the impact of which she could not comprehend. She simply had no words.

"Nathan Hackthorn, Ms. Lambert was extremely grateful for your years of devotion and dedication to her family and your discretion with her private matters. She has left her South Hampton estate to you, along with a sizable trust for its maintenance." Nathan was stunned into uncharacteristic silence as Mr. McClish handed him a manila packet and a set of keys.

"Thank you, Mr. McClish," was his only response, as he gave Thomas a look that betrayed his external bravado.

"As for you, Mr. Laird; Ms. Lambert has entrusted you to act as legal guardian for baby Emily. She has established a trust that will provide for Emily throughout her years, as well as for eight years of college, should Emily one day decide to pursue higher education. As well, Ms. Lambert's sailboat, *Wing On Wing*, has been left in trust to you, to be passed along to Emily when she reaches the age of maturity. It is currently in dry dock storage in a marina in Manassas; and it will remain there until you are ready to take custody of it." McClish handed Thomas an envelope similar to those he'd given the executives.

Slotnick and Nordgren looked at Thomas with all the contempt of a pride of lions who had just had their fresh Wildebeest carcass stolen by a single hyena. Clearly, they were unhappy. Thomas, feeling their anger begin to strangle them through their Windsor knotted ties, leaned over and said, "Guys, be happy you weren't saddled with the kid." The stuffed suits quickly deflated and deviant grins began to form on their lips. They looked at each other, eyes sparkling, sharing their new-found victory. Nathan winked at Thomas, knowing the truth.

"Well gentlemen, that seems to be all there is. Mr. Slotnick, Mr. Nordgren; additional papers will be sent to the MouseTrax resources department for your signature in the morning, along with extensive instructions for Ms. Lambert's future vision for MouseTrax and her suggested plan of action to take the company into the next decade. You and the Board of Directors are, of course, free to follow her suggestions or not. The company is now yours. I wish you every success." The two suits shook hands with Mr. McClish.

As they moved toward the door, Nathan called out, "You've been given a great gift. Don't screw it up, boys; I'll be keeping an eye on you!" Their elation quickly turned to trepidation. When Nathan watched, he saw things few others noticed; and one never knew if he would report or keep his own counsel until the information served him. The suits left the room, shoulders hunched and a look of mild dread on their faces. Tina followed modestly behind them, a smile of awe on her lips.

Nathan hung back, still watching. Thomas reached out his hand to thank Mr. McClish for his services when he was stopped in his tracks. "Mr. Laird; Ms. Lambert left additional instructions and bequeaths for you." Thomas shot a dubious look at Nathan, who shrugged his shoulders. "There is a second trust, established in the name of Logan Alexander Edwards. You are named as the guardian and executor of this trust; and you may use these funds to aid your search in finding young Logan; as well as providing for his future in whatever way you deem necessary and appropriate from this day forward." Mr. McClish handed Thomas another manila envelope with his business card attached to its inside flap. "If you should decide to formally adopt young Logan, please contact me, and I will assist with the final details."

"Thank you, Mr. McClish. I appreciate all you have done to ease us all through this process. Paige had a good friend in you." Thomas reached out to shake Mr. McClish's hand. Mr. McClish took Thomas' hand briefly, then let it go.

"Do not misunderstand, Mr. Laird. Ms. Lambert has compensated me fairly, and her lifetime retainer extends to you. Contact me if you ever have a need." He clicked his briefcase shut, punctuating his remark sharply, and left the room.

Thomas and Nathan were left alone. "Well, that was interesting." said Thomas.

"Let's go get a drink; you look like you could use one," said Nathan.

Chapter Twenty-One

"Love is but the discovery of ourselves in others, and the delight in the recognition."
~Alexander Smith

    It was ten o'clock when Thomas finally fed Emily and put her to sleep. He kissed her gently on her forehead and picked up the baby monitor as he walked out of the room, quietly closing the door behind him. Home only two weeks, still very tiny, and not yet cleared for "normal" infant life. Thomas watched over her closely, making sure she was healthy, happy and always out of danger. He headed downstairs in a sort of fog. It had been nearly a month since the craziness began. The move from the Hamptons, the scary delivery, Emily's birth, Paige's death, the reading of the will... it all happened so fast. It was difficult for him to wrap his brain around it.

    Now that things were slowly gravitating back to normal, Thomas was ready to take another look at Paige's blue box. He was having a hard time understanding why this secret box had been so carefully guarded for so long. Paige wasn't a person who usually held on to trifles. Those knickknacks, statuettes and spoon collections—the things that accumulated in the curio cabinets of his friend's houses back in Detroit did not live here. She was a pragmatic woman, keeping only those things which held great worth, or overwhelming sentimental value; and in most cases, the things she held on to had both. Most of all, Paige was a woman who hated to dust. Keeping a collection of statues and spoons did not enthrall her the way it once did his grandmother. In fact, during their stay together in the house at the Hamptons, he once asked about her sparse decorating style. She told him, "The memories one builds throughout their lifetime are far more important than the things one collects." It was a strange contradiction coming from a woman who seemed to have it all.

He hadn't picked up the contents of the blue box since the day it had made its appearance. With Paige's last hours, he was far too worried about the present to worry about the past. But tonight, he thought it was finally time. *There is another child out there somewhere who needs a family - our family - and I have to find him.*

Thomas went to the kitchen, poured himself a cup of coffee, and sat down at the table to go through the details of the blue box. He pulled out the cassette tapes, one by one, until he'd heard her whole life story from the beginning. Paige's words came across strong and vibrant. It was simultaneously difficult and comforting, but he had to do it. This was the only way he was ever going to find Logan. When he'd listen to each tape once through, he pulled out the Private Investigator's dossier, and began to read.

"Dear Ms. Lambert,
I have followed through on the project you have given me, and hired a private investigator with a notable reputation. He has spent many hours, days and weeks investigating your past, and has provided the enclosed dossier with photographs and official documents. I have read through all of the information contained within, and I believe that you will find it quite helpful in discovering the secrets you wish to uncover. As always, please let me know if you have any further requirements of my services.
Sincerely,
Nathan Hackthorn.

Thomas was stunned to see that Nathan's name had been attached to the mystery of the blue box. He'd never said anything or indicated any knowledge of its existence during the days since Thomas had shared its contents with Aaren *and* Nathan. The consummate poker face, Nathan never gave any hint of his involvement. *He's got a lot of explaining to do.* Thomas dialed Nathan's phone number.

"Nathan, hey, it's Thomas. Look, we've got to talk about this blue box Paige left behind..." Thomas thought he'd have more to say, but Nathan interjected before he could find the words, deflating his frustration.

"Yeah, I figured that was coming." Nathan said in a resolute monotone. "I'm on my way over."

Nathan appeared at the door to the brownstone about twenty minutes later. Aaren arrived just a few minutes before; Thomas called her for emotional support, just in case things got... difficult. They all sat in the living room, a heady silence hanging over them. Finally, Thomas confronted Nathan. "What's the deal, Nate? Why didn't you say anything?"

"Look, Paige told me not to come forward until I was called. She knew that once you got your hands on the blue box that you'd need someone to walk you through everything... but she also knew that you needed to do it on your own time. She knew I would be here when it was time. She never intended on using me in this way - to help you get through the story, she had always envisioned doing it herself - but she was a planner - and she knew a backup plan was essential to her success." Nathan looked to Aaren. "Remember her quip, 'Just in case I ever get hit by a bus'?"

Aaren laughed. "Yeah, that was one of her favorite morose jokes; it came from her mother, I think."

"Well, it wasn't just humor to her;" said Nathan. "It was serious business. She had a backup plan for everything."

"She never said anything to me about all of this... why did she confide in you and not me? I thought we shared everything!" Aaren was simultaneously frustrated and hurt. She reached for a tissue to stave the flood she feared would come next.

"She trusted your loyalty and your friendship, Aaren. She valued it more than anything in this world. But I suspect that if she shared this secret with you, you would have forced her to look at things that she wasn't prepared to deal with. Learning all she did... making the choices she did... keeping it close to her until she knew how she was ready to make things different... that was hard for her. She had to move at her own pace, do it in her own time, and for her own reasons. She loved you, Aaren, but she didn't want to make a decision simply based on seeking your approval. Your opinion always meant a lot to her, and she never wanted to let you down.

Me, I was easier, I was a paid employee - a friend, yes - but an employee first. She didn't need my approval; just my promise of loyalty and secrecy, and she paid me well for it. There was no emotional risk involved in having me learn the secrets of her past." Thomas and Aaren held silent, blank stares. "Let me tell you the whole story, and then maybe you'll understand." Nathan picked up the PI dossier from the table and began to explain; Thomas and Aaren hung on his every word.

"It was late on November 12th in 1995 when Mr. Smith... we don't actually know his real name... he's the private investigator I hired to look into Paige's past; well, that's when he arrived with the package.

"This journey all started with a birth certificate Paige found when her parents passed away. It was in the safe with their stock certificates, MouseTrax legal documents, and some others. The thing that drew Paige to investigate this particular birth certificate was that her name was on it... but the document was incorrect." Aaren shot Nathan a puzzled look as Nathan handed her the birth certificate.

"Her first name and date of birth were right, but the names given as her parents, and her surname were different. The copy she had in her personal papers - the one she used so many years ago to get her social security card and her driver's license, read "Paige Lambert, singleton birth, June 14, 1964; and her parents were listed as Mary and John Lambert. This document has her listed with only a mother, Melissa Sanderson. A father's name does not appear on the document. And, most interesting of all, was the birth order notation... second of two."

"Two?" Thomas said. "She had a twin?"

"It would seem so. With this birth certificate, she also found a letter from her parents." He passed the letter to Thomas. "They passed away during a skiing trip to the French Alps. An avalanche overpowered the mountain and took them when she was twenty-five years old. She was left with MouseTrax and a heavy heart. She was pretty messed up in the beginning. They were her only family. She wasn't really sure what she was supposed to do. So, she tried as best she could to regroup. Her father would have wanted her to get back to business. He had no tolerance for sniveling when there was work to be done. Paige told me that one of his favorite mantras was, 'You can cry when you get the work done - but until then, work harder.'"

"That's true." Aaren said. He wasn't a hard-nose kind of guy at all, but he was focused on the business and thought it impudent behavior whenever Paige got emotional about something. He thought she needed to keep her head screwed on straight and focus on her school work or the company. He always allowed her time with her mother to fall apart... but only after the work was done.

He had been that way since the day I met him. He was a nice guy - but very driven."

Nathan continued the story. "So, after first focusing her attention on completing her degree and taking MouseTrax to the next level; Paige spent the next few years hiring private investigators and others to help figure out her past. I'd been an employee of Mr. Lambert's for several years, moonlighting for him while working at the university. I handled currier services for the family, and other odd jobs. It seemed unfair to abandon Paige when her family was gone. I told her that I would always be around to help her in whatever way she needed. She tried to call me 'uncle Nathan' once; but I put a stop to that pretty quickly. The last thing I wanted was to be anyone's last family member. I had my own closet full of skeletons to keep the door closed on, and the responsibility of actually caring for someone, someone who could have been my daughter... well, that was a bit more than I wanted to deal with. That's when we made the agreement that I would handle any problem that came up, she would always pay me, and I wouldn't care. Little did I know just how impossible a task that was going to be." Nathan took a sip of his coffee, remembering Paige. Inside, he felt like he'd betrayed her. *Maybe I should have cared more.*

"Tell me about it," said Thomas, with a sheepish grin.

Nathan returned the smile. "Well, that's when she put me on the trail of Mr. Smith. He came well recommended, and seemed to be aware of our strict need for privacy. His fees were, in my mind, outrageous; but Paige needed answers, and she agreed to pay him whatever he wanted. Nathan stopped for a minute and looked at Aaren's and Thomas' confused faces. "I feel like I'm getting ahead of myself." said Nathan, indicating the envelope he'd given Thomas, but he hadn't opened yet. "That's the letter Paige's parents left in the safe." Thomas read it aloud.

Dear Paige,

If you have found this envelope, it means that we have passed away and you're looking through the safe. First of all, make sure that the attorney gets everything. He'll know what to do with transferring the stocks, the business, and he'll get you up to speed and fully in charge. He's got our trust, and I'm sure he'll make sure you get a copy.

Secondly, please know that we always wanted to tell you about your history, as we believe that the knowledge of where you come from is one of the most important things a person can know about themselves. However, the adoption papers were sealed, and we were unable to find any details that would be of benefit to you in learning much about your family. What we can tell you is that you were born a twin, and that your twin was a fraternal sister. We know that her given name was Gillian Sanderson, but we aren't sure if her adoptive parents changed her name when they took her in. The birth mother requested that we keep your first name, and we have, to give you the chance to find your sister, if you wanted to, someday. But we aren't sure if your sister's parents did the same. The last bit of information we have is the place where you were born, Greenwich Hospital in Greenwich, Connecticut.

We're sorry that we cannot give you more, but we hope that what we have given you throughout your lifetime has been enough. We loved you as if you were our own, and we know that your life will be rich and rewarding, both personally and professionally.

Love,
Mom & Dad

Thomas handed the letter, silently, to Aaren; who looked as if he had just handed her the original Magna Carta. "Wait a minute... Gillian? Her sister's name was Gillian?" Aaren shot a perplexed look at Thomas; Thomas looked stupefied.

Nathan nodded. "I'm getting there. As you can imagine, this was quite the surprise. Paige never had even a hint that this was her life. She always thought that mom, dad, the house in the Hamptons - it was her life, all she would ever have. Suddenly, she had something else. She was in a state of near-panic when she called me. She was very concerned about protecting everything that she and her family had worked so hard to achieve. She felt that it had taken her years to get her life in a place where she could move MouseTrax up the mountain. She was afraid that this distant sibling might muscle in on her and claim inheritance - or worse yet - a position of controlling power at MouseTrax. It was a by-product of the suspicious nature her parents instilled in her. Although it was never overt, they warned her to keep her friends close and her enemies closer. Paige internalized this idea and orchestrated her life to pay homage to it. For Paige, a probate contest would not have been an acceptable result after finding a sister she never knew she had. As she told me once, she'd lived this long without siblings, and had done quite well for herself; she could stand to continue living without them for the rest of her life."

"Wow." said Thomas. "This sounds like some story from a 1940s film noir. It just doesn't make sense. Was she really that cold - and paranoid?" The question was rhetorical.

Nathan took another sip of coffee and went on. "So, to protect Paige's interests and the company, she asked me to hire a private investigator to dig into the matter, and come up with some answers. She wasn't willing to do it herself, because she didn't know what an investigation might turn up, and she wanted to keep her image intact. This was also a difficult thing for her, emotionally. She just wasn't capable of learning everything first-hand. Information a generation removed was easier for her to deal with. So, I got saddled with it."

"Lucky you." said Aaren, shooting him a compassionate grin.

"It took Mr. Smith nearly a year, but he finally called saying that he would deliver his final report and expect payment. It was a hefty price, fifty-thousand. I met him in the middle of Boston Common, late one afternoon, all cloak and dagger-like, and we made the exchange. I can tell you this much about Mr. Smith; he was a man of few words. Standing silently by the glow of the park lamp, Mr. Smith held the package in his left hand; and held out his empty right hand, awaiting the delivery of payment. Simultaneously, I gave him an envelope with his money in it - a cashier's check - and took the package. Mr. Smith simply said, 'It's been a pleasure doing business with you;' doffed his fedora and left. I never really saw his face, and he never looked directly at me; it's probably better that way. Paige thought that if the information he provided would protect her investment, her company, and most importantly, her reputation, it was worth the money. She thought that if news got out that she wasn't a "true heir" of the founder of MouseTrax, she would be ruined and some hack would steal the company."

"That's absurd," said Aaren.

"Yeah, but consider the source. You and I would never be worried about something like that. That's just not where our heads live." said Thomas. "I think Paige's self-esteem issues ran deeper than any of us realized."

"Well," continued Nathan. "It happened. She got what she was looking for. But, she was still afraid that the media would have a field day if they got wind of any of this. The circus surrounding her parents' death was madness enough for one lifetime. She didn't want to stir up that hornets' nest again. So, she kept it a secret and made a plan."

"I've been on both sides of that equation," said Thomas. "I can understand her motivations about avoiding the press."

"When I took the package to her, she asked me to stay as she waded through it all. I remember she poured us drinks and we braced for impact. Here's the report. It's the original, nothing has been changed or redacted since we received it from Mr. Smith." Nathan handed Thomas the manila file folder, and he handed the envelope of photos to Aaren. Thomas began to read aloud.

On June 14, 1964 at 4:54pm in Greenwich Hospital, Greenwich Connecticut, Gillian Raynor and Paige Lambert were born fraternal twins, to an addled, drug addicted twenty-year-old unemployed mother, Melissa Sanderson. (see original birth certificate, included.)

"Gillian Raynor?" Thomas' face turned ghost white.

"Gillian Raynor is my wife... er... ex-wife's maiden name." said Thomas in a near-whisper. Aaren looked at Nathan, who simply nodded. Thomas kept reading.

Melissa Sanderson's parents were extremely wealthy and owned a vineyard in California. The Sanderson's didn't want the stigma of their daughter having a baby out of wedlock or the news of her drug lifestyle leaked to the press. After what the vineyard household staff describes as more than a month of heated arguments, the Sandersons sent Melissa off to a Catholic-run home for unwed mothers in Greenwich, Connecticut, where it was expected that their daughter would spend the year of her pregnancy, have the babies, and immediately give them up for adoption. Melissa did not have a choice in the matter. Her parents flew her to Connecticut on their company jet, chaperoned by the household butler, Mr. Vanguard. He escorted her to the front door of the home, and left her with the nun who answered the door. Mr. Vanguard gave a writ of instructions drawn up by the Sanderson's lawyer which clearly stated the expectation that Melissa was to give the children up for adoption immediately after their birth, without bonding (which I am told means she was not able to hold or see the children after delivery). The head-mother currently in charge at the home also indicated that the receiving nun was compelled to sign a confidentiality and non-disclosure agreement. Mr. Vanguard also provided all the necessary legal documentation for the children to be adopted without reprisal, as well as transfer instructions for Melissa to a detox house in South Carolina. (see copies of documents, included.)

Thomas and Aaren looked over the documents together, stunned at their cold, callous treatment of the birth of the children. Thomas continues to read aloud.

A week after giving birth to the children, and after being medically cleared for travel by the doctor, Melissa Sanderson was sent to the detox center for a thirty-day rehab, and then home. Her parents had accounted for her absence over the previous year to friends and colleagues by telling them that Melissa had taken a year to study abroad, living with "a lovely family in the Swiss Alps". They perpetrated this lie so that their daughter's infidelity and depraved lifestyle would not tarnish the vineyard's reputation or her parents' standing in the community. It was rumored that the young man who impregnated Melissa Sanderson had enlisted in the Army and sent to serve in the crisis in Viet Nam; and died there. Even after much attempted coercion by her parents, Melissa never revealed his name. Melissa Sanderson had no siblings and few friends.

A year later, after failing grades in her first year of college, and a string of boyfriends that her parents did not approve of, Melissa Sanderson committed suicide. She was found naked, hanging by her neck with a heavy-duty electrical cord, a bunch of grapes dangling from her mouth, in the wine cellar of her parent's lavish country estate. She left a short note that simply read "If I can't live with my children, I can't live." Melissa Sanderson's parents were branded failures by the publicity of their daughter's death in the cellar, and within three years the vineyard had collapsed in financial ruin. (see death certificate, newspaper articles, included.)

"My gosh, this is film noir." said Aaren. Do people actually behave like this in real life?"

"Unfortunately, some did, Aaren." said Nathan. "There was a huge stigma attached to wealthy families when something like this happened. First, their daughter got pregnant out of wedlock, and then she committed suicide. One of these events might have been tarnish enough on the family silver to ruin them... but both? That kind of damage was irreparable. When the press got hold of it - that was the end... and they never got wind of the detox - if they had - well, things would have been a whole lot worse for them."

"It's true." said Thomas. "The press can inflict tremendous damage on the lives of people. Freedom of the press can be a positive thing... but when it's abused... sometimes, there's no healing from that kind of disease."

"What does the report say next?" asked Aaren. Does it say anything else about the Sandersons or the children?" Thomas read on.

The whereabouts of the Sandersons today is unknown. After an extensive search through the records of the State of California, no death certificates, passports, visas or other travel documentation have been identified. A medical records search has also returned no information. A State of California prison records search has also been returned as inconclusive.

As for the twins, after some time in the foster care system, they were adopted out to two very different families. At the request of Melissa Sanderson, both families kept the girl's given first names. Gillian was placed with a middle-class accountant and his wife in Detroit, Michigan.

Thomas stopped for a moment and let out a heavy sigh. "All this time. Gillian never knew..." He wiped a tear, grieving for

Gillian and the family she would never know.

At age eight, Paige was placed with a wealthy technology and communications magnate and his wife in Boston, Massachusetts after a first, near disastrous placement (see attached dosier). There are no other children in either the Raynor or Lambert families, adopted or natural. The Raynor's have returned to Detroit, after a brief five-year move to Washington State, in a small suburb of Seattle. The Lamberts passed away two years ago. (see residency documentation, and death certificates, included.)

It was difficult for Thomas to go on. He gave the file to Aaren, and she continued reading. It was as if someone had lived in the shadows of Thomas' life, and was now playing out every detail in painful Technicolor.

Gillian Raynor married Thomas Laird on August 29, 1990, and a year later, Gillian gave birth to a daughter, Eryn Emily Laird. Gillian Laird works as a portrait restoration expert for the Detroit Institute of Arts. She is an accomplished artist and has been well-praised for her work at the museum. Thomas Laird, after spending a great deal of time writing for the Peace Corps publication department, moved on to a position as reporter for the Detroit Free Press newspaper. Eryn Laird died in a horrific train crash in a gorge in Kremling, Colorado on April 22, 1995, after visiting with Gillian's parents and extended family in Seattle, Washington. Gillian was extensively injured in the accident, and after two months of rehabilitation, returned home with Thomas Laird to their home in Detroit, Michigan after burying their daughter in Kremling, Colorado.

Six months later, their marriage ended in divorce. Gillian Laird took residence in the Detroit suburb of Rochester Hills, Michigan; and left the art world, taking a job as a junior accountant at her parent's financial firm. Thomas Laird is currently living in the family home in the Detroit suburb of Indian Village, and still works for the Detroit Free Press; although he has recently made his resume available and is in search of alternative employment. (see residency documents, death certificates, employment documentation, travel records, marriage & divorce certificates, included.)

There were tears in Aaren's eyes. "Oh, Thomas; I'm so sorry. How horrible."

"I'm sorry, too." said Nathan. "Paige told me when she hired you that you were important and she planned that you would be a major asset to the company... but I had no idea about all of this. She never shared this part with me."

"Thanks, guys." said Thomas, working hard to hide his sadness. "It was a long time ago. It's been hard, but I think I'm beginning to heal."

"I guess that explains how you were able to name Emily so quickly." Aaren said.

"Yes; it was the best way I could think of to honor Eryn's memory. I remember when I told Paige that I wanted to name the baby Emily; she smiled, saying that she thought it was the perfect name. It seemed an odd reaction from her at the time - she liked everything to be her idea, you know. But now, knowing that Paige knew about my past - and Eryn - it makes sense."

Nathan took the file from the coffee table where Aaren had placed it, and continued to read the report aloud.

Paige Lambert had a brief romantic encounter with congressional staffer, Edward Jarrett while attending college at Georgetown University in Washington DC. Their relationship produced a son, Logan Alexander Edwards. Paige chose this last name for him; lying about the true identity of the child's father, in an effort to protect his reputation. The father, Edward Jarrett, abdicated all responsibility and parental rights upon learning of the pregnancy. It was rumored that Paige was focused on climbing the corporate ladder, and Edward's focus was on climbing the political ladder. Insiders at the time state that Paige was concerned about her parents' response to the news of the pregnancy, and therefore, she hid it from them, choosing to shield them from the disgrace.

"Oh, poor Paige, said Aaren. Her parents never would have reacted that way. I'm sure they would have been surprised - but they would have loved Logan and accepted him immediately. It's sad that their daughter didn't trust them.

"Again," said Thomas; "For whatever reason, her self-esteem didn't match her outward appearances. I wonder why? I wonder what could have made her see life as so hard?"

"I don't know." said Aaren. "I always thought she led a charmed life... nothing ever seemed to go wrong for her."

"Perhaps that was part of the problem." said Nathan. "It's tough to build a thick skin if you don't have any practice, and I'm sure her first foster placement had something to do with it, too. That can't be any easy thing for a child to deal with." The trio sat a moment in silence, contemplating this thought. Together, they shared a pity for Paige that none of them would have ever suspected. Nathan continued to read.

Logan was put up for adoption through the Small Hearts Adoption Agency in Maryland, shortly after his birth in December of 1990. Paige's parents and none of her friends and acquaintances have any knowledge of the boy's existence. Logan has spent his entire young life either in orphanages or foster family situations. He has never been formally adopted. He has no physical or medical detriments, and has been evaluated to be of average psychological and intellectual capacity. Logan is currently living with a foster family in Billings, Montana. (see birth certificates, medical documents, guardianship papers, adoption records, legal records, evaluation papers, included.)

No additional information was discovered. Therefore, this investigative case is closed.

The three began to pass around the photos. They found among them, an old black and white of Melissa Sanderson. "This looks like it could have been a high school yearbook photo." said Aaren.

"She looks a lot like Gillian," said Thomas.

"This one is a photo of the Sanderson's; taken, I'm sure, for a corporate marketing campaign of some sort." said Nathan. "People don't look that perfect unless they're trying to sell something."

Other photos, some in black and white and some in color, drew attention to the bullet points of Mr. Smith's report. It's almost as if he was doing a book report for school, and had to include illustrations in order to get extra credit. But the most striking to Thomas was the family photo of the Lairds at a summer barbecue hosted by the Free Press. "This was us," he said, handing the photo to Aaren; "in happier times."

Aaren re-read the newspaper column describing the train crash again, to herself while the men looked over the photos. "You know, I think the word "tragic" did not effectively convey the situation. You should have used stronger vocabulary. I'm so sorry you had to go through this."

Taking the newspaper clipping from her, Thomas said; "Thanks. It was a difficult time. You never expect to bury a child... I did the best I could. To tell you the truth, I don't think I'll ever be done healing from that. But... having Emily makes it almost bearable." A small smile crossed Thomas' face; but there was a part of him that felt guilty for allowing it.

Aaren pulled one of Paige's micro cassettes from the stack, and pushed play on her recorder.

I wonder what it would have been like to have been there for Gillian after the train crash... to hold her hand... be a source of comfort to her? I wonder if knowing that I existed would have made a difference for her? Probably not. I'm really not that sort of person, all touchy-feely. Ugh. Still, I should probably do something - offer something that might make things better for them. I'm not quite sure just what that will be... I've never been in this situation before... but I should probably do something."

They heard the sound of the recorder clicking off and then on again. Another entry began.

Well, I did something today. I figured I should start someplace... and Dad always said, "Start with a donation to sustain the injured, and then find a solution to the problem." Okay, yes, I threw money at the problem... for now, until I figure out what else I'm supposed to do. I began by putting money into a trust fund for Logan and I hired Thomas. I'm also keeping a distant watch on Gillian. If I can eventually get close enough to Thomas to somehow get introduced to Gillian... then maybe we can be sisters. Not quite sure how this will play out. I can't let Thomas know that's why I chose his resume over all the other marketing maniacs out there; that could cause problems. I'll just tell him something like "I'm looking for a more humanistic approach" or some such nonsense, he'll probably buy that. I'll ask Nathan to keep a watch over him... help him along... make the transition easier. And then, after we get to know each other, I'll tell him who I am, ask him to introduce me to Gillian, and then maybe we can work out some way to form a family... me, Gillian, Logan... who knows... it could happen. Aaren clicked off the recorder.

"Wow. She really did have a plan, didn't she?" Thomas said, looking at Nathan.

"I told you. Paige was a planner." said Nathan. "She attacked life by the numbers, one step at a time, and always had a contingency. It saved her from the emotions she couldn't deal with after giving up Logan. It was an easier way for her."

"And you... you were just doing your job, eh?" said Thomas.

"No, it wasn't like that. Well, maybe in the beginning... but later, when you started talking about Gillian and how much you loved her... and you started writing those stories for her... I felt like I was getting to know you as a real person - and a friend. Calling you 'friend' brought it into reality for me. After a couple of weeks, it wasn't for Paige anymore. It was for me. I hope you can forgive me." Nathan held out his hand in sincere friendship. Thomas took it warmly.

"I get it, Nathan. No worries. I'm glad you're here. I don't think I could have gotten through this mess... the new job, the Hamptons fiasco... Paige's death... without the two of you." Thomas looked to Nathan and then to Aaren. "I'm just glad that the time of full disclosure has finally come and we can move on. You know, it's strange. All this time, when Paige had been cold and callous on the outside, she was really yearning, longing, hoping on the inside. I understand her need for secrecy, and her need for connectivity. I'm just not sure I agree with the way she went about it."

The photos from the Private Investigator's packet struck him oddly. It was as if he was being introduced to Gillian's family for the first time. As if it were Paige saying, *these are my family - I've never met them - but one day, if you do, tell them I said "hi"*. Thomas felt like he had a responsibility now to finish what Paige had started. If not for Gillian, then for Logan and Emily. And the first step was going to be the hardest. *How am I going to tell Gillian?*

Thomas took another long look at the photo of little Logan. "I'm still astounded that this little person - Emily's brother - even exists. Somewhere out there, there is another person who is a part of my family, but with a completely different history. This could be a gift or a curse. Either way, now that I know he's out there, I have to find him. Will you two help me?"

"Of course." Aaren and Nathan said in unison.

"Thank you." said Thomas. "How about we get started tomorrow morning? I need to spend some time with Emily and think about how I'll tell Gillian about everything." He walked them to the door, shaking hands with Nathan, and giving Aaren a warm hug. "Thank you both. You're true friends."

Thomas climbed the stairs to Emily's room, and picked her up from her cradle; rocking her gently. This mystery of finding Logan was not a dust bunny that would get quietly swept under the rug. This quest to find this little boy, Emily's brother, now infiltrated Thomas' brain like fingernails on a chalkboard - relentless and irritating. It would not be ignored.

****

I feel badly, stringing Thomas along like this. I mean, he's nice, and handsome – certainly, any woman would enjoy having him. But there's also this sensation that I've betrayed him... setting up this rouse only to get close and then spring my secret on him. It's not fair to him, I know; but how else am I supposed to do this?

And worse yet, I've stolen my sister's husband. Yes, it's true, they're divorced. But I don't think it's real – at least, not for Thomas. I get the sense that he still loves her deeply. I'm just a short-term diversion – as it should be – until he gets back to her.

Justifying my reasons for doing it, though, doesn't erase the betrayal of them both. If you add Logan to the equation, the whole thing equals an unavoidable repugnance; and me as the ultimate betrayer. I just hope the ends will someday allow for their forgiveness.

Paige's words from her own voice... it felt too much like stealing. He slept uneasily that night, tossing and turning, dreaming of Paige and her anger. Early the next morning, Thomas called Aaren and tried to work through it all.

"I spent all last night listening to some of Paige's journal tapes again. It feels wrong. I feel like I'm violating Paige's soul. Whether on tape or on paper, people keep journals because they want to keep their thoughts private, not because they want to share them openly. I feel like I'm emotionally raping her or something." There was a mix of anguish and defeat in Thomas' voice that worried Aaren. It was almost as if he was going through postpartum depression.

Thomas sat in silence, wallowing in the full weight of what felt like emotional homicide. Aaren tried to bring him back to reality. "Thomas, look, perhaps she left you all this stuff because she knew she didn't know how to give you the information you would need to find Logan. I mean, aside from some last names, which would be helpful, there's not much else she could have told you. Or maybe it was just too painful for her to relive that part of her life again so openly. But whatever the reason, you have all of this now, she gave it to you, and you need to use it. Okay, her methods were a bit questionable, but not her motives. You can't just let Logan go unknown and abandoned."

Aaren never imagined that her best friend would or could keep such an important secret from her for so many years.

Selfishly, the story was beginning to tickle her imagination and she needed to know how it ended. She needed to meet this boy. She also knew that as difficult as this might be for Thomas, however confused he was with the thought of creating a new life with two children when he only thought about on one, the truth right now was more important. *A child's life is at stake.* "Why don't we conference in Nathan?" Aaren suggested. Maybe he can help focus things a little bit."

"That's a good idea." said Thomas. He put Aaren on hold and connected to Nathan. Once they were all on the line together, Thomas continued.

"You know, after going through all these papers and tapes, I'm a little lost. I know that we need to find Logan, and soon. But I'm going to need some help. I wish there was a way to contact this Mr. Smith guy - the private investigator - but I'm not sure that's possible. Nathan, you said your one meeting with him was elusive. There doesn't seem to be a phone number or e-mail anywhere for him. Do you think you still have his contact information somewhere? I'd do it myself, but I've never needed a private investigator before. I have no idea who to call or what I'm supposed to tell them. "

"I'm not sure if I still have that stuff. I can look." said Nathan. "But, Paige was pretty insistant on cutting all ties after the job was done. Fear ran her in more ways than you can count. I'll do what I can."

"Thanks, Nathan. Money's not a problem, Paige left plenty of that, but I just don't know where to begin. This is a mess." Thomas' lack of sleep was beginning to show. His voice sounded like a fifteen-year-old who was trying to solve a simple arithmetic problem when his teacher kept trying to get him to do calculus. Frustration was everywhere.

"Don't worry about it. Nathan and I are here to help." said Aaren. "What else do you want us to do?"

"Well, I think we need to start with the adoption agency in DC. I don't have any court papers from that time; but I do have the name and phone number for the agency. Maybe if you call them, Aaren, they can give you some information. Let me know if they give you any hassles about confidentiality, and I'll call Mr. McClish. I'm sure he can help with that - he seemed to be a formidable guy. See if you can find out what Logan's status is, if he's been adopted, or if he's still with a foster family. There's no sense in uprooting him from his home if it's a permanent one, you know what I mean?"

"I get it. Look, I'll make a couple of calls and see what I can come up with; don't worry." Aaren's voice was soothing and calm. It was a welcome gift after listening to a night of Paige's ghost running through his ears. "Why don't you try to get in a nap before Emily wakes up. She'll be hungry soon."

"You're right. She's been so good the last couple of nights; and she only got up once last night; I almost forgot she was here. She's such a sweet girl." Aaren could hear the devoted daddy smile in Thomas' voice come through the phone. She missed Paige more than she could ever explain; but she was happy that her last gift was given to Thomas.

"I'll call you later this afternoon or tomorrow with whatever I find." Aaren said.

"And I should be in touch in the next day or two, as well," added Nathan.

"Thanks, guys. I owe you."

"Hey, that's Aunt Aaren to you, buddy," she giggled.

"Of course - forever. Talk to you later; and thank you." Thomas hung up the phone and re-assembled the blue box. He sat for a long moment, grateful for the gift of Emily and thankful for friends like Aaren and Nathan. He just knew that when they met, Gillian would value them both just as much as he did. And, of course, she'd adore Emily.

A small squirmy squeak came from the baby monitor. Thomas chuckled to himself. "So much for that nap."

Chapter Twenty-Two

"Grief is the price we pay for love."
~Queen Elizabeth II

After feeding, changing and rocking Emily back to sleep, Thomas returned back to Paige's tapes. It was important for him to know as much as he could about her. Gillian would have questions, and he needed to have answers. He ignored his need for his own nap, poured himself another cup of coffee, and clicked tape number thirty-seven into the recorder.

****

"Anger suffers as grief withdraws." At least that's what my shrink told me as I clutched the pillow from his couch to my chest, watching the heartless snow-pummeled window pane. He said, "Don't let it worry you too much, Paige; as your grief goes away, so will your anger. The two cannot live without each other. They feed on each other. Grief soothes anger. Anger feeds grief. When you can bring yourself to let go of one, the other will also disappear. It's the simple nature of things."

As I wrote the check and dropped it into the competent hands of his secretary, I left that session with a new appreciation for life, death, anger, grief, and the stupidity of psychoanalysis. Simply put, my Harvard educated, psych-babble wielding, one-hundred-dollar-per-hour, egomaniac-analyst was wrong. Good old Dr. What's It got it wrong. After the five months of emotionally bereft and mind-numbing grief subsided, the anger remained... and in full force just under the surface of my daily life; irritating every thought, every decision, and every joy.

Each day since I got that package from Mr. Smith, I rehash the fact that my birth mother and father, with whom I had parted company on less-than-stellar terms, are no longer in my life. I'm still angry about the facts. Not only are they gone, but they left this world in a smog of stupidity. I'm angry that our last conversation was one I was far too young to remember; and angry that my mother, in particular, had refused to do anything to improve our situation in life... when faced with the truly tough decisions. We could have had a life together - If she'd wanted it badly enough.

As I walked the snow-covered streets from Dr. What's It's office complex, back to the community parking structure, I rehashed the frustration, reinvigorating the anger with each step of boot against icy pavement. From what I read in the dossier, my birth mother had spent the last year of her life self-medicating with alcohol, drugs and non-compliance; ignoring the advice of doctors. It was reported that she claimed, "they don't really know what they're talking about and clearly, I know my body much better than they do. After all, I live with it every day, and they can only guess."

It was absurd, of course. Women in the mid-sixties were deemed too stupid to truly believe that they understood the complexities of medicine - or at least that's how they were brainwashed. I'm so glad that my parents raised with a healthier attitude. Who knows what would have become of me had I been saddled with that kind of thinking! My birth mother, it said in the report, was a maverick of sorts. She hated conformity. "She was lost to a time where she didn't fit," the investigator said. But in the end, I was here, she was gone, and blame of it rested solely on her shoulders. They tell me, and who knows if it's all true, that my father abdicated life when he heard the news, and was killed in Nam. It's ironic to think that he took the coward's way out and ended up the hero.

A year after my placement, the week of the Fourth of July, with fireworks crashing outside her window, they say that she ended her misery. It was shortly after his platoon was ambushed by the enemy. She was alone and now she knew she would always be alone. The country didn't mourn for either of them, yet celebrated another year of freedom. And perhaps she felt she was finally celebrating freedom, too. It's hard to tell.

For reasons not surpassing understanding, acceptance of the news of my adoption and the circumstances of my mother's mortality so many years later was more easily swallowed than the loss of my precious son. Yet as the grief of my mother's passing withdrew, the anger of my abandonment of Logan's still swelled within me, tainting my memory of her and the brief childhood we shared. The anger that lingered made me question the happy memories I had of my adoptive mother... my mom. It made me question my relationship with her... made me question - albeit briefly - my actions as a mother. I vowed not to follow in my birth mother's negative footsteps, and only resole the positive steps of my adoptive parents. Clearly, I have not succeeded. The anger at the discovery of my history made me question far too much. The grief no longer consoles and I find that the mistakes I have made overshadow my birth mother's... if that's even possible.

When I brought the evident failure of his theory to the attention of dear Dr. What's It, all he could offer was, "everyone grieves differently, Paige. Your process is unlike anyone else's." Then why am I paying you ridiculous amounts of money each month, I thought, to convince me there are rules to these things, and answers easily found if I sacrifice my most conflicting thoughts on your couch of absolution? That was the last time *Dr. What's It* and I spent any time together. I don't miss him, and I doubt he misses me.

It's been over two years that I've been on my own. I've made peace with my anger... I've dislodged my grief... accepted my mistakes as the only course of action available to me... and subsisted on the understanding that sooner or later, we all become comfortable with our discomfort when reflecting on the aftermath.

I was... I am... determined not to allow this two-headed monster to run me. I make my rules and either walk around the obstacle people I encounter, or simply bulldoze those who impede my progress. I'm confident that even if I don't always get it; at least I can fake it until I find a better solution. And in the meantime, I hold stories of my birth mother at great distance, and memories of Logan close to my heart. There must be a healing in all of this somewhere, otherwise, what would be the point?

Chapter Twenty-Three

"A dog will teach you unconditional love. If you can have that in your life, things won't be too bad."
~Robert Wagner

Gillian had been reading Thomas' letters for a while now - nearly a year- and sketching along as she read. The two, Thomas' words and her drawings, had always been connected. Now, she felt that they were even more so. She wanted to reach out to him... let him know that she heard him, was hearing him... and how much she missed him. She felt the need to be with him. But was she strong enough for that encounter? She didn't know... yet.

Over the last several weeks, the math had gotten to her. There were no two things farther apart in her mind than math and creativity. She'd been avoiding work the past few days - it was easy to ignore what you hated most in the world when there was no joy in it. She knew deadlines loomed overhead, and she didn't really care. She spent her weekend hours re-reading his letters and sketching. Not Thomas' stories, she'd already completed those, first in pencil and then in pastels. Now, she moved on to sketching what lived inside her brain. It was a part of her that she kept sequestered for so long, that finally, the dam burst, and the images could no longer be contained. It was liberating. She knew the IRS would haunt her into the end of October, and she didn't care. The pictures would not cease. Finally, she was at a place in her life -

again - where she didn't want them to stop. It had taken so long to find her way back into her creative castle... she wasn't going to let the path disappear into the ether again.

As she sat at the dining room table, sipping cocoa late one night, she began to coagulate the images she'd been creating into a story. She knew it lived there... she just had to put it in the right order. She spread each of the drawings across the table, left to right, top to bottom until the storyline emerged. It was clear and undeniable. She had crafted a story. Without realizing it, she had walked a step closer to Thomas... she began to write.

****

Jeni had been listening to the radio as she worked on the mountain of tax returns soon to become an avalanche across her desk. Background noise had always helped her to focus when she found the work tedious. It had been that way all through childhood, until she discovered art during her sophomore year of high school.   In those times, silence was the perfect companion to the creative process; or sometimes, if she was working on a particularly difficult piece, a little Mozart. But in order to focus on tedium, she needed background noise - to keep her brain from becoming bored and giving up completely.

On this autumn Saturday it was beautiful outside and she would have much rather been at the park feeding the ducks. Yet, here she was, chained to an uncomfortable desk sifting through monotony that meant nothing to her. She needed something to get her through the extensions her clients required because of their repeated propensity for procrastination. And what was worse, she knew a collection of shoe boxes filled with disorganized and barely legible receipts would soon follow for each one of them.

To cut through the day's frustration, Jeni relied on a gentle talk show just a few clicks down from the classical station on her radio's tuner. The precise coordinates for the "fall-back" classical station keyed into her stereo's presets was necessary, just in case she had to flee from difficult conversations quickly. Most of the time though, the topics they shared on this station were inoffensive, and just the right tenor to keep her brain engaged without getting her heart enraged. The host had an authenticity about him that Jeni found reassuring.

"And we're back. This is WKND radio Petoskey, Michigan, 90.5 FM; music, talk and a little kindness to get you through the day. For those of you just joining us, this hour we're talking about families and children and we'd like to hear your opinions, tips, tricks, hints and advice. Our in-studio guest is Dr. Kacerek, a renowned child psychologist and mother of six, an even three and three. During the break, we were talking about the situation in Missouri and their referendum on the ballot to make all abortions illegal. We'd like to know your thoughts. Jeni from Detroit, you're on the air, what do you think?"

"Well, Jim, I think that we're spending far too much time on the wrong problem. Abortion isn't really the issue. As far as I'm concerned, if people want to terminate their pregnancies, that's their choice. A fetus isn't really a person until it has a soul and can live outside of the womb, and that, I believe, begins in the moment that child takes its first breath. And that's probably a topic for a whole other show - but I believe the bigger problem here is that we already have far too many children in America who don't have families. Too many babies go unwanted and unloved. Too many parents are having children without any intention of making the commitment to care for those children for a lifetime. Why aren't we focusing our attention on those children - the ones who are already here?

"So, you're a supporter of adoption over abortion. And you're right, there's another show hiding in that topic. But how do you feel about the foster care system?"

"Well, unfortunately, I think it's a necessary evil. We must ask ourselves why it is that we need to have temporary parents for children who were supposedly conceived out of love. I spend time volunteering in a parenting clinic not far from my home. We see people of every age and every race, and every station in life come into our center and complain that they can't raise the children they have and they want resources to connect with the foster care system. It's a real travesty. Yet each time I ask them why they didn't practice birth control, invariably, both mothers and fathers alike respond that they wanted to enjoy each other's love and they believed, at the time, that having a child was the purest expression of that love.

"Now, while that may be a beautiful thought, the problem is that they never stop to think of the serious consequences a new life brings to an already struggling one. Children are expensive and they require a lot of attention and a twenty-four-seven, minimum eighteen-year commitment. Young people, especially, seem to think that having a child is a status symbol and that after it's all done, they can just put that child in a closet like a stuffed animal and bring it out when it serves their reputation or personal emotional needs. They don't seem to realize that the baby is a fully sentient person - with needs, wants, desires and feelings to get hurt, just like theirs."

"So, how do you help these new parents see what they've done, or - hopefully - what they're about to do? How do you get them to understand that the reality of the world is not as they had imagined before they discovered unprotected sex?"

"Well, for those who have already had their children - and this applies to parents of every age - we try to help them with their parenting skills. We offer classes in raising children and we build a network of other parents that they can call on for support when things begin to get difficult. We arrange play dates for the children so the parents can also spend time with each other and talk with each other while their children are getting the socialization they so desperately need. For those who haven't become pregnant yet, or who haven't had their children yet, we counsel them on the importance of making clear-headed decisions. We offer sexual education and planned parenting strategies so that they can keep their lives in order and have their children when they are really ready for it.

"We also suggest to those young people - and sometimes to older adults who aren't quite sure if having children is the right choice for them - that perhaps they should adopt a puppy first."

"Adopt a puppy, really? Why do you advocate that strategy?"

"Think about it Jim, puppies require nearly as much attention as a child does. You can't leave them alone for too long, they need to be fed on a regular basis, and they have doctor bills, costs for toys and sometimes clothes, food, and snacks. They need to be potty trained, go to school, learn good manners, learn to get along well with others, and they need constant love. We tell those contemplating parenthood that if they can successfully raise a puppy from six weeks into its third year of life, then they might be ready for all the responsibilities, financial challenges and time demands a child might place on them. Of course, we don't want to see anyone give up a dog after discovering that its not the right choice for them. But when you consider the options; giving up a dog for adoption is much more preferable to giving up a child for adoption when you discover parenting isn't a good plan for you. It's not a perfect solution, but it is a strategy that may save many children from being born into a world that is not prepared for them, and worse yet, doesn't want them."

"And for those who seem unreachable - those who want to give up their children - how to you help them?"

"Well, we connect them to non-profit adoption agencies and unwed mother hostels who will help them find a family who will love and care for their child. It's a hard thing to do, I mean, without losing your temper about it; but when you think about the fact that it's a child who you are really helping, it makes it much easier to avoid the arguments with the parents."

"Tell me, why did you decide to go into this work? My producer tells me that you're an accountant. What drove you to do this type of volunteering? Why not simply work at the local animal shelter?"

"Well Jim, I believe that children deserve more of everything I have to give; everything I can give their parents; and every ounce of my energy to give them a better life. My goal is to work with people, really have their eyes opened up to the wonderment and joy that lives in the eyes and heart of a child. Children are a tremendous gift, and we must cherish them, protect them and above all else, love them when no one else will. Being an accountant pays the bills so that I can do the real work of my life."

"Well, it sounds like you're definitely moving in a wonderful direction. Thank you so much for your call, and please make sure to give the name and phone number of the center where you volunteer to my producer before you hang up the phone. We'd like to connect more children in need with caring people like you.

"And we'll be right back after this word from our Day Sponsor..."

A twinge of guilt ran through Jeni as she hung up the phone. In reality, it was more than just a twinge. But she couldn't possibly have told them the truth. She wasn't brave enough yet to expose herself so openly. At least with the story she gave them, she still got her point across without admitting the fact that it wasn't completely true. And maybe with the website address she passed off as the place where she volunteered - that place she has thought about volunteering at for some months now - somebody out there might find the help they needed. At least she hoped it would end up that way.

Full disclosure would have meant sharing all the gruesome details about the choice she made so many years ago to give up her daughter. She wasn't proud of it, and she'd been trying to make amends ever since. That's why she put in so much time volunteering at the shelter - trying desperately to make a difference and change her karma footprint. The fact that she found it impossible to be around young children anymore, and subjugated her need to nurture by caring for dogs at the local animal shelter were details that she didn't want to divulge. She wasn't strong enough.

Jeni believed everything she told the radio show host about adoption and about wanting to help parents find a better way. But it was still too emotionally difficult - too sensitive to her heart - to do what she really felt was necessary, even after so much time. So she hid in the logical daily grind of numbers, numbing herself to her true feelings. And when she felt she couldn't make it one more mind numbing day, she shared what little emotion she could muster with the dogs. Jeni knew the dogs felt her pain, and they were a genuine comfort to her tired soul. Even though she knew she couldn't take them home - give them all - every one of them - the loving forever home they truly deserved; at least she could offer them what little she had to give. She hoped that what she did mattered, made a difference, if not to her, then perhaps to the dogs.

There was something else, too. Something told her that volunteering her time and heart to these dogs in some strange way, was a way of racking up "points" toward improving her humanity. *Perhaps if I put in enough time, extend my heart in just the right way for long enough, then maybe, just maybe, the Universe would see fit in giving me another child someday.* If Jeni were to be honest with herself, and with those who asked, she absolutely wanted another child. *I feel like because I've abandoned a child when I didn't have to, perhaps I'm not allowed to have another one quite yet. I think I have to be patient and allow my energy to recharge; allow Spirit to again find me worthy.* As she bent down to scruff the ears of her sleeping rescue mutt, MacGyver, she thought that maybe it wasn't that implausible an idea.

****

Gillian wanted more than anything to share this story and her drawings with Thomas... but she just wasn't brave enough... not yet. She hoped there would come a time when her courage would allow her this small indulgence of his approval. But this was not the day.

Chapter Twenty-Four

"You leave old habits behind by starting out with the thought, 'I release the need for this in my life'."
~Wayne Dyer

    Fear and despair have nearly consumed me now. Exhaustion is my closest companion. I awoke with a sense of such strong disquiet; it almost seemed futile to acknowledge it. Yet I feel this is my last chance to purge the isolation from within. I've tried every other option I thought was available to me. None were effective - not even with minimal influence. I'm lost, drowning in abject despair with no life vest and not one person close by to throw me a line. Words of advice float to me from their places on the shore...

    "Swim harder!" yelled one.

    "Realize that the water is only four feet deep and just stand up!" screamed another.

    And my personal favorite, "Wake up, it's only a dream - for nothing you fear is real". Their well-intentioned words fell upon my ears, deaf from the rush of each wave of depression crashing in around me.

I struggle to understand yet find no meaning in my thoughts. I struggle to let them go, yet can't, for fear has virtually overpowered me now. I am weak against the pounding sea of seemingly endless repetition of failure. My mantra no longer comforts. I reach out, one last time. Perhaps someone paddling by will lend a bit of help. I'm not expecting so much a heroic rescue, as a branch to hold on to so as not to succumb to the white water's perilous end. My effort to cry out to a passing dinghy is an ineffective attempt, and I am swamped by the wake from his paddle. Defeated, I whisper a message upon the water and set it afloat; for I no longer have the strength to scream. Hope is all I had left now, and I cling to it desperately between shallow gasps for air...

****

Gillian's eyes flooded with tears. The memories of those months of loss and sadness after Eryn's death rushed back to her with ferocity. She was angry at Thomas - angry for making her feel again. Angry at herself for not having better control over how the past still was running her. She had been excited to see the envelope among the pile of month-end bills. But now, she cursed him under her breath and growled at the letter; folding and tucking it away in a desk drawer. She couldn't believe his audacity! All the letters until now were easy - emotionally available to her - she could enjoy them. *But this... How could he!* He knew the horrific nightmares I've suffered. And this one was so close - almost exactly...

She stomped up the stairs like a heart-crushed teenager, giving Thomas and his letter the silent treatment. Achilles protested her forgetfulness of his empty dinner dish - but she didn't hear him. At three in the morning, though, poor Achilles could no longer contain his hunger, passively. She got up to his incessant howls, begging his forgiveness. She would not get it; and although one of them ate, neither of them slept the rest of the night.

At six o'clock, the sun finally broke through her night of frustrated darkness. She fed Achilles breakfast and poured herself a cup of tea. Even though her better judgement scolded her to ignore the pages, she inhaled deeply and gave Thomas' letter another chance.

*****

It was well past two in the morning when Karyn awoke a bit frightened and near crying. Her sleep had been disturbed by a host of unnerving dreams. Among them were nightmares of embarrassing encounters with people she respected and loved; blunders made under the pretense of romantic interludes; and a host of missed opportunities due to a steady shortage of self-confidence. Yet sweet calm returned to her as she turned to see Jacob nestled peacefully by her side. He seemed perfectly content, oblivious to the troubles that had awakened her. His strong, comforting arms lay gently upon the bed reaching out to her. Though she had somehow wriggled from his embrace during the night, it amazed her how his arms were still there, inviting her back to him. It was an invitation she was tempted to accept. But, she was wary of awakening him, and so, didn't move. As Karyn lay there, watching Jacob sleep, a flood of memories came cascading through her entire being and her heart smiled recalling their precious history together.

*****

Gillian stopped for a moment, remembering Thomas and his tenderness during those first few weeks after Kremmling. She paused for a moment, looking to Achilles for some sign of... she wasn't sure what she was looking for... and he was no help. Even though she'd fed him well this morning, he still hadn't forgiven her for last night. Gillian picked up the letter and her cup of tea; and moved to her sketch pad on the coffee table in the living room. She set down her tea, picked up the pad and some chalk from her kit, and continued to read.

****

They'd known each other for more than fifteen years ... from the angst of her late teen years, on into the turmoil of her twenties, and now through the transitions of her thirties. And through it all he was forever impervious in his commitment to their friendship. He had been there for her. No matter the season or time of day or night, she could always count on him. He was her confidant, her mentor, her rescuer, her dream master, her priest, her brother, and her friend. He revitalized her. He told her the truth. He believed her fears and healed her wounds. He helped her to grow into the woman she was becoming. There was so much in her life that she couldn't have accomplished without him. So much about herself she never would have learned if not for his gentle encouragement and consummate faith in the strength of her heart. She felt privileged to receive his attentions and, more often than not, a great deal unworthy.

The hours Karyn spent with Jacob were euphoric and serene; she never wanted them to end. Though, of course, they always did. The best part of their being together wasn't necessarily the wild times, as some might suspect. It was instead; the quiet moments cradled in Jacob's arms and the warmth of a few small candles that Karyn loved most of all. For there were never any expectations of her will, or criticisms of her need. Time stopped for her while lying with him. It was simple and pure. Forever untainted by the emotional corruption of those around her.

As Karyn glanced sleepily around the room, a warm spring breeze floated through the window, tickling the drapes in an angelic ballet of azure crinoline and antique lace. The energy here was beyond all compare. Peaceful. Safe. Sensuous. Exhilarating. It was everything her real life wasn't. It was perfect. The room, now basked in the cool haze of moonglow, was decorated with the mementos of a lifetime. Letters from friends collected through the years; pages of a manuscript in transition; a few pieces of artwork created by his youngest friends tacked up on a bulletin board in the corner; and pictures upon the walls of the lives he'd encountered and the souls who'd touched him and changed his life. Near the window hung a dream catcher given to him by a Native American Shaman he met on a trip out west not long ago. Its beautiful embroidery and delicate feathers dancing in the breeze mesmerized Karyn in a recollection of her mother-in-law and the profound impact that relationship had on her life. She was reminded again how it was Jacob who was helping her through this trial, as well.

She looked to Jacob, still sleeping, and smiled warmly, knowing it was he who was again saving her. It was the breeze that drew her inexplicably from the softness of his bed. She kissed him gently upon the cheek. Quietly, she gathered herself up in a blanket and moved toward the open window. The moon was full and pure white, hanging in the sky like a candle in God's window, inviting her out under the protective veil of night.

Silently, Karyn descended the stairs; pausing to stroke a sleeping cat perched on the banister. As she left the house and made her way down the dirt path, she was awe-struck with how still the world was. Every creature slept, save the occasional songs of the crickets and katydids. There was a wonderful aroma of pine, hay and wild flowers that filled her with a feeling of serenity. Like the comforting waft of hot cocoa on a cold, winter Sunday morning; it brought her peace. Still cloaked only in her night dress and a blanket, she felt at one with the wood that surrounded her. Not one ounce of insecurity or embarrassment entered her soul. For the first time in her life, Karyn felt completely at ease. She stood for a few moments, entranced, gazing up to the sky.

****

Gillian sighed contentedly as she recounted the visit she had made to the woods that night. Wondering what more of it Thomas might retell for her, she picked up her cup and returned to the kitchen for more tea. Achilles noticed the change in her energy and wound himself around her legs, purring magnificently. All had been forgiven. She stroked his panther fur and apologized gently. "Sorry catman. I won't forget you again." After refilling her tea, she returned to the letter, Achilles in her shadow.

****

There were so many stars here, so many more than in the city. And they were all here, etched into the blackboard of midnight; Orion, The Twins; Cancer; The Great Square; the two Dippers; even the Dolphin. It had been so long since she'd seen them all together like this; it was surprising to her that she had remembered where to find them. Losing herself in the moment, she reached out a hand to touch them, and indeed, felt as though she had.

This trip had been a time of immense healing for her. Back home, much of her life was in turmoil. So many problems needed solving, yet the solutions seemed far out of reach. Enigmatic puzzles encompassing the experiences of a lifetime. She felt frustrated, alone, and powerless. She had no idea which direction to go or what to do. She was beginning to feel apathetic and exhausted, completely submersed in a sea of conflict, drowning because she could not remember how to swim.

Karyn called Jacob late one evening, striving hard to explain her dilemma, yet failing desperately in her attempt. Hearing her poorly masked cry for help, Jacob invited her down for a weekend of healing and renewal. The very next day Karyn boarded a plane to this wonderfully secluded place; and to him. Both had become a great sanctuary in her life. The earth was pure and untouched here. Society hadn't intruded upon its simplicity, nor tarnished its golden fields and green forests with the scars of concrete and glass high-rise giants sprawling about the landscape. Here, the chrome and steel alligators of urban highways wouldn't snatch her up, swimming aimlessly through a swamp she never wanted to endure. Instead, horses roamed the foothills and sauntered her along on their backs, with never a care for schedules and traffic circles. Truly, this was a transforming place ... yet never transformed itself.

It was the pasture that called to her now. Karyn longed to ride through the night, leaving far behind her cares and her nightmares. Since her childhood days, riding had always offered her a solace few other things could. She felt in control and free at the same time. While sitting astride a horse, she felt completely alone and yet so much more a part of the family of nature than at any other time. Karyn could remember the very first time she went riding through these woods. She was a scared teenager, frustrated with the world and herself. She didn't have direction or a clue of who she should be, what she wanted, needed, loved or feared. It was during that summer spent riding that she found herself and discovered what it was that she truly loved about herself and the world. She found purpose that summer, and she needed desperately now to regain that lost feeling of serenity and freedom, if only for a few moments.

She glanced back at the house upon the hill and wished for a moment that she had asked Jacob to join her. But the still darkened window witnessed to her that he remained tucked in perfect slumber. She cast a long look toward his bedroom window thinking that it was probably just as well. Though a great part of her longed for his attention, she also enjoyed this brief time alone with nature.

Spirit, an Arabian gelding, neared the fence and softly snorted his welcome. Karyn stroked his muzzle gently, losing herself in the softness of his fur. It reminded her of her childhood blanket. The blue one with the satin edges that she had never let out of her sight; the blanket that calmed her bad dreams on stormy nights. The blanket she still kept in the hope chest at the foot of her bed, waiting for the day when she would give it to her own child.

****

Gillian caught her breathing and let go a small tear as she remembered the blanket... the one that had always been her comfort... the one she left with Eryn in Kremmling - for she could no longer find comfort in things now that such a large part of her soul had perished. "Oh Thomas..." she said, sipping her tea for courage. Achilles heard her pain and curled up next to her; his warm body lending his strength to her twitching legs. She stroked his soft ears, whispered "Thank you", and turned the page in her sketchbook.

****

Soft and warm, the great animal brought her tremendous tranquility. She padded silently barefoot around to the gate, and pulling a halter and bareback pad from their hooks on the barn wall, approached her mount. The sheep, goats and other animals in the barnyard paid her no heed, continuing their sleep without so much as the twitch of an eyelid. It seemed to Karyn as though she and Spirit were the only creatures awake at this hour of night; as though there had been some secret spell cast to allow her this precious time to be completely alone.

Spirit offered no struggle as she gently slipped the bridle over his head, laid the bareback pad across his withers, and tossed the reins about his neck. Almost trance-like, Karyn eased the blanket from her shoulders, and laying it upon the fence, mounted Spirit with a practiced hop, and together they trotted off into the fields. The wind tossed her short, auburn hair about her face and neck as she took the animal over small foothills dotted with evergreens and through fields of knee-high goldenrod.

It was as though she had left the entire world behind and was floating alone through a gentle fog of security and acceptance. Never before had she felt so free and so sure of herself. Forgotten was the stress and anxiety of the corporate world. Far away was the criticism and judgment of those that didn't know her heart and worse, didn't care. Gone were the accusing stares and constant internal lectures about her worthlessness and inability to be successful at every attempt to move her life forward. It was heaven realized.

Karyn had been riding for about twenty minutes when a mild rain began to fall. The silken mist landed delicately upon her body and bathed her face with tiny drops of quintessence, calming the bewilderment in her head. It affected her so that she looked toward the night sky and began to giggle out loud. It was a laugh of wonderment that exploded from her with heady excitement. She thought it amusing that this had truly become a weekend of healing and cleansing.

On the hill upon which the house sat, Karyn caught sight of Jacob watching her. Startled at first, but pleased just the same, it was like something out of an old movie. There he stood in the evening rain, in just his boxers, watching her revel in the unity and peace she had discovered. She had no way of knowing how long he'd been standing there, but she delighted in a sumptuous sensuality knowing that he had indeed watched her. It was a sensation she never thought she'd find.

She reined Spirit to a walk and approached him slowly. As their eyes met, Karyn smiled broadly, touched by his unfailing acceptance of her desires without hesitation or judgment. Without a word, Jacob vaulted up and mounted the animal behind her. He held her close to him for a long moment. Not a word was spoken between them; yet volumes were understood. She leaned into him, enjoying the feel of his warm, moist skin against hers. It was as if they had rescued an intrinsic poetry lost for centuries. As in a carefully choreographed ballet, they moved into one another. Tenderly, she leaned her back upon his chest and laid her head upon his shoulder. Holding his arms about her, she closed her eyes to the warm rain playing upon her face, tickling her eyelashes in a silent sonata.

He wrapped himself around her then... easing her into him, enveloping her in the power of his soul. It was almost more ecstasy than she could bear. Time truly stopped for her at that moment. There were no creatures, no people, no sky, and no land - only the two of them, suspended on a cloud of sweet exhilaration and sensual beauty. He took the up reins, as they began to ride off into the night's salvation.

They rode on for nearly an hour this way. Never speaking a word between them but lost completely in each other. Finally, they arrived back at the barn, and dismounted. Thunder and lightning began to punctuate the darkness. Jacob wrapped the blanket around the two of them as quickly, they ran back to the house like teenagers, laughing and playing along the way. This was a wonderment Karyn had not felt in longer than she could remember. As they approached the back door, she paused just out of reach of the awning, and turned her head to the heavens.

Lost in her own thoughts and the sensation of the warm rain upon her face, Karyn closed her eyes and tried to capture the moment for all of eternity. She feared she would never again delight in this kind of pure joy. Living in the moment, capturing the sensations of seconds, was a learned process. She had to break down wall after wall in order to climb through the rubble of denial and self-loathing to get to the now. Still not completely proficient ... at least she was trying, and recognizing its importance. This point, in itself, was an area of tremendous growth for her. And at last she felt proud.

****

Gillian felt the hair on the back of her neck stand up as she came to the very same realization captured in the words Thomas had written. It had been a very long road, with more frustration and sorrow than she thought possible. But he was right. The hot coals she had walked were simply smoldering rubble now. True, she would never forget, but at least now, she was beginning to learn endurance. Given the mountain she had climbed, he was right, this had been a time of tremendous growth for her. Although she could not yet articulate the lessons, she knew they were there... guiding her choices and her grief.

****

Silently, Jacob came up behind her and cradled her in his arms. The rain was relentless, mingling with the tears now streaming down her cheeks. She felt wonderfully released of the pain that had shadowed her over the past several months. It was nice. How she missed love in her life and the want to feel it. So much of those emotions she'd pushed away because of the frequently horrific outcome. Rejection and ridicule now lived where gentle kisses and warm bodies lovingly intertwined once dwelled.

In order to save herself from that misery, Karyn no longer allowed herself the opportunity to feel any of it. She distanced herself from the desire and the people who might offer it. She could find no other way to cope. It was for this reason that she loved Jacob's land so much. There was nothing to cope with. Everything was easy and simple. It gave her the illusion that somehow, she could muster the courage to try again.

Jacob held Karyn close until the storm which raged inside her had subsided, and then he eased her gently into the house and upstairs to his bed. She made a feeble attempt at an apology for her emotional flood, but he would hear none of it. Drawing her beside him snugly enveloped in the warmth of his body and a fluffy quilt. Jacob assured her that she was okay.

"I'm here. You'll make it through this. I'll take care of you. Nothing will hurt you."

****

Gillian remembered those words spoken to her just after... in a morphine induced haze... she remembered Thomas' voice. He had been there. And now, if she would let him - he would be there again. The thought of it scared her and comforted her simultaneously. She thought for a moment, but could not imagine it. As she continued reading the letter, she soon learned that Thomas could. Gillian sketched his words, testing the possibility.

****

Karyn buried her head in his chest, sobbed and shook, finally letting go of all the burdens she'd carried in her heart for so long. Softly, Jacob whispered words of comfort and encouragement and held her tightly to him, making her feel safer than she had ever felt in her life.

That is how she slept the rest of that night, and well into the morning. Jacob never left her side, and each time Karyn stirred, he moved a protective arm about her, drawing her close to him once again, silently reassuring her that she had nothing to fear. It was the greatest gift anyone could have ever given her. Peace. Acceptance. Unconditional Love.

Chapter Twenty-Five

"Every parting is a form of death, as every reunion is a type of heaven."
~Tryon Edwards

"Thomas, I think I've found something." Aaren's voice was muffled as she called to him from the back of Paige's master bedroom closet.   They had been cleaning out the house, getting it ready for sale, and the piles of stuff didn't seem to end. It's as if she'd never thrown anything away. Aaren backed out of the closet on her hands and knees just as Thomas came in from the spare room.

"What did you find?"

"I think it's a journal or a date book..." Aaren sat on the floor, legs crossed, cradling the book in her lap. Thomas bent down to join her. As Aaren opened the pages, Thomas sat quietly and listened to her speak with Paige's voice.

"July 5; This week is not the parade it should be... I doubt it ever will be again.   Logan left for the Small Hearts Sanctuary Orphanage today. I didn't want to let him go, but there just didn't seem to be any other option. I've got too much to do with my life to

make room for a child. Businesses don't just stop and wait every time a small child cries out. I had to choose. I think I made the right choice - but still, it's painful. I wonder if he'll be all right... I hope he finds a family to give him more than I could."

Aaren stared at the book in disbelief. In all the years that they'd been friends, not once did Paige even hint at the fact that she'd had a child," she whispered. "Why wouldn't she tell me..." Aaren's face held the disbelief of one who had just discovered that the entire Christian doctrine was simple mythology. Thomas reached over and took the book from her hands.

"July 10; I received a letter from Small Hearts Sanctuary today. 'Logan has been placed with a foster family in Washington DC. They are a nice family, who have Logan's best interests at heart. This is not a permanent placement, as the couple has four other children. However, he will be well cared for and well-loved until a suitable "forever" family can be found for him. Please rest assured that we will do all we can for him until the right family is found. More news will be forthcoming.' It sounds like they're adopting out a puppy rather than a little boy. I'm starting to doubt this decision... but... I know it will be better for Logan to be with someone else, not me. I wouldn't be any good for him. I'll just have to hope that one day he can be more than some stranger's stray puppy."

"October 15; A second letter arrived from Small Hearts. 'There was a problem with Logan's placement... the family wanted to adopt him but due to the special circumstances, instead of continuing to act as fosters, they returned him to our gentle care. The foster family was uncomfortable with a lingering future and wanted to put an end to their waiting to complete their family. Logan has since been placed with a nice couple who have no other children. This may well be the ideal placement for him, until his circumstances change.' "

"January 22; A third letter arrived from Small Hearts. 'The couple who had been fostering Logan were arrested with drug paraphernalia just after the New Year's celebration. Logan was returned to us pending trial; and is still in our care. The judge ordered the couple to jail for some period of time, and we are seeking another placement for Logan. We will make you aware when a suitable family has been found.' "

"March 6; A fourth letter from Small Hearts. 'Another family was found to foster Logan. Unfortunately, the father was tragically lost in a car accident a few weeks after Logan arrived. The family already had two other children, and the mother didn't feel that she was strong enough to care for three children on her own. We have been praying for peace and gentle healing for the family during this difficult time. Logan is back in our hands until another family can be found for him.' "

"June 14, A fifth letter from Small Hearts. 'Logan has been placed with a family in Montana. They are gentle, loving people who are willing to bring him into their household and nurture him, keeping him safe and loved until his special circumstances are resolved. We are confident that this will be his final Foster Family placement.' Well, I suppose that's the best birthday present a girl could ask for..."

****

Thomas slouched back against the cedar chest, causing the lid to thump closed. It was hard to imagine. This last year was so contrary to the Paige that he had known. He discovered that she had a regretful soul that sought redemption... and a memory that would not allow her soul the peace she coveted. *How had she hid all that behind her cold and vile exterior? How was it possible for her to have survived all these years with a dual personality - and yet achieve so much success?*

"I never imagined she could have been carrying around this much pain. She never told me." Aaren said, with a soft, penitent wail.

****

The next day, after a barrage of phone calls, Aaren and Thomas connected with Small Hearts Sanctuary in Washington where Logan's case was last noted. The caseworker, Ms. Gundry told them that she was not able to speak with them directly about Logan until they could prove power of attorney. "Those records are sealed, Mr. Laird. We are not at liberty to discuss anything about the child, his case, or his current whereabouts until we are presented with the appropriate documentation. I am sorry."

Thomas clicked off the speaker phone and looked at Aaren. "What now?"

"Didn't Paige's attorney tell you that anything you needed, he could help with? Why not call him? Maybe he could get you the papers you need." Aaren's eyes were hopeful.

"That's a good idea. Now, where did I put his card?" Thomas rifled through his wallet, finally pulling out the proper card. "Here it is, Stanley McClish. I sure hope this works." Thomas punched the speaker button on the phone again, and began dialing.

The phone connected through and a secretary answered. After giving his name, Thomas was put on hold for a moment, and then connected to McClish's office. "This is Stanley McClish, what can I do for you Mr. Laird?"

"Well, you said that if I needed any help in adopting Paige's son, Logan, you could help us."

"That's true. What do you need?" said Mr. McClish.

"Ms. Gundry at the Small Hearts Sanctuary Orphanage in Washington DC tells me that Logan's records are sealed and she can only reveal them to someone who has power of attorney paperwork. Can you help with this?"

"I can, indeed, Mr. Laird. We anticipated that this might be a problem, and so before her death, Ms. Lambert named you as personal executor of her affairs and power of attorney to handle all of her private matters. I have the documents for you at my office. I will have my secretary overnight them to you today. There are ample funds in the account for your travel arrangements. Please don't hesitate to use that account, Mr. Laird."

"Thank you, Mr. McClish."

"You're welcome, sir. Is there anything else that I can do for you?"

"Not at this time... but I'm not sure about the adoption proceedings; so when the time arises, I may need your services to assist with that."

"Very good. I will await your call. Good-bye."

"Good-bye, and thank you." Thomas punched off the speaker phone and looked at Aaren. "Can it really be this simple? Did Paige really plan this well... well enough to keep an attorney in her back pocket?"

"It wouldn't surprise me," Aaren said. "Her parents were exactly the same way... it was what she was taught. Look at everything she'd planned so far. It makes sense, given her perfectionist nature that she would try to plan for every contingency. She certainly had plenty of money to accomplish all this... and probably more... but it never seemed excessive. Aside from the house in the Hamptons, which everyone knew she inherited, and the boat that few knew was already paid for, free and clear; she never spent money without a solid purpose. All that superficial stuff, the inexpensive stuff she used to keep her image intact didn't amount to much, dollar-wise. She always had a plan running in the background somewhere. She kept telling me she was saving for a rainy day. I remember telling her that if she was always worrying about the rain, she'd never enjoy the sun." Aaren's voice quieted to a whisper. "I had no idea she was living in the eye of the storm."

"Aaren, none of this was ever your fault. I know she didn't share this part of her life with you. How could you have known? I'm just glad that we have a way to squelch the storm before it becomes too much bigger." Thomas' words brought a small smile of comfort to Aaren. "Do me a favor, book a flight for me to D.C. I think I need to make this trip in person. If those papers arrive tomorrow morning, I can leave in the afternoon. Find an inexpensive hotel near the orphanage... no use spending more money than we have to. And one other thing..."

"Sure," said Aaren, while scribbling in her ever-present note pad.

"Would you be willing to stay with Emily while I'm gone? It should just be the one night. I can't imagine that this will take longer than a day. I just think that for Emily to travel while she's still so new, isn't such a good plan."

Aaren smiled. "Of course I'll stay with her. Are you kidding! Concentrated micro-human time and nobody to have to share her with? I'm in!!" They laughed together. Babies were one of Aaren's small joys in life. She hoped one day to have her own... but she was holding out for the right guy to appear first. Although she loved children nearly as much as chocolate, single parenting was not a road Aaren wanted to follow.

****

The next afternoon, Thomas boarded a flight to Washington DC and found himself sitting in the sparse offices of Small Hearts Sanctuary. He was surprised at the utilitarian look of the office, but was pleased to see through the window, the best playground equipment money could buy. It would seem that once again, Paige had done her homework. This appeared to be a place that put children first. Ms. Gundry was a kindly woman, in her mid-forties, who genuinely seemed to have the best interests of the children at heart. After presenting his paperwork, she retrieved Logan's file from the bank of cabinets behind her and began to tell Thomas his story. She handed him a collection of photos of Logan as she spoke.

"Logan is a beautiful child, very sweet and smart. He lived with us, here at the orphanage, for the first few weeks, and then was placed with several local families of varying circumstances. I won't go into the details; it's all in the file, if you're interested. Finally, he was placed with a lovely family in Montana for long-term fostering. They are considering adopting Logan, but for some reason, have not completed the necessary steps. He's been there for two years. We're not sure why they're hesitating. They have no children of their own, and by all appearances, seem to be good candidates for adoption. According to the last report we received, about two months ago, it seems that Logan has been happy and thriving there. His case is being followed by the Montana Child Services Department; a woman named Kendra Jorgenson is his caseworker. With your power of attorney, she will be able to give you further information and put you in contact with the family... even set up an interview, if that's what you want." She gathered up Logan's file, the photos, and the contact information for the worker in Montana, and slipped it into an envelope, handing it to Thomas.

"Thank you very much, Ms. Gundry, I will contact her first thing in the morning, when I return to Boston. He stood up and reached out his hand.

Ms. Gundry took his hand and gave it a firm shake. "Good luck, Mr. Laird. And do keep us informed."

"I will; Thank you." said Thomas

The flight back to Boston had Thomas' head spinning. *This family in Montana has had Logan all this time, and they haven't adopted him yet? I wonder why?* When the wheels touched down, he wasted no time in calling Aaren to let her know he was on his way home.

"Oh, that's too bad," she teased. "I was hoping for a little more time with Emily." The smile in her voice was comforting to Thomas.

"How wonderful that Emily has people in her life that love her so much."

"Well, that's what aunts do best," Aaren giggled. "See you when you get here. I want to know everything."

"Don't worry, I've got lots to tell... and another mystery." Thomas hung up the phone before Aaren could respond. He loved dangling clues in front of her.

****

It was three o'clock on a Sunday afternoon, Mother's Day, when the phone rang. Gillian had been folding laundry and watching some insignificant game show on television. On the fourth ring, she finally made it from her bedroom to the living room, stepping over the piles of boxes still not filled as she prepared for her move in two weeks.

"Hello, this is Gillian."

"Gillian, I need to see you. This is important." Gillian's heart and breathing stopped for a full five seconds. It was Thomas. *Thomas Laird.* His voice was strong and solid, just as she had remembered; filled with emotion and unwavering at the same time. Hearing his voice was a surprise. It had been nearly three weeks since his last letter, and though she had been prepared for his words on paper, she was not yet emotionally equipped to hear his voice.

"Where are you?" She was bewildered by his voice on the other end, yet strangely comforted by it, too. Through all the months of letters... fifteen months... She had wanted to believe that somehow they would find something to bring them back together, and that she'd be there to encourage its momentum. She had always been a die-hard romantic who firmly believed in the vow of forever... despite the fact that their marriage had painfully ended in divorce... in the deepest place in her heart she knew, it was never supposed to.

"I was in Boston, working for a computer firm, but now I'm on my way to Montana. It's a long story. I'm staying at the Townsend Hotel in Birmingham for a couple of weeks. Can you come meet me here?" In a flash of doubt, she found herself relying on her logical thinking class from college. It could be disastrous for her to allow emotion to creep back into her world. She had worked so hard. She'd been doing so well this past year, despite his letters... the distance helped to keep her emotions in check. Making only rational, level-headed decisions; Thomas was renowned for his skill at infiltrating a life and filling it with emotion, and she was uneasy about what that might mean for her now.

"I don't know Thomas..." Gillian was worried about opening the old patterns of the past. Old patterns lead to old wounds, and after spending so much time with emotional bandages and psychological Mercurochrome, she really didn't want to go through that all over again.

"Please, Gillian, I wouldn't ask if it wasn't serious. Can you come right away?" There was an insistence in his voice that she'd not heard in a very long time. He wasn't fooling around; this really meant something to him. Her heart, her head, and a vow she could not forget all told her that she had to respond.

"Alright then, I'll see you in about an hour."

"This really means a lot to me. I'm in room 217. Thank you."

Gillian hung up the phone and paced the floor for a few minutes collecting her purse and her keys. "Now what are you getting yourself into, Gill? You've been doing so well..."

****

As Gillian pointed her blue Miata up the Southfield freeway from her pragmatic, yet comfortable duplex in Dearborn, she thought about Thomas and what his return to her life might mean. After the death of their daughter in that horrible train wreck, neither one would ever be the same again. Thomas knew it would take a long time to heal. He tried to tell her that it would get better for them. Gillian didn't understand how Thomas could think of the idea of healing, let alone things actually getting better. Their baby girl had been ripped from them too quickly, horrifically, painfully. There was a scar on her right shoulder - a remnant of her collision with death. She didn't think she could ever heal from a thing like that. So it was a complete shock to her when, just as her brain was beginning to believe that her wretched, painful memories were simple nightmares, Thomas called and rattled the crystal bars around her heart once more.

She had absolutely no idea what might provoke him to call after all this time; but one thing she knew, when Thomas said that something was important, he never lied. The word 'serious' was always reserved for those events that were life-changing. 'Serious' was never to be trifled with. 'Serious' could not be ignored. She couldn't deny him; for in her heart, she still loved him; and after all was said and done; Thomas was the last remaining thread of connectivity to Eryn and a life that once held such happiness and peace for her.

Gillian arrived about ten minutes early, plenty of time to grab a nerve-steadying cup of tea at the cafe across the street. 220 Merrill was known for their extraordinary food, but today, a simple cup of tea was all she needed - that and a good view of the front door of the Townsend. Gillian spent a good part of her teenage summers sitting in this very same spot, watching for visiting celebrities to pass through the Townsend's threshold to awaiting tour buses as she planned her autograph-seeking attempts. She wasn't sure what she expected to find coming and going through that door today, but she felt like she needed a few minutes to do a little emotional reconnaissance before going up.

At last, her courage restored, she walked across the street and rode the elevator to the second floor, talking to herself along the way. *Remember Gillian, whatever happens, you can't go back with him. You've worked too hard to get to where you are today. A nice place to live, a good career, no hassles. Try to keep it that way, would you please.* She often gave herself these little pep talks, and most of the time they worked. This time, however, she had her doubts. The past was a powerful adversary, especially in the compelling amber eyes of Thomas Laird.

Gillian stood outside room 217 for a full minute before reaching up to knock on the door. A little voice inside her said, *run as fast as you can in the other direction.* But she fought the urge to pay attention. She had promised Thomas she'd show, and so here she was. She rapped her knuckles upon the door twice. Thomas opened the door and invited her in. He was still beautiful, just as she remembered; a little more gray hair perhaps, but still beautiful.

"Gill, I'm so glad you came," he said, enveloping her in an embrace so warm her toes melted. "Please, come in and sit down. Would you like a cup of tea?"

"Sure, tea would be nice," she said, choosing a seat on the couch, with its pile of pillows for comfort, and a direct escape route to the door.

"Earl Gray, with a little sugar, right?"

"You remembered." Gillian smiled at the memory of Sunday morning tea and her sketchbook on the back patio while Eryn played in the sandbox.

"After making cup after cup while watching you paint, it's not a memory easily forgotten." His smile was entrancing. Gillian looked out the window, instead of at his smile, saving the rest of her appendages from going the way of her toes.

Thomas brought over two cups of tea, with accompanying saucers and spoons. Both delicately stirred their tea in awkward silence, searching for some sign of the familiar. They sat together sipping tea for a few moments, not talking, but each screaming volumes in a heartbeat adaptation of Morse code.

"So, I noticed you didn't change your last name," said Thomas, trying to find an easy lead into a risky conversation.

"I couldn't. It felt like abandoning Eryn with such finality." Gillian sipped her tea, working hard to hide her pain.

"Well, I appreciate it, it certainly made finding you much easier," he smiled.

"Are you still writing?" she asked, setting her teacup on the table next to her. "I haven't seen anything from you in a while."

"Some," he said, smiling sheepishly. "But things have gotten busy lately, sorry. Are you still painting?"

"No, working at the museum was too difficult. I gave it up and found a job that paid the bills..." Her hesitation hung low in the room. "...Accounting."

"Oh, I'm sorry," Thomas said, his voice and face pure deadpan.

Gillian pressed a controlled smile through her lips, working hard at not giving herself away. "But I've been keeping a small sketch book."

A small noise came from the bedroom, breaking the silence and adding more tension than lit match at a dynamite factory. Gillian thought it sounded like the cry of a small child, or the tortured mew of a Siamese cat, she couldn't be sure which.

"Excuse me just a moment, please. I'll be right back." Thomas jumped from his chair and nearly raced to the bedroom door. The sound abruptly stopped. When he returned a few minutes later, Thomas held a very tiny, dark-haired infant in his arms, wrapped in a purple blanket with little pink teddy bears on it.

"Gillian, I'd like you to meet my daughter, Emily." Stunned and shocked by this unexpected introduction, Gillian wasn't sure if she would throw up or faint first, so she sat down - plop - back on the couch and tried to take a sip of her tea.

"Emily... When ... How ... Are you married? Where's her mother? Thomas ..." Gillian had absolutely no defense for this moment in time. All of her logical thinking could not save her from the lava flow of hot emotions now oozing from her brain in ways she could never describe. She tried another sip of tea, but managed to spill it on her lap instead. Thomas grabbed a towel from the kitchen table and handed it to her.

"Here, take this. I'll try to explain. Emily's mother and I were together for just a short time, but things didn't work out..."

"Wait... you were with another woman? How could you!" Gillian's anger rushed from a place she'd held hidden inside herself for far too long. "I thought you'd promised yourself to me and me alone!" She was irrational, and Thomas understood. They'd both been through so much.

"In all fairness, Gillian, we weren't together anymore. I didn't know if I'd ever see you again." Thomas tried to calm her, but sensed it would only get worse before it got better. And then he did it, in spite of himself, and without thinking... "If it's any consolation, we weren't even that serious..." he'd made the fatal mistake.

"Not serious? So not only did you cheat on me... but you cheated on me with a FLING? A woman who didn't MEAN anything to you?! You're despicable, Thomas!" Gillian screamed.

"Gillian, it's a long story, I'll tell you it all, if you want to hear it, but the short version is that after Emily was born..."

Wait... this is the child from the FLING?" Gillian's face turned beet red.

"...her mother died only two days later. Our agreement, long before her birth, was that I would take full custody of Emily, and move away, no strings attached. Emily's birthday was twenty-one days ago. We arrived back in Detroit yesterday, and you were the first person I wanted to call. So now, here we are..." Thomas was talking quickly, working hard to get in all the details, rushing to the conclusion before he was interrupted again.

Immediately, Gillian's face softened and tears flowed from her eyes. Sadness rushed through her, a sadness that Thomas had only seen once before. "She gave her up, just like that," she whispered. "But how could a mother do that to her child?" Gillian's head was reeling from the story she'd just been told, and an evil box of her own painful maternal memories plundered her soul with Technicolor saturation.

"Well, it's a little more complicated than that; but that part of the story can wait until later. Would you like to hold her?" Thomas was beaming. Just as he did the day he held Eryn for the very first time. Gillian was having a hard time staying in the moment. She nodded her head in silence, trepidation filling her face.

"It's okay," said Thomas. "You're good at this stuff." He gently placed the tiny Emily in Gillian's arms. Gillian sank into the couch cushions, half celebrating the day and half mourning the loss of Eryn all over again.

"She's so small. Not even a month old. I remember..." Gillian choked back the tears that betrayed her happiness for Thomas.

"I know. And no, she's really not that small... seven pounds, eleven ounces; twenty-one and a half inches... she likes to tuck her feet up." Thomas giggled in a way that made Gillian think perhaps he'd healed. She didn't know how that was possible. "The best part..." Thomas whispered, "is that she purrs in her sleep just the way Eryn did."

"I thought you'd forgotten..." Gillian looked at Thomas with eyes that begged for his comforting words, the ones that she had relied on for so many years whenever things got hard for her... whenever she was lost... it was always his words that brought her back to strength.

"I could never forget." Thomas said with a gentle defiance. "But it is nice to know that DNA remembers, too."

Gillian smiled. *He always knows the right words.* "Uh oh, I think there's a mess to be dealt with here." Gillian smiled at Thomas and glanced down at the now awake and gas-relieved smile of a tiny little girl with big blue eyes. "Oh, she's got blue eyes. How beautiful."

"Here, I'll take her..." Thomas said, being more than willing to change a diaper now than he ever had been in his life.

"No way," squealed Gillian. "She's in my arms... I get to do it. Rules are rules, you know."

Thomas grinned remembering their diaper changing ritual with Eryn, and how 'possession meant nine-tenths responsibility'. *How easily she's falling back into motherhood.* Thomas thought. *I just hope she handles everything else as easily.*

When Gillian returned from the bedroom with a cooing Emily on her shoulder, Thomas felt the time was right. He pulled the Blue Box and his reporter's notebooks out from his briefcase, and set it on the coffee table. "What's this?" asked Gillian in a tentative voice.

"You're going to need your hands... why don't you give Emily to me." Thomas took Emily gently and cradled her in his lap as he sat in the wing-back chair directly across from Gillian's seat on the couch. "I told you that the story was a bit more complicated than you thought, and the truth is, it's a LOT more complicated. It begins with this Blue Box. It was left to Emily by her mother just before she died. In it, are secrets that may be difficult for you to accept. But you must believe me... I've done all the research, and it's all true..." Thomas looked at Gillian with his 'serious' face; and she knew this was the most important story he'd ever tell.

Gillian gently opened the box and found a dozen photos, a few newspaper clippings, official documents, and the other evidence that Thomas and Aaren were able to discover in the last week... piecing together Paige's secret past. Gillian looked carefully at it all, never uttering a word, until she came across the copy of her birth certificate, with Paige's paper clipped underneath. Her eyes fixed on the section that stated "multiple birth - twin". The look on her face was incredulous, as if someone had just told her that the painting hanging over her mantle was a daVinci original.

"What is this... I don't have a sister; certainly not a twin..." Gillian stared at the photo of Paige, attached to her certificate. "This can't be right."

"I promise you, it's the truth, Gillian," said Thomas.

"You mean my parents knew all along? How could they have kept this from me?"

****

Thomas ordered room service and a bottle of wine; prepared a bottle to feed Emily, cradling his daughter gently, as he told the whole story to Gillian, leaving nothing out. Two hours later, after all the details, photos and documents had been presented to her in details that sounded like fiction, Thomas summarized everything for Gillian's bewildering gaze. "Yes, Paige was your sister. Emily is your niece. Emily is my daughter. Emily has a brother somewhere in Montana, named Logan. It was Paige's dying wish to bring her family together, and that's become my wish too." Thomas walked into the bedroom and put Emily to sleep in her cradle, giving Gillian a few moments alone with her thoughts.

By the time Thomas came back to join Gillian, she was on her feet, standing at the window, holding a photo of Logan in her hands. He looked to be about five years old. She seemed lost, yet peaceful. Thomas was a little leery of what would come next... it had been a long time since they shared the same air space, and he wasn't sure if she would respond with anger, sadness or something else not yet imagined. He gave her the time she needed to digest everything, and simply waited for her to come to him. He poured himself a glass of wine to keep him company while he waited.

"Okay." Gillian started. "I had a sister I never knew about, we were both adopted by completely different families from different parts of the country. Our birth mother is long dead, we don't know who our birth father is... and now, her adoptive parents are dead. But, through all this, she found you, and had a child with you so that her sister could have a niece, her son could have a sister, and somehow she could be redeemed for whatever transgressions she perpetrated throughout her life as a ruthless CEO. Have I got it right? Did I miss anything?"

"Nope. You've got it all." Thomas was hesitant. He wasn't sure if there was an explosion on the horizon or a gentle breeze. He waited.

A few minutes of silence passed and Gillian spoke again. "All right. This is a lot to take in, I'll grant you. But there's something that I need to know... What do you expect from me?"

"I want us to be together, it's what I've wanted since the day we stopped being us." He moved closer to her, hoping she wouldn't reject his affection. "It's why I wrote to you all this time. It's why I told you all those stories, hoping that you'd see in my characters more of me... and perhaps rekindle the memory of us, and how good we were together. I tried to remind you of how much you mean to me... how much I love you... and how much I want you back." He stood and walked over to her at the window, gently taking her hand.

"I just don't know, Thomas." Gillian said, walking away from him. She stood just outside the open bedroom door, and peaked in at a peacefully sleeping Emily. "So much has changed between us... our lives are so different than they once were. Eryn is gone..."

"And nothing will ever change that, or change our love for her. She will always be a part of both of us. And we won't ever forget her." Thomas went to Gillian and stood next to her, sharing the vision of his newborn daughter, making those same purring noises Eryn once had as she slept. "Emily will never replace Eryn... not for me, not for you... and truly, I don't think that's what Paige had intended. But I do believe that Paige sincerely wanted us to be a family. She didn't always make the most ethical of choices... but this time, I think her heart was in the right place." Thomas turned to Gillian and put his hands on her shoulders. "She was dying, Gillian. Her last wish was that we heal her broken family."

Gillian fell into Thomas' arms, standing in his gentle embrace for a long while. She'd forgotten how comforting his spirit was... how safe she felt with his arms wrapped around her. *Oh, how I've missed you... still not brave enough to say it to out loud.*

"Gill," Thomas whispered; "I want to be with you forever... that has never changed. Please, give me another chance to make you happy."

There was a cry from the bedroom, and Thomas broke their embrace to gather up his daughter in his arms, comforting her gently back to sleep. "I remember how you used to do that with Eryn. You've always been such a good father... such a good man."

Thomas could only smile.

"But, this is a lot to take in... you and me getting back together... two new children to raise... a history to relearn. I need some time." Gillian walked over to the couch and picked up her purse and car keys. "How long will you be in town?" she asked Thomas, avoiding eye contact.

"Just until Tuesday. I've got an appointment with the adoption agency in Montana on Wednesday morning to talk about getting Logan. I have a noon flight out of Metro on Tuesday." Thomas was hopeful and worried simultaneously. Would he lose the only woman he's ever known... ever loved... again?

"I have to go." said Gillian. "I need some time to think. I'll call you." She walked out the door, only briefly glancing at Thomas and Emily as she closed the door behind her. She leaned against the wall next to the hotel room door for what seemed like an eternity. She heard Thomas singing softly to Emily, soothing her back to sleep. Gillian remembered fondly the way he used to soothe Eryn the same way. As she walked toward the elevator, she was flooded with conflicting thoughts, emotions and desires and her logical brain struggled to break through. Tonight, she needed her old friends... paint and canvas... surely, they could help her figure this out.

****

Thomas's phone rang promptly at seven o'clock in the morning. The automated voice cheerily reminded Thomas of his request for a wake-up call, greeted him to a new day, and wished him well. Emily had been such a content baby, he usually awoke before she did. They were up late last night, she was hungry and the excitement from the airplane ride from Boston hadn't completely worn off yet. Even though there was no difference in time, babies, it seemed still got jet-lag. He was up telling her stories to ease her toward sleep until well past two.

Fortunately, she was now still soundly sleeping. He indulged in a quiet cup of coffee. No matter how good a baby was, for any parent, moments of solitude were rare, and he was going to take full advantage. Also not one to give up on life-long habits, checking himself and his place in the world's scheming, Thomas went to get the morning paper from the hotel hallway. When he opened the door, he found Gillian, hand raised, ready to knock.

"Don't say anything," she said, pushing past him and into the hotel room. He closed the door and followed her in. "I need to get this out before I lose my nerve."

"Okay," he said. But she raised a finger, compelling him back into silence. With mime-like precision, he offered her a cup of coffee.

"Sure," she laughed. "I'd love coffee. But let me get through this..." Gillian absent mindedly took Thomas' coffee from his hands. He grinned, and turned to get another. "Ugh! Too much sugar... did you forget?"

"No... that one was mine."

"Oh, sorry. I'm a little frazzled." Gillian handed him back his cup and sat down at the kitchen table.

"Don't worry about it," he comforted, and poured her a second, black.

Gillian took the cup he handed her, inhaled deeply and began to talk, never once meeting his eyes until she was finished. "It's been a long time since you and I have been together, and the truth is, I've missed you... We were right together, so right... but then the accident, it was so hard. Losing Eryn was the hardest thing I've ever had to do. I blamed myself and couldn't get out of that. And when I couldn't find a way to blame myself anymore, I blamed you. It was wrong, I know, and I'm sorry. I know we both thought that we could come back from Kremmling and live through it... but it was just too hard." Gillian was crying tears she'd been saving all this time for Thomas - not because he deserved them, but because she knew he would understand them. He gently nudged the tissue box closer to her as she took a sip of her coffee.

"The letters you sent, those wonderful stories... they reminded me of exactly how in love we were once, and how strong we were together. Those stories got me back to sketching again, Thomas; and I didn't think anything could ever get me back to my art. I fell in love with you all over again, grabbing on to what we had, and hoping for something better still to come. But then you came here yesterday with Emily... and I just didn't know what to think. The whole thing caught me a little off guard, you know?" Gillian paused for a moment to take another sip of her coffee.

"I know, I'm sorry..." Thomas tried to go on, but Gillian cut him off.

"UH! I'm not done yet!" Gillian made the signal that he should put a zipper on his lips, and he complied. She smiled back, remembering their playfulness together. "But after seeing that beautiful little girl in there..." As if right on cue, Emily's muffled cry could be heard from the bedroom. Silently, Thomas stood up and motioned that he needed to go get her; never uttering a word, yet smiling broadly.

"Of course, go get her," said Gillian, radiating a smile Thomas had not seen in a very long time.

When Thomas returned to the kitchen with Emily, Gillian cooed, and Thomas placed her in Gillian's arms. "Would you mind holding her for a minute while I get her bottle?" Gillian gently took

Emily from Thomas and cradled her just as she had on Eryn's first day of life.

As Thomas came back into the room, he handed Gillian the bottle. Emily was squeaking softly, as if she had always known Gillian was her mother. Gillian put the bottle down on the table, and looked sincerely at the gentleness of the father before her. "Thomas," said Gillian, "I have something to show you. I made this after reading one of your stories... I think it was *The Griffin of Greed*. I'm not sure what got into me, but this is what came out." With a sly smirk, Gillian reached her free hand into her purse and pulled out the small book she created and had printed at Kinkos. She handed it to Thomas, who, with more than a large look of surprise on his face, took it gingerly from her, as if she had just handed him a lost scroll from the Library at Alexandria.

Thomas read the title, "Jeni and the Dogs". His face lit up when he recognized her unique artistic style on the cover. "When - how - did you..."

"Just read it. It won't take long, you can get through it easily while I feed Emily. Hand me her bottle." Gillian was once again, Mom in control. Thomas couldn't help but obey. He sat down next to them and began to read aloud. When he was finished, he closed the book, held it in his lap as if it were made of ancient parchment and looked lovingly at Gillian. For the first time in his life, he could find no words. Gillian spoke for him.

"I know that this child is not ours, but the simple fact that she is yours is enough for me. I love you, and if you will have me back, I promise to be the best wife and mother possible." Tears flooded her eyes as she watched the tiny little girl sleep peacefully in her arms. She looked up at Thomas, waiting for his reply. But he gave none. He just sat there, smiling. Mute and smiling.

"Okay, I'm done now, you can talk," she laughed.

Thomas took a deep breath and grinned. "I can't tell you how happy I am to hear you say that, sweetheart. I love you like nobody's business, and I don't ever want to let you go ever again. But before you jump back into a life with me, there are a few other things you should know." He gave her a worrisome look, not sure how she was going to take the rest of the news.

"Thomas, what is it?" said Gillian, now a little wary of what would come next.

"I can't do this without Logan..." Thomas was worried that two children might be too much for Gillian right now. "Knowing that Emily has a brother... I just can't let her grow up not having him right beside her. It just seems..."

"Too cruel," finished Gillian. "I agree. We need to go find him, and we need to do it together. Our family shouldn't be incomplete. Paige left this world believing that one day everything would be healed. I'd like to think that we are alike in that way... if in no other. Yes, Thomas; Logan should be with us."

Thomas could say nothing, but only kissed his daughter on her forehead and leaned over to kiss Gillian. It was the first kiss they'd shared in too long... how he had missed her.

****

After putting Emily down for a nap, Thomas and Gillian spent the rest of the afternoon going over the papers and tapes in the Blue Box. Thomas told her everything he could remember about his time with Paige... MouseTrax... the Hamptons... and Paige's funeral. He told her everything Aaren was able to find out about Edward - which wasn't much - and the connections they had made to the adoption agency in D.C. , and the foster care system Logan had been moved into out in Montana. They looked over all the photos again, and then, they listened to the audio tapes.

Thomas wanted Gillian to have the full story—he wanted to give her full disclosure. If she truly wanted a life with him again, she needed to know it all. When they were finally finished, Gillian sat, stunned, with a far-away look in her eyes.

"My parents never told me I had a sister; or that I was even born a twin... and now, to see her picture, hold her daughter, hear her voice... There's just so much to take in." Trance-like, she moved to the window, looking out over the Birmingham streets below. Taking a page from Nathan's book, Thomas gave her as much time as she needed to process everything. It was true. It was a lot to take in. After almost thirty full minutes of silence, Emily cried again from the next room, waking up from her afternoon nap. Thomas rose to go get her, but Gillian stopped him.

"Let me get her." When Gillian returned from the bedroom, she held a freshly diapered and cooing Emily. She sat down on the couch next to Thomas for a long moment in silence, just gazing into little Emily's perfect blue eyes.

"Well, you know, if we're going to have any hope of adopting Logan, we'll have to be married first," she said quietly.

"I can do that." Thomas said with a broad grin.

"Yes, somehow I thought you could," said Gillian. "But there's only one caveat."

"Anything." Thomas was willing to do whatever it took to make this work between them, and knowing Gillian as he had all those years, he was surprised there was only one condition - she was fond of laundry lists. "What is it?"

"I want to move back to Kremmling to raise the children. I don't want Emily and Logan to grow up knowing nothing about Eryn. I don't want her to be their dirty little secret - I want them to know her as we knew her. And I want to be close to where she was last with us." There were tears in Gillian's eyes; but Thomas couldn't tell if they were sad tears or joyful tears.

In a soft whisper he said, "I think Kremmling will be a wonderful place to raise our family."

"Oh good," said Gillian, now bouncing a very happy Emily on her lap. "When do we start?"

Thomas realized then, looking at his wife and daughter smiling at each other, that life doesn't get much better than this. "Gill," Thomas whispered.

"Yes." Gillian looked at him with the sweetest smile he'd ever seen.

"Happy Mother's Day."

Chapter Twenty-Six

"Love is a sacred reserve of energy; it is like the blood of spiritual evolution."
~Pierre Teilhard de Chardin

    Aaren arrived on Monday morning, with papers for Thomas to sign for the sale of Paige's brownstone. "How did Gillian take the news?" she asked, after all the business was completed.

    "Better than I could have expected. She's still in shock a little bit, I think; but having Emily here is giving her a little reality to hang on to. And she agreed to marry me again, too. So I guess that's positive." Thomas was working hard to reign in his excitement.

    "That's fantastic!" Aaren squealed. "I'm so happy for you both. What were her thoughts about finding Logan, and maybe adding him to your family? This has got to be tough for her... an instant family so close after losing Eryn." Even though Aaren and Gillian had never met, after all Thomas had told her about Gillian, and knowing she was the sister of her best friend, she felt as if they were already friends, and was a little protective.

    "Yeah, the first shock of it all was a little difficult for her, but she rebounded quickly - she always does. She's excited about raising Emily and she is just as enthusiastic about finding Logan and bringing him home with us. She said that she felt somehow closer to knowing Paige by raising her children. It's an awkward consolation prize, to be sure; but she seems to be handling it well."

Aaren heard Emily squirm and jumped up from her chair to get her out of bed. "You're too much!" Thomas told her, laughing as he watched her sprint into the bedroom, and return with the squiggly little cooing baby.

"Oh, come on, admit it; you're just as crazy about her as I am." Aaren chided. "I just wish I had more time with her. When do you leave?"

"We have to wait three days for the marriage license to become valid, and then we'll go to the courthouse, have the wedding, get the judge to formalize Gillian adopting Emily, and leave that day after that... so probably Thursday afternoon sometime." Thomas said, as he looked over their travel itinerary to Billings. "I'm hoping that we'll be able to get a new meeting with Ms. Jorgenson, and hopefully, get to meet Logan."

"It's too soon." said Aaren, as she gave Emily a tender Eskimo kiss. "Too soon."

"We'd like you to go with us, Aaren... if you're willing." Thomas said.

"What? Go with you? To where?" Aaren was so distracted with Emily that she only half heard what Thomas had said.

"Gillian and I discussed it, and we decided that, if you are interested, we'd like to have you go with us. We could really use your help with Emily while we find Logan and get to know him. We don't want to leave her with strangers... and we think it would be best for Logan if we do things slowly and gently. This is going to be a huge change for him... if it all works out... and we want to make it as easy on him as we can. Do you think you could take a few weeks away from MouseTrax and help us out?" Thomas knew that he was asking a lot from Aaren. She'd already given so much. He was imposing, he knew; but he also knew that Aaren would be the best choice for Emily - and for Gillian. She wanted to know more about who her sister was, and Thomas could think of no better person to introduce her to that memory than Paige's best friend.

"Yes! I would love that! I'm sure Tina can hold down the fort for a little while. There's nothing too pressing going on right now back at the office. The nerds are still trying to figure out how Paige did it so successfully. They're a little lost, I'm afraid." Aaren looked at Emily and gave her another little Eskimo kiss. "More time with the peanut. What could be better!" Aaren handed Emily to Thomas, and pulled her laptop out of her bag. "I'll need to call Tina and let her know I'll be gone for a little while... and then there's the plane reservations... hotel accommodations... And we've got to call the Montana Department of Child Services and schedule that appointment. If they're anything like Boston, the red tape will be a bear to get through..." Aaren was in support mode now, and there was no stopping her.

"Glad to see you have everything in hand." Thomas laughed. "Emily, your aunt Aaren is a little nuts," he said as he walked into the kitchen to fix a bottle.

Aaren laughed and continued to type. By the time Emily finished her bottle, Aaren had sent an email to Tina at MouseTrax to give her the change in her itinerary and some instructions on projects in motion; she called the Realtor in Boston and arranged for the staff at the Townsend to overnight the paperwork for the brownstone; she made all of the travel arrangements for the three of them; contacted Ms. Jorgenson's office and made an appointment for Thomas and Gillian to meet with her the following Monday morning; reserved a long-term stay condo in Billings for a month - they didn't know how long the process might take;

arranged for the wedding at the courthouse; and made reservations for dinner at Cameron's Steakhouse for after the wedding. Aaren was a formidable force once she got going.

****

It was three o'clock when Gillian knocked on the door. Thomas was putting Emily down for her nap, so Aaren answered the door.

"Hi, I'm Aaren," she said, offering Gillian a warm hug. "I'm so happy to finally meet you." The two women sat on the couch and began getting to know each other. "Thank you so much for trusting me to take care of Emily for you during this time."

"Of course. Thomas told me how wonderful a friend you've been to him... and to... my sister," she said hesitantly. Gillian was still trying to get used to the idea that she had a sister. "He said you were really Paige's only family; and that means now, you're a part of our family, too." Gillian's sincerity was real and Aaren knew it.

"Thank you. You look like her, you know. You've got the same eyes."

"Really? Can you tell me more about her, please? All I know is what Thomas has told me and what was in that box. But I'd really like to know more about her... know her the way that you did." Gillian felt a little like she was trying to grow leaves on her family tree... a tree she only just recently discovered. It was exciting and scary at the same time. What would she find... and would she be proud or disappointed?

Thomas came out of the bedroom as the women sat on the couch, talking as if they had been friends for decades. "I hate to break this up, ladies, but Gillian, we need to get to Pontiac if we're going to get the license in time. They close soon. Aaren, would you mind keeping an eye on Emily for us?"

"No, Thomas, watching a small baby is like torture to me, you know that." Aaren snarked. "Of course, go, do what you need to do. We'll be fine. I still have some loose ends to catch up on at MouseTrax anyway. We'll be here when you get back."

"Thank you, Aaren. We'll talk more later." Gillian said on her way out the door.

"Plan on it. I'm not going anywhere." said Aaren.

Thomas rolled his eyes at the two women. "Oh no. What have I done!" They all laughed as the door closed behind them.

****

Wednesday morning, the weather was perfect for a wedding. Nathan flew in from Boston for the day, and a few of Thomas and Gillian's old friends were invited to the ceremony. The day went off without a hitch. They got married and, after explaining the situation to the judge, were able to expedite Emily's adoption a few minutes later.

Initially, Gillian was confused about why she needed to formally adopt Emily, but as they were freshening up in the ladies room after the ceremony, Aaren explained.

"It's a technical thing... if you want to be able to make medical decisions and stuff for Emily... after, God forbid, Thomas gets hit by a bus... it would be much simpler to get things done if you were listed as a legal parent."

"Oh, well, since you explain it that way, it makes perfect sense." Gillian and Aaren laughed together.

****

"I do believe this is the fastest family I've ever built," said the judge with a grin. "I hope the three of you will be very happy together."

After the adoption ceremony, Aaren stayed at the hotel with Emily, while Thomas and Gillian went to dinner with their friends. They had a good time, mostly, but were on edge, cautious about how many details they were going to reveal. So many of their friends were still reporters, and Thomas was wary of the bloodhounds. One whiff of this story, and things could very quickly disintegrate back to the emotional flesh peddling he worked so hard to leave behind. There wasn't a reporter among them that wouldn't see this as the follow-up story of their career, and dredge up old wounds. Thomas imagined the headline... *Couple devastated by the loss of their daughter in a horrific accident reunites with a new child to replace her.* It would be disastrous for everyone. So they revealed very little about their reunion and nothing about Emily or Logan.

Gillian and Thomas were interested more, now than ever, with moving forward and starting over - fresh - new. When asked by their friends what prompted their remarriage, they only said that they both needed some time to heal, and they knew that although they were meant to be together forever, this was something they needed to heal from separately, so they could find their way back to each other. They worked hard to formulate this story, because they understood, all too well, the effects of the vulturous ways of the media. They were determined not to allow the callousness of others to bulldoze over their family again.

"Gillian, are you looking for another house in the area, Indian Village again, perhaps?" asked her friend, Maria from the accounting firm where she worked.

"No," Gillian replied. "We're thinking of heading out west. The pace is a little slower, and we can have some time to sort of rediscover each other again. Our focus now is on getting back to what brought us together in the first place; love and creativity. Time does crazy things to people... who knows, there could be a lot of adjusting - Thomas may have actually learned how to put the toilet seat down."

"Yes, and Gillian may have actually learned how to cook," retorted Thomas. The group laughed, recognizing the gentle teasing of a couple in love.

"So, what do you think you'll be doing out there, Gillian? Have you been picked up by another accounting firm?" asked Laura, a friend Gillian had met at the gym almost a year ago.

"No, I think I've done my tour of duty with the logical world." She looked over to Thomas and smiled. "I've actually been in touch with this extraordinary writer near Denver, and I'll be illustrating his new series of children's books. I'm excited about the project. Excited to get back to my art." Gillian squeezed her husband's hand underneath the table. They had always shared secrets, and this one, they knew, was something special. Not yet ready for prime time.

"That sounds like a fabulous life," swooned Maria. "No more calculators and tax forms... just the slow pace of a small town and art. How I envy you, Gillian." Laura nodded her head and smiled in agreement.

"Thanks, girls. I know I'm going to be happy. Remember, you guys are invited to come out and visit anytime you like. We'll have a little barbecue, and you could come lounge by our pool," said Gillian.

"Oh, the new house has a barbecue and a pool? I didn't know that. I thought we were planning on scaling back. You know, simplifying life just a little bit," snickered Thomas.

"Well, you do now. And besides, you can't expect a girl raised in the Great Lake State to give up water, now can you? And we are scaling back... it's just a little swimming pool, not a Great Lake with a sailboat, for goodness sake!" said Gillian. The whole group laughed at their newlywed banter as the waitress brought around desert and after-dinner drinks.

"So, what's next for you, Thomas?" asked Tim.

"Well, since Gillian got this great illustrating gig, I decided to take a job at a small town newspaper outside of Denver."

"Yeah, I knew you'd come back; face it, man, reporting is in your blood. No way you could have been happy in that marketing job writing bullet points all day. We know you." Tim said, gaining nods from his friends around the table, "you have to write just like you have to breathe."

"That's true, but this time it'll be different." said Thomas with a sly grin.

"How's that?" Tim quipped.

"Well, for starters, I'm out of the chaos game. I picked up a cushy little column writing simple small town features, just three days a week... no blood, no guts, no gore. I'm actually looking forward to it."

"You? After all these years, doing the small town beat? I don't believe it." said Mark.

"Well it's true. Small town, simple writing... maybe I'll even finish that novel I started years ago. Who knows. But I can tell you this much, I'll never let the scent of a fresh kill dictate my writing again. The damage isn't worth the column inches."

"Oh come on, Thomas." Stan chided. "We know you... you won't be able to stay away for long. You love the limelight of crisis reporting." Stan punctuated his statement with a sip of his drink. "Oh sure, you'll go write your small town comfort pieces... but soon enough, you'll be back to the earthquakes and train wrecks, mark my words." Mark socked Stan on the shoulder. The crowd got quiet. Gillian looked mortified.

"You're an idiot, Stan." said Mark, as he pulled out his credit card to pick up the check. Mark had always been a good friend and Thomas appreciated his loyalty.

"What'd I say?" stammered Stan, as he took another drink. "You all know I'm right. He'll be back." Stan declared.

Thomas squeezed his wife's hand underneath the table and laughed, dismissing Stan's drunken remarks; knowing that both he and his writing are now headed down a very different path.

"We'd better get out of here," said Mark. "It looks like Stan has had a little too much celebrating. I'll make sure he gets home. Sorry about that."

"Don't worry about it, Mark." said Thomas, standing and pulling out Gillian's chair. "We should get going too. Thanks for getting the check. I'm glad you guys could make it." The others at the table stood, too; shaking hands, offering hugs, and saying their good-byes.

"You're welcome; and congratulations. I always knew you two were meant to be together." Gillian smiled and hugged Mark good-bye.

Chapter Twenty-Seven

"Each child is an adventure into a better life –
an opportunity to change the old pattern and
make it new."
~Hubert H. Humphrey

    It was a good thing that Thomas had asked Aaren to come with them to Montana to help with the adoption process. It turned out that while they were busy with meeting Logan and his foster parents, the Garrisons, they needed someone to handle all the legal details and work as a liaison back to Mr. McClish. It turned out that the adoption process was far more complicated than any of them had realized. There were so many papers to fill out, conversations back and forth with Ms. Gundry at Small Hearts Sanctuary, and legal wrangling that none of them had been prepared for. And through all of this, they still had to make sure that Emily's needs were met, and that somehow, Gillian and Thomas had some time alone, to rekindle their love affair.

    Aaren had been with Paige for a long time, and she had learned the nuances about business and the expedition of important matters. She was a perfect advocate for them. During their first few days in Billings, Aaren and Gillian spent hours talking. Aaren told Gillian about her sister and helped Gillian to feel a little more like she knew Paige... it wasn't the same as talking directly with Paige, of course; but learning about her through her closest friend of thirty years was the next best thing. Gillian and Aaren became close friends, and more than that, Gillian began to truly see Aaren as a member of their family.

****

After three weeks of working through the Montana State Welfare Department and the Child Protective Services Department... countless meetings with counselors, case workers and lawyers... more supervised playtime than they expected, and even a parenting class mandated by the State, the Lairds were finally close to the day when they might be able to bring Logan home with them. One day, when they were at the Garrison house, visiting Logan and introducing him to Emily and Aaren, Gillian and Thomas took the opportunity to have the conversation they'd been delaying since the day Thomas discovered where Logan was living. Aaren, Emily and Logan were outside, playing in the tree fort in the Garrison's backyard.

"Mr. and Mrs. Garrison, if you don't mind my asking; why haven't you adopted Logan yet?" Gillian asked.

"Oh it's not that we don't want to, Logan is an amazing little boy, and we love him very much... it's just that..." Mrs. Garrison's voice trailed off, unsure of what she should or shouldn't say. Thomas and Gillian looked to Mr. Garrison to complete the story.

"We were asked not to adopt him just yet," said Mr. Garrison, a solemn look on his face.

"By whom?" asked Thomas, curious, and knowing there was more to this story than a simple request.

"Each month, we are given a check - equal to my monthly wages, and separate from the check from the State - with the expectation that we will care for Logan, love him, and keep him safe until someone comes to ask about adopting him. We were told that if by his sixth birthday, no one came to adopt Logan, then we would be able to bring him into our family forever."

"Who gives you this check?" asked Thomas. He could hear his old reporter habits clicking in again... so he worked hard to squelch them. He didn't want to become that man again. "I'm sorry, it's not my place to ask - it's just that, well, so much has happened lately, and we're trying to make sense of it all."

"We understand your frustration. We were very confused in the beginning, too. Until Mr. Smith told us the whole story."

"Mr. Smith... is he by chance, a private investigator?" Thomas thought that he was beginning to connect the dots.

"Yes, he is." Mr. Garrison looked to his wife and then back to Thomas. "Do you know him?"

"Not personally, but I know of him." Thomas shot a worried glance at Gillian, not sure where this new rabbit hole might take them.

"Of course. Well, we he told us recently to expect you. He said that you and your wife would be asking about Logan, and that we should be prepared for the possibility that you would want to adopt him. Well, you can imagine our surprise, after three years, to hear this. And yet, we knew this day would come - eventually. It's difficult. But as we understand it," Mr. Garrison looked at Gillian; "You're family. And we believe that children should be raised by their family, no matter how distant that relationship might be."

"There are special things about your family that we would never be able to give Logan," said Mrs. Garrison. "He deserves to know you and to know about his mother. If you can promise us that you will take care of him, and help him to know who his mother was... we will support your adoption request with the courts. We would, of course, like to visit..." Mrs. Garrison hung her head and rubbed her hands together before looking back up at Thomas and Gillian. "But if you don't want us to, we will completely understand." Mr. Garrison nodded in agreement.

Gillian didn't hesitate. She reached over and took Mrs. Garrison's hands in hers. "Of course we would want you to visit... and often. It's important to us that Logan knows that his family extends far beyond the constraints of blood and DNA. If not for you, Logan might still be at Small Hearts Sanctuary, living in a dorm room with ten other children, never knowing what a real family is like. You have given him a very precious gift, and we are tremendously thankful." Tears welled up in both the women's eyes.

"We'll be making our home in Kremmling, Colorado... that's not too far from here. We can easily come for visits and we would love to have you come and visit us." Thomas' enthusiasm made the moment a little lighter, and all four smiled. "As Gillian said, birthdays and holidays, and summer vacation wouldn't be the same without the entire family!"

Mr. Garrison reached out and shook Thomas' hand. "Thank you, Thomas. We are most appreciative. Logan is a very special child, and he feels like a part of our family."

"He always will be." Thomas and Gillian said in unison. The four laughed together.

*****

That evening after dinner and putting Emily to bed, the trio called Mr. Smith and Mr. McClish to discover more about what they had learned from the Garrisons. Mr. Smith was, of course, unreachable. What they learned from Mr. McClish was that although only two others - Mr. McClish and Mr. Smith - knew about the arrangements for Logan, Paige had thought about this for a long time. Just as she had been watching Gillian and waiting for what she thought was the best time to meet her... she knew that one day, she would get her son back. But she didn't want to do that until the rest of her family was also part of the story. Her intention was not to remove Logan from a loving household until she knew she had something just as great or better to offer him.

"Ms. Lambert believed that, with a little guidance, she would one day be a good parent. But as she said to me, she didn't think that was possible unless she had an extended family to support her and give her the direction she needed. She believed, Mrs. Laird, that you would be that guiding force in her life. She watched how you raised Eryn, and believed that you would be a good mentor for her in her own quest for motherhood. She had not figured Emily into the equation until after she met your husband. I must be clear with you, Mrs. Laird; it was never Ms. Lambert's intention to break up your family... her intention, all along, was to bring it back together. When the pregnancy occurred, she believed it was in the best interests of both of you to carry the child and give you a niece. Of course, she never planned to lose her own life in the process. But I must be clear... it was certainly her intention to bring your family together; however that manifested."

"Thank you, Mr. McClish," said Gillian.

"And what of Mr. Smith? What happens now?" Thomas asked the question that was on everyone's mind. They needed to know if they would continually be watched... was there more to this agenda that Paige had orchestrated?

"Now that you have made your request to the courts to adopt Logan, Ms. Lambert's wishes have been fulfilled. Mr. Smith's services are no longer needed. He has been fairly compensated and he has signed a very firm, very binding confidentiality agreement. I can assure you that your future privacy will not be invaded; and none of the details he holds regarding your family will *ever* be released." Mr. McClish was firm in his tone. Thomas knew he was serious.

"Thank you for your time so late in the evening, Mr. McClish." Thomas said into the speaker phone.

"Not at all, Mr. Laird. Remember I am on retainer, so if there is anything you need, now or in the future, do not hesitate to contact me."

"We will keep your contact information close at hand, sir. Thank you." The phone disconnected and the trio stared in amazed silence at each other.

Finally, it was Aaren who broke the quiet. "Paige had always been a planner... but I never would have thought that she would have pulled off something this involved. She must have really wanted this badly. And, she must have really believed in the two of you to make her plan work, even after she was gone. That woman... she'd been a friend for more years than I can count, and still, she continues to surprise me."

"All that planning," said Gillian. "Imagine all the lists!"

Thomas laughed. "I'd rather not, thanks." The three laughed; and all three thought the exact thing. *I wish she was still here to share in our happiness.*

****

Two days later, everyone appeared before the Judge at the Family Services wing of the courthouse. When the judge asked everyone to relate their side of the story, each in turn, gave an accounting of what had brought them to this moment. The judge listened intently to each, taking notes and nodding his understanding, but saying little.

"Ms. Jorgenson, do you have any issues with the petitioner's request to adopt?"

"No, your honor. We have performed a complete background check; we have witnessed supervised visitations, and have received positive reports from the Garrisons. All information points to the fact that this would be a suitable adoption, and in the best interests of the child."

"Very well. I have been privy to a file of additional information sent to me by one Stanley McClish, Esquire." Thomas, Gillian and Aaren all glanced at each other, surprised at this announcement. They had all assumed that his involvement was done. They were uneasy as to what he could have sent to the judge.

"In the accompanying dossier, which will remain sealed by the courts, ample information is provided regarding the wishes and motivations of the birth mother and her intention that suitable adoption not be hindered." The judge said the word 'suitable', in a way that anyone listening might have believed it to be a secret code name. Thomas was sure the stenographer would type that part of the record in italics.

"And so, if there are no further objections, the court grants the petition of adoption by Mr. and Mrs. Thomas Laird to adopt Logan Alexander Edwards. Logan's name is officially changed this day to be Logan Laird." A broad smile crossed the judge's face. "In a world where there are so many challenges in raising children, and in a world where I see too many of the failures, it is a nice change to have been witness to one of its successes. I hope that your family is very happy together for many years to come." The judge pounded his gavel, signed the appropriate documents; the clerk handed the adoption certificate to the Lairds.

Afterward, there was a small gathering in an adjacent room, where an informal reception was held. Emily and Logan, who had been playing in another room during the courtroom proceedings with a Department of Child Services baby sitter, were welcomed to the party with balloons, cheers and a small cake. The judge was there, too, not willing to miss out on one of the few celebratory moments of his job. Photos were snapped and smiles shined brightly from every face. Just as he was leaving the party, the judge leaned down to Logan and said, "You've got a wonderful family... your story will be incredible." Logan giggled and gave the judge a "high five".

Chapter Twenty-Eight

"The interpretation of dreams is the royal road to acknowledgement of the unconscious activities of the mind."
~Sigmund Freud

Maybe it was the combination of melatonin to help me sleep and the Aleve to relieve my chronic joint pain, and the Dickens novel I've been reading; but I had a very vivid dream last night that I was visited by a couple of spirits. Okay, not really spirits, but rather, people; or perhaps not really people, but rather whispery visages of my life. They were fuzzy images of themselves, but absolutely identifiable nonetheless. I have hidden their names in this telling, to protect them - from what, I'm not sure - but it seems requisite to telling the story.

She said, "I am the memories of your past. I am the touches of past love, the laughter of past games, the tears of past heartaches." I remembered her vividly. Her voice rang in my ears as though it were still singing to me in those years of my newly discovered ability to love with depth and conviction, complete abandon and tireless attention.

She said, "Do you remember the spontaneity with which you once lived? Do you remember the connectivity you had with those who ran with you, played with you, and held your head while you threw up?" Of course, I remembered. Those memories were etched into my psyche so deeply; they had become integral parts of who I had become. I could no more erase those memories than change my social security number on a whim.

"You can have those parts of you back again, if you want them." She hugged me - strong and hard - with a deep resonance that stirred desires I'd daringly flirted with into a froth of craving. Without realizing it was happening, I found myself entranced in her song, like a Siren from the Greek seas; unable to fight the current of youthful temptation.

"You can have it all again. You can be that person completely filled with wonderment and spontaneous abandon. You can relive all the best parts of your memory... the romance of your youth... the captivation of not knowing what might lay in your future... the exhilaration of the newness of a world undiscovered. You can be there. You can have it. You can relive everything as if it were new and fresh and perfect."

"Yes", I murmured, eyes closed, head dancing, body floating to the sounds of the music of the time. "I miss it so much. I want it so much". The emotional orgasm was near overwhelming. "How ..." was all I could utter in a voice that purred with a chocolate-brandy induced relaxation.

"It's easy. All you need to do is give up everything you've experienced since those years have passed. Give away the pain and the frustration of the past twenty-five years and transport yourself back to those years of wonderment, warmth and laughter. Let go the responsibilities of a life you never really wanted. Banish the stagnant anger that lives deep in regret and the choices others made for you. Release the connections to the people in your life that don't know you now, never really knew you then, and have no real desire to understand who you truly are at the core of your being. Who you have always been. You were the man who changed like a chameleon to suite everyone else's dreams and aspirations, never giving your own dreams the attention they were due. Come with me, I know you can do this. I know you want this."

My hypnotic foray into the gentleness of remembering the past with selective service was interrupted by the reality of those other milestones that begged to be noticed. "But the passing years haven't all been pain and frustration. Some equally interesting and exciting things have been a part of my life in the time that has gone by. I have grown and changed, I believe, for the better. Can I take those memories back with me too? After all, they have helped to make me that man I am today."

She got angry then. It's odd to watch the cloud of your wistfulness respond in frustration and exasperation when you challenge its relevance. "Well, of course not. Why on Earth would you want to bring this tired, frustrated, angry, conflicted man back with you to the precious wonderment of youth? The past and the present can never intermingle, that would ruin everything! Come on, let it go, it's not really all that important, is it? Think of where you once were. Think of the perfect happiness you once held in your heart. It can be yours again, just say Yes..."

Her words were mesmerizing. I felt as though I could truly transport myself back in time and be at home again in that world of my early twenties. The cityscapes of St. Louis, Seattle, Detroit, and Boston and Billings, filled my brain with so many flashes of ecstasy. The images, sounds and aromas of those moments stunned my imagination into slow motion. And the people... Eryn, Gillian, The Freep, MouseTrax, Paige, Nathan, Aaren, Logan, Emily ... it was hard to imagine the thought of never having known them, never having touched them, loved them. The invitation was so tempting. And the more her whispers of encouragement and longing filled my ears, the more I felt like I should take the plunge ... just let it go ... after all, I was just a tired old journalist, who would miss me here, really?

And then, just as I was about to fall full-force into the warm pool of my past with all the empathy of a thousand long good-byes, from some distant place, I heard the whimper of my dog ... our dog ... the dog Gillian had chosen from a litter that would soon be euthanized. We saved this little pup, and he saved us. After all we'd meant to each other, I just couldn't leave him. As I pulled away from the arms of desire, I heard the cloud's desperate pleas...

"Don't do this, Thomas. Things are different now. I want you again. I need you again. My life has turned upside down; I need your love and devotion - I don't know if I will be able to go on without you by my side. I can't wait any longer!" Her words became more frantic then, as I moved still further away from the envelope of the past's entrapment.

"You won't get another chance like this one. An offer like this only comes around once in a lifetime. Don't be foolish! I'm offering you a second chance... a chance to do it all over again, to do it right this time, with me. Thomas ... come back here!"

But as her last hysterical words reached my ears, my eyes opened and I found my hound, gently nudging my elbow with his little wet nose. Again, he had saved me, the least I could do was let him outside to go potty.

As I groggily made my way back to bed, I thought of the many times I had wished for the chance to go back. Take a do-over, and fix whatever it was I had done wrong with that pure, first love, and make it mine again. How many times, especially recently, when my self-esteem lacked luster, had I flirted with the idea of reliving those days of what I thought was perfection, and improving on them - as if that were actually possible. I giggled to myself, glancing at the clock: 11:34pm. Still a full night of sleep ahead of me.

    I snuggled myself back under the covers of my present day comfort, and took with me a dash of peace as I drifted off to sleep again, my pup curled up, paw gently tucked over his nose, on the flannel cushion next to my bed.

    I'm not sure how long I had been sleeping, when another wiry figure presented himself at the foot of my bed. In his left hand, he held a travel suitcase, you know, one of those carry-ons with the convenient wheels and handle. In his right hand, he held a paper ticket and my passport. "Well, don't just lie there, get up," he said. "We've got miles to go before we sleep, and you've got a plane to catch."

    I stood up out of bed and was instantly smack in the middle of the busiest airport you could ever imagine. Think JFK International on the day before Thanksgiving, and you might have an idea of what I'm talking about. There were lines of people going everywhere and nowhere, as that's how it works at the airport - slow and steady. Tickets, security check-points, tram rides, boarding lounges. Hurry up and wait is usually the motto of any American airport, though those in charge would flatly deny it.

    "Where are we going?" I asked, not wanting to sound ungracious for this spur of the moment vacation, but curious nonetheless.

    "Your Golden Years, of course. It's about time that you get there, don't you think? I mean, you've been dreaming about them since you were about sixteen, am I right? Well, I'm here to offer you a non-stop flight to the Age of Leisure. You won't have to wait in any of those lines; we've got an expedited ticket for you."

The sidewalk beneath me began to move, and I noticed that we were now looming high above the lobby below. It was then that I realized that the lines of people below were all actually going someplace. Large, brightly colored signs hung above each security check-in station, and throngs of people were waiting impatiently to move on through. Our conveyor led us easily over Concourse Y; a yellow sign with bold black letters that read *Youth*.

"See all those snazzily dressed people? They're traveling to reclaim their lost youth. Some are going for broke and heading all the way back to kindergarten - usually the weakest of the bunch, desperate to regenerate their lives into something completely unlike anything they know or want. Some, the mildly daring, are revisiting their adolescence - still trying desperately to regain some control over the decisions that ultimately got them to where they arrived when adulthood hit. As you can see, most are in their college years, still battling some form of hysteria or rebellion. It is their hope that by going back; they can change their path and bring success to their door."

Next, we glided over Concourse M ; a bold burgundy sign with stark magenta lettering read *Mid-Life*.

"The older people you see standing in line there are like recalcitrant icebergs - forever bobbing up and down with no real direction or understanding of what life should be about for them. They're going back to their wonder years to recapture lightning in a bottle; and of course, each thoroughly believes that they created that lightning in the first place. The hope of each traveler is that some new car, new condo, or new spouse will bring them the peace, success and fulfillment that maturity can't give them."

Finally, we hovered over the emerald green sign with bright gold lettering, Concourse G.

"But you, you've got a first-class ticket to the Golden Years. You won't have to put up with all that nonsense about getting through these last forty years or so of boring maturity. You have a get-out-of-dullsville-free-card directly into the hallowed halls of seniority. You'll be revered, admired, and envied wherever you go. You'll be the wise elder statesman who has all the answers; but without any of the nitpicking, mundane processes required along the way. No memorization, no new formulas, just simple easing into a comfortable existence."

Instantly, we were standing in front of a nice looking lady, who was asking for my ticket and passport. She seemed to be very intent on getting me to board the aircraft soon, constantly glancing at the old analog clock on the wall and nervously surveying the concourse as if security might arrest her at any moment for dereliction of duty.

"So, what do you say? How about you just stop playing all these silly little "I'm a creative writer" games and join in the fun of relishing the finality of lifelong sufficiency."

"But I still have things I want to do," I said. "Goals that I want to achieve, books that Gillian and I have yet to create together, years to spend with my wife, daughter, son, and perhaps grandchildren someday. I don't think I'm ready to just leap willy-nilly into my future without a plan."

"A plan! You really think anyone has a plan? You're nuts." His face grew a little purple and his eyes bugged out of his head just a little bit. "Listen, I'm trying to save you from forty years or more of grief, frustration, rejection and debilitating illness. Wouldn't you rather just skip all that and enjoy the finish line? The journey's not so great, you know. The destination's the thing."

I felt strangely compelled to step over the threshold of the aircraft jetway. The thought of a life filled with ease and gladness was alluring. It would be nice to finally be at a place in life without struggles, without tears, without the malicious vanity hounds attempting to ride my coat tails to wealth and notoriety. I thought of the many struggles I'd been through and how debilitating they had been to my spirit. *I could easily do without more of that.* I thought of the many years of work ahead of me to finally finish my manuscript and get it published. *It sure would be nice to jump to a happy ending*, came the whisper in my brain.

I was about three seconds away from taking that second step that would secure my passage through Concourse G; when a gentle thud hit my rib cage. It took me only a moment to recognize my wife Gillian's arm lying across my chest. I took two steps backward. Her unyielding love, loyalty and support had gotten me through some of the most difficult times in my life. We shared a life; raised two daughters, one in our hearts, and one in the world. We welcomed a son into our lives and loved him as his mother would have wanted. We were connected as no two other souls could ever be. I would never give that up - I made a vow, twice. I was intent on keeping it, forever.

"So, what'll it be, Thomas? It's an easy passage to easy street. Why not just jump on that plane and get out of here."

"No, actually, I think I'd rather enjoy the slower ride along the way. I've got books to write, and that takes time. There's no point in going to the signing parties if you can't remember what you wrote. I have many more steps that I want to take, horses I want to ride, and hands to hold before I'm willing to fade off into the sunset. Thanks for the offer, but I think I'll pass."

"What! Has your little choo-choo train of thought just derailed?! Have you lost all intelligence? Do you know how many people would kill to get the opportunity I'm handing to you!"

I find it fascinating that when those who offer you perceived bliss get rejected, how quickly their beguiling charm turns to rancid sewer water; even those ghostly visages of your own imagination. I backed out of the airport, fully confident that in the next fleeting moment, I would find myself next to my wife in bed, her body delicately draped about mine in a protective cocoon of sinewy love and affection. I was right. I opened my eyes to meet my wife's, gently holding my esteem in hers.

"You okay," Gillian asked.

"Sure," I said with still a little numbness in my voice. "It was just a weird dream."

"Do you want to talk about it?"

"No, let's just go back to sleep. I'll tell you about it in the morning."

I glanced over at the clock; 3:47am. Our pup was still sound asleep next to our bed, as he had been just a few hours before; but now, his feet were strait up in the air, as if reaching out for a hug. I giggled to myself as I heard Gillian's kitten-purring snore fill my ears with peace, reminding me of Eryn.

Yes, all things end eventually. One age moves into the other; sometimes with abrupt changes, and sometimes with the gentle breeze of a summer's evening. The end of any year in our lives can be a difficult thing; but always, we learn, grow, and evolve through the process. Little comfort in the intensity of the moment, I know, but these are important, supportive beams to the temple of our soul that we are building, as we venture forth and learn to take new risks in love.

So, I'll be leaving the paper today, this is my last column. Retirement beckons from a sunny window seat well-appointed with a writing desk, computer and puppy curled at my feet. I am crossing the next bridge in my life, from journalist to author. Watch for a new series of novels and a collection of children's books illustrated by my beautiful and talented wife, to hit your bookstores soon.

After much reflection, I am glad to say that my life is not filled with great regret or a specialized yearning for something more. I have made peace with my past, and I am confident that the decisions I made are, still today, the right choices for me.

I have looked at the longing of the future, and although hints have been given to me regarding what is possible, I am comfortable waiting until the future reveals herself, in her own time. I am not in a hurry to speed up the clock.

I am at home with my present. I am focusing with intent on living in the moment, and relishing the surprises around every corner. After all I have seen, done, wished for, sacrificed and sequestered, it is where I need to be. Here, with my own demons, and my own dreams.

I hope that someday you will find peace in the now, as I have, free from regret and confident in your own identities.

Epilogue

The excitement of their wedding day was over, and now, they charted the course for their future together.

It was a simple blue and white sailboat, about thirty-five feet long, with a wooden tiller and a small cabin below. Forward, there is a berth with a few pillows and a soft down quilt - navy blue with white lettering, the boat's name, *Wing On Wing II*. It was moored at dock, in a small, unassuming marina not far from Nantucket.

Quietly, Emily and Bennjamin walked down the finger dock, hand in hand, caressing each other's palms in anticipation of the wonderment ahead of them. As they move below decks, Bennjamin reaches behind to fasten the hatch. The best part of harbor neighbors is that all recognize the need for privacy - and although there are only a few short feet between moorings, it might as well be miles. Sailors; they are good people.

She poured them each a small glass of brandy, which he tersely took from her hands, and set them on the table. He waited long enough - seduction was no longer a necessity. He nuzzled the softness of his beard against her cheek, and in that moment, she was lost to him. As she wrapped her arms around him, she whispered to his ear, "You can have anything you want ... anything."

With a trail of clothes behind, they made their way through the galley and to the awaiting berth. Giggling as they climbed up amongst the softness, they enjoyed an easy banter, teasing and tickling; they found a warm place beneath the blankets, lying together ... fingertip to fingertip ... skin to skin. He fondled delicately her teal blue leopard print lingerie, as it clung to her breasts and hips. He liked the feel of her shoulders beneath the straps, and gently replaced them as they fell over her arms. He wanted to enjoy her with it on ... this seduction he would have. She smiled, knowing that they would remember this moment forever.

Emily traced the outline of Bennjamin's face, reveling in the softness of his beard, enjoying the touch of his kiss on her lips, and she cradled his face in her hand - the silky softness brought her serenity in a way few things ever could. He matched her movements, and held her face in his hands. She closed her eyes in rapture, and let out a small sigh of elation. His tenderness was beyond her imagination ... intuitively he knew what would bring her joy, and peace. She gave herself to him completely.

The generosity in his eyes was almost more than she could bear, and she had to turn away to stifle the joyful tears. She turned her back to him, and he held her gently, wrapping his arms around her with heroic strength. She arched her back and buried her head in his shoulder, finding comfort in the safety of his protection. She felt his beard soft against her neck, his breath warm in her ear, and she shivered with anticipation.

Over the next two hours, he learned things about her that he had never known, even after seven years of living together. But his favorite was that when she was really happy ... happier than she thought she was capable of ... she squeaked. Not the squeak of a door in need of repair. Not the squeak of a well-worn spring. No, it was the squeak of the happiest mouse you could imagine. A mouse on helium. She couldn't control it - and he was glad. He liked her best when she wasn't censoring.

When it was over, she snuggled next to him, gasping for air and writhing with the spasms of ecstasy. Her whole body was lost to him, her heart pounded and her muscles twitched with the overwhelm that only romantic perfection can bring.

"Will this come again for us, do you suppose?" she asked.

"Well, maybe," was his answer, "but you'll have to give me a few minutes." She giggled into his chest, delighted with the miracle of the day.

Diana Kathryn Plopa

Diana Kathryn Plopa is the associate publisher, editor-in-chief, and writing coach at *Grey Wolfe Publishing,* an independent publishing house headquartered in Oakland County, Michigan.

She has published a book of poetry, *Ideate Avail* (currently out of print) and several other books from various genres. Her personal goal is to write one book in each of the major genres, and then choose a favorite - if that's possible. She spent time as a features writer for a Detroit newspaper, wrote copy for several websites and blogs, and wrote copy for a popular radio program.

Writing, and a sincere love for the written word, are passions that have followed Diana Kathryn since early childhood. Whether poetry, fiction, memoir or any other genre; her words create worlds to step into with enthusiasm and wonder. She doesn't write because it's necessarily fun—although, for her, it truly is—she writes because, "Like breathing, if I don't do it, I will die!"

Diana Kathryn's Muse, Drake (a small mallard duck), helps her with the tough stuff, quacking inspiration in her ear whenever necessary. Her imagination is fueled by an abundance of hot cocoa whenever she writes.

Currently, she lives in Michigan with her husband, Dave, and their two dogs, Alex and Finnigan. She enjoys writing; sailing; kayaking; escaping to her cabin to write; spending time with her family, especially her son, Zachary; chocolate; *Carmina Burana*; nearly anything written by Mozart, especially *The Magic Flute*; and cheese in large quantities.

Writings by Diana Kathryn Plopa:

- Wolfe Cub (a memoir)
- Free Will (a satirical novel)
- The Griffin of Greed (a children's book)
- A Tryst of Fate (a romance novel)
- Encore Writers (an anthology; editor & contributor)

Coming Soon:

- American Plague (a conspiracy novel)
- The Last Strand (a science fiction novel)
- Boys Night Out (a crime novel)
- The Wizard of Alcazar (a young adult novella)
- Elephant Ways (a children's book)

Made in the USA
Middletown, DE
14 March 2019